WHISPERING WIND
THE MIST

CIN J. MEDLEY

MED'S PUB
PUBLISHING

Whispering Wind
The Mist

Cin Medley

Published by: Med's Pub Publishing
Copyright © 2015 C. J. Medley
All Rights Reserved
ISBN-13: 978-0986117824
ISBN-10: 098611782X
Cover by: Amanda Walker PA & Design Services
Editing by: Kendra's editing and book services-Kendra Gaither
Formatted by: Med's Pub Publishing

For McKenna
My Loua
You will always be my Princess
I love you always
Nana

My Beautiful Britt, without knowing you and learning from you, I would have never known the patience I needed to write this story. I love you

My beautiful friend Jenny (Lady Sapphires) thank you for being a pony girl with me and for inspiring Rebecca's personality. Without knowing you this story would not have so much girl power. Autobots transform and let's roll out!!

And to all the rest who have read this story, given me your thoughts and critiques. I am thankful that you loved it so much and helped me decide to go through with it. You know who you are!

For my fallen Guardians...You will forever be in our hearts!!

Edited by Kendra Gaither. Thank you so much for your insight. I am honored to call you my friend.

Amanda you never cease to amaze me with your mind, keep being you and never change.

PROLOGUE

As I turned to look back at my home, the place of my birth, my mind flooded with the memories of my life there; the happiness, the love, and the death that once filled the halls of Whispering Wind. I closed my eyes to absorb it all, to hear the voices of those I loved and those who are now gone. My mother, my father, my brothers Ardes and Simon and my sister Jenna all played a part in my training for what my future was to hold. They all died because of me. I could feel the tears as they fell on my cheeks; they were tears of gratitude for their sacrifice, tears of sorrow for my loss, tears of exhaustion.

I opened my eyes to a horror far worse than that day I heard the thunder. Whispering Wind was shrouded in a thick green mist. The castle, the village, the fields; it was the strangest thing. I swear you could almost feel it. The mist was death.

The past three years have felt like a lifetime to me. My journey has been one that no princess should ever have to take. I should have been given in marriage to a man my father, King Stephan of Whispering Wind, had chosen for me at the age of just sixteen years. I should have a child or be ripe with one now, in a kingdom of my own. Instead, I watched as death rode across the plains lying before me, with the sound of thunder, and took all that was dear to me. It set me on a journey filled with fear, determination, and the need to find those who murdered my family. I was driven by revenge. My mind wanted an adventure, but I think I got more than what I wished for.

My beloved Jared was brought back from the hands of death itself, my love Juliana lives with the passion of her parents, Jenna of Wellington and my beloved brother Ardes, in her being. I sit here surrounded by men who secretly, in their youth, swore to protect me, long before they knew who I was. It all seemed so far from the truth that it made me giggle.

I sensed their eyes upon me as I sat on my horse, Raiden; a horse who most believe is the spirits of those who have ridden him before me, possibly even the great sorcerer Merlin himself, gazing out at the thick green mist that now engulfed my beloved Whispering Wind.

CHAPTER ONE

The light of the day was new and rising above the hills as the green mist seemed to thin. I could not take my eyes from it. *Could this be more trickery from the witch Devious?* I knew what I saw, the birds falling to their death as they flew over the kingdom. It was impossible to know; her body was lying lifeless in the dungeons along with her head. She seemed so convinced that Raiden was going to stop us. I sensed him as his ears twitched beneath me. I looked down at him.

"Do not tell me you can hear my thoughts as well?"

He did not move. I could not help but wonder what he might be thinking himself. As with everything that had happened, I was sure that in time I would discover it. I looked to Rebecca. Charles said that we must figure things out on our own now, that he could in no way disclose the outcome of future events. His sole purpose was to protect me. Again, a giggle escaped me as I considered just how preposterous that thought was.

"My lady?" Charles said softly from behind me.

"It is nothing, Charles."

I knew he was worried about me, worried about my silence, worried of what may lay ahead for us. Tearing my eyes from the green mist, I gently pulled on Raiden's reigns, turning him to face my Guardians.

"Charles, I am going to ride alone. I am sure that Raiden knows the way."

"I would feel more at ease, my lady, if you would allow us to accompany you."

"Raiden can outrun any horse that would try to pursue me, and he knows where the cottage is. I think we will be fine."

"As you wish, Sabine. Please be safe."

I did not mean to, but I giggled, and before he could respond, I kicked Raiden in the sides, and we were off. I was sure that Raiden could sense my desire to be free, so he did not hold back. The wind in my face was like nothing else I have ever known. As he reached his full run, I could feel the gentle way his body moved effortlessly beneath me, the trees in the forest flying by so quickly. If I had not been looking for them, I would have believed that they were not there.

My mind began processing all that had taken place. I had felt such a range of emotions, and anger was the one that stood at the fore front of my mind. I was angry, amazed at all that had happened, but angry as to why it all happened; angry that my family was dead, angry that I had been forced to become this killing machine, with the blood of thousands of men on my hands. I looked down at them as we flew through the forest. I saw nothing but small, delicate fingers covered with pale skin, which was layered with dirt. These small hands of mine wielded a sword most men had a hard time lifting above their heads. *How is any of this possible?* I was angry that my beloved Jared had been tainted by that witch, angry that Juliana would be forced to grow up without the love of her parents. Anger was the emotion that filled my being. It was what courses through my veins. As I sat upon Raiden and flew through the forest, a tear fell on the hands I studied, smearing the layers of dirt, then another and another. I did not realize that I was sobbing until Raiden slowed, and I had to grab his reigns or be bounced off. He pulled to a stopped, turned his head to look at me, and neighed.

"I am all right, boy." He neighed again and nodded his head, wanting me to look forward. I looked up to see that we were no longer in the forest but on a plain. Ahead of us were the hills that led to the cottage. Confused, I turned to see if anyone was behind us, but it was just Raiden and I. "This cannot be. We are here already?" I heard myself say.

Raiden stomped his hoof and neighed at me, nodding his head. This was impossible. It was at least a four-day ride when you only stopped to sleep two times, and that was at a full gallop. *Have I been so involved in thought that the light of day has passed without me seeing?*

"Raiden, did I miss something? How did we get here so quickly?"

I heard a sound come from deep within him, almost like a giggle. We started across the plain and up the hills. I could hear the familiar horn to warn the others that someone was coming. Shortly after, I heard the light thunder of the horses as they approached. Raiden continued his ascent to the top of the hills. Fast approaching was Blake and about twenty guards.

"Sabine, is everything all right? Where are the others?"

"They are not far behind. I needed to ride and, well, Raiden brought me here."

Looking at Blake and the others, I could not help but notice the solemn looks on their faces, but a giggle escaped me any way.

Blake looked at me and asked, "Sabine, again, I must ask. Is everything all right?"

"Well, let me see. My family was murdered. I was marked for assassination from my father's neighboring kingdoms. I mass murdered tens of thousands of men. My beloved Jared was grabbed from the hands of death. I traveled across the known lands to the edge of them, and I cut the head off of a witch. So, let me ask you this, Blake. Does it sound as if everything is all right to you?"

The bite in my words hit him as if I had slapped him across the face. I did not want to look at any of them any longer. I kicked Raiden in the sides and he took off. Down the hills we flew, across the plain, and in no time, we were stopped in front of the cottage. Before my feet could hit the ground, Westin came running out the door and scooped me up in his arms.

"Oh, Sabine, you are here. I was so scared that you would not come back." He hugged me so tightly I could not breathe.

I giggled. "Breathe... Westin, I cannot breathe."

He laughed as he released me. My hand found his face. "I will always return to you."

His arms were around me again as Blake and the others rode up.

"Sabine, can I talk to you please?"

"Blake, I am tired and wish to bathe, eat, and then sleep. Another time perhaps?"

I turned and walked arm and arm into the cottage with Westin. Inside, Juliana squealed and ran into my welcoming arms.

"I missed you," she whispered in my ear.

"As I have missed you, my love," I whispered back.

The feel of her warm embrace hit me so hard. *How was any of this possible?*

"Are you staying with us now?"

"Yes, my love, I am."

I put Juliana down, hugged Camille and Stephan, and then made my way to my old room. I could not close the door fast enough. I leaned against it and slid down to the floor. I did not know where the tears came from or why they came, but I could not stop them. I was not aware of how much time had passed, but there was a knock on the door, so I quickly wipe my eyes and stood to open the door.

"Sabine, can I get you a hot bath?" Camille asked as I peered out.

"That would be lovely, Camille, but someone else can do it. You are my sister now, and you need not fret over me."

"Sabine, I would not want anyone else to care for you. Yes, we may be sisters in marriage, but you are still my queen, and I would love nothing more than to care for you."

"Thank you, Camille," was all I could say. I walked over, sat in the big chair in front of the fire, and waited for Camille to fill the tub.

"I will have the cook prepare a meal for you. I will be back in a little while."

I nodded at her and gave a forced smile. She closed the door behind her, and I walked over and locked it. I undressed and submerged myself into the steaming water.

I had no idea how long I was in the water, but there was the thud, thud, thud in my head that startled me awake. I heard voices and crying. *What in the world is all the noise?* As I stood to grab a blanket, the door slammed against the wall, and Blake rushed forcefully into my room, looking at me blankly. I was standing before him, completely without clothing or a blanket around me. His face changed and turned red like the flowers on the plains. I turned so my back was facing him, and I heard the door shut softly. It was Camille who wrapped the blanket around me.

"Sabine, I am sorry. I was scared when you did not answer the door. I have been knocking for some time."

"I.....ah.....I must have fallen asleep. I am sorry, Camille. Could you please go? I would like to be alone."

"Yes, my lady. I will put your food on the table. Will you be down for the morning meal?"

I did not have an answer for her. I just could not make myself move. I stood staring blankly at the floor. I heard the door close as she left. I climbed into bed, still wrapped in the blanket, and let the darkness surround me as sleep engulfed my mind.

My eyes fluttered as the light of the day warmed my face. I heard people talking. *Are they in my room?'* Sleep took over again, and I welcomed the darkness.

There were those voices again. *Who is that?* Darkness surrounded my mind, and I was not sure if I wanted to wake.

I felt someone close to me before I felt the blanket fall against my skin. Someone must have been covering me up. I could feel myself smile, and whispered, "Thank you." Then the darkness took over.

"Sabine." I could feel someone's hand on me. "Sabine, wake up."

Who is that? Why do they want me to wake up? My eyes fluttered, and I saw that someone was standing next to my bed, a man. I could just barely make out his shape. I should have been scared, but I was not. I could not fight anymore. I did not care. I forced myself back into the darkness. My mind did not want to wake.

I heard voices again, but this time, they were loud. "I do not care. There is something wrong with her. Now let me pass, Blake."

Blake? Why is Blake not letting anyone in? Who wants to come in? I tried to force my eyes open, and my voice came out in a grumble. *What is happening to me? Why can I not wake? I feel like I am stuck in sleep.* It came out of nowhere, the ice cold wetness. My eyes flew open, and I was gasping for air. Between my choking and sputtering, I could hear someone gasp and then movement as the door closed. As I gathered myself, I realized that I had no clothing on. I was sitting in my bed, soaking wet, with nothing on, and it happened again. I giggled.

There was a knock on the door. "Sabine, may I come in?" I heard Charles say.

"No, Charles, you may not. I will be down when I have dressed."

There was no response. I managed to get out of bed and find something to put on, deciding to wear a gown. I had been in my boy clothes for far too long, and I wanted to feel like a lady, not the mass murderer that I had grown accustomed to being. Camille knocked on my door and announced herself as she made her way in.

"Sabine, is everything all right?"

"I just wish everyone would stop asking me that," I snapped at her. Immediately I apologized to her. "I am sorry, Camille. I should not be taking this out on you. I have no idea what has come over me. I just want to sleep, but apparently my Guardians seem to think I should not have that luxury in my life."

"It is all right, my lady. Do you want me to comb your hair?"

"That would be lovely, Camille. Thank you."

I sat in the chair while she combed through my hair. "Camille, how long have I been asleep?"

"The light of the day has passed six times, my lady."

Six times? What has come over me? I just sat there and waited for her to finish. I made my way down to the room where we had our meals, and Charles was sitting in a chair at the head of the table all by himself. He did not look pleased at all.

"What is it that you found so urgent that you needed to wake me? And in such a manner as you did?"

"You and I need to have a talk. Sabine, one where there are no ears to hear us. Would you please accompany me to the center of the plain? Raiden is saddled and waiting for you in the front of the cottage."

"I believe you have passed a line here Charles, assuming that I would want to talk to anyone to begin with. Can you not see that I am tired of all of this, and I just want to be left alone?"

"I was being kind in requesting, Sabine. If you do not come of your own free will, I shall indeed remove you from this cottage by force and take you there myself." He stood and waited for my response.

I was not sure if I should challenge him or not, but after a moment of thought, I decided not to. I turned and walked out of the room and to the door, which I flung open and walked out. I climbed on Raiden as I looked around. There were plenty of people standing in amazement, just looking at me. *What is with everyone?* Charles followed me out and climbed on his horse.

"Lead the way," I said in a curt voice.

He looked at me the way my father would have if I had been so curt with him, and it escaped me with no warning at all. I giggled.

We rode for a bit until we were far from those we left standing at the cottage. Charles dismounted his horse, and I followed.

"So, what is it that you need to say to me that warrants your threat to bring me here yourself?"

"First of all, you will begin by telling me what is wrong with you. You take off from Whispering Wind, and when I arrive here, you have been locked in your room asleep for several days."

"So it was you who dumped the bucket of water on me?"

"Yes, it was, so start talking, Sabine."

"First of all, Charles, let me point out the obvious to you, just in case you have forgotten. I do not answer to you. In fact, I do not answer to anyone. Second, you are not my father, or my husband, and I hate to tell you this, but if you were either of those things, I still would owe you no explanation as to what is in my head, or my heart for that matter. Thirdly, let me remind you of the fact that you chose to be my Guardian. I did not choose you, and well, as far as I can see, there is no more danger, so I would like to relieve you of your duty. Now, I would like to return to the cottage and continue my sleep."

I turned to mount Raiden when Charles grabbed my arm. That was his second mistake. My instinct was to throw him to the ground, which I did. I think, if I had my sword with me then, I might have ended his life.

I screamed at him, "Do not EVER think you have the right to lay your hands on me!"

I climbed up on Raiden, and off we went, leaving Charles to lie in the grass. As I rode up to the cottage, I saw Rebecca sitting on Spirit.

"Would you care to ride with me?" she asked.

"I would love to be any place else other than here."

She smiled and handed me my sword. "Shall we?"

We took off in the opposite direction away from Charles. Raiden and Spirit did what they do, and before we knew what was happening, we were flying across the plain. They did their usual and turned in an arch, repeating this process a few more times, and then slowed to a walk.

"Listen, Sabine, if you do not wish to talk, that is fine, but I just want to say that I miss my friend. I am here for you, even if it is just to do this, even if we do not say a word. Charles is not the only one who is worried about you. I have been in and out of your room these past days, and it is frightening to see you just lying there. It is as if someone put a sleeping spell on you. Charles should not have thrown that water on you," she leaned over, "but I am glad that he did." She giggled.

The tears just came. I have no idea why, but before I knew what was happening, her arms were around me, and she held me while I cried. I do not know how long we sat there on our horses, but when I finally stopped, she let me go.

We climbed off. "Raiden will you please take Spirit and go back to the cottage? I will call you when we are ready to come back." He neighed at me and stomped his hoof on the ground as if he was telling me no. "Go!" I said, and they left.

We walked for a while, saying nothing, then I found a nice spot under a tree for us to sit.

"Rebecca, I do not know how to explain how I feel or why. It is as if my whole body is filled with dread. It is a feeling I cannot explain. I do not know why I slept for as long as I did, and I do not know why I have been so mean to everyone. I mean, poor Charles grabbed my arm, and I threw him to the ground."

She tried to stifle a giggle. "Well, it serves him right for being so forceful, but in his defense, Sabine, he is very worried about you. We all have been, and with Blake standing guard over you, not letting anyone near you, it has been difficult at best."

I felt my cheeks go flush. "He saw me with no clothes on," I whispered.

"What? Are you serious?"

"I am afraid so. I just wanted to die. Jared has not even seen me like that."

"That would explain a few things."

"What do you mean?"

"Never mind, but speaking of Jared, Sabine, you have not seen him yet, have you?"

"No, why, and what do you mean, that would explain things?"

"We can talk about Blake later. Jared is not well, Sabine. He just sits in the corner mumbling."

I was not sure that I heard her right. "What do you mean, mumbling?"

"It is as if he is speaking, but no one can understand what he is saying. He will not eat, he will not drink, he has soiled himself, and he will not let anyone touch him."

My beloved Jared, what had that witch done to him?

"When did this happen?"

"Well, Blake said it happened right around the time we cut her head off."

It was in that moment that my body froze. I put my fingers to my mouth and whistled for Raiden. A moment later, he was standing in front of me.

"Take me to Jared," I said to him, and we were off.

I turned to talk to Rebecca, but she was heading in the direction of Charles. Raiden did not go to the barracks where we kept Edward. He went to the farthest end of the valley, to the caves, where I once put the jewels. Standing outside were guards, and there were bars along the entrance.

I climbed off Raiden and said to the guard, "I need to see Jared."

"My lady, we were told that you were not to enter without an escort," said one guard.

I put my hand on my sword. "You will let me pass, or I will make you let me, and you will tell me what this place is."

It was Blake's voice that answered me. "Sabine, we needed a place to put Wellington and Blackmore, and well, now Jared."

I turned to face him as he spoke. "I would like to see Jared."

"With all that I am, I beg you to change your mind."

"Blake do not force my hand. Take me to see him."

He held out his hand, directing me to the gate. All along the walls were torches to light the way. We turned and walked down slope after slope until we reached a door at the end of a long labyrinth of caves. As I peered through the bars, I could see Jared sitting on the ground in the corner, chained to the cave walls.

"Open the door, Blake."

"Sabine, it is not safe."

"Open the door Blake!" I screamed at him.

He produced a key, unlocked the lock, and then removed a very heavy chain before opening the door. My whole body was shaking as I stepped through the doorway.

"Jared," I whispered.

I do not think I could have spoken louder. I wanted to run to him, but the look in his eyes made me freeze in my spot.

"Jared," I whispered again.

His eyes wild and murderous as he gazed at me, he licked his lips.

"Princess, how nice of you to join me." I heard the words, but they were not Jared's.

"What has happened to you?"

WHISPERING WIND THE MIST

"You happened to me, Princess. You brought me out of the darkness and into the light, and now you keep me locked in this cave."

I could not move. I felt Blake directly behind me. If Jared moved, I knew Blake would end his life. I reached behind me to grasp his hand. He took it gently in his and squeezed it, and he did not let go.

"You are not my Jared," I whispered. My voice would not go any higher.

"No, Princess, I am your Jared. I am just the improved version. You are quite beautiful, Princess. Why not come closer, and I can show you just how improved I am. You are to be my wife, and if you would like, we can start now."

I felt Blake tense as the words came out, and I squeezed his hand to calm him.

"You are not my Jared. He would never speak to me in this manner. I do not know who you are, but this is the place you shall remain." The tears started. "You shall never lay eyes upon me again."

"Oh, do not cry for me, Princess. Cry for yourself, because I will come for you, and you will have nowhere to run."

I heard the guards yelling all the way down here, and then I heard Raiden.

"You will die," was the only thing I could say.

He let out a guttural laugh. "I am already dead, Princess. You brought me back from the depths of death itself. Now come to me and let me show you how wonderful it is to be me. Let me show you the union of a man and woman."

He moved toward me. Blake wrapped his arm around my waist and lifted me, pressing my back against his chest, backing out the door. He sat me down and locked the door. I am not sure when it happened, but I felt the world leave me and darkness take over. As I fell to the ground, Blake caught me and carried me up and out of the cave. I woke lying in the grass away from the entrance. Blake, Charles, Rebecca, and Raiden were all there looking at me. I was half lying in Blake's arms. As I looked at the faces above me, I could see that their eyes were full of concern.

"What happened?" I asked them.

"One minute you were standing there, and the next I was carrying you out of the cave," Blake said, smiling at me. I felt as if his smile held more.

I started to get up, and Rebecca reached to help me. As she pulled me up, I suppose the look in my eyes said what I was feeling. *I want to be any place but here.*

"Come on. Let us go for a ride, shall we?"

I was grateful for her intuition and gave her a nod.

"Wait a minute. You are not going riding." Blake said.

"You seem to have forgotten your place, Blake. Let me remind you that it is not telling me what I can and cannot do." I turned and climbed onto Raiden.

I heard Rebecca say softly, "She will be all right."

I turned Raiden and leaned into him, saying, "Ride," and he did. We stopped by the tree again, and I sent Raiden and Spirit back to the cottage.

"You will tell me, Rebecca, what you know about Jared and about Blake."

"What I know of Jared is pretty much what you know. He left Whispering Wind, and on the journey here, he seemed to lose his mind. He tried on several different occasions to harm Juliana, so they chained him and kept him from the camp. When they arrived here, he started with the strange words, but when we killed the witch is when he really went mad. They built the bars in the caves to house Wellington and Blackmore, so they just extended them into another cave for Jared." Her voice became softer, and she reached for my hand. "He is gone from us, Sabine. I am so sorry, but your Jared is no more. We should have never brought him back from the hands of death. We should not have listened to that witch."

"I felt him leaving me long before this. He was not the same when we left the battle. He was more forceful with me, trying to pressure me into... I am at a loss, Rebecca, and my heart is broken."

"As for Blake, I think he thinks he is in love with you."

At the oddest times, it seemed to happen. I heard myself let out another random giggle.

"That is preposterous. He knows nothing of me. I do not wish to discuss Blake. He is not of my concern right now. He just needs to stop trying to protect me and stop ordering me around. What is it with everyone telling me what I can and cannot do? I need to find out who I am, Rebecca. My life, our lives have been torn to shreds. The things we have done and the things we have seen; my mind cannot wrap itself around it all. I think I am going mad, and everyone wants to know what is wrong with me. I want them to just leave me alone. I want to be alone, Rebecca. Would you please just tell them all to leave me alone?"

"I will tell them, but you have to promise me something in return. You have to promise that if you need me, you will come to me."

"I promise. Now, can we go? I am hungry, and I want to sleep."

With that, I whistled for Raiden. When he arrived, we rode back to the cottage, and I ate and went to bed without saying a word to anyone.

CHAPTER TWO

Days passed by, and I did not leave my room. I sifted through my mind all that had taken place in the last three years. I found myself amazed that I was alive, and that I was who everyone believed me to be, The Bringer of Peace. It all sounded like a tale one would tell a child, yet I had lived through it all. Now, I sit here in my room, locked away from those who love me.

I could not make myself go out and face them. I did not know what to say. As I paced the floor, there was a gentle tapping on my door. I knew it was not Camille, for she did not knock.

"Sabine, I need to speak to you."

I opened the door, and Westin threw his arms around my neck, nearly toppling us both to the floor. The giggle came again.

"Oh, Sabine, I am so sorry that you are so sad. Camille told me that you do not want to see anyone or talk to anyone. She said you do not even talk to her. She said that you are either walking the floor or sitting in the chair. Please, Sabine, do not be sad any more. You are missing everything with Stephan and Juliana," he whispered with his eyes full of tears.

"Oh, my love, I am sorry. Westin, I fear that I am not well. I know that you do not understand what has happened to me. I am just trying to make sense of it all. I promise to try and do better."

"Sabine, I know a lot of things. I just do not want to know them. I like my life with Camille and the children. I am happy, and I want you to be happy like me."

The tears just fell, "Oh, Westin, how can I be happy? My beloved Jared is gone, never to return. I am never going to know love, to know what you know."

He wrapped his arms around me and kissed my head. "Sabine, you do not need Jared to be happy. You have me."

It came again. The giggle escaped with the tears and the sobs. My brother, my simple loving carefree brother; only he could make me giggle like this.

"I love you, Westin."

"I love you, Sabine. Now will you come and see the children? You do not have to see anyone else. I will tell no one that you have left your room. Juliana misses you, and Stephan is starting to crawl. Come, Sabine, you are missing everything."

I let him guide me out of my room, out into the world again. We walked down the halls and into his and Camille's room. Sitting on the floor were Juliana and Stephan. With just one look at the beauty and the innocence that these two faces held, I somehow knew that life would get better; that all I had endured was to save them. My chest filled with love, a different love, one that was unconditional and pure.

As the days passed, I stayed with Juliana and Stephan. I ate my meals in my room and kept to myself. I do not know how many times the light of the day turned into the dark of the night, but soon the seasons were changing, and the winter months were upon us. I had not been back to the caves to see Jared, and no one spoke of him, not even Juliana. It was as if he never existed. I knew that I was having a difficult time dealing with everything. It was hard, pretending that Jared was never a part of my life. I just could not stay in the cottage any longer. I needed to ride. I walked to the stables, hoping to see Rebecca along the way, but she was nowhere in sight. Only the guards were out to watch me. I knew that they were going to report back to

Charles and Blake, but I did not care. When I walked into the stables, Raiden was happy to see me.

"Hi, boy. It has been a long time. Would you like to go for a ride?"

He nodded his big head and stomped his foot. I put his saddle on, led him out the doors of the stable, and climbed on him. I could feel eyes upon me, and it made me feel uncomfortable. I knew they were all talking about me, the poor little princess who had lost her way, but I did not care.

I leaned into Raiden and whispered, "Take me away from here," and with that, we were off.

Before we hit the plain, he was in full gallop, the world around me becoming a blur. Only this time, he did not hit the arch. He headed straight for the hills. Before I knew it, we were at the top and descending the other side. I could see the plain stretched out before us, and I knew what he had planned. He hit the ground running. We rode for what seemed like a long time. He never tired. I just knew I needed to be free. Raiden only slowed as we came to a river, where he took his time crossing it. I found that odd, as I did not remember a river such as this. *Where are we?* When we hit the other side, he was off again, the world passing us by.

As I sat on top of my magical horse, I could not help but think about who he was, why he was. I leaned into him as the world around us sped by unnoticed.

"Who are you?"

I did not expect an answer, but I could not help but ask the question. When I looked into his eyes, I could have sworn he was smiling as if he was going to tell me. I lay on his neck, just hugging him and enjoying the freedom. His pace slowed, and when I sat up, we were in front of a mountain, a huge mountain. He nodded his head, a sign for me to sit up right, so I complied. He started his ascent, and up and up we went. The cold air made me shiver. I had on nothing but a gown. We came to a cave more than halfway up the mountain, and he made his way into it.

Further into the darkness he walked, and then I saw it, a small ball of light. As we moved further, the light became brighter. The closer we got to it, the easier it was to see. It was not a light at all, but an opening on the other side of the mountain.

"What is this place?"

I asked him, half expecting him to answer me, but he just neighed at me. As we came through the opening at the end of the cave, lying before us in the center of this mountain was a valley, a valley of beauty beyond my comprehension.

He made his way down the mountain to the valley floor below. The second his feet hit the valley floor, he was off again, stopping only when we arrived in the middle. I sat atop this magnificent magical horse and looked around me. We were at least a day's ride from the edge of the mountains that surrounded us, and the only thing here was a tree. I climbed off him and stood, turning in a circle and looking at the beauty that was before me. It was when I turned full circle that I heard it.

"Sabine."

I spun around, looking for the person whose voice called my name. My chest was racing. How could anyone this far from my home know me. I saw no one.

"My beautiful Sabine."

I knew that voice. My eyes searched in panic. This was trickery. I spun around to face Raiden.

"Why did you bring me here? Are you taken by the witch as well?"

He just nudged me and pushed me toward the tree. I stumbled and fell, landing under the canopy. I sat there staring up at him, but he turned and walked away.

"Where are you going?" I screamed at him, but he did not turn.

"He is doing what I asked him to do."

I scurried around, my chest pounding. Where was the voice coming from? Could this be the witch's doing?

"What is this trickery?" I said out loud.

That was when I saw him. I had to close my eyes because I could not believe what my eyes were seeing.

"No, you are not real."

"No, Sabine I am not real as you are real, but I am here. By whatever magic, I am here."

"No, this is not possible. This is not real. You are dead. I did not see your body, but you are dead."

"Yes, my child, I am gone from this world, but I exist on a plain of another world."

"Father?" was all that I could say, and then the world went dark.

CHAPTER THREE

I had no idea how long I was in the darkness, but when my eyes fluttered open, I was alone. The light of the day had left the sky, and the dark of the night had taken its place. I stood up and looked around for Raiden. My back was to the tree when I felt the warmth radiate from it as my whole body warmed. The fear was like no other I had ever felt before, not even when I said good-bye to Jared.

Then the voice came again, "Sabine."

I could not make my legs move.

"You are not real. This trickery will not work on me."

"I am sorry that I could not be there for you as you came of age, as you were thrust into this life, I tried so hard to protect you from."

I said nothing, nor did I turn to face the voice. I would not allow this trickery to have a hold on me. It was the warmth that caused me to move. It was as if it was turning me to face it. I closed my eyes as I struggled against it to no avail. The warmth engulfed me, embraced me, and for the first time since that day on the hill, I felt safe.

"My child, you are who they say you are. Together, you and Rebecca will bring peace."

The tears fell over my cheeks.

"I do not wish to be this person. I do not wish to be the Bringer of Peace."

"It is your destiny, my child. It was your destiny long before you were born. I am sorry I did not tell you. I am sorry I did not have the time to train you, to explain it to you. Now you must travel this road alone. You and Rebecca must figure it out on your own. I understand now why we were taken from this world. It was foretold. You will be great, Sabine. You are strong, and you are stubborn like your mother, and you will succeed. Raiden will never leave you. He will guide you just as Charles will. You need to come full circle, my love, and you must never stop until peace has come to Whispering Wind. Then you will find true happiness."

"My happiness lies in a cave touched by death."

"No, Sabine, Jared was just a stone on this path you are on. Your true happiness lies before you, unseen by you."

"You know nothing of what I have seen or what I have done."

"Open your eyes, child, and look at me."

"I cannot. I will not let this trickery take control of me."

It was the second voice that forced my eyes to open.

"My beautiful Sabine."

I felt the breath within me leave. I felt my breath stop. My eyes opened, and before me was my mother, my beautiful mother, and next to her was my father. Beyond them were Ardes, Simon, and Jenna. The tears flowed freely. I wanted nothing more than to run to them, to stay with them.

"You must protect Westin and Juliana. They are still in grave danger. The evil forces know they are your weakness, and now baby Stephan. You must never give up, Sabine. Your father speaks the truth. Only in the end will your true happiness come, and it will be so much more than you know. Then and only then will we be at peace."

"I miss you," I said in a whisper.

"As I do you, my love, but we are not destined to be together yet, not for a very long time. You are always in our hearts, Sabine, and we will always be with you. It is only because of what is coming that you are here now. You have lost your faith. You have lost your will to live. You must find it. You must protect them, Sabine."

Jenna spoke next. "Juliana is the key, Sabine. She is the key," was all she said.

"You must protect her, Sabine. Take care of my little girl," Ardes said with urgency.

"Father's sword combined with mine, Sabine, together they are forged," Simon said in a whisper.

My father reached to touch my face. I could not feel his hand, but I felt the warmth. "You are my greatest accomplishment, my child. I could not have asked for anything more in this world. I love you."

And just as they appeared under the tree, they disappeared. Gone. I stood in the darkness alone. Raiden walked up behind me and nudged me, but I was still in a trance like state, unsure of what I had just seen, or if I had seen it at all. *How strong was that witch's hold even after death?* I mindlessly climbed on Raiden, and he began our journey back to the cottage. I remembered nothing of our journey back. The only thing I could hear or see in my mind was them, all of them. My family, the people I loved most in this life had all been taken from me. It was not until we started our decent into the valley of the cottage that I snapped out of whatever trance I was in. The shouts and the flickering light of the torches rushed toward me. There were hundreds of them. I leaned into Raiden.

"Take me to the cottage," I whispered.

Before I knew what was happening, the torches became a blur. Raiden slowed as we approached the cottage. I jumped off him and made my way to my room. Closing the door behind me and bolting it, I closed my eyes and cried. I found myself curled on my bed shaking. The next thing I knew, the door flew off its hinges, and Blake was at my side. He climbed on the bed and wrapped his arms around me.

"You foolish girl, we have all been searching for you. Where have you been?"

I said nothing. I buried my face in his chest and let him hold me while I cried.

I had no recollection of time or how long Blake held me. I was aware of nothing but the thumping in his chest. I felt his head move a few times, but no words were spoken. I cried myself to sleep in his arms, and it was the warmth of the light of day that woke me. I sprang up in a panic, throwing myself on the floor and backing away from the bright warmth of the new day. I could not take my eyes from the light. It was instantaneously that he was at my side.

"Sabine, it is all right. You are home."

I forced myself to look at him as the light surrounded his great form. He reached up to touch my face, and I closed my eyes.

"How long was I gone?" I whispered.

He looked at me in a quizzical manner as if I were speaking in a foreign tongue.

"You do not know?"

"How long was I gone?"

"The light of the day came and left five times, Sabine. Where were you? We have been frantic looking for you."

"I am afraid that I was in a place that no man has ever been and returned."

"What sort of place is this you speak of?"

"A place of trickery, a place of nothingness, a place where only the dead go," I whispered.

Blake sat down in a huff in front of me and reached up to touch my face.

"Sabine, what you say makes no sense. What happened to you?"

I could not take my eyes off of him. He was quite beautiful; his hair was curly and yellow like Rebecca's, his teeth were straight and white, his jaw was chiseled like it was formed from stone, and his eyes were the color of the green meadows of the plains.

"I am not sure," I whispered into his face.

He leaned closer to me, so close I could feel his breath on my mouth.

"I was so frightened. I thought you were dead."

I closed my eyes and swallowed. I felt it come from deep within me, and I did not want it to escape, but the second I opened my mouth it was there. I giggled.

"No one can kill me, not yet anyway."

Blake pulled away from me, staring at me like I had just slapped him.

"Charles is beside himself. He has been in here many times wanting to talk to you. I would not allow him to wake you, but he will be back, and you will have to face him. I must warn you that he is not happy."

I proceeded to gather myself up and stand.

"Consider me warned. Now, if you will excuse me, Blake, I would like to change and have a meal."

I hated to dismiss him like that, but I was feeling uncomfortable being in a room alone with him. He bowed and excused himself as he backed out of my room. I would have closed the door behind him, but it lay on the floor. I just stood there, amazed at what had happened to me. I took a deep breath to steady myself. I found a gown, changed, and then made my way down to the meal room, where I found Charles sitting at the table. I do not know what came over me, but I could not stop the words I spoke to him.

"The last time I checked, you did not live in this cottage. I find it offensive that every time I come in here, you are sitting alone waiting for me. If you have not figured it out, Charles, let me say it to you in a simple manner. You are not my father..." I paused, remembering what I had seen. "Nor are you my husband. You will stop trying to control me."

He slammed his hand down on the table, which made me jump.

"You, Princess, will have a conversation with me, and you will keep me informed as to what is going on. I cannot protect you, Sabine, if I do not know where you go."

"I go where I choose, Charles," I snapped back at him.

"You are an impossible girl."

"In case you had not noticed, Charles, I am no longer a girl. In fact, today is the nineteenth year of my birth. You forget your place here. Your services are no longer required by me, so, by all means, please feel free to leave whenever you choose."

With that, I turned and left the room, heading for the kitchen. As I passed the staircase, I heard a crash and then glass breaking. I could not hide the smile on my face. Walking into the kitchen stopped all activity. Charlotte was standing at the huge table.

"May I have something to eat please?"

All the kitchen maidens were scurrying about, trying not to fall over one another to gather me food. I sat down at the huge table across from Charlotte.

"Are you all right, Your Highness?"

"Please call me Sabine, and no, I am not all right. I just spent five days talking to my dead family. How could anyone be all right after that?"

"What did you say?" The words came from behind me.

I turned to find none other than Blake.

"Nothing, I said nothing. Would you and your brothers kindly leave me alone? I would like to eat my meal in peace and then find Rebecca. Go report that back to Charles, so he knows just what I am doing and where I am at."

I turned around to find food in front of me, and I proceeded to eat. I did not hear him move, so I was sure he was standing there watching me. I cleaned my plate and asked for more, and then I cleaned that plate, thanked the kitchen maidens, and rose to leave. Blake was still standing in the doorway, so I went out the kitchen door to find Rebecca. I did not have far to go; she was in the courtyard with Charles.

"We need to talk, now." I said to her as I stormed past.

As I made my way out to the front of the cottage, I just kept walking. I could hear Rebecca's footsteps running up behind me.

"What is going on, Sabine?"

"I am fearful that you will not believe me when I tell you, but before I say one word, you must promise me, Rebecca, that none of what I am about to say to you leaves your lips. You must give me your word that it stays with you. You cannot tell Charles. You must not tell Charles. No one must hear these words."

"Sabine, you are scaring me."

"Your word, Rebecca."

"My word, Sabine. What you say to me here and now will not leave my lips."

I walked and walked further away from the cottage and all that it held. I could not risk anyone hearing these words. I stopped and turned to face her. Looking past her, I could see Charles, Blake, and a few others standing watching us. Then I turned my eyes on hers.

"I was frustrated and wanted to ride, so I asked Raiden to take me. He rode to the hills, over them, then across the plains to a river. We made our way through the river and proceeded to some mountains. He climbed the mountains, and half way up, he entered a cave. We walked for a very long time in the darkness through this cave, through the mountains, and at the end was an opening. We passed through it into a valley of such beauty, something I have never seen before. He rode into the center of the valley where a lone tree stood."

Rebecca said nothing.

"As I stood there and looked around, I realized that the edge of the mountains was at least a full day's ride on an ordinary horse. Raiden proceeded to nudge me until I fell to the ground, which in turn placed me under the canopy of the tree, and then he just walked away."

I turned and started walking.

"Sabine, why would he do that to you?"

I just kept walking. I needed to get away from the words I was about to say to my friend, words that would, under ordinary circumstances, find me locked in a cave such as Jared's. This was crazy. Saying those words would make me crazy. *No, saying these words will make them real.* I stopped and turned to face my friend.

"The tree was some sort of channel. Some sort of trickery took place under the canopy of that tree, Rebecca, for what I experienced makes no common sense. It could not have been real, but, seeing what we have seen, doing the things we do, and being who we are, it had to be real."

I just could not say the words, so I sat down in a huff, buried my face in the skirts of my gown, and cried. Rebecca wrapped her arms around me, holding me close.

"Sabine, we have seen and done more than any one person is

capable of doing. Things that scream trickery, scream magic of the darkest kind. What you have to say to me cannot shock me."

It happened yet again. The giggle just came from deep within me.

"You have no idea what I have seen."

"Then tell me."

"My family, Rebecca... I have seen my family, and I spoke with them."

She let go of me and landed on the ground next to me in a huff. I was afraid that she would run, so I reached out and touched her hand. In turn, she held onto mine.

"Is that at all possible, Sabine?"

"I know what I saw, and I know I was wide awake."

"What did they say to you?"

"They told me that this is not over, that I have lost my faith, that Juliana is the key, and that danger still lies ahead. Simon's sword and my fathers are forged together. They also said that my happiness is not with Jared, and that I will find it at the end of this."

"Did they say anything else about what is to come?"

"No, just that together, we are supposed to figure it out, and that we will bring peace. Rebecca, could this be real?"

"I do not know, Sabine. Do you think we should tell Charles?"

"He will surely think I have gone mad."

"No, he will not. While you have been so withdrawn from all of us, he has told me things."

"What things?"

"That word has traveled the lands about what we had done to the barbarians, and that there is an uprising coming. No one knows where we are, Sabine."

"The barbarians found us. Who is uprising and why?"

"We should go talk to Charles. He can tell you."

I could not bring myself to move, so I just sat there looking at her. She stood and reached for my hand.

"We are in this together, Sabine, and if your father was really in that meadow, and if the words he spoke were the truth, then this is far from over. I think it would be better if we were, at the very least, informed of what could possibly come of all of this."

I reached for her hand. "I am not so sure that I can do this."

"We will do this together. We must do this. We must protect Juliana and Stephan. They are now the future of Whispering Wind."

"Whispering Wind is no more, Rebecca. You were there. You saw what happened."

We walked back to the cottage, where we found Charles and Blake standing at the door waiting for us. I did not say a word to either of them. It was Rebecca who spoke.

"We need to talk, and we need to be far away from here."

Without speaking another word, Blake went and retrieved the horses, and we rode to the farthest point from the cottage.

"Charles, you need to tell Sabine the things you have told me, and then Sabine needs you to trust her, for she has something to say."

I climbed off Raiden and sat in the grass, waiting for him to begin. We sat there in a circle; Rebecca next to me on one side, Blake next to me on the other, and Charles across from me.

"I have sent scouts out to all the lands over these past weeks, and they have all come back saying the same things. People think that we were not good but evil, all tainted by the witch's spells. They say that her magic is what allowed our small army to conquer all that we have. The rumors are that we took Wellington and Blackmore hostage to control the lands. They were started by Jared and Rebecca's mothers. I believe that they were, or still are, in fact being controlled by the witch. I believe that the connection lies with Jared. Sabine, I cannot and will not end his life without your permission, and before you say anything, you must remember that he is not Jared any longer. There is no way to save him from his hell. The scouts have said that the people of the lands are forming an uprising against you and Rebecca, against all of us. There is a new band of barbarians that have entered the lands, hired by the kings of the known kingdoms. They are known as blood-gutters, and they are said to drink the blood of their conquests and eat their guts. We have a serious problem forming. If the barbarians found us here, these new barbarians will eventually find us as well. We need to consider leaving this place."

"There is nowhere for us to go, Charles. They want me and Rebecca, no one else but us."

"They want us all, Sabine. They believe that we have all been tainted by your trickery."

"I suppose you are right, Charles. We need to leave this place, soon, and I think because we are the only ones who can stay in Whispering Wind without the mist affecting us, that is where we will make our stand against them. Westin, Camille, Juliana, and Stephan must remain here. They must remain safe. You need to devise a plan for them to be taken to safety should they be found here. Your best men must protect them, especially the children. They are the key. Juliana is the key to this all."

"She is just a child, Sabine, I believe you are the key."

"Charles, what I am about to say to you did in fact happen to me. It was as real as you are sitting in front of me. When I was gone with Raiden for those five days, he took me to this place, to a place I will never see again. While I was there, I spoke to my parents, to Jenna and Ardes, and to Simon. Juliana is the key. Simon's sword and my father's must be forged together. My father assured me that we will succeed. It is up to me and Rebecca to figure this all out, so whatever you think you know about what is to come, you must not tell us."

No one said a word. Charles just stared into my eyes, looking for the truth of what I had just said to him.

"You know what I say is the truth, Charles. I can see it in your eyes. I also know that Jared cannot live another moment, but I just do not think his life should end here. He must die in Whispering Wind with the witch. I am fearful that, if we end his life here, this valley will become as Whispering Wind. Have him taken there as soon as possible. Your brothers, Rebecca, and I are the only ones who can go. We are the only ones who will live."

It was Blake who spoke, saying, "I will not leave you, Sabine. I will send Steven and Joseph with Jared. Aidan, Edward, James, Charles, and I will accompany you and Rebecca."

"We are but an army of nine, Blake. I fear it will not be enough."

Charles spoke then. "The others can come and camp outside of Whispering Wind, in the hills that surround the castle. Anyone who enters will die, I am sure of it. We will need to prepare and leave as soon as possible, but I will have them take Jared immediately."

We all got up and mounted our horses. "Sabine, may I speak to you alone please?" Charles asked.

Blake and Rebecca started back to the cottage.

"I am sorry for the way that I have been with you, Sabine, but you need to understand my role in all of this. I am sworn to protect you with my life. When you disappeared within yourself, and then for real when Raiden took you away, you not only jeopardized yourself, but you made a mockery of what we stand for, what we believe in. We, I am your Guardian, and you must never forget that. I will die for you, Sabine, and would not even hesitate to kill for you."

"I know, Charles. I have no idea what came over me, or what has come over me. I think I was just a bit more than overwhelmed. I believe that is why Raiden took me away. I needed to be reminded of who I am and what it is that I must do. I still do not know, but I, we, will figure it out together. Charles, can I ask you a question?"

"You can ask me anything."

"Does my happiness end with Blake?"

"What kind of question is that?"

"Well, you said it was foretold that you would be Rebecca's husband. Was it foretold that Blake would be mine?"

"I am not allowed to give you the answers to what the future holds, Sabine. You must find them for yourself," he replied with a smile.

CHAPTER FOUR

I rode back to the cottage to find Westin. I knew he was not going to like that we were leaving again. He was in the kitchen with Stephan.

"Hello, my love."

He looked up at me with a huge smile on his face. It was the look that was in my eyes that made it fade.

"What is wrong Sabine?"

"Will you go for a walk with me?"

"Sabine, I have learned that when we go for walks or rides, it is never a good thing."

"I know, my love, but will you please come with me?"

Camille walked in just as he was standing.

"Will you take Stephan, Camille? Sabine wants to talk to me."

She smiled at him, and I knew that Charles had already told her we were leaving. Westin walked out into the courtyard with me.

"My love, I am sorry, but we have to leave you again. It is not safe for us here yet. It is Rebecca and I who are in danger, and as long as we stay here, I fear that they will find us. I cannot risk you and the children. Do you understand?"

"Sabine, I am not afraid of anyone, but I am afraid that this will be the last time that I see you."

I could not help myself. I grabbed him and hugged him tightly, whispering in his ear, "I promise you, Westin, you will see me again. I will return to you, and when I do, we will return to Whispering Wind, and we will stay there for the rest of our days."

When I pulled away from him, he was crying.

"Oh, please, Sabine, do not go. Do not leave me here alone."

"You will not be alone. I need you to look after Juliana for me. The guards will stay with you, and when it is safe, I will send Blake to get you and bring you home. I promise."

"All right, Sabine, you never tell me promises unless you mean them. I love you."

"I love you too, Westin. We are leaving in a day or two, so we have until then. Come on. Let us go play with Stephan and Juliana. I want those giggles in my mind when I leave. I will need them to see me through all of this mess."

With that, we headed into the cottage to find the children. Jared was removed from the caves and taken back to Whispering Wind to the dungeons. Two days later, we were ready to go, leaving behind guards to take care of Westin, Camille, and the children. Sitting on Raiden in front of the cottage, I looked down at my brother, at Juliana, and at the ever-playful Stephan.

"I love you, Westin. Please do not worry. You stay happy, and you take care of them."

"I love you Sabine, and I will."

I smiled at him and then turned to Camille. "It is with great honor that I leave my brother and these children in your care, Camille. You are as Jenna was, my sister."

The tears fell from my eyes as I turned to face Rebecca. "Let us go."

She nodded, and we made our way back to Whispering Wind.

As we climbed the hill to Whispering Wind, the feelings of dread filled me once again. Raiden was the first to the top, and just as I had left it months ago, the mist still hugged the land. *Here we go again.* We made our way to the fields and then proceeded into the mist. It was as cold as I would imagine that death would be. As we came out of the fields to the gates of the village, I saw on the ground what looks to be the bones of wolves. *I knew this mist was death.* We continued through the village to the castle. Sitting in the courtyard were Steven and Joseph who came with Jared.

"Your Highness," Joseph said.

"Joseph," I said as I nodded toward him. "Have you secured Jared?"

"Yes, my lady, and I am fearful to say this, but while we were down in the dungeons, we checked on the witch. Her body is still there, as is her head."

I could not stop the giggle from coming out of my mouth. With everyone looking at me, I said, "Well, did you think she was going to get up and walk away?"

"No, my lady, you do not understand. There are no bones as we expected. It is her body, exactly the way we left it."

I was not sure if I heard him right. "What do you mean, Joseph?'

"Come, my lady, and see for yourself."

We followed Joseph and Steven to the dungeons. Down we went through the labyrinth to the witch. As I walked to the door, Raiden put his massive head on my shoulder, as if to stop me from entering. I reached up to pat his nose, saying to him, "It will be all right, boy."

I did not pass across the threshold of the doorway, but Joseph was right; her body and her head lay in the exact spot we left them, untouched by time. No one said a word. We just looked back and forth at one another. It was Raiden who reacted, neighing and rearing up on his hind legs as he thrashed his front legs in the air. We moved out of his way. When he landed, he pushed me toward the stairs and continued until we were out of the dungeons.

"What is it, boy?"

I asked, expecting him to answer me. His eyes were enough of an answer; I saw fear in them for the first time. Raiden was afraid.

"I am not sure I understand what that was about. It is as if he is human or something," Blake said.

I climbed up on him and leaned into his ear.

"Take me for a ride." I looked up at Charles and said, "I will be back," and Raiden bolted.

He took me up to the top of the hill where I climbed down off of him.

"What is going on, boy?"

I was expecting him to answer, with all that I had seen and all that we had done. I found myself on top of a hill outside my father's kingdom, expecting a mystical horse to speak to me. I thought I should be in the dungeons with Jared. I felt that I must be mad.

Raiden just stood there with his ears twitching, looking at me. If he had opened his mouth and spoke, I would not have been surprised, but he did not. He just stared into my eyes. Our eyes locked for however long, and then I heard it in my head. I heard one word.

'Evil.'

I stepped back and tilted my head. *There is no way that just happened.* "You cannot be serious," I said to him.

Raiden just stared at me, and without any notice, he turned his head toward the castle and nodded, and then I heard it again.

'Evil.'

The light left me, and I fell to the ground. I had no idea how long I was lying on the hill, but, when I opened my eyes, Blake was holding me, and Rebecca was crying.

"What happened?" I asked.

"Oh, Sabine, Raiden came flying into the courtyard, neighing and snorting and stomping his feet. We followed him here and found you lying on the ground. What happened? Are you all right? I thought you were dead."

"Rebecca, I am fine. I... what happened?"

I looked up at Raiden. He was standing there, obviously nervous about what had happened.

"We do not know what happened. Raiden just came running into the courtyard, and we followed him up here and found you. What happened to you?"

Blake was obviously concerned, but Charles did not say a word. He just stood there watching me, watching Raiden.

I sat up and gathered myself. "The light of the day is leaving. I think we should figure out what it is we are going to do." I stood and climbed on Raiden. "I am tired and hungry, and I need to be alone. I am going to my room. I am sure Raiden will accompany me. When the light of the day returns, we will discuss what is happening here and what we should do with Jared."

Charles nodded, and I turned Raiden and went back to the castle. When I reached my room, Raiden stood in the hall.

"You are not coming in there with me. If you insist on staying with me, you will stay out here. I really do not know what happened on that hill, but I am tired, and I will figure it out tomorrow."

Raiden just nodded his head. I went into my room and climbed in my bed, closed my eyes, and sleep took over. I saw images in my head while I slept, horrible images of fire, and giant balls of fire reigning down on Whispering Wind. There was no color in the images, but I saw Jared laughing, the witch Devious holding his hand, and Juliana standing in the middle of a fire. When I woke, I was soaked with sweat. Sitting up, I put my head in my hands. *What in the world was that?* I climbed out of bed and went to the window to get some fresh air. Looking out over the courtyard and beyond, I saw that the mist was still hanging just above the ground. I watched as Aidan walked from the barracks, and the mist swirled around his feet, and then I remembered what Devious had said just before we cut her head off. She looked at Raiden and said, 'You will not allow this old friend. You know what will come of it if you allow her to kill me. He knows more than you, Princess, and he will not allow this.' Quickly, I changed into a gown and opened my door. Standing outside was Raiden.

"We need to talk," was all I said to him.

I walked down the hall, and he followed. I made my way down the grand staircase, and he followed. I made my way through the great hall and out into the courtyard, and he still followed. Charles and Blake were there.

"Charles, I am going for a ride. I will not be long."

"Sabine, I wish you would not go alone."

"I will not be alone. I will be with Raiden, and I will not be long."

I climbed up on him and kicked him in the sides. He knew I was angry with him. I never kicked him unless I was mad. We made our way through the village and the fields to the top of the hill. I dismounted him and walked away, and he followed.

"I remembered what that witch said to you and to me when we cut her head off, and if I am not mistaken, you smiled. Now, I do not know how any of this is possible, how you managed to put that word in my head, but if you can pull this trickery on me, then I would have to assume that you are evil as well, that you are tainted by the witch. What you did is impossible."

I stood there looking at him, waiting. This is so stupid. He is not going to speak to you. He is just a horse.

'I am more than just a horse, Sabine.'

The world went dark. Again, I woke in Blake's arms with Rebecca crying next to me. As my eyes fluttered, I could hear her moans of agony.

"Oh, Sabine, what is happening to you? Are you ill?"

I just lay there looking at her, and it happened. I giggled. Everyone just stood there watching me. I sat up and could not control myself; the giggle just kept coming.

"I think I am going mad, Rebecca. I think that I should be locked in those dungeons with Jared. I am seeing things and hearing things that are not possible in this world. I have seen and spoken to my family, who are dead. I have been seeing visions in my head while I sleep. I am hearing things in my head when there is nothing or no one around to say them to me. I have gone mad. It must be this place. This mist must have some sort of power over me." I looked at Charles. "You are my Guardian. It is your duty to lock me away."

He did not move or smile or speak; he just stood there looking at me, like he was willing me with his mind. I stood, as did Rebecca, and then he spoke.

"Would you all please leave me and Sabine alone? I will make sure she returns to the castle safely."

"But, Charles, there is something wrong with her. She should be in bed," Rebecca said, sounding frightened.

She very well should have been, for I knew not what was happening to me.

"Please, Rebecca, Sabine is fine. Trust me."

She took one look into his eyes and smiled. Without another word, they mounted their horses and left the hill top.

"You know, do you not?"

"It all depends on what you are talking about."

"Do not play games with me, Charles. You know, and you have known all along. You know because he talks to you as well. Is this part of what you cannot tell me? Is this what we need to figure out on our own? Exactly who are you, Charles?"

Not one word did he say; he just started to walk. I stood there watching him as he walked away and then turned and walked back. He continued to do this several times before he came to a stop in front of me. Looking deep into my eyes, I heard him in my head.

Yes, I have known all along.'

"What? How are you doing that? How is this possible? Has this mist got ahold of you as well? We are all doomed, Charles. If you can do this trickery as well, then all that is being said about us throughout the lands is truth. We are under the witch's spells, and we are all doomed for death. Jared and Rebecca's mothers, have it right, do they not? I cannot imagine this to be truth, Charles. I cannot deal with this."

"Sabine, you are not under the witch's spell. None of us are. It was Raiden who chose to reveal himself to you. I cannot tell you what is to come, you *must* figure it out for yourself. What Raiden did, taking you to the valley, to the tree, revealing himself to you, it only happened because it is time for it to happen. The legend is what it is, and as I have told you many times before this, it is not my place to tell you what will come. You and Rebecca must do this on your own. As time progresses forward, the truth will be revealed. You will know what to do. My job in all of this is to keep you safe. What is to come must happen in order for the legend to come to an end. You are who we say you are. I can tell you this, Sabine, what is coming is nothing you have ever seen or will ever see again. What your father, Ardes, Jenna, said to you is the truth. Juliana is the key, Sabine."

"How can a child be the key to any of this, Charles? She is just a child."

"Her birth was foretold. Samuel knew this, and that is why she was not killed. It had nothing to do with anything else. It is why the witch had her. The witch knows. Juliana is the key," he said this with a sense of exhaustion.

"Well, if she knows, why then did you let us cut her head off?"

"Because I cannot interfere, Sabine. My job is to protect you, not make your choices for you. You and Rebecca must figure this out. Now, you need to talk this out with her. She has knowledge you do not, just as you have knowledge she does not. I will go back to the castle and send her to you."

"Charles, do you know what Simon meant when he said his sword and my fathers are to be forged together?"

"I believe he said 'Father's sword combined with mine, Sabine, together they are forged.'"

"What does it mean?"

"Do you have Simon's sword?"

"Yes, it is back at the castle."

"When you return from talking with Rebecca, we will discuss this. I will send her to you."

CHAPTER FIVE

I stood there with my mouth hanging open as he mounted his horse and rode away, down the hill, across the fields and into the village. It did not take long before I saw the dust from Spirit as he flew through the village. A moment is all it took for Rebecca to be standing next to me.

"Charles said we needed to talk." She held out her hand for me to take.

We walked a bit, not saying anything. How was I supposed to tell my friend that my horse, and now her love, could speak to me without saying any words?

"Rebecca, there are things I must tell you, but I do not know how to say them."

"Sabine, there are things I must say to you as well."

I stopped walking and turned to face her. "We should say them together."

She nodded, we both took a deep breath, and we said the same things, "Raiden/Spirit can talk to me."

I could not be sure how long we stood there staring at one another, and I could not help but think. *Did I hear her right?*

"You just said Spirit can talk to you?"

Rebecca nodded her head, and in a whispered voice, she said, "And Charles can as well."

She just stood there looking at me. In my mind, a million thoughts just suddenly exploded at one time.

"Rebecca, are we tainted by this witch like everyone thinks we are? How is it possible for this to be? What sort of trickery has this witch put on us all? A horse who speaks with no words, a man who says things without ever moving his mouth, and I hear no sound, yet I hear him in my head. I think we are all mad. We are doomed, Rebecca, doomed to live here in this place, in Whispering Wind, for all eternity, never to have a normal thought again." I started walking back and forth. "This cannot be truth, Rebecca. How long has Spirit been doing this?"

"Since you left us and rode with Raiden to the valley, but it was Charles that I heard in my headfirst, and that was just after we brought Jared back from death."

"Why did you keep this from me? Why did you not tell me?"

"Well, to be honest, Sabine, I thought perhaps I was going mad, and then, when I figured it all out, I came to tell you, but Charles told me that you needed to figure it out for yourself. You have been so withdrawn, Sabine. For such a long time you stayed away from us. I thought Raiden had spoken to you and you believed yourself to be mad, but Charles assured me that he had not. Then Raiden took you to see your parents, and I was going to tell you then, but again, Charles stopped me. So when did Raiden finally speak to you?"

"The day before this one, when you found me on this hilltop. I was so sure I was going mad."

"Charles explained it to me that you had to open your mind in order to receive Raiden's thoughts."

"Are you telling me, Rebecca, that you can do this as well?" I remembered what happened in the dungeon. "When we were in the dungeon, is that what that was when I heard you in my head?"

"Yes, I was not sure how or why that happened. In the beginning, I could only hear them in my head. It took some time before I could project my thoughts back to Charles and then Spirit. With you it was easy. I think because we are so connected. I never tried again, not until Spirit."

"So, do you think you can do this to me again?"

Right after I said it, I heard her in my mind.

Yes, Sabine, I can. Now that you have opened your mind, I can project my thoughts to you.'

"Okay, you need to stop that. Can you see what I am thinking?"

"No, it does not work like that. I cannot hear what is in your head unless you want me to hear it, just as you cannot hear me unless you are listening. You have to want me to hear you."

"So can I ask you what Spirit has said to you?"

"He just reassured me that you were safe with Raiden. Sabine, I have been so worried about you. You locked yourself in your room for so long, and then you removed yourself from all of us. When Raiden took you away for those days, I thought you had left me, left us all. I was so frightened." She threw her arms around me and hugged me.

"Can you hear Raiden in your head?"

She pulled away, looking at me. "No, Sabine, I cannot. He is your Guardian, not mine. I can only hear Spirit and Charles."

I turned and looked at Raiden. "So you are indeed a magical mystical horse. You can speak to me in my head. You ride and never tire. You never sleep. Do you eat?"

Yes, I do. When I am hungry.'

"You really need to stop doing that. I am not so sure I am comfortable with you in my head. You are just a horse, and I am mad."

The only thing I could think to do was walk away. I was not sure if this was real, so I started walking, and he followed.

"Please, Raiden, I would like to be alone."

But he kept coming. Halfway down the hilltop, I turned and screamed at him.

"Please leave me! Go back to the castle!"

He stopped and just stood there, and I kept walking. As I made my way down the hill, the memories of that fated day when the barbarians came flooded my memory. *How could all that Father said to me be truth? What is this destiny that has been forced on me? How is a tiny child the key?* I had nothing but questions and no real answers.

"Sabine!" Rebecca yelled.

I kept walking. I really did not want to talk to anyone, especially now that I could hear them in my head. This was more than I could bear, and I just needed to get away from everyone, from everything. I worked my way down to the fields and back into the mist, through the village, and finally to the courtyard where Charles and Blake were in a heated discussion. I tried not to hear them, but I could tell that Charles was angry.

"You have no right telling her anything. You must not interfere. Everything must happen naturally."

I stopped in my tracks, knowing this is about me. Rebecca had said in the valley that Blake thought he was in love with me. As I changed direction to walk up to them, Charles stopped talking and turned to face me. I was not about to let him speak first, so I did.

"I would assume that since you both stopped talking when I walked up, that your conversation is about me."

No one said a word. Blake just stood there, trying with all that he was not to look at me. I had to try very hard not to giggle at him.

"No, Blake, you do not have any right to tell me anything. You may think you feel something for me, but just let me point something out to you. I am the only other woman in this tight little group of ours, so it is only natural that you would think you have feelings for me, but I need for you to know that I do not share those feelings. I love Jared and only Jared, and it will be a very long time before I do not. So, please stop thinking you are my savior, and please stop hoping that I feel the same way. I am sorry if this is uncomfortable for you, but I did not ask for your protection, and I certainly did not ask for your feelings." I turned to walk away as he spoke.

"Sabine, please stop and listen to me."

"Blake, you are about to cross a line here, and as your brother and your superior, I am telling you not to say a word."

"Forgive me, Charles. I know that all of this," he waved his hand through the air, "is supposed to happen naturally, and that we are living and breathing a legend that was told through generations of time but keeping them in the dark is not only reckless but cruel. I will not allow her to believe that we were talking about my feelings for her when we were not."

I turned to face him, trying my hardest to look angry. "If you were not discussing his feelings for me, Charles, then what secret is so important that you have to order your brother not to tell me?"

"Sabine, I have told you time and time again…"

I had to stop him. "I know you cannot reveal the path. We must find it on our own. I know this, Charles, so now please let him speak."

Just then, Rebecca came walking up from the stables.

Blake looked at Charles. "I am sorry, brother, but this must be said." He turned back to me and continued, "Sabine, it is because of my feelings for you that I feel the need to tell you this. I know what I am feeling is real, and it has nothing to do with any of this." He waved his hand in the air again. "There is something going on with Jared, but Charles does not want you burdened with this. He thinks we should just end his life and be done with it, but I think," he paused, turning to give Charles a strange look. "I think you should at least be given the opportunity to have some input into ending the life of the man you profess to love."

"What about Jared?"

"Since he has returned here, he has changed yet again. We know that it is from being here that this transformation has taken place, but perhaps you should see for yourself." He turned and swept his arm in the direction of the dungeons.

Charles stepped into my path. "Sabine, I would not recommend this. What is happening to Jared is not real. You must remember that the influence of the witch still has a hold on him."

"Do not think that you have the ability to stop me, Charles. I have seen just as much as you, and I shall not be fooled again by her. Besides, she is dead. What power could she possibly have over us?"

I started to walk away when Raiden stepped in front of me.

'No, Sabine, you must not go.'

"I told you to stay out of my head and move out of my way. I will go, and I will see Jared, and none of you will stop me."

I side stepped Raiden and continued on my way. When I reached the gate, Steven and James were standing guard.

"Excuse me," I said as I pushed my way past them.

As I descended the stairs and worked my way through the labyrinth of hallways, I could hear them behind me calling my name. I had no idea where Jared was, so I had to stop and listen. I heard the others coming after me, and I heard Raiden's hooves clicking on the stone, and then I heard him. He was humming. *I know that tune. What is that?* Then it hit me; it was the lullaby that my mother used to sing to me. *How did he know it? I had never told him that melody.* I followed the song, and it led me right to him.

"Hello, Princess. I have been waiting for you. James told me that I would never set my eyes upon that beautiful face of yours. I told him he was wrong, that you would come for me, and here you are."

I could not believe what I was seeing. It was my Jared. He looked like Jared, and he sounded like Jared, not at all like the man I saw in the caves in the valley.

"My love, hurry and unlock the door. The others are coming. We can finally be together, and they will see that I am fine."

I heard Raiden in my head.

'Sabine, no, he is not your Jared.'

My hands instinctively reached for the lock, but I had no key.

'Stay out of my head,'

I thought, hoping he would hear me.

"I do not have the key," I whispered into the room.

Jared smiled at me. "You are the princess. You do not need a key. Just concentrate, Sabine, and you can unlock the lock. I know it is in you to do so."

Is he kidding me? How was I supposed to unlock a lock with my thoughts? I looked at the lock, and I concentrated. Raiden's thoughts jumped into my head.

'NO, Sabine, he is not your Jared.'

Just then, the lock popped open, and I started to remove the chains. Just as I opened the door, I felt an arm around me, lifting me off the ground and pulling me away from the door.

"Get your hands off of me!" I screamed.

"No, you must not enter that room. You must not get close to him, Sabine. He is not your Jared."

"Blake, if you do not let me go, I will run my sword right through you." I heard Jared laugh.

"That is my princess, feisty as ever. You cannot hold her, my friend. She is stronger than you know."

It was Rebecca who I heard then. "Blake, let her go. She must do this on her own. She must see for herself. Otherwise, she will not believe."

Blake's grip loosened, and I wiggled free, making my way to the door of the cell. There he was, looking just like my beloved Jared, and his smile brightened my whole body.

"Oh, my love, I have missed you." I whispered.

"As I have missed you. Come here and let me hold you."

I hesitated. "Jared, I am not sure that is a good idea."

He smiled. "My love, I would not harm you."

He put his arms out, beckoning me to come. I moved closer, my eyes never leaving his, and the closer I moved toward him, the more I felt complete. I was just out of his reach when he blinked. In the dim light of the room, I was not sure that I saw what I saw in his eyes. They were still the blue that I remembered, but there was something different, something more in them. My feet stopped. The silence was tremendous. I could hear nothing but the thumping in my chest. He smiled at me as my foot rose to take a step. I tilted my head to get a better look at him and to return his smile, but then I saw the green swirl in his eyes, and I froze.

"Come, my love, and we will be reunited."

I heard him say, but I no longer believed him, and I shook my head.

"No, I cannot come to you, Jared."

His face changed, and he became angry.

"You will come to me, Princess, and we will be together. It is what is meant to be. Ask your beloved Charles. Ask your damn horse. They will tell you," he said, and then he lunged toward me.

I nearly fell trying to get away from him, but Blake caught me and moved me from his reach.

Charles stepped in front of him. "You will not have her, Jared. No matter what that witch has made you believe, you will not have her."

Screaming at Charles, he said, "You will not stand in my way. You know this, Charles." He calmed his voice. "You know it is foretold that she will be mine. We will consummate our union, and you will not stop it."

"No, you will not, Jared."

I did not think I had ever seen that side of Charles before, this stern and forceful man.

"I will be on the ground dead before I allow you to lay one finger on her, and you know that is never going to happen. She is not yours because you are not Jared. I know you, witch. I would know you anywhere. I know what your plan is, and we will stop you."

Jared laughed, but it was not his voice that followed.

"Oh, you think you know what is to come, but you do not. They will come for you, all of you, and if you think that pretty little princess and her horse are unstoppable, you are just as mad as you think I am."

"Yes, witch, they will come, and they will die just like your band of barbarians died. You cannot stop us. You will not stop us. Peace will be had, and you will be no more."

The guttural sound that came out of Jared's mouth shook the walls; it was as if he was growling. I managed to work my way out of Blake's arms to move in front of Charles.

"Witch, I will end you. Your hold on Jared will be no more, nor will your hold on Juliana."

"Ah, my Juliana," she slithered.

"No, she is not your Julianna!" I screamed at him.

Jared laughed again. In his voice he said, "Do not worry, Princess. You will be mine. Come closer, and we can consummate our promise to marry. You will be ripe with my seed, and this will all end."

He slipped his tongue out of his mouth and licked his lips, making them glisten in the pale light.

"You will not have any other but me. I will plant my seed within you, and you will belong to me forever. It is foretold in your legend that you shall bore a king, and that it shall be my bloodline. You know this to be truth, my friend." He looked past me to Charles.

"I will die before I allow you close enough to touch her, witch, and as I have said before, that will not happen. You cannot kill me," Charles said.

The walls shook as he let that guttural growl escape again from deep within him. His eyes fixed on me; I felt drawn to him, my body moving closer to him against my will. I could feel the love deep within me stir. He reached for me, his fingertips barely touching the flesh on my arm. The fire I felt as his fingers brushed my skin wiped out every fear, I had of him. My foot rose to move forward, but it never touched the ground. I was flying through the air to the opposite side of the cell. Before I had a chance to gather myself and my thoughts, the voices in my head were loud.

'Well, old friend, we are face to face again.'

'We have never been friends, crone.'

'We are born of the same bloodline. You chose this ridiculous path of righteousness, the path you know will not win. It is foretold that we will rule these lands, and I will see it through to the end. Our father did not want this.'

'You know nothing of what our father wanted. You were led astray by your greed for power, by your desire to hate. You wanted the power that was not intended for you. You are the one who murdered our father to possess his knowledge, but it did not work, did it? Instead, you became this evil crone you are now.'

Jared growled again at Raiden.

'I will win, brother, and you know this. That is why you stand before me. You are scared of what is to come. You will die as our father did, trying to protect the secret, trying to harness a power you know nothing about. I will win, and you will not be able to stop me.'

I managed to stand, disbelief warring with what I was hearing in my head. As I looked around, I locked eyes with Charles, who was watching me. He nodded his head at me, as if giving his permission.

"No, Raiden will not be the one to stop you. I will."

Before I realized it, I was moving toward Jared, toward the witch Devious, my hand on my sword.

"I killed you once. I will kill you again, and again, until I am sure you are dead."

Jared spun to look at me. "Oh, Princess, you cannot kill me. You will not kill me. Without me, your precious Juliana will never come to her full potential. She needs me to guide her, to teach her how to harness that power that lies within her. You know it. Your Jenna told you."

I drew my sword. "You know nothing of Juliana, and you will never know her."

Before I knew what was happening, my sword went flying through the air. The brilliant light that followed knocked me to the floor and lying there in a heap was Jared without his head. No one moved; the silence seemed to go on forever. I just sat on the floor, looking at my love, looking at his lifeless body, when I realized that I felt at peace.

CHAPTER SIX

I managed to pull myself up off the floor of the cell and worked my way to the door. I did not look back at Jared, nor did I look at anyone else. My mind was numb with the loss of my love and with the reality that I just cut off his head. I slowly worked my way up through the labyrinth of the dungeons and out into the bright light of the day. James was the first to notice me.

"Sabine, is everything all right?"

"No, James, it is not."

Was the only thing I could say before I felt the panic rise in me. I stood there only for a moment before the urge to flee won out. I ran. I ran as fast as I could. I did not know where I was going, only that I just needed to be any place but there. I needed to be away from Raiden, away from Blake, away from all the eyes that watched me with guarded caution. My legs slowed only when I came to the edge of the hedge that ran along the rocks at the end of the back courtyard. *The cave.* I moved with swiftness, so no one could see me, along the rocks behind the hedge. I made my way to the cave, where it was dark and cool and secluded. I knew that Raiden would figure out where I was. I just hoped he would have the manners not to follow me and not to put it in someone's mind where I had gone.

I collapsed on the ground and soon found myself crying. How is any of this possible? My horse was not always a horse. He was, in fact, the brother of the witch who swore to murder me and my family. How is it possible that he was once a man? Who turned him into a horse? How much did Charles and the others really know? Am I but a pawn in a murderous game between siblings? How did I unlock that lock with no key? What trickery is being played on me? None of this is real; it cannot be real. Oh, Father, why is this happening to me? Why were we left behind? My head was aching, and I felt ill. I lay on the ground weeping, wanting no more of this madness. I wanted Westin and the children. I wanted to be like him, happy and without a care in the world. I did not want to be this girl who had just murdered the only man she would ever love.

I do not know how long I cried, I just know that, when I awoke, I could hear my name being called out. It sounded as if there was panic in the voices. I did not want to see them, and I did not want to talk to them. Raiden, I was sure, knew where I was, and I was thankful he had not let on. I closed my eyes and let the darkness take over. I just could not face the fear or the pity in their eyes when they looked at me.

But as the darkness came this time, that was exactly what I saw; the fear in their eyes as the sky lit up with fire. It was coming right toward us from all directions, but I was not afraid. I heard screaming, but it was not from me. It was Juliana. As I looked around, I could not see her. I did not understand why she was here; she should have been with Westin. As I searched for her, the sounds of the fire grew closer. Without warning, the castle walls started exploding around me. Fire and bricks were flying through the air as I searched for Juliana. The screams were getting closer. Without any warning, I saw her. I saw little Juliana, but she was not little. She had grown, and lying on the ground in front of her was Rebecca. I rushed toward them, only to see that Rebecca was lying at her feet. She was dead. I woke unable to breathe, unable to move. I scrambled up, gasping for air. The screams were so fresh in my mind, so much so that I realized they were not in my mind. I was the one screaming. I felt arms around me. I could not be sure whose they were, or if they were even real. I just felt them holding me, and then the darkness came.

I felt myself being lifted in the air. I could only hope that I had died, and I was going to be with my father and mother. My body was being jostled around. I was floating, and then I was laid on a soft place; perhaps it was a cloud, perhaps I was with them, and when I awoke, I would be with my family. Unfortunately, that was not the case. As my eyes fluttered against the light of the day, I could make out my old room. I was in the castle. *Who brought me here? It had to have been Blake.* I rubbed my eyes and began to sit when I noticed them sleeping in the chairs; Rebecca, Charles, and Blake. I sat there watching them for a while, then Rebecca's eyes opened, and she smiled. As I put my finger to my mouth to silence her. I motioned to the door and she nodded. We quietly left the room and made our way down to the great hall before we spoke, our words in whispers.

"Sabine, what happened to you? Why did you run?"

"Come, I will tell you everything."

We walked out into the courtyard and proceeded to the great gates and down into the village. When I knew we were far enough away, I spoke.

"What did you hear right before I cut off Jared's head?"

"I did not hear a thing. Why? What did you hear?"

"Come on. Let's go to the hill and talk. There is much we need to discuss."

We walked through the village, or what was left of the village. As I looked around, I could see the work that had been done before we left, before we cut her head off and the kingdom filled with mist. We made our way through the fields and up to the hill. I sat down on the ground, facing Whispering Wind, and Rebecca sat beside me.

"Why did you run?"

"I could not and did not want to deal with the inquisition that would, and will, surely follow. I just needed to be alone. I am sure that Raiden knew where I was, and I am sure he knew I wanted to be alone. Did he not tell Charles where I was?"

"I am not sure that Charles can hear him in his head like you can."

"Oh, I would not be so sure of that, Rebecca. While Raiden and Jared, or the body of Jared, were face to face, you did not hear anything in your head?"

"No, but I suspect that you did. Are you going to tell me what happened, or are you going to torture me by withholding that information?"

"It was the strangest thing. Apparently, Raiden and the witch Devious are brother and sister. According to Raiden, Devious murdered their father to gain the knowledge that he had, but instead, it was given to Raiden, and Devious went to the dark side. She became evil. That is why she had said that Raiden would not let us kill her. She was counting on the fact that they were siblings and thought he would save her. I guess she was wrong." I could not help but giggle.

"Wow, so how did Raiden turn from a man to a horse?"

"This is knowledge I do not have, but I will by the time the dark of the night approaches. Rebecca, I had a vision in the cave. I do not know what it means, or if it means anything at all. I just do not understand how it could possibly be anything but my overactive imagination."

"Well, from the sound of the screams that were coming from you, it had to be pretty frightening."

"Oh, Rebecca, it was about you."

"Me? What about me?"

I looked her in the eyes and just said the words, "You were dead."

We sat there looking at one another. I thought I saw a flicker of fear in her eyes, but I could not be sure.

"You seem unaffected by my words."

Carefully, she answered, "I too have had similar visions. Mine are full of fire, and in them, I die. But, in my visions, it is Juliana who kills me."

"She is in mine as well, but I have not seen her as the one who kills you. Oh, Rebecca, how could our beautiful little Juliana be the one who ends your life?"

"In my vision, she is not little. She is not grown either, but she is not little. I do not know Sabine, but I cannot let this interfere with what we must do. I know nothing about visions, or even if they are visions and not just our minds playing tricks on us. Remember where we are. That witch's magic is very powerful. Perhaps she is just trying to keep us occupied with these thoughts, so we are distracted from the real task at hand."

What she was saying to me made sense; the witch was very powerful, so much so that she had inhabited Jared's body and mind, not to mention she had entered my sleep through Juliana.

"You are right. We should just put this aside and focus on what needs to be done. And right now, I need to find my horse and have a conversation with him." We both laughed. "How silly does that sound? This is so unreal, Rebecca. Our horses speak to us through our minds. It is trickery and magic at best. Should we be cautious of this? I wish I could speak to my father. Raiden was his horse, as Spirit was your father's. Perhaps your father would know where they came from."

"Spirit was not my father's horse, Sabine. My mother gave him to me when I was a child. She said that she found him in a field one day when she had gone for a ride. I never questioned it."

This made no sense to me. Raiden was my father's horse, and his father's horse before then. He had been with my family through generations. Would Spirit not come from the same line as Rebecca's father?

"How is that possible? Spirit must have been your father's horse, Rebecca. If Raiden was my father's, and we are these so-called Bringers of Peace, it would make sense that the line of Spirit would follow the same path."

"So, it would seem. Perhaps Charles knows."

I whistled for Raiden. "Perhaps we should go ask him."

As we looked toward the castle for Raiden and Spirit, we both noticed the mist. It seemed to be thinner today, almost as if it was disappearing. Things were not what they seemed to be there.

As we entered the courtyard, Charles, Blake, Joseph, Steven, Aidan, Edward, and James were all standing by the fountain as if they were waiting for us. Rebecca and I climbed off our horses.

"I think it is time that we shared information, Charles. Some things have come to light, and I think it is time for you to tell us what you know."

"I am bound by my oath, Sabine. I can only tell you what you already know, so perhaps you and Rebecca should tell us what it is you have discovered. Then, and only then, will I be able to tell you."

I looked at Rebecca, signaling for her to begin.

"Charles, who is Spirit? I mean, Raiden came from Sabine's father when he died, but my father is still living, so where did Spirit come from?"

Charles just stood there looking at her as if he did not know what to say. His eyes never left hers, and I wondered if he was talking to her in her mind. I would have to ask Rebecca later.

"It is true that when Stephan was murdered that Raiden became Sabine's, so it would only be fair to say that Spirit came from your father when he died," Charles spoke very carefully.

Rebecca turned to look at me. "What does that mean?"

I turned to Charles. "What you are saying then, if this is truth, is that Rebecca's father, Gerald of Blackmore, is not Rebecca's father. Gerald is still alive and was alive when Rebecca received Spirit."

"It would seem that way, Sabine. The horses you ride are bonded to you both. The legend speaks of the two of you and the lineage of your horses. It is not specific of which lineage you were to come from."

"Then who is my father?"

"I cannot say, Rebecca. I fear that the only one who knows that answer would be your mother." Charles reached for her hand.

In as calm of a voice as she could muster, Rebecca said, "Charles, would you be so kind as to send your brothers to retrieve my mother for me and take her to the hilltop?" He turned to them and nodded. We watched as they rode off.

It was now my turn. "Charles, did you hear what happened right before I cut off Jared's head?"

"No, Sabine, I did not. What did you hear?"

"I am not sure what to make of it all, but it would seem that Raiden and Devious are siblings. Well, they were siblings, brother and sister.

Devious murdered their father to obtain his knowledge, but instead, it went to Raiden and she fell into the darkness."

Charles turned and walked away. Rebecca and I just stood watching him as he walked back and forth. Looking up, he said, "I have heard this fable. It was just a story, one we all believed to be fabricated, but apparently it is truth. Do you know any more, Sabine?"

"No and I am not sure that I want to know how a man would become a horse; one with magical powers, one that can speak to me in my head, one that never sleeps, never needs to eat, and can run faster than the wind can blow. Charles, I am afraid that there is more. I have had a vision in my sleep, one filled with fire and Juliana and resulting in the death of Rebecca, and she has had the same. What does it all mean?"

"I am not sure about Raiden, but your vision, well, I have had the same. I thought, at first, that it was the witch who was putting these things in my head, but, last night, I had the vision again, after you cut her head off."

"As did I," said Rebecca.

"Myself as well, while I was in the cave. I thought we could not be killed, so how could this vision be truthful?"

"Yes, it is the legend that the two of you cannot be harmed in any way, but you had said that Juliana is the key. That is what Jenna said to you. Let this keep with me. I need to speak to my father. When my brothers return, I am going to Wellington to see him. I do not have all the information that I need. I think things are happening here that I know nothing about, and if it is my position to keep you safe, then I need to be informed."

"Charles, Rebecca and I will be fine. Raiden and Spirit can out run any horse, and the mist prevents anyone from entering the kingdom. You can go now. We will be fine."

"This is true. Are you sure you will be all right?"

"Yes, so go and seek the information from your father. We need to be prepared if what you have heard is the truth. We are going to need it to survive this."

Charles kissed Rebecca and left.

CHAPTER SEVEN

We watched as Charles rode off to see his father. I could not imagine how Rebecca must have felt, knowing now that her father really was not her father.

"Are you all right?" I asked her.

"I am not sure if I am or not. It is not every day that you discover that your father is not who you thought he was. My mother was unfaithful, so what does that make me now?" she said softly.

"I do not know. Perhaps Spirit knows. I cannot believe I just said that. How is it that we can hear their thoughts in our heads?"

"I remember that first time I heard him, when we were riding back to the valley. I do not think it was as much of a shock as it was for you, because Charles had already been in my head."

"Do you hear him often?"

"No." She giggled. "It is not as if we have conversations. In fact, he rarely does it. It is more like he tells me to get ready or hold on, things like that."

"Do you think we should try and talk to them, to see if they can or will? How is it that we are talking about talking to our horses with the hope that they talk back? Rebecca, I am still not sure that we are not under the witch's control. Perhaps your mother and Jared's mother are right. Perhaps we are tainted by her trickery."

"I would be inclined to believe you, Sabine, but not after all that we have seen and all that we have done. You did not imagine your family being murdered, you did not imagine Samuel plotting to kill you and Westin, and we certainly did not imagine defeating tens of thousands of barbarians. Those things happened. I think we should do as Charles asked of us, and that is to believe. These men have been raised for generations, through specific bloodlines, to watch over us. Even though they were expecting us to be men, it is still you and I who have turned up in this generation and who have been what everyone has been waiting for, for a very long time. You know me. I am right there with you, Sabine. Whatever you think we should do, I shall not argue with you. Perhaps we should just bow out and let things happen the way they would have happened if you had actually been here when the barbarians came."

"I have been thinking the same thing. I would love nothing more than to go into hiding with Westin and Camille, keeping my hair covered and not letting anyone know who we are. But at whose expense would that be? It seems that there are those who believe and those who are counting on us to bring them out of this barbaric time to live in peace. As you and I both know, fear is not a good emotion to have these days. I mean, do we really want to live in fear for the rest of our days, to be on the run and always hiding? I do not think I would like that at all. I know I would like to marry someday, to have children, and to know love, but you and I are known now. My hair will never change color, and people will know me no matter where it is I go. I will never have the things I desire, not until this is done. If we die in the process, then so be it. At least I will be with my family, and at least we will have tried. As farfetched as this all is, I think it would be best to see it through to the end."

"I agree. Even if our visions say that I am to die at the end of this, there really would be no place to hide, and I do not think I could live with myself if I did not at least try to save these people. If it is our destiny, our fate, or whatever was foretold, we must see it to the end.

All that has been told to us has been truth. All that we can do is beyond any reasonable explanation, so it cannot be trickery. It is magical, and I am not sure if trickery and magic are the same thing, but I think perhaps we should at least attempt to figure out these horses. No one is about, so it would not look so silly for us to try and talk to magic horses," she said with a giggle.

I could not help myself; I had to laugh as well. I can almost hear my mother's voice in my head, telling me it is all just a story someone made up, that a horse could not possibly talk. We started walking to the stables. It was a bit eerie walking through the courtyard in such silence. The wind was not moving around the buildings as it did on any other day. I could not hear the birds, nor hear the stream. It was as if all time and movement had ceased. I listened, the only thing that I could hear was the thump, thump, thump in my chest. I stopped, and Rebecca looked at me. I held my hand up for her to stay silent as I picked up my foot and stomped the ground, there was nothing; no sound, no dust, nothing. It was then that I heard him in my head.

'Do not move.'

I looked at Rebecca, and her face said that she had heard the same thing. A million things were running through my head. *How is this possible? Is this more of the witch's trickery? Are we going to die if we move?* As the last thought passed through my mind, I saw movement just beyond Rebecca. My eyes shifted to see what was there and landed on Raiden. I was seeing him, but then I was not. It was as if he was fading right in front of me, and then, all of a sudden, it was not Raiden, but a man standing in the distance. The air left my body as the words started to flow into my head.

My name is Raiden of Westbrook. The land you stand on was once my father's kingdom. I was to inherit this land and carry on the work set before my father, but, before I came of age, my sister, Diana, you know her as the crone Devious, became obsessed with the gifts that were instilled to our father. She was not happy with the knowledge that she would not inherit our father's kingdom because she was a woman.

She was the first born, but she was not a man. She plotted against me and my family and endeared herself to a witch to achieve her goal of total destruction and domination of the knowledge. The witch lied to her and assured her that she could remove my father's knowledge from him and give it to her, making her the most powerful. In return, Diana had to commit her life to the witch: and Diana agreed. She would have done anything to stop me from getting what she believed was her birthright, but when my father was murdered by Diana's hand, it set into motion the events that changed both our lives.

The knowledge was never meant for Diana. Her heart was not pure, and the witch knew this, but she took Diana anyway. When Diana realized what had happened, she cast a spell on me, turning me into a horse. Her reason of thinking was that I would not be able to carry out my father's work as a horse and not a man. What Diana did not know at the time was that my mother was with child. She was swept away by those you know as the Guardians, and was kept hidden, as was her child, a son, my brother Tristan. He was kept hidden until he became a man, and he fought to take this land back from the barbarians who moved in and claimed it when my family disappeared.

Although he was not a huge man, he wielded a sword that was nearly his height in length, and his hair was the color of yours. The knowledge that was instilled to my father was in turn given to Tristan when he came of age. He could not be defeated. I became his horse and fought along with him, and I have been here with his son, with his son's son. I was with your father, and now with you. Sabine, we are distant relations. We are of the same bloodline. I am here to finish my father's work, to carry out his task. You are pure of heart. You are who they say you are, and it is up to you and Rebecca to finish this, so this land will finally be at peace.'

'What is this? What are we supposed to do? You must tell me.'

Just as it began, it ended. I could feel the soft breeze on my face, and the sound of the birds filled the air as I exhaled. Neither of us moved, but just stood there looking at one another.

"Did that just happen?" I asked.

"I heard everything, Sabine. What did you see?"

"I saw Raiden as a man, and now there is nothing. This has to be trickery, Rebecca. I am not so sure this is what it is. How can any of this be truth? A man turned into a horse. A sister possessed by a witch."

"It would explain how Jared became possessed by her, how she moved into his body. She must have done the same to his sister. Maybe that is why she called him old friend."

Just then, we heard a horse. We both turned toward the great gates to see Joseph riding in.

"Rebecca, we have your mother. She is on the hilltop."

On cue, Raiden and Spirit appeared, and we were off to find out just who Rebecca's father was. One way or another, we needed to figure this out. As we reached the top of the hill, it was apparent that Rebecca's mother had been taken by force, for she sat on top of a horse bound and with a sack over her head. Rebecca moved closer and reached up to remove the sack.

"Hello, Mother."

"What is this? You stay away from me. You are possessed by a witch," she hissed.

"Funny you should say that, Mother, for it is not I that is possessed. It is you being misguided and told untruths, just as you have filled my life with untruths. But now, Mother, it is time for you to tell the truth. It is time for you to reveal to me what it is I wish to know, or I am afraid that you shall suffer the same fate as your husband."

"Do not threaten me, child. I shall have your head, for it is the only way to stop a witch."

"Well, Mother, let me assure you that is not truth at all. I am afraid that I have a rather uncomfortable question to ask you, a question that shall surely shatter your virtue."

"You know nothing of virtue. You sleep with men you are not bound to by marriage. You roam the countryside with armies of men. You are a blemish on our kingdom."

The shock on Margret's face as Rebecca slapped her hard was quite comical. I had to stifle my giggle.

"The only blemish, Mother, is you. Passing off a child to her husband that was not his holds a death sentence, does it not?"

Margret sat on her horse staring at Rebecca. I could not determine whether it was shock or fear in her eyes.

"You know not what you say."

"Well, Mother, let me tell you what I do know, and we shall see if you will speak the truth, or if you shall suffer the same fate as Gerald. Let me first present you with a query of sorts, Mother. Where did Spirit come from, and how did he already have a name?"

"I told you. I found him on a ride, and I named him Spirit because he was hard to catch."

Rebecca's laughter startled me. Her Mother, on the other hand, looked terrified. "That is one mistake, Mother. I shall allow you three. I am going to tell you a little story, and then you can try again. The horse that Sabine rides was her father's, and his fathers before him, and his father's father, and so on. Do you see where I am going with this? Raiden is a very old horse. Spirit is just as old as Raiden, and I believe that he was my father's horse who was sent to find me when my father died. Are you with me so far, Mother? So, it would be safe to say that Gerald is not my father, seeing as how he is still living, and I was given this horse in my fifth year?"

Her mother did not move.

"You see, Mother, you know who I am. You know who my father is, and to save yourself and your virtue, you have ordered my death, just as Gerald has. He did not know that I was not his, not until Wellington murdered Sabine's family. How am I doing so far? So, my Mother, Queen of Blackmore, is nothing but a lying, cheating whore who would murder her own child to save herself."

"You know nothing of who I am. I loved your father, but my father sold me to Gerald for a king's ransom. I did not love Gerald. I do not love him. End his life. I do not care. He is nothing to me. He abused me and tortured me my whole life, committed acts of sexual deviance against me time and time again. He was the one who had your father murdered when he discovered that I would secretly see him on my rides. Your very existence will destroy Blackmore. You may have done me a great justice by imprisoning Gerald, but you will not be the downfall of Blackmore. All that I have suffered from that barbaric filth will not be for nothing. You will die, Rebecca, if not by my hand, then by those who are coming."

"I shall not ask you again, Mother. Who is my father?" Rebecca screamed.

"Stanford of Whispering Wind," Margret said in a very soft whisper, so soft that I was not sure I heard her correctly.

Rebecca turned to look at me. I shook my head, for I had no knowledge of my father having a brother.

"That would be your second mistake, Mother. There is no brother to Whispering Wind."

"There was... Stephan's younger brother. Gerald had him murdered before Sabine was born. Her father knew of our love, and he would not intervene on our behalf when my father sold me to Blackmore. Stephan knew you were his brother's child, and he did nothing to stop Gerald. The way I see it, Whispering Wind got just what it deserved in the end."

This was news to me. I felt Raiden twitch beneath me. It was truth; Rebecca and I were cousins. Raiden did not mention this Stanford or Spirit. *How is this possible?* I said in my head, hoping Raiden heard me, but there was no response.

"I have had enough of these untruths from you, Mother." Turning to Joseph, she said, "Would you please escort my mother to her destination, and please keep her head covered. I would like her to visit my father for a while. Perhaps spending some time with him will bring her to the realization that the truth must be told. Not to mention, she must never forget that we hold all the power, not her and certainly not Wellington."

"As you wish, my lady," Joseph bowed his head.

As Rebecca turned to face me, I could see the look in her eyes and that smile. I knew exactly what she wanted. I nodded at her, and we were off. Raiden and Spirit took off in a dead run, heading out onto the plain. We did not speak until the horses slowed. Rebecca was off first and landed on the soft grass with a thump. I sat next to her.

"I am afraid to tell you that I know nothing of this Stanford, but if it is truth, then we are cousins. We are of the same blood. It would explain a great deal... why our horses are who they are, our swords, the bond we have."

"I just do not know what to believe anymore, Sabine. No wonder my father found it so easy to order my death. There has got to be someone somewhere who knows the truth, Sabine. Did your father keep any family records?"

"I do not know, but, if he did, they would be in his study. We should go back to the castle and have a look around. I found all those jewels in a hidden place, so perhaps there is something somewhere else in the castle that is hidden as well. I never knew there were dungeons, but there are."

"Yes, I agree. Come on. We still have some light left in the day." She said.

CHAPTER EIGHT

We rode back to the castle. Walking into the great hall I said, "My father must have had a study."

"I know that Gerald had a study, but I cannot say that I have ever been in it."

"I was in Samuel's study a great deal while I was in Wellington. It is strange how men have these secret places that women and children are not allowed, but, I suppose, when you are running a kingdom, you would need a place to run it from."

We wandered around the halls until we came to a doorway. I looked in and it was obvious that it was my father's study.

"I do not think that I have ever been in this room." I said as we walked into the room.

The walls behind his desk were lined with tall book shelves, floor to ceiling, and each shelve was packed with books. My father's desk sat against the far wall; it was huge, bigger I think than the table we ate our meals at. The fireplace dominated the opposite wall, so massive that I could literally duck a bit and walk into the firebox, and the windows were covered with dark velvet drapes. On the wall to the left of the fireplace hung a tapestry.

"We should start with the desk," I said as I moved across the massive room.

My father's chair was tumbled over, and there were papers thrown all over the floor. The drawers had been pulled out and the contents dumped on the floor.

"I guess the barbarians were looking for something as well. My guess would be the jewels."

We began our search. Sitting on the floor, we worked our way through everything that we found, replacing things in the drawers as we went along, and then replacing the drawers back in the desk, drawer after drawer. When we finished, I pushed the bottom drawer in, but it did not shut all the way.

"Something is stopping it." I pulled it out and looked into the hole, but there was nothing in there.

"Put your hand in the hole and feel along the ridges. Maybe there is something you cannot see," Rebecca said with idle curiosity as she rose from the floor to look at the books on the shelves.

My hand slid in the opening at an awkward angle, and I leaned in, so I could feel all the way to the front of the desk. My arm just was not long enough.

"Rebecca, my arms are too short. Come see if you can feel to the front."

She giggled but stuck her arm in with her fingertips just brushing the wood. Her arm went in and out four times.

"Nope, nothing."

I tried the drawer again, but it still would not close, so I put my feet on the drawer and kicked it.

"Did you hear that?" Rebecca whispered.

"No, what did you hear?"

"A click or something. Did you break the drawer?"

I pulled it out, but there was no obvious damage.

"No, it is fine. Why would it matter if I did or not? It is just an old desk."

Putting the drawer back in presented the problem again. Once more, I kicked it with my feet.

Rebecca whispered, "There, did you hear that?" I sat there shaking my head no. "It came from back here," she said, turning to look behind her, but the only thing there was the tapestry.

I got up and walked to the tapestry looking up the length of the wall to the ceiling. The piece of cloth was the biggest I had ever seen. Grabbing the side of the cloth, I pulled it back, revealing the wall behind it. A memory flashed in my mind of the hedge. I stepped behind the tapestry and put my hands on the wall.

"What are you doing?"

"I have a feeling. Come on."

Rebecca joined me behind the cloth. I moved one step at a time, pushing on the wall as we moved. We must have been halfway when the wall suddenly gave way. I froze.

"What is it, Sabine?"

I smiled at her and pushed with all my might. Her face lit up when the giant stones began to move.

"A secret passageway," she whispered.

The wall swung away more easily than it should have, opening up into a dark hallway.

"We are going to need some light." I whispered back.

We worked our way back along the wall into the study.

"There has to be some candles around here with a striker." Our search turned up nothing, so we moved through to the kitchen where we found lots of candles and one striker. "Take as many as you can carry," I said.

We gathered them and went back to the study and along the wall to the passageway. Stepping inside, I lit two candles. As we moved down the passage, it felt as if the ground was on a slope. We actually stepped down a few steps and then into a room about half the size of my father's study.

There were shelves on every wall and another smaller desk in the middle of the room. There were candle holders with numerous candles in them, we lit them all. It was amazing that Father had this room, and no one knew about it. I was sure that the barbarians searched for this place, for its contents.

"Well, I guess this is where the secrets are," Rebecca said.

"I guess you are right, so let us get busy and find them."

I sat down at the desk and proceeded to work my way through the drawers. There were all kinds of little trinkets, pages of written text, drawings of things I had never seen before, and drawings of the castle; things I am sure had some significance to my father but meant nothing to me.

"Sabine, I think you should see this." I turned to see Rebecca standing on a ladder with a leather-bound book in her hand. "I think this is for you."

"What do you mean, for me?"

"Well, it has written here, 'My Dearest Sabine', so I think it is meant for you."

I reached up and took the book from her. Inside were pages and pages of my father's writings. I took the book back to the desk and laid it down. Sitting down, I began to read.

My Dearest Sabine,

Today is the day of your birth. We were blessed with a daughter who possesses such beauty as I have never seen before. But with your beauty, I am afraid, comes much danger for you. Your life has been foretold for generations. The shock of it all is that you are a daughter and not a son.

"What does it say?"

"Well, he says that my beauty comes with much danger."

"What does that mean?"

I giggled. "I do not know, but I think my father was just being proud. I see not the beauty he does. Now let me read. Better yet, come and read with me. This is about you as well." Rebecca came and sat in the huge chair next to me, and we proceeded to read.

Our family has been safe from the stories of time, for they have all been just stories until today. I started to think just the same, that what was foretold, I would not see in my lifetime, that the next generation would hold the legend, your generation. I thought one of your brothers' children perhaps, or one of your children could be the one, but today it was made apparent to me that it is you. I know now that I will not be alive when you come of age, for it is a road you must travel without my guidance. I will do all that I can while I am here to ready you for what lies ahead of you. I must apologize to you now in these pages for what is going to happen to you, and for the things you must live through and do before it all ends. I hoped you would be a son, for men handle such travesties with much less emotion than women.

You are less than one day, and I am finding myself working a plan to keep you hidden from Wellington and Blackmore. They must never know that you are who you are. Once you are discovered, it will set into play a sequence of events that have been foretold and cannot be stopped. There are many who will seek you out to destroy you. My heart breaks at this moment in time, knowing the things you will endure. My hope is that I succeed in keeping you safe long enough to train you, but with your hair the color of the sky as the light of day breaks, I am fearful I will not succeed.

"He knew the minute you were born. Oh, Sabine, he must have been so tortured through your life, trying to keep you hidden."

"It was the marriage of Ardes and Jenna. That is how Wellington discovered me," I said, and we continued.

My Dearest Sabine,

You have been with us for an entire season. You are such a happy child, so loved and so filled with love. You have the kindest demeanor. What lies ahead of you will be difficult at best. Today I did as I was instructed by my father, as he was by his father, to take the block of steel and have your first sword pounded by Julliard Porter. I had one pounded for your counterpart, your cousin Rebecca. She has been hidden away as well, and I bear the weight of guilt every day for not stopping my brother's murder. Stanford knew what lay ahead for him once she was born, with her golden hair and crystal green eyes. You will know her someday, and you will be as sisters.

Your mother wants us to pack up and move as far away as we can from this. She is afraid. Not that I mean to make light of her fears, but she is the strongest woman I have ever known. It seems odd that she would be afraid of anything, but I do understand. You are our daughter, and we know that we have to leave you, and we know what lies ahead of you, and no parent would ever want that for their child, especially their daughter.

"I am so sorry, Rebecca. My father knew and did nothing to stop Gerald from murdering your father."

"It is all right, Sabine. I am finding it hard to feel for a man I never knew."

My Dearest Sabine,

Today marks the end of your first year. You took your first steps today, while in the courtyard with your mother. Westin accidentally pulled your bonnet from your head, exposing your hair to a guardsman. I saw his face and knew instantly that he knew who you were, and I could not have him telling anyone. I immediately took him into my study and took his life. You must remain secret for as long as possible. If the truth of your existence were to get out before you could defend yourself, then your death would be imminent. I have taken many lives in my time here, but never one of an innocent man. I will compensate his family and make sure his children want for nothing. Please forgive me for the things that I have done, and for the things you will discover in this journey that I have done. It has all been for the greater good.

I swallowed hard and looked at Rebecca. What could I say? My father was a murderer of innocent people, and no matter how I looked at it, there was no reason for it.

My Dearest Sabine,

Well, today marks the end of your second year, and things are becoming even clearer now as you grow. Out of all of my children, you have excelled in everything; your speech is more advanced and your ability to obtain information is beyond your years, so it must be true. The legend is real, and you, my beautiful daughter, are the savior these lands have been waiting generations for.

There is an evil that dwells here; an evil that, if not stopped, will bring nothing but pain, suffering, and death to the people of these lands. This land that we live on is sacred ground. It is said that this is where life began, and the evil that fights for it will bring nothing but death. You will find, or at least I hope you will find, the jewels that I have hidden within these walls. There are many, but there are only a few that you will need to discover. You will know them when you see them, even if you have no knowledge of what is happening to you. They possess an energy that you will need to harness through your swords. As you grow, I will embed in you clues. As you discover the things I secretly write in this journal, you will flash on those memories, and it will become clear to you what needs to be done.

No one knows the whole truth, but Raiden will guide you. I hope that if you discover this room before I am gone that you do not think your father to be mad. We are, after all, talking about a horse, but you will find that he is not just a horse. He was a man a long time ago, a man who could have and who would have stopped this in his time, but his fate was sealed by the dealings of this very evil I speak to you about now. This evil knows no bounds and will use every means it can to stop you. You cannot kill it, and you cannot stop it without Rebecca. It is with hope that you find her, and that you two together discover this journal. Then, and only then, will these ramblings of this mad man make sense to you. Sabine, my heart saddens as each day passes, knowing that I will not be here to see you become the incredible woman you are destined to be. It is with hope that you find this in time. If I have trained you right, you will find the clues I have left for you, you will have discovered this journal, you are still alive, and there is still hope.

"I found these jewels he speaks of. I touched most of them, but none of them were as he said. This makes sense now, why the barbarians wanted the jewels, and why Samuel wanted to send them with me. He knows something about them, but if the ones my father speaks of were not with the ones I found, then that would mean that they are still here."

"Where did you find them?"

"In secret compartments at the bottom of my mother and Jenna's chests. I tried Simon's chest, but there was nothing."

"Do you have a chest in your room?"

It never occurred to me to check my chest. I smiled at her and replied, "Yes, I do."

I closed the journal and we started to blow out the candles.

"We need to close this room up. No one must know we have discovered these things."

We worked our way out of the secret room and closed the wall behind us. In my room, we found ourselves standing at the foot of my bed, looking down at the chest. Rebecca moved first, slamming open the lid and throwing everything to the floor.

Looking down, she said, "Nothing. It is empty."

I smiled at her. "There is a secret to opening the bottom."

I raised my foot and kicked the lock, and there was that oh so familiar sound. Click. We just looked at one another smiling. I dropped to my knees and reached in, and in the corner was a small hole, just big enough to slip my finger in. As I pulled the bottom up, Rebecca gasped.

"Sabine," I heard her whisper.

I looked down. These jewels were not like the others; they were, but they were somehow different. As I reached in to pick one up, I could feel the energy.

"I do not think you should touch those yet."

"You might be right."

I put the bottom back in the chest, and we filled it with my gowns.

"What does your father say we should do with them?"

"He mentions that I or we need to harness their power through our swords. I do not know what that means. Simon also told me, when I was under that tree, that his sword and my father's should be forged together. So, it would seem that we have bits of an intrigue but no real solution." I picked up the journal. "Shall we see what else my father has to say?"

My Dearest Sabine,

Time has moved quickly. It is nearing the end of your fifth year. You have started and excelled greatly at swords. Ardes is enjoying teaching you, and Simon has been training your young mind with intrigue after intrigue. I think you may be smarter than he is. They are both aware of the legend and of how important it is for you to learn all that they have to teach. Your mother, on the other hand, wants to teach you to sing and to be a proper lady, so that one day you will be able to teach your own daughter.

Sometimes I feel so barbaric, training my only daughter to become something no woman should ever be, a warrior. I have drawn up the layout of this castle for you. You will find the drawings in the secret room. There are many drawings, but you will know which the true ones are. You will find many passageways that no one is aware of, not even your brothers. You and Rebecca will need to figure out the clues I have left for you in the drawings in order to gain access to these rooms. I thought it best not to put all the information that was instilled upon me in one place, and remember, Sabine, you already know how to solve the puzzles. Only you and I have this knowledge. It was the only way I could keep it from the evil that lurks beyond these walls. If you become confused, Raiden and Charles are there to help and guide you, but do not forget that you and Rebecca must solve this yourselves in order for you to be able to defeat this evil. Never forget and never divulge the information or the knowledge that this land is where life began. No one must know what you are trying to protect. Trust only each other with all the information. Even those who seem pure at heart can be swayed. Keep your mind closed when you are with others. The magic that surrounds you is easily accessed.

I closed the book and looked at Rebecca. "This means we tell no one not Charles, not Raiden, no one, and we must not speak of these things out loud. I believe it is time for us to take this seriously. Our fathers gave their lives to protect us and to finish what Raiden's father tried to do all those years ago."

"Charles should be back soon. Should we continue, or should we wait to hear what his father told him?" she asked.

Just then, we heard his horse. "I guess we hear what Charles has to say."

We both laughed. On our way out, we stopped by my father's study and replaced the journal. Charles was just climbing off his horse as we walked out into the courtyard.

I bumped Rebecca in hopes that she would not reveal the knowledge we had obtained from Raiden and the secret room we found. Her look told me I need not worry.

"Was your father helpful, Charles?"

"Well, yes and no. He had heard of the story pertaining to Raiden, but there is nothing but a story. He did, however, know of Rebecca's birth right and of her father, long before Blackmore discovered her true bloodline. Apparently, Sabine, your father had a brother, Stanford. He and Margret were in love and wanted to marry, but Margret's father's kingdom had fallen on hard times. Blackmore needed a bride for his barbaric son, so her father sold her into marriage, for quite an amount so it is said. It would seem that the two of you are cousins, which would make sense with the connection you have."

We pretended to look excited and amazed.

"Charles, do you have any knowledge concerning those jewels that I found? I only know what Samuel had told me, and I am inclined to think he was not telling me the truth."

"I am afraid, Sabine, that the jewels are a mystery. No one seems to have any information concerning them. As far as I know, Samuel just thought they were the wealth of Whispering Wind, and if he had them, then he would be the wealthiest. Oh, and my mother sent this for us."

He pulled a sack from his horse that was filled with food and drink. We sat and ate as the light of the day set over Whispering Wind.

"Well, I am going to retire and leave the two of you alone. Goodnight, Charles. Goodnight, Rebecca. Enjoy the evening."

In unison, they said, "Goodnight, Sabine."

I climbed the stairs and made my way to my room and standing outside my door was Raiden.

"Goodnight, Raiden. I would suspect you will be here when I wake?"

He nodded his head, and I giggled. My bed was a welcome sight. The days had been long, and I felt relieved for some reason. Perhaps it was because I could feel my father with me, or perhaps because his fear for me was greater than my own. This momentous task that was laid before me and Rebecca would have to wait until the light of the day returned because I was sleepy. Climbing into my bed was a task in itself, but sleep came easy.

CHAPTER NINE

I must have been tired; the light of the day was high in the sky when I woke. I washed my face, opened the door, and of course Raiden was there waiting for me.

"Good morning," I said, and I swear he smiled at me.

I worked my way down to the dining hall to find everyone seated around the grand table. Greetings were passed around as well as bread.

"We have much to discuss this day," Charles said.

"Do we have any idea what is coming for us, or better yet, when this might all take place?"

I really wanted to know how long Rebecca and I had to locate all the things Father had left for me.

"When Aidan and Steven return from the valley, they are bringing with them our men to camp on the hilltop, and Aidan has orders to send out as many scouts as we can spare."

"Charles, I am not so sure that we will need those men. It is apparent that no one can enter the village or the castle grounds without being killed by the mist, so would we be putting all their lives at risk? I mean, Rebecca and I are unstoppable."

"I agree, Sabine, but we must remember that these blood-gutters that Blackmore and Wellington have sought out and hired may be immune to this mist. We just cannot take that chance."

"Well, my concern is for Westin, Camille, and the children. Will there be enough men to protect them and to take them away to safety?"

"Yes, they are our first priority. I am wondering how you are, Rebecca, with what transpired with your mother."

Rebecca giggled, which was something I did not expect. "Oh, my dear mother will get just what she deserves, and as for Blackmore, his time will end soon enough. Charles?"

"Yes, Rebecca."

"Sabine and I have much to do and much to discuss. Would it be acceptable if we had the day together? If we leave the castle, we will be sure to inform you."

"I have no say over you, Rebecca, nor do I of Sabine, but in answer to your question no, there is nothing to do but wait." Charles smiled.

"Charles, would it be acceptable to you that no one enters the castle? The things we need to discuss, as I am sure you already know, must be kept private." I did not want to alarm him.

"Understood but remember that I am here to help and guide you, so if you have any questions or need any guidance, please seek me out. I will not be far."

"I am sure that we are going to need your help, so thank you. Rebecca, shall we?"

As we walked out of the dining hall, so did everyone else. We waited at the bottom of the grand staircase for them to all leave. Running seemed to be the fastest way to get to Father's study. We managed to get the secret door open and worked our way behind the tapestry.

"We should figure out how to close this door and then open it from inside, so if anyone comes looking for us, we will remain hidden."

As we entered the passageway, Rebecca lit the candle.

"You would think that Father would have put a lever or something in here to re-open this door. Do you see anything?" I asked.

Looking around, Rebecca said, "Well, there is this rock here that seems out of place. Here, hold this."

She handed me the candle, and as she pushed the rock, the door swung shut. I tried to grab it, but it moved too quickly.

"What do we do now?"

She slipped her fingers along the sides of the rock and pulled it out, and the door swung open.

"That, I would guess," she stated, and we both giggled as she pushed the rock again.

We were secure in the secret room, so we made our way down the passage to the room with all the maps.

"There are a great deal of drawings here. This is going to take some time," I said as I started to lay them out on the floor while Rebecca lit all the candles. When she finished, she came to help.

"Now, it said in the journal that you would know which ones were the true ones."

"Yes, it did, but that does not mean that I can. Looking at these is not bringing any memories up."

So, we began the arduous task of shifting through pages and pages of drawings. Father was not kidding when he said there were many. How in the world am I supposed to figure this out?

'Just be patient. We will do this.'

I looked up at Rebecca and smiled. "Is this going to be a regular thing with us?"

"It was very easy to do. We must be linked somehow, more so than before. Perhaps it is because now we are cousins."

I could not help but laugh. "We have always been cousins."

We searched through many drawings, when I happened upon one that seemed different than the others.

"Rebecca, look at this."

She scooted over to me, where I was holding it up against the light of the candle.

"Do you see that?"

"What is it?"

"I am not sure, but I do not think it is on the other one that is the same as this one. There, get that one by your foot."

She picked it up and held it to the light. "No, it is the same."

"Here, let me have it," I said.

She handed me the drawing, and I placed it on top of the one I was holding, and then held it up to the light.

"See, look here. There is a passageway on the bottom one that is not on the top. This must be one of them. Shall we go investigate and see what we will find?"

Her eyes were huge. "I love a good intrigue."

We gathered up the remaining drawings that were the same as the one with the new passageway on it. I grabbed the journal while Rebecca blew out all the candles, then we made our way back to the door. After listening carefully to make sure no one was in the room, we let ourselves out and resealed the wall. I made sure to conceal the drawings and the journal in the bodice of my gown. Father was very specific that we did not share any information we may acquire.

As we wandered through the castle, we noticed that there was no one else about. Charles kept true to his word that we would not be disturbed. I made my way to the second floor, which is what was on the drawing, and then pulled them out of my bodice.

"This seems to be the hallway that leads to my room." I pointed to the drawing. "It has the numbers two and five next to it and then the letter L. What do you think?"

"Well, perhaps we take two steps then turn left and take five steps."

We did just that, but nothing. "Perhaps it is twenty-five steps then left."

So we counted then turned left, and I was standing in front of Simon's door. I opened the door, and we went in, closing it behind us. I stood there looking around; all of his things were still there. His room and mine were the only two rooms that were not destroyed by the barbarians. I still did not understand that.

"Is anything coming to you, Sabine?"

"No, but perhaps Father has left a clue in the journal."

We sat on Simon's bed and read.

My Dearest Sabine,

Today you displayed your uncanny ability to disappear. I thought that you had been discovered and were taken from us. It makes me shudder to think of the torture you would endure or even the possibility of death. You are becoming more and more curious about your surround-ings, and I think it might be time to consider putting out a decree. The people must be informed that they are not to speak of you. The legend has been folklore for generations, but the people still hold the belief that the Bringer of Peace is real. I chuckle to myself, thinking 'yes, she is real, and she gave her mother and father a terrible fright this day'.

Rebecca leaned into me, and I could not help but smile. "I remember this day he speaks of. I was hiding in the cave. I must have fallen asleep in there."

Having sent Ardes and Simon on business for me, it gave me time to prepare his room. The drawings will show you where to go, but I am fearful to write anything more in here, just in case the room where you find this is discovered. Use your memories, Sabine. To others, it will never be discovered, but to you, it will seem the simplest task.

We just looked at one another for a moment before Rebecca asked, "Do you have any idea what he is talking about?"

"No, but he is sure that I will remember, so I am going to sit in the chair by the fireplace and think of all the times I was in this room with Simon and without."

"I think it might be best if I leave you alone. I know I will not be able to sit still, or be quiet for that matter." She smiled. "I think I will go find Charles and see what we can do about some real food. This bread supply is not enough for us. We are going to wither away to nothing. If you discover anything, wait for me, all right?"

"I will indeed. Father said we must do this together. I promise I will find you."

I hugged her, and she left me, so I sat in the chair by the fireplace and let my mind wander. So many good times were had in this room, and so many times I had hidden there. Pulling the drawings out, I examined the room, turning the page over and over in my hands. I could clearly see the space father indicated on the drawing as being secret, but I just could not place it in this room.

I moved the chair around to many different angles and locations to see if something would arise in my mind, but nothing. The light of day was leaving. Soon it would be the dark of night. I looked for a candle, but there was none. It would be dark soon, and I would be struggling to see my way around, so I decided to go find the others and come back to this after I had some sleep.

I found Rebecca, Charles, and Blake, along with Joseph, Edward, and James in the kitchen. They managed to hunt a deer and were arguing on how to cook it. I stood in the doorway laughing at them because they did not even have a fire ready. After some discussion, it was settled, and the deer was cooked. We sat in the kitchen and ate, talking and laughing. It felt good to not have to worry about anyone coming to murder us. I thought about Westin and Juliana, and my heart ached to see them, to hold them.

"I think I might go to bed, if you will excuse me," I said as I rose from my chair.

Blake stood, or tried to stand, but lost his footing and fell into the hearth, hitting his head. As he was trying to stand, he grabbed a rock dislodging it from the wall. It was like a million arrows were pointed at that spot, and a memory flashed in my mind.

I remembered hiding in the fireplace in Simon's room. He could not find me for a long time, and it was my giggle that eventually gave away my secret spot. I shot Rebecca a look, and she knew I had figured it out. The fireplace; the secret space was behind the fireplace.

"Blake, will you be all right?"

"Yes, I am fine. No blood."

"Good. Then I shall see you all in the light of the day."

Everyone bid me goodnight, and I left the kitchen. At the door, I looked at Rebecca and raised my eyebrows at her. She smiled and nodded, but not enough for anyone else to see.

"Wait up, Sabine. I will walk with you," she said as she rose and kissed Charles goodnight.

"It is very difficult not to run," I whispered as we climbed the stairs as slowly as we could manage.

"I know. When we get around the corner and out of sight, we will run."

We managed to make it to the top of the grand staircase without exploding into a dead run. A few more steps and we would be out of sight. I could not remember ever having run this fast, with the exception of that time I raced my brothers through the village. I was victorious that day, but Ardes was not so fortunate. The thought made me giggle. Rebecca just laughed with me.

We made it to Simon's room with no incidents, no blood drawn, and no gashes. We managed to grab a candle and a striker along the way from my room. I shut the door quickly and quietly and then bolted it.

"What did you remember?" Rebecca said winded.

"Well, when Blake fell, and the stone fell out of the wall, I remembered that as a child, I hid in the fireplace for a very long time. No one could find me. So after spending most of the day in here, turning this drawing around in my hand and sitting in the chair in every possible place, I never once thought that the space could be behind the fireplace. Father must have had the whole wall rebuilt."

We both just stood there in front of the fireplace, not moving. I could not even be sure we were breathing. Rebecca started to push on the rocks that made up the face of the fireplace. I got inside the fireplace, just as when I was a young child. I remembered climbing up into the chimney, so my feet were hidden.

"What are you doing?"

"When I was a young child, I hid in here. I remember climbing up like this to hide my feet."

I put my feet on the ledge of the frame as I slowly walked my hands up the inner chimney. That is when I felt it; just above my waist, a brick was sticking out a bit further than the rest. I put my feet back down.

"I think I found something."

Rebecca popped her head up into the chimney. "What is it?"

"Well, it is a rock that is sticking out further than the rest."

"Push it. Maybe we will hear a click."

I pushed, but nothing happened, so I grabbed it and pulled it out.

"It came out."

I reached into the hole to feel for a lever or something, but instead, I found a paper. I grabbed it and pulled it out.

"It seems to be a paper."

We climbed out of the fireplace, covered in soot, and sat on the floor. I slowly unrolled the paper.

"It looks very old."

I laid it flat on the floor, and we used pieces of wood to hold it flat. It was another drawing, only this one was of the entire kingdom.

"Look, there is writing here. What does it say?"

"I do not know this language. Do you?"

Rebecca turned her head and then turned the paper every which way.

"I have never..."

There was a knock on the door. "Sabine, are you in here?"

"Blake," I whispered to Rebecca.

Quickly, I rolled the paper back up. She wiped smudges off my face as I started to take off my clothing, and then I walked to the door while she was un-plating my hair. I pushed her behind the door as I went to open it.

"Yes, Blake, can I help you?"

"I went to your room to speak to you, and you were not there. I was worried, and then I saw the light from under this door. Is everything all right?"

"Everything is fine. I was just missing my brother, so I thought I would sleep in his room. What did you need to speak to me about?"

"Well, I wanted to know if you would go for a ride with me tomorrow after we have our morning meal."

"Blake, I am not sure that would be a good idea."

"Sabine, we need to talk. I can do it now if you would like."

"No, tomorrow is fine. I have just my undergarments on, and it would not be proper for you to be alone with me in this bedroom. I will meet you at the stables after we eat. Goodnight, Blake."

"Goodnight, Sabine."

He backed away from the door as I closed it and silenced Rebecca, who was standing next to me with her mouth open, ready to squeal.

"What was that about?" Rebecca whispered.

"You would know more than I. Rebecca; I do not want this with him. You told me in the valley that he had feelings for me."

"No, what I said was that he thinks he has feelings for you. Apparently, he is struggling with them. Be kind, Sabine. He has a good heart."

"This is not what I want to think about right now. Let us have another look at this drawing."

We sat on the floor and studied the drawing, but the wording was baffling. I wished I knew what it said. We must have fallen asleep on the floor, as I was awakened by thumping on the door, loud thumping. I scurried around, gathering up all the drawings. I jumped up and shoved them under Simon's coverings on his bed, and then rumbled the blankets to make it look as if I had slept in it.

"Who is it?"

"Sabine, it is me, Blake. Are you all right? Is Rebecca with you? Charles is going quite mad searching for her."

I opened the door. "Really, Blake, this is becoming troublesome, the way we are watched. Yes, Rebecca is here with me. Where else would she be, and frankly, it really is no one's business,"

I said and shut the door. Turning, I looked at Rebecca.

"Your boyfriend is becoming a problem. He is going to hear me out."

I gathered my clothes and the drawings, got dressed, and headed down to my father's study. I put everything in the secret room and then made my way to the dining hall. Sitting at the head of the table like he belonged there was Charles, with his brothers on either side of him.

"Your obsessive behavior concerning our whereabouts is becoming a problem for me. I am in my family home, which is covered in a mist that will kill anything and anyone but us, with a horse that can outrun the wind, and you want to know our location at every turn. Charles, you really need to stop this. It is getting out of hand. I am a grown woman, and I am pretty much a killing machine, so I would greatly appreciate it if you would please end this."

I turned around and headed to the kitchen. As I was leaving, I heard a crash come from the dining hall and the chair slam to the floor. I could hear his footsteps behind me. I looked up the grand staircase and saw Rebecca's worried face, and then I felt his arm around my waist.

"Not so fast," he growled.

My natural instinct was to fight and fight I did. When it was over, Charles was on his back with my sword at his throat.

"Do not ever assume it is acceptable to touch me without my permission!" I screamed at him.

I turned and continued my path to the kitchen. I grabbed a few pieces of fruit and a skin of water and kept right on going out the door. Raiden was there; he must have sensed my mood. I jumped up on him and kicked him in the sides, and he was off.

I leaned into him, saying, "Do not stop. Just take me away from here." We were gone so fast, not even dust was raised in our wake.

CHAPTER TEN

"Charles, what has gotten into you?" Rebecca rushed down the stairs to help him up.

"Where have you been?" he shouted at her.

"Well, let me just say this to you I do not answer to you. There is something going on here, and you will be telling me what it is."

"I believe you have stepped out of place, Rebecca. You never speak to a man in this manner. I think that all this time you are spending alone with Sabine is rubbing off on you. Mind your place."

Rebecca reached up and slapped him across the face.

"You seem to have forgotten YOUR place. Do not assume you can speak to me in this manner."

She turned to walk away, but the brothers were standing in her way.

"Move or I shall move you!" she yelled.

Just then, Charles grabbed her by the waist. Rebecca threw him to the floor and whistled.

"You have taught me well, Charles. Next time I will not be so kind."

Spirit came running through the kitchen door and into the great hall. Rebecca jumped up on him, and they were gone.

"Take me to Sabine," she said.

Spirit ran; it took only a few moments before she spotted me, and she whistled. Raiden slowed and waited for Rebecca to catch up.

"Something has gone wrong at the castle, Sabine. Charles is out of control."

"I know. I cannot believe he grabbed me."

She giggled. "I cannot believe you beat him and laid him on the floor. He grabbed me as well and found himself in the same position. The brothers are acting strange as well. They would not let me pass. They just stood there like they were statues or something."

"Things are not right. We cannot go back there. Raiden knew something was wrong as he was waiting for me outside. I can only think that the witch has somehow gotten to them, and with no one else being able to come into Whispering Wind, I do not know what to do. We need to figure this all out, and we will not be able to with the seven of them keeping watch or possibly imprisoning us."

"What about their father? He was a Guardian as well, and Charles did go speak with him. Perhaps he would be able to help us."

"Rebecca, I am fearful that if their father were to enter the kingdom the same thing would happen to him."

"That is true, but we could at least go and speak to him."

"You must keep in mind here that there is a price on our heads, thanks to Wellington and Blackmore. We cannot just go wandering around."

"Well, you cannot, not with your hair being so well known now, but I can. There are lots of people with my color hair. I shall go and get their father and bring him here. We do not have to take him into the village or the castle grounds. We can draw Charles and his brothers out, so that their father can speak to them and help us figure out what is going on."

"I am not so sure that this is the best idea. We are strongest together."

"Agreed, but our horses can outrun any horse known, and you will know where I am. Besides, Raiden and Spirit are linked together. They will be able to find one another. I will be back before you know it." She turned Spirit, smiled, and said, "See you in a bit. Spirit take me to Charles' father." And just as quickly as she arrived, she was gone.

Taking off in the opposite direction of Rebecca, we were gone. I do not know how long we rode, but Raiden slowed as we came to a river. I cannot ever remember a river being this close to the castle before. I climbed down and looked around, but there was nothing that looked familiar. I could not help but smile. Sitting by the water, I caught my reflection; my face was filthy, as I had not bathed in days. I washed my face and hands, splashing water on me to remove some of the soot and dirt from my body. The locket Jared had given me came dislodged from my bodice and dangled on my neck. Leaning into the river, I noticed the reflection; it was backwards. I froze looking at it, and then it came to me the writing on the drawing from Simon's fireplace was written backwards. Thoughts raced through my head. My mother had a looking glass. I remembered when Father gave it to her, and she was convinced that it was some kind of trickery on his part. I could remember her yelling at him. She was very frightened, and he just laughed, calling her silly. But after time she accepted his gift, and it sat on her mantle. I did not recall it being there when Westin and I cleaned up their room.

I must have been sitting there for a long time, because Rebecca came riding up with Charles' father behind her on Spirit.

"Good day, Sabine," he said as he climbed down. "Rebecca told me that the boys are acting strange. This is worrisome indeed. These boys were trained from infancy to carry out their role in all of this, just as my brothers and I were, so for them to become violent is a worry. Rebecca had said that you were worried that I could not enter the kingdom, but I believe that I can."

"No, sire, I will not allow you to risk your life. We will bring them to you. All we have to do is send one of the horses in, and they will follow it, thinking one of us is in harm's way."

"That might be a better idea. Sabine, I need to ask you a query, but first, let me say this, I know much more than I have let Charles or the rest of them know. It is not for us to interfere, nor are we allowed to change anything that must take place. Even the purest of hearts will be challenged. What is to come is very powerful, and it will change who you both are, but because you are who you are, it will be for the good and not for evil. Now to my query… you have found the stones, have you not?"

I was shocked. I looked at Rebecca, and she gave a little nod, telling me that I should be truthful.

"Yes, we found them."

"I see," he said as he started to walk to and fro.

"What do the jewels have to do with the behavior of your sons?"

"Well, first of all, they are not jewel's. They are disguised as jewels, but they are in fact stones. They are summoning stones, and they hold within them a great energy. When they were hidden away many years ago, there was an incantation that was passed down through your family to settle the stones. Once you discovered them and exposed them, they became active again. The energy from these stones is what is altering my sons. You must discover the incantation and calm them again until it is time. Each time you expose them…"

"Excuse me, sire, until what?"

"I can only say that you will know. But each time they are exposed, you must say the incantation to settle them. Remember that even those pure of heart can betray you. I will keep my sons from Whispering Wind until you discover the incantation and settle the stones. You can send one of the horses, and I will send them back to you."

"Raiden, will you please go and draw them out? Make them follow you here. Is this a good idea to have us here when they arrive?"

"Once they leave the castle grounds and the village, the enchantment will be broken, but they cannot return until the stones are settled. They have no knowledge of this, and they must never know. Remember, Sabine, this knowledge is only for you and Rebecca. No one else must know what you uncover. If it gets away from you, then life as we know it will be no more. This is a great task set before you, and being women, it only makes it harder. Now go Raiden and bring them to us."

With that, Raiden stomped his foot. "They are safe with me. Trust me, old friend," he said. He patted Raiden on the neck. Raiden nodded, turned his head, and I heard him in my head.

Trust him,' he said, and he was gone.

"Sabine, you cannot rush this. It was all set into motion when your family was murdered. It will take time and you, both of you, must never lose faith. Rebecca, Charles has told me of his vision, and he mentioned that the two of you have had the same vision."

"Yes, of my death. What do you know of it?"

"I cannot tell you what I know, but I can tell you this there will be more visions to come, and you must take note. They are important, and they are intrigues that you must decipher. Remember, things are not what they seem. Sabine, all that you will learn and all that you will uncover is hidden within you. Your father set this all into motion the day you were born. You already have the knowledge within, so now you must bring it all out into the open, and the two of you will decipher its meaning. Then, and only then, will the land change."

"Thank you, sire, for your input. We shall do our best."

"I am afraid, Sabine, that your best may not be enough. I am afraid that it will take every part of your spirit and soul to finish this. Both of you have a fight ahead of you, and you must trust no one."

Just then, I felt the ground rumble and said, "They are coming."

We all turned in the direction in which Raiden left, and I could see the small cloud from the horses. We waited. Upon their arrival, Charles dismounted and ran to Rebecca.

"I am sorry, my lady, for the way I acted toward you," he pleaded, then turned to look at me. "Sabine, your forgiveness is all I ask."

"Charles, we understand why all of this has happened," his father spoke up, causing Charles to look at him.

"Father, what are you doing here?"

"Well, the girls suspected that something has gone awry, so Rebecca came to get me to see if I could help. How are you feeling, Charles?"

"I feel remorse for the way that I acted and the things that I have done. Why do you ask this of me, Father?"

"How did you feel when you were at the castle?"

"I felt angry and deceived. I felt anxious, but mostly, I felt as if I wanted to punish them for keeping things from me. I do not understand."

"Well, we do. Listen, you cannot go back to Whispering Wind. Only the girls can enter the kingdom now. You must stay with me until it is safe to return. They must deal with what is happening there first. Do you understand?"

"No, Father, I do not. I know you have knowledge I do not, and I respect you for that, but we have vowed to protect them."

"Yes, you have my son, but going back there will only bring harm to you, and then you will not be able to fulfill your vow. Stay here with me until they have cleansed the kingdom. Besides, I would love to spend some time with my sons. They will be safe. I assure you that their horses can carry them away to safety if need be."

Charles had no other choice but to listen to his father. Rebecca and I went back to Whispering Wind in hopes of finding this incantation and settling the jewels so Charles and his brothers could return.

As we made our way into the castle, I turned to Rebecca. "I think I figured out the language on the drawing. Come, we need to go to my parents' bedroom and retrieve something."

She smiled at me and we ran up the grand staircase and through the upper part of the castle to my parents' room. I quickly searched the room with my eyes, but the looking glass was nowhere to be seen.

"It has to be here, but I do not remember seeing it when Westin and I cleaned up this room."

"Well, if you tell me what it is that we are looking for, I can help you find it."

"A long time ago, my father gave my mother a looking glass. When I was getting a drink from the river and washing up, my locket was dangling, and I saw the reflection in the water. It was backwards, so I thought perhaps the writing was backwards, and the way to read it would be through the looking glass."

"That is brilliant. Where did your mother keep this looking glass?"

"It was always on the mantle, but as I look, it is not there. I hope it was not broken." We rummaged around the room, but it was nowhere to be found.

"Perhaps it is in Jenna and Ardes' room."

We made our way there and searched the room, but there was nothing. I sat down on the hearth to think of where else it could be. If it was broken, I would have found pieces of it on the floors. Rebecca opened the shutters so the light of the day could come through, and that is when I saw the light reflect off it. It must have been knocked to the floor and kicked under their bed. I got on my hands and knees and made my way across the room. I was just small enough to fit under the bed. I scooted back out with my prize in my hand.

"Got it. Now let us go see if we can figure out what those writings on that drawing say."

Back in the secret room, we lit all the candles and laid all the drawings on the floor. We sat down with the looking glass and carefully rolled out the drawing from Simon's fireplace. To look at it, you would see lines and what looked to be gibberish.

"Okay, you ready?"

"As ready as I will ever be. Sabine, before we start, Charles' father said it was an incantation. Would that be some sort of trickery?"

"I am pretty sure that it is. When I went to see Jared, I unlocked the lock with no key. He told me to just think and concentrate on the lock and it would open, and it did. I do not know if it was I who opened it, or if it was the witch working through me, but she has no power over us, so I am inclined to believe that it was me. Am I a witch? I think not. I am just Sabine, so whatever this is, it is what needs to be done. We cannot go this road alone, Rebecca. Each of us holds a piece to this intrigue, and it maybe you and I who are destined to bring peace, but I think it is all of us who will figure it out."

"I suppose you are right, and I could not imagine us doing this without Charles. He terrified me today, and if those jewels did this to him, I want to calm them and stop their power."

I held the looking glass up to the words.

Blue, Violet, White
Burn them from left to right

Three points match in equal length'

We looked at one another, and Rebecca asked, "What does that mean?"

Raising my shoulders, I shook my head.

'At the dark of night
With the whole orb alight
Fill the space with white'

"Okay, so I think this means we have to do this at the dark of night with the orb full of light, but I do not know what the white is," I told her.

"Could it be salt? Witches use salt, I think."

"Yes, it could be salt, or possibly sand."

Thrice disclose these words you seek,
Thrice disclose unheard to thee'

"What does this mean?" she asked again.

"I believe we need to say whatever these words are three times out loud and then three times to ourselves."

'In this time,
In this place,
Seek the refuge that brings you peace'

"So now we know what to do and what to say to calm the jewels, but what are violet, white, and blue?" Rebecca thought aloud.

"I would think that they are something that burns. Maybe they are candles. It says to burn them from left to right, and candles burn. Let us look for the candles."

We searched the secret room and found only white ones, but they were not really white. They were a golden color, like Rebecca's hair. We moved out into father's study, but there was nothing.

"Maybe there is a clue in the journal." Rebecca turned back to the tapestry.

"I think that it is in the drawings. Father was very clear. He said.

The drawings will show you where to go, but I am fearful to write anything more in here, just in case the room where you find this is discovered. Use your memories, Sabine. To others, it will never be discovered, but to you, it will seem the simplest task.' "

"Yes, I remember now. Then let us go sit and study the drawings. If what Charles' father said is truth, then we need to calm the stones. We have no idea how long it will be until those who are coming will come. I know that no one can get to us here, but what about all the others in the lands? I think my mother and Wellington have no mercy, and I am fearful that we will not be the only targets for these blood-gutters that are coming." Rebecca said.

We made our way back into the secret room. Lying on the floor were the drawings, so we sat down and began searching once again.

"All right, I think the best thing to do is to take all the drawings that look the same and put them in separate stacks."

"There are a lot of drawings," she said, spinning around the room. "There are more over there and some more here."

"Yes, it seems that Father tried to make sure that whoever found this room would not know what to make of it," I said with a giggle.

We spent a great deal of time putting all the drawings in order. It was not until I realized that I was hungry that we stopped.

"I wonder if there is any food left. I am quite hungry."

Rebecca agreed, so we decided to take a few minutes to eat. We made our way out of the secret room, and when we reached the main hall, I heard arguing coming from the top of the grand staircase. It was Blake and Joseph.

"We must find them. We know they have got be in the Castle!" Blake was yelling.

"We should not be here. We must leave now, Blake. You know this is not what Father wanted."

We froze. Looking around, I could not see any way to go without being seen, so we just stood there.

"Blake, we have got to get out of here."

"There are so many rooms in this damn place. They have got to be in one of them."

He turned and ran toward my room, Joseph following him.

I turned to Rebecca and whispered, "We need to get some food and get back in that room before they find us."

She nodded, and we ran as quickly and as quietly as we could to the kitchen. Rebecca grabbed the meat that was left over from the night before, while I grabbed the bread and the water skins. There was a noise at the door going out into the back courtyard. We froze and looked at one another. Too terrified to look, we turned our heads, but it was Raiden.

'Run now,'

I heard in my head and took off running toward Father's study with Rebecca close behind. Coming around the grand staircase, we heard them again. Blake was calling my name in a very menacing tone.

"Sabine, I know you are in here. You can come out and talk to me." Then, in a very chilling tone, he said, "I will not hurt you."

It sent chills up my back. I looked at Rebecca and could see she was just as frightened as I was. We moved as one toward Father's study. We made it past the staircase without being seen. Running as hard as we could, we made it to the study and closed the door quietly. Rebecca opened the secret door, so we made our way in and closed the door behind us. Looking at one another in the darkened passageway was when we finally dared to breathe.

"What was that about?" she whispered.

"I do not know, but we really need to calm those jewels. We have got to find those candles and get this done. The power that they have is definitely dangerous to everyone. I cannot even imagine what they would or could do in the wrong hands. No wonder Samuel wanted them. He would have gone madder than he already is."

"Well, we really need to figure this out. If those jewels or stones or whatever they are can do this to our Guardians, then I can only imagine what they would do to a regular person."

I could not stop the giggle. "In the past two years, Rebecca, what actually defines normal?"

She laughed, answering, "I really do not know."

We made our way down the darkened passageway to the room, Rebecca lit the candles, and we sat and ate.

"There are so many drawings in here. It makes me wonder when my father had time to do all of this."

We sat for a very long time looking at them all. One stuck out to me, from the smaller pile that was of my mother and father's room.

"I think this one is a bit different from the rest."

"Where is that?"

"I think it is my mother and father's room."

"Should we go up there? I wonder if Blake and Joseph are still here."

Just as Rebecca said those words, I heard in my head

'No.'

'Are they still here?'

'Danger.'

"Raiden just told me no. He said danger, so I think they are still out there. Maybe we should just finish with these drawings. They will have to sleep soon, and we can go then to get the candles and do the incantation."

We went through all the piles and discovered eight differences, so we gathered our drawings and the journal and prepared to leave the secret room.

'Is it safe yet?' I said in my head.

'Do not go the usual way. They are sleeping on the grand staircase, waiting for you. Find another route.'

"We cannot go up the grand staircase."

"We need to work our way through the castle to the kitchen. There is a back stairway there, hidden behind a pantry. We used as children."

Rebecca nodded, and off we went. It was easy getting to the kitchen and up the back staircase. We first went to my mother and father's room. I closed the door and bolted it, just in case. We had our swords with us as well. I really did not want to hurt Joseph or Blake, but I was not about to let them harm us in any way. I sat with the smallest of the drawings on the bed.

"All right, according to this drawing, the difference from the rest of them is that there is an extra line drawn here," I said, showing Rebecca the line.

"It looks to be a space of sorts beneath the floor."

"That is what I thought as well. Now we just need to find an opening."

We walked around the room but found no markings or loose stones. I sat in the chair and searched my memory for what Father said was already in my mind. I closed my eyes and let the memories roam. We were children, and we were hiding from each other. I was maybe in my tenth year. I remember coming in here to hide from Simon. Searching the room, I could not find a place that was not obvious, so I chose to hide under the bed. Mother and Father's bed was high off the ground, and there was a loose board at the base. I remembered that the board was easy to remove and then put back on. I fell asleep in there because Simon could not find me. I could hear Mother's voice in my head. *Sabine darling, where are you? It is all right to come out now.* I woke hearing her sweet voice. My eyes popped open, and I smiled at Rebecca.

"I remember," I said.

I got out of the chair and moved toward the bed. I went around to Mother's side, got down on the floor, and removed the panel.

"As a child, I hid under here from Simon. This must be where the hiding place is."

I was too big now to crawl in the space, so I put my hand in and searched around on the floor, but I felt nothing. Moving my hand up to touch the bottom of the bed itself, I discovered a little piece of wood sticking out. I moved it back and forth, but nothing happened. I looked up at Rebecca.

"I am not sure what I am supposed to remember or what I am supposed to do." Just then, the piece of wood came out, and I heard a click. "Did you hear that?" I whispered?

"Yes, what was it?"

"I am not sure." I reached around the floor again, and this time a piece of stone was higher than the rest.

"I think I found it."

I tried to slip my fingers around the stone to lift it, but it was too big, so I pushed it and it lifted.

"There is something here."

I reached into the space the stone left and felt something long and round. I wrapped my fingers around it and pulled it out.

"The violet candle," Rebecca whispered.

"Let me see if there is anything more in the space," I said.

I put my hand back under the bed and into the space, but there was nothing there.

"No, it is empty."

"Well, we have one, so now onto the next drawing."

I took all the drawings of Mother and Father's room, folded them in half, and stuck them in my bodice. We grabbed the next stack and studied them.

"This seems to be a passageway, but I do not recognize its placement. The doors along it do not match any in this part of the castle."

"Well, there are many passageways and many floors. Have you been through this entire place as a child? It seems that everything is linked to a memory you have as a child, a place that you have hidden."

She was right. I wondered if I should just sit and try to remember every good hiding place I had as a child.

"Perhaps that is the key, that he hid everything in all of my best hiding places. It would seem that my father was a very clever man."

I could not help but smile. Of course, he was.

"Lay the drawings out on the floor. We can do this in order, so we are not running all over the place."

Standing and looking down at them, the drawings looked different. "This one here," I said, pointing to the one in the middle. "This is definitely Westin's room. The passageway has three doors on it, so that is the closest." I bent down and took it off the floor. "This one here is the tower, so it should be last. I think it is the farthest away from here." Rebecca picked it up.

"That one there by your foot, I think that is the servants' quarters. See all the doorways? Their rooms are smaller than the rest. That one is on the way to the tower, so put that on top of those drawings." Rebecca pointed out and picked them up.

That left four more. Walking around in a circle and looking at the drawings made them all look different. Somehow, they seemed the same, but different. I started walking a bit faster, my eyes never leaving the drawings, and noticed the markings were becoming one. Rebecca stood there watching me. I think she thought I was mad, but it seemed that the faster I walked, the more the drawings became one. I knew this place. Where was this? Then it hit me the cave; the cave behind the hedge in the back courtyard. I stopped walking, and the drawings became separate again. I looked up at Rebecca.

"Did you see that?" I asked

Shaking her head, she replied, "I did not see anything but you walking around and around. What happened?"

"Well, as I moved, the drawings became one and formed one drawing. I think it might be the place where we are to do the incantation."

"Do you think we should take the jewels with us?"

"No, I think we need to gather everything first. I do not think we are supposed to remove the jewels yet. It was us uncovering them that caused them to do whatever it is that they are doing. I think we need to just leave them where they are."

"Agreed. I really do not want to be touching them. If they can do what they are doing to Charles and his brothers, just by being uncovered and locked in the trunk, I cannot even think what they would do if we touched them."

"Westin's room is next, so get your mind working on your memories," she continued with a giggle.

Quietly and quickly, we made our way through the castle to Westin's room. I needed to know if Blake and Joseph were still sleeping on the grand staircase.

Raiden are we still safe?'

Yes.'

In Westin's room, we closed the door and bolted it. I knew just where this memory was. I discovered the secret passageway to Ardes' room when I was in my eleventh year, tucked behind his bed head. I slipped between the wood and the stone, and it seemed tighter than I remembered. I could not help but chuckle to myself; of course, it would be because I am grown now. I felt for the rock sticking slightly out from the rest and pressed on it. The rocks moved just below my bodice. Yes, I was much smaller back then. I sank to my knees and crawled in. I remembered as a child not having any fear of the dark, but now the darkness was a bit frightening. I felt my way along the floor. My hands in a sweeping motion in front of me, I felt something as my fingers brushed against it. I was expecting it to be a candle, but this was a satchel, a big satchel. I grabbed ahold of it and dragged it back with me as I worked my way back to the opening. Standing proved to be harder than slipping down, but I managed. I pulled the stone, so the secret door swung closed, and then worked my way out from behind the bed.

Rebecca could not help but giggle. "You are filthy. You look like you did when you climbed up the chimney."

I looked down at myself, noting that I was indeed filthy. "Yes, but I found this," I said, sitting the satchel on the bed.

I untied the leather strap from around the neck, and we both looked in. It was filled with white powder or sand. Looking at one another, we smiled. I tied the satchel back up, and we made our way through the castle to the upper floors, to the servants' rooms.

"All right let us have a look at the drawings," I said.

Rebecca unrolled them. Looking at them, I pondered aloud, "This door here is darker than the others, so we need to figure out which one that is. Come on. We need to go back to the end of the hall."

Walking back, we turned and counted; eight doors on either side. It was the third door on the left, but if we were coming from the other end of the hall, it would be the third door on the right.

"Third door here," I pointed.

We made our way into the room. It was small, smaller than it should have been. Our servants did everything for us, and all they had to call their own was this small room. As we entered and closed the door, the memory came flooding in of a night of one of my parents' parties. I remembered that I was not feeling well. This was Sarah's room, and she took care of me that night. She sang me songs and brought me fancy bread from the party that tasted so sweet. She hid it in her bag she carried around her waist. I spun around the room, searching for the bag, and there it hung on the chair by the little firepot. I rushed to it, but after picking it up, I realized that it was empty. Father would not have been able to hide it here. Sarah always had this on her, except for when she was sleeping or bathing. Then I remembered, on that night, she had given me a bath to cool me down. I went out into the hall and raced to the other end, the third door on the other end. In this room was the tub. I lay on the floor, looked under the tub, and there it was. Wedged into the leg of the tub was the white candle. When I pulled it out, Rebecca just shook her head.

"Your mind is very scary. It is bizarre the way your father knew just how you would think."

"It was my father who taught me to think this way. That is how I figured out that Samuel was the one who murdered my family, and that his plan all along was to murder me as well." I smiled at her. "Now to the tower."

The dark of night was in full, and seeing was difficult without any torches or candles, but the moon was rising and was full. We needed to hurry. Reaching the tower made for a difficult task. Many of the passageways had no windows, making them as dark as the secret one behind Westin's bed, but we made it. The memory I had of this place was not such a nice one. I was maybe in my thirteenth year, and I wanted to go riding with my brothers, but Father had forbidden it. We had such a fight. I was so angry at him, and I wanted him to suffer, so I made my way here and stayed here for three days, sleeping on the floor. He was beside himself when hunger finally won, forcing me down. He made Sarah tell him where I was, for she had seen me coming from this side of the castle.

"Oh Father, how sorry I am for making you worry," I whispered.

"Are you all right, Sabine?"

"Yes, I am fine, just remembering, but my memory has no real significance here. I did nothing here but hide from my father, so I do not know where to look."

"Well, all the others were in secret places, so perhaps one of the stones in the walls or the floor is like the others."

We started searching and feeling the walls and then the floor.

"Nothing, there is nothing here. Father, where have you hidden the last candle?"

I sat in a heap in the center of the room, then lay down to look at the ceiling. There was a candelabra hanging from the roof, so I stared at it. I could not place it in my memory. Was it there all those years ago? I followed the rope that it was attached to, across the ceiling and down the wall, to the hook it was wrapped around.

"Could it be?"

I jumped up and ran over to the rope. Untying it, I slowly lowered the candelabra to the floor, and there it was. The blue candle was right in the middle. I looked at Rebecca with a smile.

"Now that we have all the parts, we need to make our way to the cave."

'We need to go to the cave. Is it safe?'

'Yes, go the way you came, and hurry.'

"We are running out of time. We need to hurry," I said.

I ran to the door. We moved as quickly as we could through the castle, to the hidden stairs that led to the kitchen, then out the door to the back courtyard. Just as we hit the bushes, I heard Blake and Joseph screaming our names in voices that were not their own. As quietly as we could, we made our way along the rock to the cave.

"In the drawing, I saw the center of this cave, so that is where we must set it up, but what is equal length? Rebecca, let me have the journal. Perhaps Father wrote it in there."

I opened the journal and started flipping through the pages, reading but not reading. On the last page, I turned, and there were these words. '

From the palm to the bend.'

I looked at Rebecca and then my arm, from the palm to the bend. I laid it out on the ground and placed the candles just as he directed. Rebecca lit them in order, and then we poured the white powder in the center to fill the space. Together we said the incantation three times.

'In this time, in this place, seek the refuge that brings you peace.'

Then we said them in our head's equal times. The flames of the candles grew larger and larger, so much so that we had to back away and just as quickly, they went out, as if the wind had blown through the cave. We sat there looking at one another.

"Did it work?" Rebecca asked.

"I have no idea," I replied.

Yes,' I heard Raiden say in my head.

"Yes, it worked."

We made our way out of the cave and along the hedge. When we entered the courtyard, we saw Blake and Joseph lying on the ground. We ran over to them.

"What happened to them? Are they hurt?"

Then I heard the horses, Charles, and his brothers, as well as his father, come riding into the courtyard.

"What happened?" Charles demanded.

"We do not know. We came out of the castle and found them like this."

I hated to tell untruths, but I could not tell him the truth. Just then, Blake's eyes fluttered open.

"What happened? How did we get here?"

Their father spoke then, saying, "It is a mystery as to what has happened here today, just as this mist is a mystery. I am sure, in time, we will all know what is happening."

He looked at me, and I knew the look I saw in his eyes. It was fear.

CHAPTER ELEVEN

The day had been long, and the only thing I wanted to do was sleep. I went back to my father's study and put all the drawings and the journal in the secret room before making my way up the grand staircase to my room. Sitting in the chair next to the fire was Charles' father. He startled me when he rose.

"Sabine, the task that has been set in motion will bring much sorrow for you. We are not allowed to tell you what is to come, but you will see things that will disturb you and make you doubt yourself. You must ignore these things and stay on the course that has been set before you. Never forget that things are not as they seem. You have accomplished settling the stones, and now the real battle will begin, for they are coming. It will not be easy to win this one. I have sent Blake and Joseph to remove Westin, Camille, and the children. Word has reached the ends of the lands that the valley is where you have been, and that it holds magical powers for you, so I believe that Westin is in grave danger."

My heart stopped beating in my chest.

"I must go and protect him. I promised my brother that I would not let anything happen to him."

"You cannot go. You cannot leave Whispering Wind, for I fear you will surely die. This has been foretold for hundreds of years. This coming is going to happen, and only you and Rebecca can stop it. Do not fear for Westin. He is married to my only daughter, and her brothers will make sure they are safe."

"How can they possibly be safe if I am not there to protect them? Where will they be safe if all the lands are against us? Where could they possibly go?"

"I have instructed Blake to take them to the valley where Raiden took you to see your parents. It is a very long journey, and it will be some time before my sons return to you."

"No, I will send Raiden and Spirit. They can get there and then to the valley and back here in no time. We are safe here. No one can enter the kingdom with the mist, and there are places for us to hide if they do. I will write a note for Westin. He will go, and then Blake can bring the rest. I must make sure my brother, his wife, and the children are safe."

I ran to the table and penned a note to Westin.

My Love,

You must leave the valley. Raiden and Spirit will take you to safety, and then you must not leave the place they take you. Take Camille and the children and hold on tight. Remember, Raiden is Magic. Bring with you the jewels in the cave. Remember where they are? Take with you enough supplies to last a fortnight. I love you, and I will come to you when this is over. Bring blankets and supplies.

I love you, Westin, with all that I am. Please do not dispute this. You must leave now.

Sabine

"I must warn against this, Sabine. You and Rebecca will need Raiden and Spirit."

"You do not understand the power of Raiden. He is faster than the wind blows. He will make it in time."

I ran out the door and down the hall to the grand staircase. I whistled, and before I hit the great hall, Raiden was there.

"Listen to me. You must take Spirit and go to the valley to get Westin and Camille. You must take them to the cave to get the jewels, and then to the valley where you took me to see my parents. They are in grave danger. You must hurry."

'I cannot leave you.'

"You must go. I will be safe here."

'I have found my father's secret room. I will be safe. Now go and take this note with you.'

I tucked the note in his bridle. "Go, my friend, and get them to safety. I will be waiting right here for you."

With that, he turned and neighed, and then made his way to the door. Spirit was waiting for him, and then they were gone. I ran back upstairs to Rebecca and told her what was going on, so we then went back to my room to talk to Charles' father, but he was gone. We ran out to the barracks to find Charles.

"Where did your father go?" I asked.

"My father went back to Wellington shortly after we came back to the castle. Aidan took him. Why, Sabine? What is wrong?"

"No, that is not so. Your father was just in my room. He told me that Westin and Camille were in grave danger, and that Bla..."

Just then, Blake came out of the barracks.

"It was trickery. Someone wanted the horses gone. Who?"

We then heard a very eerie bellowing laugh from deep below the earth. All of us whispered at the same time.

"The witch."

I closed my eyes and cleared my mind.

'Can you hear me? It was trickery. Come back.'

I waited but heard nothing.

"I cannot reach Raiden. Charles, you must hurt me. Put me in danger. Hurry."

Charles drew his sword and swung it at me, catching my arm with the tip and drawing blood. I fell to the ground and tried to scamper away, but he swung again and again, catching my leg. Blood poured out, and Rebecca was screaming at him to stop, but he did not. Two more swings, and I heard Raiden.

'RUN!'

"Stop!" I screamed at him, but he did not stop.

It was Rebecca who swung her sword at him, and the flash of light was so brilliant that it lit the whole courtyard. I shielded my eyes as I got to my feet, and then I ran, just like Raiden said to. As I moved through the courtyard, the light from Rebecca's sword kept flashing. Charles was fighting her. I stopped, I could not run and leave her. I turned, drew my sword, and went back. By the time I made it to Charles, they were all fighting her, and she was holding her own. I engaged Blake and Joseph. It was easy to put them down, and then came Steven and James. When we were done, the only one left standing facing the both of us was Charles. I was not sure if it was Raiden's presence that caused him to drop to his knees and lay his sword down, but he did.

Rebecca yelled, "Come on! Get up! Let us finish this!" I reached out to touch her arm.

"We must leave this place, all of us. The witch has cast some trickery here, and it is no longer safe for any of us. We must not stay here."

"Agreed," was the only word Charles spoke.

"Come with me, Rebecca. We need to prepare." I reached out for her hand.

We went back into the castle, with Raiden and Spirit close behind us, straight into my father's study and into the secret room to retrieve the journal.

"We need to be someplace safe while we figure this out, and I think I know just the place. Do you trust me, Rebecca?"

"Always." she replied.

We left Father's study and went to pack our clothing and to get some food and water. When we finished, we went back to the barracks to find Charles and his brothers.

"Rebecca and I are leaving, and you will not follow. You need to go somewhere that this witch has no control over you. We will find you when we figure this all out. You need to trust me, Charles. Everyone keeps telling me that things are not what they seem, so I am going to remove us from this place, from this hold that witch has over us, and I suggest you do the same."

"Sabine, I am sworn to protect you. I cannot leave you."

"Charles, you just tried to kill me. I think we need to leave this place. If I need you, Raiden will find you. Please, Charles, this is what needs to be done."

He knew I was right, so he just bowed his head.

"You and your brothers must leave this place, and do not return until we come for you. The final battle will be fought here, but we cannot stay here. There is much Rebecca and I must learn, and I believe it is out of your control now. Until we meet again."

Rebecca did not say a word to him. She turned on Spirit, and we left them standing in the courtyard. After we were far away from Whispering Wind, I spoke to her.

"We need to get Westin, Camille, and the children. They are not safe."

"Agreed. We also need to talk about what happened back there, and my need to kill him."

I smiled at her. "That need will soon leave you, and yes, we need to talk."

I leaned into Raiden, saying, "Take me to Westin."

Rebecca did the same, and we were off. Riding him this way was like nothing else I had ever known. My thoughts went to Westin and how happy he would be to see me. I could not wait to see Stephan and Juliana, and I was sure they were much bigger than when we left. Before I knew it, Raiden was in my head.

'Hold on.'

I looked up, and we were at the hills to the valley. I turned, but Rebecca was not there. I moved in my saddle, turning around just in time to see a whiff of wind as Spirit came up.

"Wow! That was different." She was excited, her eyes wide and her smile grand. "How long has Raiden been able to do that?"

"For always, I suppose. Spirit has never done that?"

"No." She giggled.

We started our way up the hills, but halfway up, Raiden stopped.

'No, No, No, No! Sabine, something is wrong.'

'Go. You must go, and hurry'

When Raiden reached the top of the hill, I realized there was no horn, and then I saw the fires. Everything was on fire.

"Oh no," was all I heard Rebecca say before I was gone.

"Take me to Westin."

There is much danger here.'

"Take me to Westin."

We were flying again across the plain to the caves. If there were people here, they did not see us. Raiden did not stop until he was in the cave, and moments later, Rebecca and Spirit showed up.

I jumped off Raiden and took off running deeper into the caves.

"Westin!" I screamed. "Westin, where are you?"

I could not hear him, but Raiden did. He ran up behind and around me, so I followed him deeper and deeper into the caves. Raiden was way ahead of me when I heard him neigh. Then I heard Camille scream. I ran as hard as I could forward. Rebecca had drawn her sword and was right behind me. I ran past Raiden to see Westin standing in front of Camille and the children with his sword drawn. He dropped it and ran into my arms crying. I hugged him so hard.

"I am here, my love. I am here," I whispered.

We stood there for what seemed days, hugging while he cried. I pulled away from him and grabbed Camille, who was holding a teary Stephan and Juliana.

"I am here. I came for you. We are all safe now," I whispered to them.

Rebecca held Westin while I comforted the kids and Camille. When everyone was calm, we sat, and Westin told us what had happened.

"We were getting the children ready for sleep when we heard the horns blowing. I thought you were coming, but Camille did not think it was you. She was frightened, so we gathered up all that we could and ran outside. Everyone was running around, and the horses were running around. I knew it was bad then, so I grabbed a horse. Camille climbed up, and I handed her Stephan and Juliana." I squeezed her just a bit tighter in my arms; it felt so good to feel her hand on my face. "Then I climbed on, and we raced here. I wanted to go out a few times, to see what was happening, but Camille would not let me go."

"I am glad she would not. She was right for you to stay here where it is safe."

"I waited and waited for you, Sabine, but you did not come."

"I did not know, Westin, but we are here now, and you are all safe."

"We were not sure how much time had passed because it is so dark in here, but many times we slept, and there was nothing. I thought I heard voices once, while the children were sleeping, and we put out the candles, so no one would find us, but the voices went away. So, when Camille fell asleep, I was very careful, and I moved through the caves. When I got to the opening, I could see the black smoke from the fires. The light of the day was here. I tried and tried to see if anyone was moving around, but I could not see anything. We were running out of food, and the children needed to eat, so I was very cunning, and I worked my way back to the cottage. While I was gone, Camille woke up, and boy was she mad at me when I got back." He looked at her and smiled. "When I got to the cottage, I saw them all. Everyone is dead again, Sabine. Why does everyone have to be dead all the time? It was just like at Whispering Wind, only this time I did not almost kill Camille," he said with a small smile. "There was no one here, no one except for everyone that was dead, so I made my way into the cottage and found a bunch of food that was not rotten, and I put it in a bag. I found a bunch of water skins and filled them with water, and I made my way back to the cave. I do not know why Camille was mad at me. I just went to get food and water."

"Because you scared me. I thought you had been killed as well. What would I have done if you were gone?"

"But I am not dead. I did not get dead at Whispering Wind, and I did not get dead here. I saved Sabine, and I saved you and the children. I would not get dead and leave you."

I did not know what to say to them. My brother was beyond brave, and he was very cunning; two of his very strong points.

"Westin, do you know who it was that did this?"

"No, Sabine, I do not, but everyone that is dead out there was cut open like this," he said, and he ran his finger from his mid-section to his neck, showing me how they were all cut.

"Well, we are here now, and we are leaving while the dark of the night is here. Camille and Juliana will ride with me, and you and Stephan will ride with Rebecca. Westin, did you get the jewels?"

He jumped up and went to the back of the cave, and when he returned, he had many satchels with him and a big smile on his face. "Just like you told me to do, but Camille was too afraid to leave here to go someplace else like you said we should."

"Well, I am glad that you did not go anywhere else, for it is not safe here anymore. We need to gather as much as we can carry, and we need to do it now. We need to leave this place."

"Sabine, we can take this horse, so we do not have to ride with three of us on one horse."

"That is a good idea, my love, but do you remember what I told you about Raiden?"

He whispered, "That he is magic."

"That is right, my love, so your horse, as nice as he is, will not be able to keep up, so let us go."

We took as much as we could carry. I got on Raiden, followed by Camille, and Westin handed Juliana up to me, and I put her in front. Then Rebecca climbed on Spirit, and Westin handed her Stephan before he climbed up, putting Stephan between them.

"Westin, you must hold on to Rebecca. Do not let go of her for any reason. Hold Stephan between you, so he does not fall off, and do not be scared."

"I will, Sabine, and I will not be scared."

"Camille do not let go of me," I told her, and her arms tightened around my waist.

Juliana looked up at me and whispered, "Are we going to go fast again?"

"Yes, my love, we are, but we are going to go faster than before, so you hang on. Do not be frightened, and do not let go. If you get scared, just close your eyes."

She nodded.

Take us to the valley where we saw my father. It is the only place to be safe.'

We made our way out of the caves and up the hills at the far end of the valley. Before we hit the plain, I reminded everyone to hang on, and then we were off. Juliana squealed with delight as Raiden hit top speed. I heard Camille wince with fear. In no time at all, we were at the river. We slowed so Raiden could cross safely as his load was bigger than the last time. When we hit the ground, we were off again. Time disappeared in front of us. Soon we were at the base of the mountain, and Raiden slowed to climb.

"Sabine, you were right. He is magic, and so is Spirit. Father's horse is magic. Who would have thought that?"

"Not I that is for sure." We all laughed.

Halfway up the mountain, we came to the cave. It was still the dark of night, so we could not see a thing once we entered.

"Sabine, I am frightened," Juliana whispered.

"It will be all right, my love. I am here with you. We are almost there."

Perhaps it was the dark of night, but it seemed to take a very long time to get through the cave, but we made it, then down the side of the mountain and across the plain we went, stopping in the middle by the lone tree. We all dismounted the horses. Stephan was asleep, and Camille was shaking.

"Are you all right?" I asked her.

"What just happened could not have happened. Where are we?"

"We are hidden from the danger that came to the valley. No one will ever find us here. Now come. Let us make a place to sleep, and when the light of the day comes, I will tell you everything that I can." Camille smiled at me and started to get our make-shift beds ready. This night we all slept together, all touching, while Raiden and Spirit stood guard over us.

CHAPTER TWELVE

When the light of the day broke, I was the first to awaken. I sat up and looked at my brother with his wife and son wrapped in his arms. It was amazing how strong he was. He could have been king; he should have been king. Juliana was wrapped in Rebecca's arms. She had changed so much since we left. I could see Ardes in her, in her jaw mostly. This was all that is left of my family. Jared was gone, and we had to fight a fight that those who were protecting us were not sure we could win.

They will be safe here, Sabine, forever. No matter what happens, I will stay with them. No harm will ever come to them.'

Thank you, Raiden, but I am hoping that I will be with them for the rest of my days, as well.'

There are those who believe that is not possible.'

What do you believe?'

I believe you will live a long and happy life.'

I smiled at my friend. I slid away from them all and took a walk. There was a small lake nearby, so I thought I would at least try to wash up. It had been far too long since I had bathed. I peeled off my clothing and gently walked into the water, then lay down and let the cool water rush over my body. As best I could, I rubbed my hands and face.

"I managed to bring some soap along. Would you like me to wash your hair?"

"Camille, you startled me, but that would be lovely. How is it that you managed to bring soap?"

"Well, I have two children that I need to tend to, after all, and the little things are what matters in this life, Sabine. Knowing you and Westin has taught me that. Before I met you, I had no thoughts of anything except doing my work to the best of my ability, either that or suffer the wrath of Samuel."

"Was he a cruel king?"

"If you crossed him, yes. Otherwise, he did not bother with you, especially if you were a woman. I remember his daughters would cry and cry, wanting the attention of their father. I remember one-time Kaitlin wanted her father to hold her. She tried climbing in his lap, and he shoved her to the ground, and rather hard. Her skin on her backside turned purple. So yes, he was cruel."

"Camille, you saw more than you are saying about what occurred in the valley. Will you tell me please?"

"Oh, Sabine, it was terrible. They came out of nowhere. One minute, the horns were blowing, and the next, people were dying right in front of us. It seemed impossible that they got from the top of the hills to the valley center in such a short time. It was as if...."

"As if what?"

"As if their horses were magic, like Raiden and Spirit. There was no way to outrun them."

"But you all managed to escape."

"After it all happened, and we were in the cave, I started thinking the same thing. They had to have seen us running. But then we heard the voices, so perhaps they needed to kill all the guards before they got to us."

"Do you think Wellington and Blackmore still live?"

"I was thinking the same thing myself." We turned, and Rebecca was wading into the stream to wash with Juliana.

"Well, I think that Camille and Westin were allowed to leave, that they were not to be harmed but captured and used against me. It would seem that the guards needed to be taken care of first, and then perhaps when they came to the caves, they discovered Wellington and Blackmore, so the search was called off. The thing that seems strange to me, however, is the fact that their horses were faster than most, the same as Raiden and Spirit."

"So, I guess it would be safe to say that Wellington and Blackmore are no longer alive, considering it was my mother and Jared's mother who started this in the first place."

We bathed and played in the water with Juliana, and it felt so good to just be me. I was not worried about anyone finding us. This is the enchanted valley that Joseph was sent to find, but he never did. Raiden assured me that Westin would be safe here forever, and I had to believe him.

We finished, dressed, and made our way back to the make-shift camp. Westin and Stephan were still fast asleep.

I looked at Raiden and asked, "Do you think it is safe to build a fire?"

'No fire.'

'How will we cook the food or warm the water, or keep warm for that matter?'

'The tree will provide you with all that you need; warmth from the cold, heated food, warmed water.'

I just looked at him, giggled, and shook my head. "Would I expect anything less?"

'You should not.'

Westin jumped up and frightened us all.

"Oh, Sabine, I was dreaming you were not here," he cried. As he grabbed me and pulled me into a huge hug.

"Westin, breathe. I cannot breathe," I struggled out.

He laughed as he let me go. "I am so happy you are here with us, and you are going to stay with us."

"Oh, my love, I cannot stay with you. Rebecca and I have something very important to do. Father needs us to finish something for him and his father before him, and his father before him. We are going to stay for a while, as we have some things we need to figure out before we can go back to Whispering Wind, but you are safe here. No one will ever find you, ever."

"Will we live here then, instead of Whispering Wind?"

"Hopefully, when we are finished with our task, then we can go home, all of us, but there are some things that I need to tell you. Remember when we left Samuel's, and I told you that Joseph had found a magical place for us to live where no one would ever find us? Well, I was wrong, this was the valley that Joseph should have found. This place is magic, Westin, and it is secret. Remember when we went through the cave to get here?" He nodded his head. "Well, we had to go through the cave because the mountains that surround this valley are too high for any horse or man to climb and cross over, and the entrance to the cave seals when we pass through it, so only Raiden or Spirit knows where it is. You must never light a fire here. I am not even sure you can light a fire, but do you see that tree behind me?" He leaned over to see the tree and nodded. "Well, that tree is the magic in the valley. If you are cold at night or during the day, go under the tree and it will warm you. Sleep under it when the seasons change. It will warm the water, and it will cook your food. You can eat the fruit that grows on that tree. In fact, it will probably be the only food you will have. I do not know if you can hunt in this valley."

Yes, he can.'

"Well, yes you can hunt here, but do not, no matter what, Westin, do not start a fire. The smoke will rise above the mountains, and they will come looking for you."

"Sabine, I will not start a fire ever. I give you my word. I wonder if Father knew of all this magic, and of Raiden."

"Oh, I think he did. That is for sure."

We did not rush and hurry to do anything. We just enjoyed being together for the day. Stephan was beginning to walk, and Juliana was filled with stories of her and Westin's tricks on the house staff. The children had grown so much while we were away. It did not seem we had been gone long enough for this amazing transformation.

I wandered off to have some time to myself and to try and figure out what was happening. All the times someone had said to me that everything was not what it seemed stayed in the forefront of my mind. I thought back to my room, the person who I thought was Charles' father, and the things he said to me. They were truth in part; Westin was in danger, but no one was on their way to help them. Then Charles tried to kill me. The power of the witch was strong, and I wondered if it could reach this far. *Could she penetrate us here?* Then there were the jewels. I did not know what we were to do with them. They must have had something to do with the drawings of the kingdom, and with our kingdom being the place where life began. *What did this all mean?* Perhaps the jewels were what would save us all. The power they held, and the mystery as to what they did to others, needed to be understood. Perhaps Father had left me clues in his writings. Charles and his brothers were affected by both the witch and the jewels. They were the Guardians, but yet they changed. *Were Rebecca and I to do this alone?* Perhaps we would not survive this. Perhaps we were not strong enough to do this. *'Oh, Father, I wish I had enough confidence in myself to carry out this task, this huge undertaking that has been set before me.'*

I heard Jenna in my head, saying,

Juliana is the key.'

I turned to look at her. How was it possible that such a tiny little girl could be the key to all of this? What did that witch know that I did not? Was she magic as well?

'Yes,'

Jenna's voice said in a whisper.

It must be truth. Why else would the witch keep her close? There was so much I did not know, so much we needed to discover, and so much we needed to figure out.

I walked back to Juliana and sat with her, looking, observing her. *What was hidden within this beautiful little girl? Was my whole family blessed with magic?* Ardes and Jenna, Wellington and Whispering Wind; Rebecca, Blackmore and Whispering Wind; Father and Mother, Ridge Manor and Whispering Wind; the only link was Whispering Wind well, that and Mother's family's kingdom, Ridge Manor. Did I know anything about my mother's family? My grandfather, who was he? Did I ever meet him? I could not remember ever meeting him. I only knew him from the stories of my mother. What ever happened to him?

"Westin, do you remember our mother's father?"

"No, Sabine, I do not think we ever met him. I think he died when Ardes was born. Why do you ask?"

"Oh, no reason... I was just thinking about our family, and I could not remember ever knowing him."

He went back to playing with Stephan, and I back to my thoughts. I was playing with Juliana's hair while my mind wandered. So Whispering Wind was the one thing all of us had in common, the place where life began. What did that mean? My hands were entwined in Juliana's hair, putting it up on her head, when Jenna's voice popped in my head.

'Look.'

This place had to be magic. I kept hearing her voice. Was it wishful thinking or was it real? I looked down at Juliana, leaning forward and giving something to Stephan, and there just above the hairline on the back of her neck was a mark. I could not make out what it was. I did not want to alarm anyone, so I decided I would wait until she was asleep to look at it again. I looked across the plain and saw Rebecca sitting alone.

"My love, I am going to go and sit with Rebecca for a while. Will you stay here with Westin please?" Juliana smiled and nodded at me.

I wandered over to where Rebecca was sitting in the grass.

"Everything all right with you?" I asked as I sat down.

"I was just thinking about the night we left Charles. What do you think happened? He was really trying to hurt you, even kill you."

"I do not know," I paused, bumping her shoulder, "but you took him down, along with the others. You held your own."

"I know, but it should not have happened that way. There is some powerful magic going on there. I do not think it wise of us to go back."

"We cannot go back until we are ready, until we know what it is we are supposed to do with those jewels. Since we have been here in this valley, I have been hearing Jenna's voice in my head. I do not know if I am imagining it or if it is really happening."

"After all that we have seen, it is real." She half smiled. "What is it she is saying to you?"

"She said that Juliana was the key, and then just now, while she was sitting in my lap and I was playing with her hair, Jenna told me to look. When I looked down, just above Juliana's hairline was a mark."

"What kind of mark?"

"I could not see it clearly, but I will look again when she sleeps. We need to figure this all out, Rebecca. I am fearful now that these blood-gutters have made themselves known. It means that the time is coming for this battle we are to fight. I am also fearful that we will be fighting it alone."

"I think it is time for us to read your father's writings."

"Yes." I got up and went back to our make-shift camp. "Rebecca and I are going for a ride. There is much to discuss. We will not be far, so if you need us, just whistle. Raiden will hear you if I cannot."

"It is all right, Sabine. We are safe here now."

Westin looked at me and smiled. I hugged them all and climbed up on Raiden. He did not do his usual quick departure, but it was a casual ride. We only needed to be far enough away so that we were not over-heard. We climbed down.

"I need for you and Spirit to go back to Westin. What we will be talking about is for our ears only."

Raiden nodded, and they were off. We sat in the grass and opened the journal.

CHAPTER THIRTEEN

My Dearest Sabine,

There is much to teach you as you grow. My only wish is that I have enough time. I do not know when the coming will take place. I just know, have known, that it was truth since you were born. I had hoped that it would not be my children or their children, but looking at you and watching you grow, and the ease at which the skills of a warrior come to you, I know it is you. You are the chosen one. You and your cousin will be the Bringers of Peace to this unsettled land.

Whispering Wind is named this for the way the wind blows through the trees, and if you listen, you can hear it whisper. Sometimes it helps when I wander through the forest down by the river. There is a certain rock that I like to sit on, just below the bend in the river. You can really hear the whispering there.

This land has been with our family for generations. No one is sure of the length of time in which we have been here. Some say it is written in books, but these are books I have never seen. You have excelled well in your reading, so perhaps one day you will find these books to read. I know not of any place they would be, or even that they would be, but perhaps one day you or even your children will find them.

"I believe he is saying that somewhere by this rock at the bend in the river is a place we should discover."

"Do you know this place?"

"It is not a familiar place, but I am sure we can find it."

We continued to read.

My Dearest Sabine,

Today has been a day of lessons for you. With your knowledge, Ardes has set you upon the course of training. One day, you will wield my sword according to the legend. I have to chuckle Ardes can just lift it above his head. Such a large sword for such a small girl, you have big shoes to fill, my darling daughter. Simon's sword is more the sword for you. The steel that forged them came from the same place, this place, the land in which you stand. Its beauty is of nothing you have ever seen.

"This is what Simon said to me the day Raiden brought me here. 'Father's sword combined with mine, Sabine, together they are forged.' Somehow, I think what Father is saying has a different meaning. Do you think it would be possible to forge two swords together? Who could we get to do it? Everyone is dead? Or is Father saying I should wield Simon's sword instead of his?"

"I wonder if he is talking about this place, Sabine. Its beauty is like nothing I have ever seen before. Do you think the steel came from here?"

"I do not see how my father would have known about this place, but then again, Joseph and Charles knew of this place. They just could not find it, but Raiden did, and Raiden was my father's horse. It makes me wonder, Rebecca. I know I am supposed to understand all of this, but I am not so sure that I do."

"I know. Let us go for a ride. That always makes you feel better. We can read more later."

I put the journal back in my bodice, and we walked back to the camp. I noticed that Juliana and Stephan were taking a nap.

"Sabine, would you stay with the children while Westin and I go for a swim to wash up?"

"Yes, of course. You go have fun."

I thought this would be the perfect time to look at Juliana's head, so I lay softly next to her, moving her long hair out of my way. I could not believe how long her hair had gotten. I lay so that my head was flat on the ground, and my eyes were level with the back of her neck. Rebecca sat there watching me, trying her hardest not to laugh. I suppose I looked silly. Gently, I separated the strands of hair so I could see the mark clearly. It was brown and looked sort of like a flame from a fire. *What in the world was this?* I motioned for Rebecca to look. She was just as stunned as I was. I put her hair back and sat up, and we moved a bit away so not to disturb them.

I whispered to Rebecca, "What do you think it could be?"

She whispered back, "It looks like a flame from a fire."

"Yes, I thought so as well, but why would she have a mark like this on her head? Look and see if I have one."

Half joking, I lifted my hair so she could search my hairline for one.

"Wow."

"What?"

"It is a perfect circle. Here, look and see if I have one as well."

She flipped her hair and lowered her head so I could look.

"You are not going to believe this!"

"What?"

"You have one that looks like the sliver of the moon." She sat up, and we just stared at one another.

She whispered, "Just like on our swords. What does this mean?"

I had no idea what it meant, so I just looked at her.

"I do not know. On our swords, I am the sun and you are the moon."

I looked at Juliana, and a chill ran through me. The wind kicked up, swirling around us.

"Fire," I whispered.

Looking at Rebecca, I could see it in her eyes that she was thinking the same thing I was.

"Do you think she is fire?"

"Perhaps that is why the witch wanted her. Could this be why

Jenna told you she is the key? What key could fire be? Is she going to burn?"

"I do not think she is going to catch on fire. Maybe she can control fire. Maybe she has the ability to do what our swords do."

"Our swords make lighting, not fire."

We sat there looking at Juliana. After a while, she stirred and opened her eyes, and I know what I saw in her beautiful amber blue eyes; I saw fire.

"I need to go, and I need you to stay here with them. Can you do that?"

"Sabine, we should not be separated. We need to stay hidden until we figure this out, until it is time."

"I cannot stay here right now. There is something I must do, and I believe I need to do this alone. I will be back soon."

Before she could object, I got up and went to Raiden.

"I need you to take me back to Whispering Wind, back to the river in the forest."

'We should not leave here.'

"Everyone keeps telling me we need to figure this out on our own, so I have some information that does not make sense, and I need to go where my father told me to go. I need to listen to the wind. Now, please take me."

He neighed and stomped his hoof on the ground, but he did not argue with me when I mounted him. Westin came running up when he saw me get on Raiden.

"Sabine, where are you going? Rebecca said you were leaving. Please do not leave us, Sabine."

"I will return soon, my love. I have something I need to do. Rebecca will be here to keep you safe. Remember, do not start any fires, and take care of the children."

"I will always take care of them. I would die for them."

"I know you would. Now please do not worry. I will return soon."

I did not look back as Raiden flew across the valley. It seemed like no time at all had passed when I arrived back to the green mist of Whispering

Wind. Raiden seemed to know exactly where it was I wanted to go. I was sure he had been here many times with Father. I climbed down and found the rock Father spoke of, and I settled in for whatever was to come. Raiden made himself scarce, as if he knew what was going to happen.

I climbed on the rock, which was bigger than I had thought it would be. I closed my eyes to listen, but the only thing I could here was the babbling of the water as it trickled over the rocks in the river. Then I felt a soft breeze come across my face. The wind was cool, signaling the change coming. Soon it would be the cold months, which only meant more passage of time. I thought I heard something in the wind, but I thought maybe it was just my imagination or wishful thinking.

Everything had been such a fantasy. I was not sure how anyone could believe all that we had done, all that we had seen, and now here I sit on a rock that I read about in a journal my father hid in a secret room that he started writing when I was born into this world. None of this was right. None of this could be real. Perhaps I was living in a vision, and I would wake to find my family intact and ready for the fight I should have had with my father about the man he had chosen for me to marry. At that thought, my eyes popped open. *'Who would have been chosen for me?'* I supposed I would never know. The wind blew again; it sounded like soft whispers, no real words, just an enchanting unsung song. It was a very calming, almost hypnotic chant. I could not make out any words, just a tune. I sat there for some time, just listening and feeling the calm over take me, when I thought I heard my name. I opened my eyes and looked around. I could see Raiden in the distance, so perhaps it was just my imagination playing with me.

I looked at my surroundings. Even with the mist hovering just above the ground, this was a beautiful place. I really did not think I had been there before. In fact, I knew I had never seen this place. The forest was not a place I was allowed. Father really went to extremes to keep me hidden. He had to have known that Samuel would have discovered me when Ardes chose Jenna. Maybe he thought that Samuel would be fearful of moving against him. I closed my eyes. I could not stop my mind from wandering, and the thoughts of the past years kept flooding in. I was trying to make sense of it all. The wind blew through the trees, and I heard my name again so soft and gentle that I was not sure I even heard it.

'Listen with your eyes.'

What? How do I do that? I opened my eyes as the wind started to stir. The trees were swaying with each gust, the leaves on the ground swirling in the air, and then they went flying away. I watched them blow down the river and come back, and then blow down the river and come back again. It continued to do this over and over again, as if the river was breathing. I stood amazed at what I was seeing, and then I heard Raiden in my mind.

'Follow.'

So, I followed them. There came a point in the water where it was less than most parts. It looked as if I could walk across without getting too wet, but as I started to cross, the water seemed to become less, and rocks appeared for me to step on. When I reached the other side, Raiden was standing on the bank.

'Go,' he said.

So, I followed the leaves. Raiden walked on the opposite side along with me. The leaves came to a stop and started to swirl in a circle, as if they were telling me something. I remembered what he said to me. 'Listen with your eyes.' Then just as they started, they ended by disappearing into the rock face along this side of the river. I just stood looking at the wall of rock in front of me. *Where did they go?* I took a step forward and could see nothing. Closer and closer I got to the rock wall, and still I saw only rocks. I reached up to press my hand against the rock, and instead of feeling it, my hand went through it. As I turned to look at Raiden, I heard him in my head.

'Go.'

I stepped forward into the rock face, and as I passed through the rock, I felt a coolness take over me, the chill going to my bones. I turned to look at the rock I just walked through, I could see Raiden and the river. I walked back out to the river and turned back to the rock face. It was just a wall of rock. There was no way of telling there was a cave beyond. Shaking my head, I smiled and walked through it again. The cave was lit from the opening. As I walked in, it opened up into a huge cavern. In the center of the room was a circle, with eight pedestals of sorts sat in equal distance from one another to make up the circle's boundaries. In the center was a place to start a fire.

As I looked around the cave, I noticed writings on the walls, but they did not make any sense. They were written the same way the writing on my father's drawing was, backwards, so I would need the looking glass to read them. As I moved to the back of the cave, there seemed to be what looked like holes cut in the wall. Most of them were empty, but some held old tomes of sorts. I was afraid to disturb them; the dust and moss led me to believe they had not been touched for a very long time. Then I saw on one of the holes high up something shining, glimmering from the reflection of light. I could not reach it, so I look around for something to climb on, but there was nothing. I stretched to reach, but just my fingertips would touch it, it felt very cold. Perhaps Raiden can help. I walked back out to the river. He was just standing there looking at me.

"I need your help."

'I cannot enter.'

"I do not understand why I am here or what I am supposed to do here. I need to talk to Rebecca," I said to him as I started across the river. I climbed up on him. "Take me back please."

Before I knew what was happening, he was blazing across the land. I could not help but wonder what that place was, and what it had to do with me. I reached into my bodice to feel for Father's journal, making sure it was safe. Perhaps there was something in there about that place. Maybe Rebecca had some clue. Before I realized it, Raiden was climbing the mountains. We made it through the cave in record time, and then we were flying across the field to our little camp.

"Where have you been, Sabine? I was giving you one more day, and then I was coming after you."

"What do you mean, one more day? I have been gone only a few hours."

"No, Sabine, the light of day has come and gone six times. Where were you?"

I turned to look at Raiden. "You move so quickly that the light of day and the dark of night pass without me seeing?"

He just stomped his hoof and neighed at me, bobbing his head up and down.

"I am sorry, Rebecca. I had no idea that time passed so slowly for you. I went to the river my father spoke of in his journal, and you will not believe what happened. I cannot speak the words, even Raiden cannot. It is something we need to do together. We can leave in the morning, if that is good with you."

"Are you all right? Nothing happened to you, did it?"

"Oh, my friend, very much happened to me, and yes, I am all right."

I looked around for Westin and Juliana. I spotted them down by the river and made my way to them.

"Sabine!" Juliana screamed as she ran toward me.

I laughed as I bent to catch her in my arms. "My love."

She hit me so hard we tumbled to the ground laughing.

"I missed you," she said as she showered me with kisses.

"As I did you, my love. Every time I leave you, I cannot wait to see you again."

She pulled back, and with a very serious face, she said in a whisper, "You are leaving us again."

"I am, my love, but I will return. Rebecca and I have much to do before we can all go home to Whispering Wind, so you can grow up where your father and mother lived. I promise that I will not be gone so long this time."

"As long as you promise to come back." Her smile held my heart.

"I will always promise you. You are my love, and nothing will keep me from you again."

I wrapped my arms around her, and we rolled around in the long grass, laughing and giggling.

As the light of the day lit up the sky just below the top of the mountains that surround our little valley, Rebecca and I packed what we needed in our sacks, said our goodbyes, and left the valley. We blazed across the lands to the river.

I told Rebecca, "You must believe and open your mind to listen with your eyes. If you do not, you will not see."

"What does that mean, 'Listen with your eyes'?"

"You will see."

I could not help but smile. I knew how silly it sounded. I followed the same path down the river to the rocks, and as I approached the water's edge, the water receded and the rocks came into view. I crossed first, and Rebecca followed. She did not say anything. We moved down the opposite side of the river with Raiden and Spirit following. As we reached the place where I walked through the rock wall.

Turning to Rebecca and, in a very low voice, I said, "What we are about to do is impossible, but do not be afraid. You must hear with your eyes."

She swallowed and nodded at me, not saying a word. I turned to face the rock wall. Slowly I moved forward and reached out to feel the wall. When my hand went through it, I reached behind me with the other and grabbed Rebecca's hand, and we moved through the wall together. I felt her tense up as I passed through and she was still on the outside, but as she came through it, I felt her breath on my neck as she released it.

"Sabine," she whispered. "What is this place?"

"I do not know, but I think this is where Father wanted us to come."

We made our way into the cave.

"These writings on the wall are like the ones in Father's drawings. They are backwards, and over here are these holes." I moved to the back of the cave. "Some of them are empty, and some hold what look like old tomes."

"Should we read them?"

"I do not know, but up there..." I pointed, and she looked. "Up there, do you see the glimmer?"

"Yes, should I lift you?"

I climbed up on Rebecca's back and reached into the hole. What I felt was cold and heavy. I grabbed it with my hand, but it was heavy, so I slid it to the edge and took it out with both hands. It was a block of silver. Rebecca slid me down her back and faced me.

"Is this the silver your father spoke of? Is this what your sword was forged from?"

"I am not sure, but if I had to say, I would say yes."

"What is this place?"

"I thought that my father's journal would give us a clue, so I came to get you. We are supposed to do this together."

We sat down, and I took out the journal. As I opened it, I said, "All right, Father, what do you have to tell me now?"

Rebecca giggled. "We will soon discover it."

My Dearest Sabine,

Time will move across the land, but for you and Rebecca, it will stand still. The seasons will change, and the ground will be covered in white, and it will seem that no time at all has passed. The bend in the river where the wind whispers to you has no boundary of time. It seems to stand still, so be wary of this. You will need to take possession of Simon's sword in the land of beauty.

"So, is he saying that we need to be in the valley?" Rebecca whispered.

"I believe so. He mentioned old books, and over there," I paused and pointed to the holes in the back wall before continuing, "are old books. Do you think we should read them? And what of this writing on the walls? We need the looking glass to read them. Do you think we should go to the castle and get my mother's looking glass?"

"Would it be safe to go there? Whoever found the valley rode magic horses like Spirit and Raiden. Do you think they would be able to withstand the mist as well?"

"Together, they cannot touch us, but if we were alone or separated, I fear we could be overcome. We need to go together, Rebecca. We cannot leave one another."

"Agreed. Let us go to the castle and get the looking glass and then return here." We made our way out of the cave and back to Raiden and Spirit. "Take us to the castle. We need to retrieve something there. Is it safe?"

Raiden nodded his head, and we were off. It was as if I blinked and we were at the great doors of the great hall. We jumped off our horses and we ran as fast as our legs would carry us to my father's study. Rebecca triggered the latch, and we bolted into the secret room. She grabbed the looking glass, and I grabbed all the papers that were left lying about. Just as fast as we entered the castle, we left it and were back to the river before we knew it.

"All right, so where do we start?" Rebecca said spinning around.

"Well, I think it might read like the journal, so I think we should start here." I pointed to the right side of the cave opening."

"Top or bottom?"

"Top."

"Do you want to read it, or should I?" Her eyes were wide.

"Go ahead. You can start."

Rebecca held the looking glass up to the wall and started reading.

"Here is where time began. Here is where life began. Here is where no time moves."

Rebecca turned to look at me. "What does that mean?"

"My father's journal said we must be wary of time while we are here, that it stands still for us."

"And that we must be in the valley when the cold months come."

"Rebecca, perhaps we should go back. We can take the metal and one old tome and go back to the valley and wait for the cold months to pass. I have a bad feeling about this place. I am not sure we should be here."

She looked at me and nodded. "I think you are right. Which tome should we take?"

"Well, as with the wall, we should start at the right top."

She went over and removed the old tome. "This is heavy." Looking in the hole, she said, "Hey, look at this."

I went over to her and looked in the hole. It was dark, but it looked like there was a shape carved in the back of the stone.

"It looks like the shape of a jewel. I wonder if the other holes have shapes as well."

We went around the wall looking in the holes. There were sixteen of them, but only eight of them had shapes in them, and they were all different.

"I think the jewels fit in here somehow. Each one has a different shape to it. In fact, they are all different shapes and sizes. We need to leave this place with our minds so full of this intrigue. We need to get back to Westin and the children, and if time stands still for us in here, we do not know how long we have been away."

"Here, help me put this in my sack, and we will go."

We walked out of the cave to see Raiden and Spirit standing across the river. We crossed and climbed on. "

Take me to the valley," I whispered as I leaned into Raiden. I stayed lying on his neck, hugging my old friend. "I am fearful, my friend. I do not know what is expected of me."

He did not answer. He just ran, and soon we were climbing the mountain and passing through the cave. As we neared our camp, I thought I was seeing things. Stephan was running alongside Juliana, and she had grown a great deal. How was that possible?

Westin came running up. "Sabine, you have been gone for so long I feared you were dead. We stayed here, just like you told me to, and no one came. We did just as you said and lit no fires. The tree has kept us warm, and the cold months are coming fast now. I am so glad you are back."

He startled me when he said I had been gone for so long. I turned to look at Raiden, though I did not know what I expected him to do or even say.

"Westin, how long have we been gone?"

"For a long time, Sabine. Look, Stephan can run, and Juliana is growing, and Camille is having another baby." His eyes were huge. "I am going to be a father again, Sabine."

I looked over to see Camille walking up from the river, her belly swollen huge with a baby.

"How is this possible?" I whispered. I looked at Rebecca, and she just shook her head.

"Westin, I did not realize that we had been gone for so long. I am sorry. We will stay with you until the baby comes." I put my arm around him. "You are going to be a father again. How exciting! Are you nervous?"

He hugged me tightly.

"No, I am happy. I hope it is a little girl. Do you think it would be all right if I named her after Mother, if I named her Julia?"

"Oh, Westin, I think that would be wonderful, and I think Mother would love that you named your daughter after her, but what if it is a boy? What will you name it then?"

"I have not thought of it being a boy. I should ask Camille," he said, and away he went to sit and talk with Camille.

I stood there watching my brother, watching the children. Juliana was so big and looked just like her mother. Stephan was so much like Westin. I could not help but think of all the games and trickery the two of them would share. We had to end this. They needed to be at Whispering Wind. It was not fair to leave them here to grow up. I looked again at Raiden, but he was avoiding my eyes.

There is much you must tell me,' I said in my head to him.

He did not respond. He walked away to the tree, which prompted me to remember that the tree was the source of heat and comfort. *The swords... would the tree be how I forged them together?*

"Rebecca, could I have that metal we found?"

I went over to pick up Simon's sword and then went back to Rebecca. I took the metal from her and went to the base of the tree. I laid Father's sword on the ground, placed the metal on top of that, and then balanced Simon's sword on top of that. I did not know what I was expecting; a flash of light, or maybe a mystical blacksmith to appear and pound them together, but there was nothing. I giggled to myself and turned to walk away. It was then that the whole valley disappeared before my eyes. It was as if I was standing in a blinding light, and nothing would penetrate it. I heard nothing and saw nothing, just the light. I felt like I was magically transported to another place in time. There was no sound, no movement, just the light. I stood there unable to breathe. The fear was overpowering. *Was I losing my mind? Was I imagining all of this? Had I perished?* So many thoughts flowed through my mind. It was the smallest of sounds like the tink, tink, tink sound of metal, and then I heard a voice like no other, saying.

'Together they become one. Together they stand. There is no other who can defeat the power, when two become one.'

The light slowly disappeared, with the valley coming back into view. As I looked at Rebecca and Westin, I saw that they were not alarmed. *Had they seen the light? Did they hear the voice?* I turned to look at the swords I had laid on the ground, but they were gone. There was nothing.

Raiden was standing nearby, so I ran up to him and whispered in his ear, "Did you see that? Did you see what happened to the swords? They are gone." He just neighed at me.

'What did I do? I cannot fight this fight without my sword,' I thought to *myself.*

"Rebecca!!!" I yelled.

Running toward me, she asked, "What is it, Sabine? Are you all right?"

"No, I am not. I put the swords and the metal by the tree and look! They are gone."

She ran up to the tree and walked around it, looking for the swords, but found nothing. "No one was here but us, and I did not take it."

"Did you see the light?" I asked.

"No, Sabine, the only thing I saw was you standing there." She pointed to the spot I was standing. "I saw nothing more. What happened to you? Somehow you seem different, as if something has changed."

She walked around me, looking me up and down. Her hand reached up to touch my hair.

"Uhh," she whispered. "Sabine, your hair..."

She slid her fingers through it, keeping some between her fingers and bringing it around so I could see it. My eyes did not believe what I was seeing. The strands of hair in her fingers were white.

"How is this possible? How did this happen?"

We stood there looking at my hair and then looking at one another.

"Sabine, what happened?"

"I put the swords and the metal next to the tree. Nothing happened, so I turned to walk away, when this light came. Everything that was outside the canopy of the tree disappeared, and it was nothing but light, and then I heard a voice that I did not know, and it said, *'Together they become one. Together they stand. There is no other who can defeat the power, when two become one.'* And then it was gone, along with the swords. Rebecca, I have no sword to fight with. We cannot leave this valley, ever."

"I am positive everything will turn out all right. We have much to do before we leave here again, and Camille is having a baby. Can you believe we have been gone for so long? I mean, to us it just seemed like a little bit of time, but outside the cave, almost a whole year has passed. Look how big Juliana and Stephan have gotten."

I reached up to stop her. I had discovered that when Rebecca got scared, she would talk without taking a break. It was not often that she was frightened, so she must have really been scared. I did not blame her, but I was worried. She is right, however, that we had much to do, much to learn, and we were going to have another baby.

We stood there looking at one another. I was sure we were both thinking the same thing that this was never going to end, that time was going to go by us, and the lands outside of this valley were going to suffer greatly. We turned to look at what was left of our family, and I wondered out loud, "What is going to come of us?

CHAPTER FOURTEEN

Time seemed to get away from us. Camille gave birth to a beautiful baby girl, and Westin named her Julia after our mother. The cold months had come and gone, and the ground was becoming new again. Rebecca and I had been gone from Charles and his brothers for a very long time; more than a year had passed, so I knew they must be worried about us. We had been through the old tome more than once, trying to figure out what it all meant. Most of the pages were empty, but there were some that had a few words on them that made no sense, and some of the pages were faded and unreadable. For the most part, there was no information at all. We needed to regroup with Charles, and we needed to gather information about what had been going on outside the valley, but without my sword, we could not leave here for fear we would perish. So time moved forward, the ground became green again, and the wild flowers sprouted out of the ground. The air became warmer, and we just lived out our lives.

I kept going back to the tree, back to the place my sword disappeared, hoping something would happen, but nothing ever did. Day after day, so many times the dark of night came and went. One night as we slept, Raiden came over and nudged me awake.

"What is it, boy?"

Of course, he did not answer me, but I did notice a glowing coming from the tree. As I sat up, I saw my sword leaning up against the tree. It was not the tree that was glowing but my sword, only it was not my sword anymore. It was a different sword, a much bigger sword. I got up and walked to the tree, and as I reached down to touch this new sword, that voice came into my head again.

'It is time. Take this sword and wield it with the power of the kings who came before you. It is time to bring the peace to the land, to settle the evil. Go now.'

I touched the sword, and I could feel the energy that pulsed through it. As my hand curled around the hilt, the energy pulsed through me, deep into my body. My mind was no longer clouded. I knew what needed to be done, and I knew how to do it. Father was right; everything I had learned, everything I was taught, even the things I was unsure of, all made sense. The knowledge unfolded in my mind, in my heart, and in my soul. I became one with it, just as I had become one with the sword.

"It is time," I said, looking at Raiden. "We must go. We must finish this."

He stomped his hoof and neighed at me.

I woke Rebecca and Westin, and we said our goodbyes. "When I return to you," I told my brother, "it will be done, and we can go home. Remember what I told you do not leave the valley and do not set a fire."

"I will remember. I love you, Sabine." He hugged me, and I felt his tears on my neck.

"I love you. Stay safe, Westin, and protect them with your life."

We said our goodbyes to Camille and the children, and I assured her that I would let her parents know that they had another grand-child and that she was safe. As we rode away, I hoped I would one day see my brother again. I hoped that one day I could bring them to our family home to live out their lives.

Once we were through the cave and down the side of the moun-tain, I leaned into Raiden and told him, "I need you to find Charles. Take me to him please."

I closed my eyes and hugged his neck. So many things ran through my mind, but there was one thing missing; there was no fear. I felt alive and confident. I knew what we had to do. I knew that Rebecca and I would survive this, and I knew that this was the end of all the hatred and evil that had plagued my family, that ended my family. I needed to fight for Westin and his children and for Juliana, and I needed to fulfill my word to my father that I would avenge his death. Raiden slowed, and I sat up. We were climbing the hills that surrounded the valley where the cottage was. As we hit the top, I heard the horns sound, and then I saw the horses coming.

Looking at Rebecca, I said, "They have been waiting for us." She smiled her wide-eyed smile.

Charles and Blake came riding up with about a hundred men, and before I knew what was happening, Charles was off his horse and running to Rebecca. She barely had time to dismount before he had her in his arms and was kissing her.

"I have been so worried about you. Where have you been?" he managed to get out in between kisses.

I had to laugh, looking at this brave fearless man reduced to this mushy gushy man before me. We rode to the cottage, and as we got closer, I noticed that it had been rebuilt. I could see the new lumber meshed with the old. There were new cooks and new men.

"You have been busy," I said to Charles and Blake.

"We have indeed. Listen, Sabine, I need to apologize to you about the way we treated you at Whispering Wind. Something happened to us."

"It is not necessary, Charles. I understand. Please tell us what has been happening while we have been away."

"May I inquire as to where you two have been for so long?"

"Yes, you may inquire, but I am sorry to say that we cannot divulge our whereabouts. Camille and Westin are fine, and they have a daughter now. They named her Julia after our mother."

"So, they did not perish with the others? When we finally made it here many months ago, Blake went to the caves and found that they had been there. We hoped that you had found them and took them to safety. But where have you been? It has been more than a year."

"I can tell you this," I started, looking at Joseph. "The valley you were sent to find for us was not this valley. Raiden knew the valley in which we were supposed to live. Westin, Camille, and the children are there, and they will remain there until this is finished. Much has happened since last we met, Charles. You know that I cannot tell you any of what we have been through, but what I can tell you is that this is it. We will finish this. I do not know what is to come of any of us, but I do know for sure that Westin is safe and will remain where he is until I come for him. No one will ever find them."

Charles nodded and turned to Rebecca. "I have to tell you of the outcome of your father's fate, of Blackmore's fate. Your mother and Katherine had them murdered. The both of them seem to have a calling for being monsters themselves."

"The vile hatred my mother has toward Gerald is great. I am not surprised by her actions, nor am I surprised by the fact that she is trying to have me murdered as well. Trust me Charles, my mother as well as Wellington will get their just dues."

"So, who are these men who have come to fight with us?" I interjected.

"They are volunteers from all the kingdoms in the land. The strange blood gutters have been marching through the lands and terrorizing the people, looking for anyone who may know your whereabouts. They kill everyone who they deem to be untruthful."

"Charles, I do not know these men, and I can assure you that their presence is not necessary. What lies before us is for us alone to face. I really think it would be best if you sent them all back to where it is they came. I will not have anyone else's blood on my hands, and I will not take the lives of these men."

"Sabine, they are here of their own free will."

"Yes, that may be so, Charles, and excuse me if I seem ungrateful or rude, but I trust no one but Rebecca and our Guardians. There is a spy among them, and we are not safe here."

"How do you know this, Sabine? You have only just arrived."

Rebecca interrupted me and spoke. "Charles, Sabine has seen things I have not. She has been empowered with great knowledge, and she has been given the path in which we must not stray," she said as she reached up and ran her fingers through my hair, producing between them the white hair to show Charles. "It is in the best interest of us all that you listen to her. It will take the nine of us to complete this, no one else."

Charles stood there staring at my hair, his eyes giving away the truth of what he knew. He nodded his head and walked away. Rebecca and I entered the cottage to find men sitting around the table where we had our meals. I stopped, putting my hand on my sword. "May I inquire as to who you are, and exactly what it is you are doing in my home?"

The man at the head of the table stood, and the rest followed. "Well, well, well, if someone had told me one day I would be standing in the same room as the great Princess Sabine of Whispering Wind, I would have laughed at him."

"Again, I ask, who are you, and what are you doing in my house?"

"It is not necessary for you to know who I am, Princess. What is necessary for you to know is that you will fail at your quest for peace. We have seen what these men who seek you can do. Our families have been slaughtered, and they will continue to be slaughtered until you are served up to them on a silver plate. We have all come here to make sure that will happen. You are but a waif of a girl, and those who protect you, or try to protect you, are fools. You cannot stop what is to come. We have been promised many riches for bringing you to those who seek you."

I do not know where it came from, but I could not stop the giggle. The look on the man's face turned from sureness of his conquest to fear. I tilted my head and smiled at him.

"What you were promised is untruth, and you will be rewarded with death, just like everyone else. Those who seek me are the bringers of death. The only reason you are standing here in my house is because you are a means to an end. Go home, sire. Go home and hug your children and pray that I am successful in my quest. I do not wish to kill you, but if you force our hands, we will do just that."

Now he bellowed. "You are but a mere child. I will wager my life that you cannot best me."

Rebecca laughed now. "It will be your life you pay with if you challenge her."

It was fast, his movement. With his sword drawn, he was on me. I drew my sword and swung one time. The light was brilliant, and his head rolled back into the room. The others stood still. No one made a move, and of course, Rebecca could not stop herself from saying, "Next?"

"It is not my wish to kill all of you. My wish is for you to leave this place. Go home to your families as I have asked of you. I do not require your assistance, and you will only die if you stay."

They bowed and made their way out.

Rebecca turned to me. "What was that?"

I smiled at her. "I do not know, but it was easy, easier than ever before to wield this sword. I know what we need to do. When I picked up this sword, everything made sense to me. I cannot tell you now, for I fear the walls have ears, but trust me."

"With my life. You need not tell me, Sabine, for I know as well what must be done."

I looked into her eyes, and I could see that she was being truthful. I smiled at her, and we followed the men outside. Charles was on his way in when he ran into the men.

"I was just informed that you killed one of my men."

"Were you informed as well that they wanted to take Sabine back to the blood gutters or whoever they are calling themselves? They said that they would be paid handsomely for bringing her to them. All of them, every one of these men, were sent here with one mission, and that was to take Sabine back. So, in the morning, I think it would be best if we went back to Whispering Wind, where we will make our stand, just the nine of us, and we will end this."

Charles just stood there looking at her. I was not sure if he wanted to kiss her or face off with her. He did neither and just walked away. It was Blake who spoke instead.

"Well, it would seem that the two of you have gotten a bit braver in our time apart."

Rebecca smiled, and we went back inside to find some food.

In the kitchen were a cook and a few maids who bowed when we walked in.

"Please, it is not necessary for you to serve me. I am just a girl who is looking for some food."

The cook nodded and said, "If you would like, I will bring you some in the other room."

"If you do not mind, we would like to eat in here. There is a dead body in the hall."

One of the maids smiled and said, "Then it is truth. You are the princess everyone is talking about."

"Well, I am Sabine, yes, and what might they be saying about me?"

"Just that your sword is magic, and you can best any man."

I smiled at her. "Do not believe all that you hear. I am just a girl like you."

The cook made us some plates, and we sat in the kitchen with the helpers and ate, and ate, and ate. When we were finished, we made our way upstairs to the new rooms and fell in a bed to sleep. It was the light of day warming my face that woke me, Rebecca beside me still sleeping. I shook her.

"Hey, we need to get going. Those men are going to bring those who seek us back here."

"Can I just sleep until it is over?"

I laughed. "Would that just not be the best thing ever?"

We made our way downstairs and into the kitchen where the cook had prepared a feast for us, so we ate. Charles and his brothers arrived.

"All the men are gone, and I think it is time for us to go now. Ladies…" he said to the cook as he turned to face her, "you may stay here if you wish, but your services are no longer needed."

"Thank you for your kindness," I said to them as we got up and left the cottage.

I turned to look back at it, and I knew it would be the last time I would ever see it or this valley. We all rode together. I needed to stay close to Charles as I knew there was much he needed to tell me. We rode for two days without stopping. When we made camp, Charles came to me.

"I think it is time that you and I had a talk."

"I could not agree with you more, Charles."

We walked away. "So, what has been happening with you and Rebecca whilst you have been away?"

"Charles, you know I cannot tell you much. When we left you, we went to the valley, where we found Westin, Camille, and the children in the caves. Westin told me that they came, and they came on very fast horses, horses like Raiden and Spirit. I think they let them run in hopes that I would return to the valley to get them. If they were there waiting for us, they did not make themselves known, but then again, as swiftly as Raiden and Spirit move, I am not sure they would have seen us enter the valley. It was the dark of night, and we left right after we found them. They are safe, Charles."

"Would you tell me where they are?"

"You know I cannot. Your mind was compromised, and I must keep them safe, and even if I did tell you, I could not tell you exactly, but they are safe."

"So, what else is there for you to tell me?"

"You seem a bit controlled, Charles, as if you wish to say something but you are holding back. Are you angry with me?"

"Anger would not even be close to the word I would use to describe the way I am feeling toward you, Sabine, but I know that it was necessary for you to find Westin. I just did not realize that you and Rebecca would be gone for more than a year's time."

"Charles, the task that has been set before us is one that will take great confidence to achieve. If I cannot count on you to stand with us, then I am fearful all will be lost. You know that we needed to figure all of this out on our own, and you know what lies ahead for all of us, so how is it that you can stand here and act as if I wronged you in some manner or another. I did what you and everyone else had been telling me to do. I went and figured out what my role in all this is. Have you done the same?"

"I already knew my role, Sabine, and that is to Guard you, to protect you, and for over a year, I have searched all the known lands for you, and still I found nothing, no trace of you. The time that has separated us has led me to believe that you and Rebecca were dead."

"If we were dead, Charles, I am afraid that you would have known it. A great evil is alive and in our midst. If we fail, nothing will survive, nothing. I have learned a great deal while we were away. I have been given a great deal of knowledge, the knowledge that started all of this some two hundred years ago. My father was a brilliant man. He knew who I was and has trained me from birth to fulfill this quest. I just did not know it, not until things started happening, and the memories came back. The pieces of this intrigue began to fall into place, and I did what I had to do in order to make sense of it all. So if you really want to stand here and quarrel with me over something this trivial instead of the important things, then so be it, but you are going to be standing here alone. Either we discuss what is to come, or I am going to sleep."

He stood there looking at me. "Well, I am in agreement with Blake. You have become much braver in our time apart."

"No, Charles, I have become inpatient. For years now I have been on the run, running for my life, and I miss my home. I am just tired, tired of all of this death that has become my life."

"I agree. Well, as you already know, Samuel and Gerald are dead, and Katherine is not happy with the fact that Jared has chosen you over his rightful place as king. She does not know the fate that her son has endured, and it is probably best she not know until this is over. As far as I can tell, no one has entered the kingdom, so you are right to believe we would be safe there. These blood gutters seem to be many in their numbers, and they are everywhere you turn. I must apologize to you about what took place at the cottage. Not once did I have any indication that you were the reason for them being there."

"It is fine. I told you before that things have changed within me. I do not trust anyone."

"Sabine, you must trust me to guide you."

"Forgive me, Charles, but you turned on me as well. I know you were enchanted by the jewels I uncovered, but it just means to me that your mind as well as your brothers' can be tainted. Rebecca is the only one who has my full trust."

"Understandably so, but, Sabine, without communication between us, we could very well fail."

"Oh, Charles, we will not fail. My worry is that many will perish, but I cannot concern myself any longer with the loss of lives that will inevitably take place. My concern is to end this, by whatever means possible. I may even lose my own life, but in order for Westin, Camille, and the children to live a safe and happy life, I am willing to do that. No matter what, Charles, I will end this."

"Well, it is my duty to make sure you do prevail, even if my life ends while doing so."

"What do you know of these magic horses they ride?"

"I have heard what Westin has told you, but I have not seen it for myself."

"There are just nine of us to stand against them. I think I know the answer to this, but I have to ask it anyway are your brothers willing to die for us?"

Blake came walking up just as I finished, and he answered, "Yes, Sabine, we are. That is a query that should never need to be asked."

I turned to look at him. "Excuse me, Blake, but it is. I need to know that if I need it, you will stand beside me. What is coming is like nothing you will ever know again. Rebecca and I are going to be doing things that will sway your judgment of us, but know this it is what must be done to achieve peace."

Just as he opened his mouth to speak, I heard Raiden scream in my head,

'RUN!'

I turned away from them and ran toward Raiden. Blake and Charles were calling after me, but I did not turn to see if they were following. I just ran. Raiden, Rebecca, and Spirit met me halfway. I jumped on Raiden, and we were gone. As we blew through the forest, I saw them. I saw the blood gutters, and the scene was unreal. They were moving quickly, but as we passed each other, the world seemed to stand still. I was not sure if they saw us, but we saw them riding toward our camp. Raiden did not slow. After what seemed to be minutes, we were entering the village at Whispering Wind, and then he slowed. I turned to Rebecca.

"How were we found so quickly? Those men had less than a day ahead of us."

"I do not know. I hope that Charles got away."

"Do not fear. They cannot be killed. Those men will lose their lives. What bothers me is why Raiden took us from the fight." Looking down at him, I had to ask, "Care to explain why we left the fight?"

I really did not expect an answer. I knew the answer already. It was not time for us to display the power we now hold. It was to be kept in the shadows until it was time. As we walked through the village, I heard a man's voice shouting.

"Princess Sabine of Whispering Wind!"

I turned in my saddle, and I could see about two hundred men at the edge of the village. Raiden turned and walked to the edge of the mist.

"Sabine, we should not be here alone," Rebecca whispered.

"They cannot enter the land. We will be fine. Raiden would not let us come here if he thought we would be harmed," I whispered back as we approached the men.

"I am Sabine."

"Oh, I know who you are," the lead man said and smiled. His teeth were rotten and covered in black. "And I know you, Princess Rebecca of Blackmore. Your mother is not happy with your choice. She has sent me to find you and give you the opportunity to come home unharmed and take your place at her side."

Rebecca laughed, which startled the man. "You can tell my mother that she shall meet the same fate as Wellington and Blackmore. I am not Princess Rebecca of Blackmore, and my mother knows it. I am Princess Rebecca of Whispering Wind."

One of the men lunged forward on his horse. He crossed over into the mist and dropped to the ground, just like the birds the day we left here, after cutting the head off the witch. The lead man laughed.

"Believing this mist will save you will be your demise."

I could not stop it. I giggled, "Oh, sire, I do not need this mist, and you know it. You also know that you were sent on this mission because you are of no importance to whoever leads you, for your mission is a death sentence. I can see it in your eyes. You have heard the stories of what we can do, and you are fearful that you will burn from the light."

Bellowing laughter came from this man. "You are but a mere child, a waif of a woman. You cannot bring harm to me."

"You heard the men you sent after me, and you know what they say is truth. Otherwise, you would not have this army with you. If you thought you could just hit me on the head and carry me away, you would have come alone."

The man just sat there on his horse looking at me, and then he said in a very deep voice, "Remember my name. When I end your life, you will be screaming it and begging for me to spare you, for I am Toddzwga." He turned on his horse, and they rode away.

"Well, I think you angered him," Rebecca said with a chuckle.

"Yes, I do believe you are right," I replied and laughed. "I believe we are going to have some company, and soon. We need to get back to the secret room. We have much to discuss. I fear it is the only place that we are truly safe."

"Sabine, do you know what we are supposed to do?"

"I believe that I do. Come, let us go before we are interrupted again. I am sure Charles will be here soon. I think we need to leave him a note. He is not happy with us, and if he cannot find us, he will surely have our heads."

Giggling, she said, "I know you are right. He told me that he has never been frightened, but when he could not locate us, his heart became hard."

"Leave it to Charles. You know, I never figured him to be such an emotional man. It must be love."

We both laughed as we made our way back to the castle. Rebecca left him a note and hung it on the great door for him to find.

Charles,

We are safe, and as you have seen, no one but us can enter the kingdom. We had a bit of a confrontation with someone who calls himself Toddzwga. We are here in the castle, so trust me when I say that we are fine. When we finish figuring this out, we will emerge, and we shall have a great deal to discuss. Please do not be angry. Just promise you will wait for us.

Yours Always

Rebecca

"That should do it. I know they will look for us, but he will just have to wait."

I could not help but smile at her. We made our way to my father's study and into the secret room. It was time to tell Rebecca what I now knew. I just wished I knew how I knew, but I stopped wondering about that a long time ago. We lit the candles and sat on the rug in the center of the room.

"Well, you know what happened with the swords." I laid my sword on the floor between us. "When I put my hand on the hilt, I was empowered with knowledge. Things made sense to me. I did not feel that it was time to share this with you, but it is time now. Rebecca, you and I have been set on a path, the same path as Raiden was. This is the end. One way or another, this is the end. This sword holds new meaning and a new power."

"Should we test this new power?"

"Yes, and we will, but first I must tell you what I know. The old tomes in the cave hold the truth, the story I suppose, of how this all happened. This land we sit on is where time began. The evil that is coming wants to possess it. In possessing it, they can and will own time, and they will never die. Life began here, I believe in that cave. We are privileged to have this knowledge, and no one must ever know this about our very existence. If evil takes control of time, the lands will be plunged into darkness. The good will become evil, and death will run rampant. Nothing will survive, not even light. Only, those who seek this power do not know this. They are like us, acting on a legend and greedy for something more, greedy for power. No one wants to be ruled by tyrants, and these people, people like Wellington and Blackmore and Collingwood, they believe that this power will make them the richest of the kingdoms, but it will only destroy everything. We have been chosen through time itself to be the keepers, so to speak, of time. Only you and I are allowed in the cave. Even Raiden could not enter. Only you and I can stop this. Charles and his brothers can do nothing to help us. They are indeed our Guardians, but that is all they are. When we disappeared, I believe Charles knew then what his fate would be, and I think he has reacted out of fear, knowing now his true fate."

"What are you saying, Sabine?"

"I am saying, Rebecca, that they cannot help us. I do not know what will become of them, but this is not their destiny. It is ours and ours alone. Although there is another, but I am not sure how she fits into all of this."

"She? Are you talking about Juliana?"

"Yes, Jenna told me she was the key. The witch knew. There are some things we still do not know, so the time for all of this is not yet. I do not know when, but I do know that there are things that need to happen before it is over. Time is something we need not worry about as it is out of our control. I know that we will enter the cave again. When we leave the cave, for us, time will have stood still, but for the rest of the land, it will have passed. People will die, kingdom's will fall, and our enemies will be great. I think we need to figure out the writings on the walls of the cave. They will be our guide now. When we enter, Rebecca, I fear that you will never see Charles again, and I believe he knows this."

"Never see him again? I think I know this. I just do not want to know this, Sabine. I love him."

"As he loves you, and that is what is hurting him. I thought that they would all stand with us when we fought this fight. I believed it was like the barbarians, but this is something more. These are not just men we are fighting, but it is evil in its darkest form. It is not trickery, not magic, but evil. It is not time for us to go yet. I am not sure when we will go into the cave, but I do know that when we do, there will be no turning back."

"I know. I thought for sure he was my match in this life, Sabine. I cannot begin to think of a life without him. I was convinced we would grow old together. I did not know the depth of any of this."

"Rebecca, Charles will grow old, but you and I will not."

I sat looking at my friend, and I could see the tears drop off her cheeks. The man she loved would grow old without her.

"Come, I am sure they are here now. We still have time to spend with them. They mean the world to me as well. I have come to feel toward Charles as I would my brother. Rebecca, we will find our happiness when this is done." I hugged my friend for a long time.

"Come now. We should go. I am sure that the dark of night has arrived, along with Charles and his brothers."

Rebecca nodded, and we made our way out of the secret room. When we reached the grand hall, I noticed the door was open and Rebecca's note was lying on the floor. I reached over and touched her arm. It was instinct to draw our swords and put our backs together, something we had never done before. As we moved in a circle in the darkness, searching for anything, I heard Raiden in my head.

Drop to your knees.'

Just as I did, I heard a swishing sound pass over my head. I do not know why I did it, but I slammed my sword on the stone floor. A brilliant light filled the hall, and the ground beneath us trembled. I saw them then. There were about twenty of them coming at us from all sides. I swung, as did Rebecca, and the light lit the entire courtyard outside. It took only moments for them all to fall. We did not move, standing, listening for footsteps. Then I hit the floor again. We were alone.

"How did they get into the kingdom?" Rebecca whispered.

"I do not know."

"Well, it would seem that your new sword does a great deal more than your old," she said, and I could hear the smile on her face.

"What frightens me is that I know what to do with it. I would not have been able to tell you it could do that, but when we were being threatened, I just knew. It was instinctive. If they got into the kingdom, then others will be able to as well. We are not safe here any longer."

"We need to find Charles and tell him."

We walked back to back out into the courtyard. Raiden and Spirit were waiting. We mounted them and started to ride out into the village, only to be stopped by the hundred or so men at the village entrance.

This Toddzwga spoke, "Well, Princess, it would seem that your mist is no longer a problem for us."

He waved his hand across our path. I looked down and noticed that the mist was gone.

"You are but a fool to think you can defeat us," Rebecca shouted.

"No, Princess, you are but a fool to think I want to defeat you. I was sent here to talk, to present to you a bargain."

It happened again. I could not stop the giggle.

Toddzwga tilted his head and looked right into my eyes. "Do you find something amusing, Princess?"

"In fact, I do. You sit there on your horse with these men behind you, and you spew untruths out of your mouth out of fear. You know we just bested twenty or so of your men. If you were here to bargain, as you say, you would be here alone. I am sorry, sire, but you are to try and capture us. Whoever sent you would like Rebecca alive and me dead. I laugh because you shall have neither of these things."

"One would say that in a situation such as this, one laughs out of fear."

"Oh, sire. I am afraid you are mistaken. You have been misled into believing that you could achieve either of those tasks. Whoever sent you, sent you knowing you would die."

I think I hit a mark. He yelled, "I FEAR NO ONE!!! Especially a woman."

"Then say your peace and leave my land. That will be your only warning."

"Come peacefully with us to speak with our leader, and I will see to it that you are returned to this land safely."

"There will be no one leaving with you this day," Charles said from behind us.

"Well, the infamous Guardians have arrived. You should do a better job of guarding these two, Charles, for they have murdered a few of my men."

"Better your men than you, right?"

"I suppose, Charles. I was just asking Sabine if she would be so kind as to accompany me to our camp to have a chat with our leader."

"You can tell Lord Roman that he will not be honored with Sabine's presence, not now or any time in the days to come."

"He will not be pleased with you, Charles."

"Well then, I suppose you should move out of the way when he wields his sword in your direction for failing him."

"I think you are outnumbered here, Charles. Let us say I just take her."

Charles' bellowing laughter made me jump. "You can do your best in trying but let me just warn you it will be your own head you take back in your arms to Lord Roman."

I felt Raiden twitch beneath me. I looked at Rebecca as she looked at me, and we reached for our swords. As we drew them, Toddzwga rushed forward with his men. Raiden was up before I knew what was happening, and instinctively, my arm went in the air. What happened next took my breath away. Not only did our swords shoot lightening, but the whole sky lit up and turned the dark of night into the light of day. When we landed, I was witness to this new power my sword now held. Nothing stood except for Toddzwga. There was no fire like before, and there was no smoke. In fact, there was nothing but ash. When I looked at him, his hair was white, and his face was frozen with fear. He did not say a word he turned his horse and disappeared.

"That was different," Charles said.

"What was different, Charles, is that you knew that man. You know who sent him. Why would that be?" I tried not to let my anger leak through in my voice.

"A great deal has transpired while you two were away. I told you before that there was much to discuss and seeing as how the mist seems to have been lifted from Whispering Wind, it would be best if we discussed it sooner rather than later."

"I could not agree more," I said with a bit of disdain in my voice as I turned Raiden and started back to the castle.

We rode into the courtyard, and I climbed off of Raiden and sat at the fountain in the middle, where I waited for Charles and his brothers to arrive. Charles paced back and forth on the cobblestones that made up the walkway, his hand on his chin. To me, it was a signal that he was deciding whether or not he should disclose all of the information he had.

"It would be best if you told me all of what you know, instead of deciding what I should know."

"You are right, Sabine. The mist is no longer able to protect you, so I think that the only way to keep you safe is to keep you informed."

I wanted to laugh at him. He really did not get that I did not need him to protect me any longer, but I kept quiet and waited for him to decide.

"While you were gone and we were searching for you, we had several encounters with this man, Toddzwga. He knew who we were and was very surprised that you were not with us. At first, he thought we were not telling the truth, and he proceeded to try and force us to tell him where you were. He failed miserably, to say the least. Every encounter was the same. I have seen what this man and his men are capable of. I have seen him in the act of killing. It is truth what they say about them when they kill, they cut open their victim and eat their insides right in front of whoever is watching. Sometimes they do not even kill the person. They just gut them while they are alive. He told me once that he would find great pleasure in eating me one day. I challenged him to try. Needless to say, he has not attempted it. His response was that Lord Roman would not have it, that we were to be spared because we would ultimately lead them to you."

"Well, it would seem that this Lord Roman was correct. How is it that the mist is gone, now that we have arrived back here?"

"Lord Roman is a great sorcerer. I am sure that once you were located, he did something to remove the spell the witch had cast on Whispering Wind, which would leave you unprotected. I am afraid to say this, Sabine, but you can no longer hide from what is coming."

I could not stop the giggle. "Charles, we were not hiding. We were learning. We were being imbedded with knowledge. We can hide, as we did for over a year's time, but hiding is not going to end this. Yes, we can leave here and never return, but all the kingdoms will suffer worse than what they are now. No, we will not be hiding, for there is still much for Rebecca and I to learn. This is not going to end soon. I now know where the rest of the knowledge is, and we will be going to retrieve it. This Lord Roman knows what needs to be done, and now he knows where we are, so instead of learning more from you, we are going to have to leave again and seek the knowledge that will end this."

"So, if you are leaving again, will you be going back to Westin? I only ask this because I would like to go with you and see my sister."

"No, Charles, I will not see Westin again until this is over, not until I can bring my brother and his children home. Where we are going no one can go. I cannot tell you. I am fearful, however, that I will never see you again. Where we are going, time does not exist for us."

His look was one of shock and dismay. He looked at Rebecca. "I cannot let you go," he whispered.

"I love you," Rebecca said. "But this is bigger than our love. It has been my honor to have been loved by you, but when we leave here, Charles, you must keep it in your heart that I will survive, and you must love again."

"I cannot imagine my life without you. It was foretold that our love would last a lifetime. I just thought we would spend that lifetime together."

"As did I, but it would seem that is not how it will be."

They stood there in one another's arms. "I do not wish to make this any harder on the two of you, but if Toddzwga's horse is a fast as

Raiden, then he has reached this Lord Roman, and I am sure that he will be back."

"I would not fear him, Sabine. After seeing what you can do now, filled with this knowledge, I am sure he will not make the same mistake again."

"Either way, it is time for us to move on. I want my brother and his children here. I want them to grow up in our childhood home. The only way to do that is to finish this. Thank you for your service," I said, looking each of them in the face. "It is time for us to go. Charles, I hope your life is filled with much happiness. Please do not spend it looking for us. I do know that in your lifetime, you will see the end to this."

"I will raise an army to help you with this war when it is time. I will not let either of you down."

He turned to Rebecca and kissed her. "I will love no other as I love you."

With tears streaming down her cheeks, Rebecca climbed on Spirit. I hugged each of them and climbed on Raiden.

"Until we meet again, my lord," I said, and we rode out of Whispering Wind.

CHAPTER FIFTEEN

When we reached the top of the hill, I turned to look back. I could see them standing there, and just as the day this all began, I heard the thunder. Tapping Rebecca on the arm, I pointed to the horizon. We could see the cloud moving across the sky.

"Horses," she said.

"Yes, just like the day this all began."

"Should we go back and help Charles?" I could hear the desperation in her voice.

"No, we cannot go back. They will not be harmed, and we need to go to the valley. I need to see Westin, and I need for him to know that we are going to be gone for a very long time. Once we enter the cave, it is the beginning of the end. We will not come out again until we know what is going to take place and how we are going to end this. For us, it will seem just days, but as we have discovered before, it will in fact be years. Westin needs to know that I am not dead and that he must keep Juliana safe. I did not tell you this before, Rebecca, but I think she has the ability to manipulate fire. I am not sure what it all means, but I need for Westin to know that I am not dead."

"I love him, Sabine."

"I know you do, and I know he loves you, but it is not your time, not anymore. We have to end this, Rebecca. Just know that he will be alive to see it end."

She nodded her head, waved goodbye to him, knowing she would not see him again for a very long time, and we turned and left them to deal with the army that crossed the plain heading toward Whispering Wind.

❦

Charles stood there watching as they left his life just as they came into it.

"How is them leaving going to help anyone or anything?"

"Brother, you as well as the rest of us know that this is what is supposed to be."

"I know. I just thought we would have more time."

"As did I," said Blake.

"Joseph, the valley you found for them was not the valley of the legend. Do you think you could find it?"

"Charles, it was not meant for me to find. As much as I would love to see our sister and her children, she is best to stay hidden. I feel your pain as well as our parents', but if we find them, we will only be putting them in grave danger. They must stay safe, and Sabine and Rebecca must not be compromised."

"It is Juliana who needs protecting. That child is the key to the end of this. Sabine and Rebecca are the Bringers of Peace, but the child is the key. She holds a gift within her, and we should be the ones who teach her how to use it. I do not think Sabine knows what the child is capable of. I do not think she would have left her alone if she did."

"We cannot interfere. It could change the outcome."

Just then, Aidan said, "Do you feel that?"

No one moved. The ground was humming. "It sounds like thunder."

"That is not thunder. It is horses, and a great many of them."

Charles and his brothers mounted their horses and started to the village. As they came out into the fields, they could see the army coming toward them. "Lord Roman," Charles said softly. They sat there waiting for what would come. They knew they would die in a fight with this man, but Charles also knew that Roman would not kill them, for he feared Sabine.

The small army rode up with Roman at the lead. "Well, Charles, we meet again."

"Roman, what brings you to Whispering Wind?"

He laughed. "I think you know." He turned to look at the many piles of ash. "It would seem that the legend of Sabine and her companion is truth."

"It would seem."

"Well, I would really like to know how a waif of a girl could obtain such magic. Who taught her, Charles? I would like to meet this person."

Charles chuckled. "Roman, you know as well as I do that this is not magic. Toddzwga here saw it all happen. You will not win this battle, and you being here now tells me that you know I am right. You cannot stop this."

"You may be right, Charles, but I can do my best. It is my destiny to rule these lands and to absorb the power they hold. Everyone knows what Stephan did to obtain them. The birthright does not belong to this girl."

"The birthright does not belong to you, Roman. You know this legend. You know this is what has been foretold for generations, and you will not accomplish anything but your own demise by coming here. This land is hers and hers alone."

"No, there is another. Samuel was the fool to hire barbarians to take care of this, and we both know of the child he tried to manipulate instead of ending her life along with the others. Only a greedy fool would have missed this girl and her brother. Perhaps you know where they are?"

"I have not been privileged to that information, Roman. You should know that."

"Well, I will search until I find the brother and this child. She should not have been allowed to live. She will be the end of us, Charles, you included."

"Well, you see, Roman, when you are true at heart, evil does not seem to hold on to you. If I were you, on the other hand, I think I might be worried about my future."

Roman bellowed laughter. "Oh, Charles, you know that it will take a lot more than a waif of a girl and a child who can manipulate fire to end me."

Charles looked past Roman to the ash. "Believe what you may, Roman." He nodded his head toward the ash, "But I think you and I know better."

"Until we meet again, Charles, but keep in mind that I will find them, both the child and Sabine, and then you will answer to me. The whole of these lands will answer to me." He turned with his army and left.

Blake looked at Charles. "The child can manipulate fire? Does Sabine know this?"

"Yes, Juliana is gifted in a way other would deem trickery. I am not privy to what knowledge Sabine has. Samuel wanted to harness Juliana's powers. That would be why he gave her to the witch. He discovered the mark on the child's head when he came to see her at her birth. I am sorry to have withheld information from you, brothers, but it is not mine to tell. What is coming will be the end of life if they do not succeed. We will be thrust into darkness, and evil will rule. No man will be able to fight it, and Roman knows it. That is why he seeks them. Only Sabine, Rebecca, and Juliana will be able to finish this and push the evil into its own darkness and destroy it. I will tell you this Juliana has not come of age as of yet, and she cannot control what is inside of her, so for Sabine to hide them and keep them safe from harm tells me she knows. We shall not see them again for a very long time. I had this knowledge from the beginning. I just did not know that it would be so soon. I thought that we would all live in harmony until the child became of age."

"Charles, this burden of knowledge you carry must be heavy. What is it that we can do to help you?" Joseph said.

"There is nothing, but thank you, brother. We can do nothing now but carry on, build them an army, and wait. The years will pass slowly. Roman will not move now that he knows she has been imbued with the knowledge that has been hidden for generations. He will wait for her to come to him, and she will, so we need to stay ready."

"Charles, what you are saying will not take place for many years. The child is but in her fourth or fifth year. What you are saying is that our children will grow to become this army you speak of."

"Yes, that is right, Blake. Our children will be trained just as we were, and it is our duty as their Guardians to see this through to the end. Just as we have been raised to give our lives to them and for them, so will our children. Our work is done for now. It is time to return to our father."

"Just like that, you are yielding?"

"Blake, you have always questioned me. Why is that? Roman knows, and he will not move on the lands. It serves him no purpose. He knows as well as I do that Sabine will find him. It is time to return to our father and carry on with life. There will be much to do in the years to come."

CHAPTER SIXTEEN

As we rode up to our little camp, I could not get off of Raiden fast enough. I hit the ground running to scoop Juliana and Stephan up in my arms.

"Oh, I have missed you," I yelled, almost on the brink of tears.

I knew that I would not see them grow up, though I knew we should all be together.

"Sabine!!!" Westin yelled as he appeared from the river. "You have come back."

I let go of Stephan and Juliana and ran to my big brother.

"Oh, Westin." I could not stop the tears from flowing.

"Sabine, why are you crying? Is everything all right?" His concern made me giggle.

"As right as rain. I am just happy to see you. There is much we need to discuss, all of us."

"Well, come then, and we can talk," he said, sounding just like father.

We walked over to the camp and sat around in a circle. I held Stephan while Rebecca let Juliana sit in her lap. Looking at Stephan, I could see so much of Westin in him. He was beautiful and happy; they all were.

"So, what is it we need to discuss, Sabine? Do we get to go home yet?"

"Not yet, Westin. I am afraid that it will be a very long time before we can go home. Camille, I have told your brothers that you are fine and that they have a new niece. They wanted to come to the valley to see you, but I cannot let them. You are safe here. You are hidden from all that is taking place. I am going to tell you as much as I can, and you are going to be frightened, but I need for you to trust me and to know that as long as you stay here, you will be safe. None of what is to come will touch you."

"Sabine, you are frightening me," Westin whispered.

"I know, my love, but that is not my intent. I need for you to know that, no matter what happens, I will be fine, and you will be safe as long as you stay in the valley and never start a fire."

When I said that, I looked at Juliana. I knew what she could do. I had not told Rebecca that I knew, but I knew she was magic.

"You know how Raiden is magic?" It was the only place I knew to start this fantastic tale from. They all nodded their heads. "Well, his magic is real, just like the tree, just like the valley, just like me." I looked at their faces. Westin's was crinkled up.

"You are magic?"

"Yes, but I am not magic alone. Rebecca and I together are magic. Rebecca is our cousin, Westin. Her father was our father's brother."

"Uncle Stanford had a baby?"

"You know of Uncle Stanford?"

"Oh yes, Sabine, he was murdered when you were a little girl like Julianna. Father was very angry. I remember Mother trying to calm him down. He was fun. He liked to play tricks with me."

I sat there looking at my brother. "Why did I not know of him?"

"Why would you? He died when you were very little, and we never talked about him," he said, then looked at Rebecca. "We are cousins." His smile was more than enough to let me know he was thrilled.

"Now listen carefully to me, Westin. There is a terrible thing coming to the lands, and Rebecca and I, along with Raiden and Spirit, have been destined to stop it. Father knew this when I was born and has trained me my whole life. I just did not know it, not until I found a secret room in his study where we discovered this." I pulled the journal out of my bodice. "It has helped us figure out a great intrigue, and I am afraid to tell you all that we are not done. There is still much that we need to learn. The land that is Whispering Wind is special. There are some terrible people who want it, and the only way they can get it is to figure out how to harness the power that dwells in our land. Rebecca and I have to stop them, and then we can all go home. Do you understand what I am saying, Westin?"

"Yes, Sabine. You are leaving us again, and you and Rebecca are going to take your magic horses and fight evil with your magic, and then we can all go home."

I smiled at him. I reached over and grabbed his hand.

"There is more, my love. When Rebecca and I leave this time, we will be gone for a very long time. Many years will pass before we return, and you and Camille will have to raise Juliana. Can you do that for me?"

"Yes, I will, but how many years, Sabine? Why could we not come with you? I know how to fight."

"Yes, you do, and I love you so much for that, but these people who want our land would use you and the children to get me to do what they want. That is why Raiden brought us here. No one can find you here. No one can enter this valley. This is where you need to stay. You see, Westin, your children, along with Juliana, are all that is left of our family. They need to be kept safe. I need you to keep them safe."

"I will protect them with my life, Sabine."

"I know you will, Westin, but you must not fight them, for you will lose. If you are ever in danger while I am away, Raiden and Spirit will come and take you all away. Do you understand me?" He nodded. "You know how the seasons change?"

"Yes."

"When the seasons change, look for Raiden and Spirit by the entrance to the cave. He will come to you four times a year to let you know that I am still alive, so you will know that we are safe. If he comes down into the valley, you must go with him. That will mean it is over or that we failed, and he will either bring you to me or stay here with you. I give you my word, Westin, I will do my best not to perish. We will not leave you, but look for him so you will know. Father has assured me in his writings that we will succeed. I do not know how many years will pass, but they will be great. Where we are going knows no time, so when you see me again, I will look just like you see me today. Do you understand me?"

"I am not sure that I do, but I will trust you, Sabine. You are my sister, the chosen one," he paused and giggled. "You have not been untruthful to me. I will stay here, and we will wait."

Juliana reached up and touched my face. "You said that you would never leave me again, and you keep leaving me."

"I know, my love, and for that I am sorry. I will return for you. I give you my word. I found you once, and I will find you again. Never doubt my love for you."

She climbed into my lap and hugged me hard. "When will you leave?"

"We can stay for a little while. Just remember that the sooner we go, the sooner we will be together, but we shall stay for a bit."

And we did. The light of day came and left seven times, and on the eighth day, we parted ways. It hurt to know that the next time I saw my brother, he would be so much older, yet we will not have changed at all.

"I love you all, and please remember what I told you. Look for Raiden so you know we are still alive."

"I will, Sabine. I love you as well," he said as he waved goodbye to us.

Rebecca and I left the valley. I knew it would be a very long time before I would see my family again, and if I failed, if we failed, I knew he would live his life out here, untouched by the evil that would reign beyond these mountains.

It was no time at all before we reached the cave by the river. It was the dark of night, and if the big rock had not been there, I would not have known where we were. As I dismounted Raiden, I patted his neck.

"You cannot stay here. If you are seen, then Lord Roman will know where we are, and please do not forget to go to the valley. Westin will worry when time starts to pass. I know time will move forward, but we will stay the same. What seems like moments to us will in fact be years. I will miss you, my friend."

He was in my head.

Time has stood still for me, and it will stand still while you are gone. I will go to the valley, and I will not be far. When you are ready, I will be here, and we will finish this.'

I smiled at him, hugged his neck, and they were gone. Rebecca and I made our way down the river and across the stones. Standing at the entrance to the cave, we looked at one another.

"You ready?" I asked her.

"I am. Are you?"

"Let us finish this."

We held each other's hands as we passed through the rock face and into the cave where time did not exist.

CHAPTER SEVENTEEN

Once we entered the cave, Rebecca took the old tome and put it back in its place. We had brought food and water skins to sustain us, my father's journal, his drawings, my mother's looking glass, and a quill to write down the writings that were written on the walls.

"Sabine, can I ask you something?"

"Of course. You can ask me anything you like."

"Do you doubt this legend any longer?"

I was not sure what she meant or why she was asking me this.

"I think I no longer view it as a legend, but more like something that has to be done. I am still so very angry at what Samuel and Gerald did to my family. The justice in them being dead seems not to satisfy me. Now we have your mother and Wellington trying to design our end, and this man Lord Roman. Charles said he was a great sorcerer, and I know nothing of his kind of magic or if we can defeat him, but my father seems to believe that we can."

"I agree with you. My mother… let us just say that I know nothing of who she really is. I am just not sure that she and Wellington did this. I think this Lord Roman has been waiting for us."

"You know, I think you might be right. Somehow, I know that he cannot obtain the magic here unless he defeats us. I know now that this is the way it has always been meant to happen. Good and evil will fight to the death, and that is the only way to end this."

"Do you think we will die?" she whispered.

I reached over and took her hand. "No, Rebecca, I do not. Everything that has happened for whatever reason was meant to happen. Am I happy that it has happened this way? No. I miss my family, and I miss the life I should be living right now. Would I be happy with the man my father had chosen for me? Probably not, but I would live the life he felt best for me just to please him. No, Rebecca, I do not believe we will die."

"We should get busy then. Where do we start? "

"I think, first, we need to read the walls."

Rebecca picked up the looking glass and started again by the entrance to the cave.

"All right, we know what this says here. I shall read it again, and you write it down."

I nodded as she began to read.

Here is where time began
Here is where life began
Here is where no time moves
Here is where it will come to an end

"So we know what that means, seeing as how a whole year in time passed while we were here before, and this is where it will come to an end, when whatever comes next is over."

I still was not sure what was coming next. She moved to the back wall of the cave.

In the caverns below, place the stones

Rebecca turned to look at me, asking, "Do you think this means the stones we found, the ones that came alive?"

"I would have to agree."

She turned to face the wall again. Holding up the looking glass, she read,

Blue White Green Violet
Red Pink Amber Black
Harness the power with the metal forged

"So, we need to retrieve the stones and put them in these holes here." She looked in the hole in front of her. "Each one has a different shape in it, so each stone must be in a different shape." She turned to look at me. "I cannot remember if they were different."

"Yes, they are. Each one has its own shape. Something must happen when they are all set into place, and I am going to have to somehow harness the power with my sword."

"Can you do that?"

"I am not sure, but we do not have the stones with us. I think we are going to have to go back to Whispering Wind to retrieve them."

"We cannot do that. The mist is gone, and we would be in great danger if we went on our own."

"Let us see what else the writings say. We have much to learn before we can do this."

She moved on to the next wall and started reading.

Burn the stones of color one by one
Blue White Green Violet Red Pink Black Amber
When fire touches fire the flames are
Blue Green Yellow Black Amber

"All right, I am lost now. What does this mean?" she said.

I did not answer her. I sat there reading the words over and over. The words just came to me.

"The color of fire is amber, the color of Juliana's eyes. The mark on her neck looks like a flame, so she must be fire. Raiden moves faster than the wind, so he must represent air. I am fighting for the land, so I must be earth." I looked up at Rebecca. "You must then be water, the four elements of magic. That is why Roman fears us and why he wants us all. He knows that we are the only ones that can stop him."

"How do you know this?"

"I do not know how, but if you think about it, it makes perfect sense. We did not know we were magic; not magic you learn but magic within us. No one else can make our swords do what they do but us."

"You got all that from what I just read to you?"

"I think it was there all along. I just did not see it."

"So, now what should we do?"

"Read the rest."

She moved to the next wall, away from the holes with the tomes and stones.

Strike five the forged to the ground
Thrice is said what calms
Thrice is heard by all who came
Thrice is heard by all who went

"So, you hit your sword on the ground five times, then we say what we said in the cave to calm the stones. This third line do you think it means all who have died?"

"No, I think it means all who have come and all who have gone, so in a sense, yes, all who have died, but also all who have lived. Read the last wall, and it should tell us how it ends."

Rebecca moved to the last wall, the wall with the entrance to the cave on it.

Time is here for all to share
No man must own
When all is done
Calm will come

As she turned to face me, she said, "So when we do this, then it is over and the battle is won."

"I do not think it is that easy, Rebecca. I believe this is how it all ends, yes, but it is not that simple. We have been trained for a great battle, the battle of good and evil, and one must fall. I think this is how we settle the land after that. Only we can do it. If Roman wins, then the evil will remain. It will be over."

Rebecca and I stayed in the cave reading Father's journal and reading what we could of the tomes. There was much to learn and much to do. What seemed days for us were in fact years for everyone else. As they moved onward, Charles and his brothers married and had children. Each of them had seven sons. As they were taught, they taught their children. Raiden and Spirit roamed the lands, doing their best not to be seen. At the change of every season, they went to the valley and stood at the opening, waiting for Westin to see them.

Westin and Camille had more sons, six in all, and Juliana grew up to be a young woman, with the beauty of her mother Jenna and the personality of her father Ardes. They lived in the valley, untouched by the outside world.

Lord Roman had grown tired of waiting. He was pillaging and torturing the people. Charles and his brothers could do nothing to stop them. All of the kingdoms had suffered greatly. Many of the kings had been murdered, and Roman took many of the women for his slaves. All but Wellington and Blackmore were put to ruin. They were the two most powerful kingdoms left. Jared's sisters, Kaitlin and Francine, were given in marriage to Roman's commanders, and Eloise was given to Roman.

Rebecca's sister Kate had ended her own life when she heard of the marriage of Eloise. Her mother sat on the throne and was hated by all. Jared's mother was the same; they had become bitter and angry and very wealthy by allowing Roman to rule them. The world that we lived in had become dark indeed.

We had read and learned all that we could from the tomes in the cave and from Father's writings, and it was time for us to go and face Roman.

"I think it would be best if we left everything here."

"I agree, Sabine. The things that are written here cannot fall into the hands of Roman, or anyone else for that matter."

"We will need to seek out Charles, and then we need to get to Whispering Wind and wait for the battle."

"I could not agree with you more."

I looked at my friend. "You do know that Charles is not the same as when we came in here, right?"

"I know he is probably an old man now, but my heart still loves the man I left. It will be hard not to love him still."

"I know. It is going to be hard to see Westin and Juliana as well. I found these," I said, handing her a cloak. "They were in the back of the cave. We need to wear them. We must hide who we are when we go into Wellington. As much as I would like for Roman to take apart that kingdom, I cannot put those innocent people in harm's way."

"Agreed. Now how do we find Raiden and Spirit?"

"I think once we leave this cave they will find us. Are you ready?"

"Not really. How much time do you think has passed, Sabine?"

"I do not know, but I think it is time to go find out."

I reached out for her hand, and just as we entered the cave joined as one, we left it. The chill in the air told me that the cold months were leaving and the new had arrived. We made our way down the bank and across the stones to the other side. We walked back to the big rock and sat down. I searched for Raiden in my mind, and I am sure Rebecca did the same for Spirit. The light of the day was anew, and the sun was rising in the sky. The birds were singing as they were to begin the day. It was when they stopped that I knew Raiden was close.

'Hello, old friend,'

I said to him in my head. He did not speak to me, but just appeared. I jumped up as Rebecca did and flung my arms around his neck, whispering in his ear, "I do not think I have ever been this happy to see you. Is Westin still safe?"

He nodded his head, and I swear he was smiling.

"We need to see Charles. Will you take us there?"

He stomped his hoof on the ground and nodded his head. I climbed up on this giant horse, and before I knew what was happening, we were flying through the forest, only we did not go in the direction of Wellington. We headed instead to the valley that Joseph had found for us. I did not understand and leaned into Raiden, asking.

"Why are we going here? Charles should be in Wellington."

Raiden slowed when we reached the hills, and up he went. I heard the trumpet as we climbed. When we reached the top, I could see the valley, only it was not as we had left it; it was in fact a small city. There were horsemen riding up as we descended the hills. There was a young man sitting high on a horse next to an older man. As my face came into view, I heard him gasp

"It cannot be. What trickery is this?"

I was confused at his response. Raiden's ears were twitching, so this could not be good. He sensed danger for us. Before I knew what was happening, we were running straight into this new town in my valley. The way Raiden was turning this corner and that one I had to hang on tightly. I nearly fell off a few times. I was looking around at the people, but none of them looked familiar. 'How long have we been gone,' I asked myself. We turned the last corner, and I could see the cottage, only it did not look the same. Next to it was yet another cottage, and beyond that a whole line of cottages. Raiden stopped, and I sat there next to Rebecca, looking at our surroundings and looking at all the people rushing about looking at us. Only a few moments had passed when I heard him.

"Who are you?"

I turned in my saddle to see the men walking up to our horses. There were seven of them. The men before me were not the same men that I left what seemed only weeks before. Standing in front of my cottage were Charles, Joseph, Blake, Steven, Aidan, Edward, and James, but they were not the young men I knew. I heard Rebecca draw in her breath as I reached up to grab the hood of my cloak, slowly pulling it back over my head to reveal my face.

"Sabine," Charles said in a whisper as his eyes darted past me to Rebecca. When she removed her hood, his eyes came alive. "Rebecca."

Then I saw the tears that fell from his eyes. Rebecca was off her horse and in his arms before I knew what was happening. She nearly knocked him to the ground. I climbed off Raiden, and his arms were around me as well.

"I thought I would never see you again."

He was squeezing me so hard that I could not breathe. Finally, he let go, and I smiled at him.

"Charles," is all I could say.

The man that stood before me had many years behind him. He was not the same man we left a few weeks before.

"How many years have passed?" was all I could get out of my mouth.

"Come inside and we can talk there."

He walked us into the cottage. It looked exactly the same as when we left it. I took off my cloak and laid it across a chair. We made our way into the room that we ate our meals in and sat down at the table.

Charles spoke first to Rebecca. "I never thought I would see you again. You have not changed a bit. You are still as beautiful as the last time I saw you riding away from me at Whispering Wind all those years ago."

She just smiled at him. "Charles, it would seem we have a lot to talk about, but could you please tell me how many years have passed."

He looked at me, and as I glanced around the table, I saw they were all looking at me.

"Many years have passed, Sabine. My oldest son is in his eighteenth year."

"You have a son?" Rebecca said to him. I could hear the sadness in her voice.

"I have seven sons."

"So, what you are saying to me, Charles," I said, swallowing the rock in my throat. "Is that twenty years or more have passed?"

"It would seem that, yes. Where have you been that you have not aged?"

"A place where time stands still for us. Charles, there is much to talk about. We came to find you to help us with Roman. Is he still here?"

"Oh yes, Sabine, he is, and I am sure that sooner rather than later he will know you are back."

I could not help but giggle. "Charles, we never left. We have been here well, at Whispering Wind, the entire time."

His look said a thousand words. "I shall get my son to gather our horses, and we shall go for a ride. We have much to talk about. Are you hungry?"

"No, we are fine. Thank you."

He got up and went to the door. I heard him speaking, but I could not see who he was speaking to.

"Come, we can ride out to the plain."

We all walked out the door to our horses and proceeded through the tiny village to the plain. We rode to the middle and dismounted. Sitting in our circle as we did, I decided to speak first.

"Looking at you all, I cannot help but wonder how you all are, how you have been, and what brought you to this valley. Who are all these people?"

Blake answered, "We are all well. We are all married, and believe it or not, we all have seven sons. A great deal has taken place since you have been gone."

I could not stop the giggle. "It sounds so strange to hear you say that, Blake. We did not go anywhere, but I suppose that it surely does seem that way, considering the fact that Rebecca and I have aged just weeks."

Joseph spoke next, directing his words toward Rebecca, "I am sorry to tell you this, Rebecca, but your sister Kate has ended her own life." Rebecca did not respond; she just sat there holding Charles' hand. "Wellington sold off her daughters to Roman and his men. Eloise went to Roman himself while she was just in her fifteenth year. Kate knew your mother was going to do the same, so she ended her life."

"My mother will surely pay for this, as well as Wellington."

"That may not be as easy as you think. Wellington and Blackmore are the only two kingdoms left intact. All the other kings have been murdered and their kingdoms given to Roman's men. These are dark times for the land."

"How have you managed to stay intact?" Rebecca asked.

Charles spoke, looking right at her, "My love, I told you when we saw one another last that Roman would not harm us. These people are the ones who survived. They came from the known lands. Roman wants you, and he knows that he cannot kill us. He will come for you, and I am sure that there are those here who would trade information to Roman for his favor. He does not give favor, though, only empty promises. I will give him a few days at most before word gets to him where you are."

"So, what you are saying is that in order to save these people, we are going to have to leave here? But I have just found you."

"Rebecca, my love, I have a wife now, and I am an old man."

She laughed at him. "You are not old, Charles, and my love for you will be with me when I draw my last breath. You were meant for me. You said it yourself, and it does not matter to me if you have a wife or not. You are my love."

His hand reached up to touch her cheek. "As you will always be mine."

As they sat there looking into one another's eyes, a horse approached with a young man on it. Actually, he was my age.

"Father, Mother is concerned and wishes for you to come home."

We both looked up. It was an amazing sight. This man looked just like Charles

Charles did not take his eyes off Rebecca when he spoke.

"James, please inform your mother that I am fine, and when I finish my business here, we will be back."

"Yes, Father, but may I inquire as to who these women are?"

"You may inquire, but you will not believe me when I tell you."

I looked at the young man. "I am Sabine of Whispering Wind, and this is Rebecca of Blackmore."

He sat there on his horse, staring at me.

"How could this be truth? You are just a story. You cannot be real. If this was truth, you would be old."

I could not stop the laughter as it bellowed out of me.

"As you will learn, James, all is not what it seems."

"Enough of this inquiry. We have much to discuss. James, return to your mother with my words, and then get to the barracks and round up all the men. The time we have prepared for is here."

James nodded to his father and turned to go.

"Father, these cannot be the women you spoke of. They are but waifs of girls. What could they possibly do to stop Roman?"

"You have your orders, now go."

I watched as he rode off to the village.

"I believe it is time for the two of you to tell us what has happened to you," Charles said.

"Well, when we were at Whispering Wind, I discovered a secret room in my father's study. There we discovered a journal that my father started writing when I was born. It has guided me to discover many things, one being a cave where the knowledge on how to calm the lands was bestowed upon us. That is where we have been. In this cave, time stands still for us. What seems like days is actually years. We know now what is to come and what will need to be done to end this, to end Roman. The magic that Rebecca and I have is just two parts. Juliana and Raiden are the third and fourth parts. I am earth, Rebecca is water, Raiden is air, and Juliana is fire."

I heard Charles' intake of air. "You know then?" he asked.

"Yes, Charles, I knew when we parted company. She is indeed the key, and Samuel knew this. We will need her to finish this. Whispering Wind is magic in itself. It is where time began. It is where life began. The power, if harnessed correctly, can bring evil or goodness. It all hinges on who completes the ritual. Roman may think he knows how to do it, but I can assure you he does not."

Joseph spoke, "So what you are saying is you and Rebecca can stop this?"

"Yes."

"Then, why do you not stop it?"

"Well, in order for Roman to complete the ritual, he needs my sword, which he would have to kill me to get, and for Rebecca and I to complete it, we need the jewel on his sword. So, this battle of good and evil must take place. I am sure he is not going to give it up without a fight."

"There is much to do, Sabine. I have kept your cottage for you. The two of you must go and rest. I will take care of everything else, and we can leave in a few days' time."

"Charles, I am going to have to go get Juliana, and I want to see my brother."

"Sabine, I am sorry, but now that you are here, I am sure that Roman will follow you, and that would put my sister and her children at a great risk. We should just gather what we will need and go back to Whispering Wind. The time is now. We must not prolong this."

"Charles, I have trusted you with my life, and I shall not stop now."

We all stood. As we did, Blake came over and wrapped his arms around me.

"You are still the most beautiful woman I have ever known. I have missed you."

I did not know what to do, so I just hugged him back. It felt good to be close to him. "Thank you, Blake."

We went back to our cottage where a feast was waiting for us. As we finished, there was a knock on the door. I do not know who opened the door, but when I looked up, there was a woman standing in the doorway.

"Charles, what are you doing here? Who are these girls?"

The look on his face was one of love. He loved this woman, and not like he loved Rebecca. He looked from the woman to Rebecca and then back.

It was a soft whisper, but we all heard her ask, "This is her?"

Charles nodded his head. "This is Sabine of Whispering Wind and Rebecca of Blackmore. Sabine, Rebecca, this is my wife Margret."

Nothing was said; she just stood there staring at Rebecca and then at me, and finally she stopped at Charles. She was a beautiful woman. Then I saw one single tear fall from her eye and down her cheek. She smiled, turned, and left the room. Charles got up and ran after her, calling her name. I just sat there, not saying a word. Blake rose first.

"Well, ladies, the dark of the night is upon us. You are safe here for now. You should get some rest, for we have a great deal to do tomorrow."

He bowed his head, and they all left. Rebecca and I just sat at the table looking at one another.

"She was hurt by what she saw," Rebecca said softly.

"He is her husband. I am sure that she knows he loves her."

"Yes, but I love him as well."

"Rebecca, you cannot have him, not now, not ever. We cannot allow ourselves to get distracted. Our happiness comes when we finish this." I tried to be as soft as I could.

"I know, Sabine. I suppose I am just in shock. How did so many years pass us by? Juliana must be older than we are now. Stephan and Julia must be grown as well."

"It is just too much to bear, knowing we missed everything. I am tired and looking forward to sleeping in a bed." I smiled.

We walked arm in arm up the stairs. As we reached the top, a gentle knock came on the door.

"I will see who it is," said Rebecca as she turned to go down.

I think she might have wanted it to be Charles, but when she opened the door, it was Margret.

"May I come in?"

"Yes, of course," Rebecca said as she moved out of the way so Margret could enter.

"I will not keep you, Princess. I just wanted to tell you that you have never left my husband's heart. I knew this when I agreed to marry him, but I love him nonetheless. Over the years, he has called out your name in his sleep. He has sat starring at those hills waiting for you. Please do not get me wrong he has been a good husband and father, but I have never had his heart, not the way you have. You are very beautiful, my lady, and I can see why he loves you still. I must be truthful in telling you this, but I have dreaded the day you returned. I do not despise you, for I do not even know you. I just knew that this day would come, and this would be the day I lost my husband completely."

"No, my lady that is not the truth. I did not come here to take your husband. You must understand that where Sabine and I have been felt to us as weeks, not years. My love for Charles has not had as many years to fade. He does not love me that way. He could not possibly hold the same feelings. Please understand that I do not wish to break up your union. I know you must know a bit of what is happening here. He is Sabine's Guardian, as are his brothers. They will leave here with us, but I promise you that he will return to you. It is not our time any longer."

I should not have been sitting on the top stair listening, but I could not help myself.

Margret bowed her head to Rebecca. "Your Highness," she said.

"No, please, my name is Rebecca. I am not above your station. I am just a girl. Please call me Rebecca and do not bow to me. I am not better than you. In fact, it is you I should be bowing to. Charles is a happy man. I can see it in his eyes. His love for me is not anything you should feel regret about."

"Thank you, and again, I am sorry for keeping you. I can understand why he loves you. You are a very remarkable woman."

"Thank you, Margret. Please feel free to come here at any time. There is nothing we have to hide."

"Goodnight, my lady."

"Goodnight, Margret."

She left, and Rebecca closed the door behind her. "Well that was interesting," she said looking up at me.

"It sure was. Come on. Let us get some sleep."

When we entered my room, there was a young girl taking a pot off of the fire. "My lady," she said. "I have drawn you a bath."

I smiled at her. "Thank you. My name is Sabine, and this is Rebecca."

With her eyes down, she said, "Oh, I know who you are, my lady. I just did not believe you were real."

Rebecca laughed so loud it startled even me. "Oh, she is real all right."

I giggled. "I am going to take a bath. I was going to be nice and let you go first, but now I am."

"That is fine. I am going to see that Spirit and Raiden are being taken care of while you bathe." Looking at the young girl, she said, "Are the stables still out and to the left?"

"Yes, my lady, but my brothers will make sure that your horses are taken care of. I can go get another tub and draw you a bath as well."

"Your brothers? Who is your father?"

"My father is Joseph, my lady."

"No need to get another tub. I will wait for Sabine." Looking at me, she smiled and said, "I will be back in a bit."

Knowing Rebecca, the way I do, that smile could only mean trouble. "Have it your way," I said shaking my head.

"I always do," she said giggling as she walked out of the room.

The young girl took the pot and poured it into the tub. "What is your name?" I asked.

"My name is Camille. I was named after my Aunt, whom I have never met.

I giggled. "Camille, well thank you. I know your Aunt. She is married to my brother Westin."

"Yes, that is what we have been told, but no one knows if they are still alive or not. I shall leave you now, my lady."

"Thank you."

She left my room. I took off my gown and climbed into the tub; the water was hot and felt so good. I could not help but wonder about what she said. They must still be alive. Why would they not be? I needed to know, so I cleared my mind and concentrated on Raiden.

'Can you hear me?'

'I am here.'

'Are Westin, Camille, and the children still alive?'

'They are all fine.'

'Thank you.'

I would rest a bit easier now that I knew they were alive and well. I closed my eyes, and the darkness took over. I felt my body being lifted and then the softness of the bed. The light of the day was on my face, warming me. My eyes fluttered open, and it took me a few seconds to realize where I was. I sat up, and the blanket that was around me fell to my lap. I was naked. *'How did I get in bed?'* My question was answered when I heard him clear his throat. I reached up to grab the blanket as I looked across the room to see who was here with me.

"Blake. Again, I find you standing guard over me. Was it you who put me to bed?"

"Yes, Sabine, it was, under the careful guidance of Rebecca. You are still as beautiful as you were all those years ago."

I really had no words. This man still believed he was in love with me.

"Would you mind stepping out so I can get dressed?"

"I will wait for you downstairs," he replied as he got up, crossed the room, and went out the door.

I jumped out of bed, searching for something to wear.

"What happened to my clothes?"

Just as I said that, there was a knock on my door.

"My lady, it is Camille. I have your gown. May I come in?"

"Yes," I told her. As she entered, she turned her head so that she could not see me. "Camille, I was in fact looking for my satchel. Have you seen it?"

"Yes, my brother brought them in this morning from the stables. You left it on your horse."

"Would you be a darling and go retrieve it for me please? The clothes I wish to wear are in it."

"I did not mean to search through your things, my lady, but they were all boys' clothes."

I giggled. "Yes, I know. They are my clothes. Would you get them for me?"

She crinkled up her nose and left, returning a few minutes later with my bag.

"Thank you. Could you please tell Rebecca that I will meet her to have our morning meal?"

Camille stood there looking at me.

"What is it?"

"My lady, it is midday."

I looked at the window. "Really? Well, I would like something to eat nonetheless."

I changed into my boy clothes and asked her to plait my hair. It was amazing to look at her. The memories of her aunt flooded my mind; they were so similar.

"Camille, do you have a man in your life?"

"Oh no, my lady, I am just in my fourteenth year. My father would not allow such a thing."

I could not help but giggle. "No, I suppose he would not. Can I ask you something?"

"Of course, my lady. You can ask me anything you like."

"Your uncle Blake, is he married?"

"He was, my lady, but his wife died during childbirth with his last son, about ten years ago."

"That is so sad. Thank you."

I went down to the room where we had our meals, and it was as if nothing had changed, except for the obvious fact that everyone except me and Rebecca had aged. Charles chuckled.

"As usual, you are late." I just smiled at him and sat down. "We have much to discuss and much to do. When you are finished, I would like to take you two to the barracks so you can meet everyone, and then we can prepare to leave for Whispering Wind."

"Charles, may I speak?"

"Sabine, when have I ever been able to stop you?"

"Well, never. I just want to say this, not that it will make a difference anyway, but it needs to be said. Since Rebecca and I have stood still in time, and all of you have moved forward with wives and children, would it be best if the seven of you stayed behind?"

There was a long silence, but Joseph finally spoke, "Sabine, as you already know, we were born your Guardians. We were raised to protect you. We were trained by our father, whose father trained him, as we have trained our sons. We are still alive, and we will fulfill our sworn oath to protect you to death. If we survive this and it ends, then and only then will we return to our families. When we married the women we chose, they knew that this day would come, and they knew that we would eventually leave them to protect you and Rebecca. You forget that this is not about us as individuals. This concerns the lands and those who dwell in them. This is bigger than all of us. If we fail, there will be no tomorrow. Roman will bring the darkness, and we will fall into a submission of the most vile. When we win and the evil is put in its place, then and only then will we be free. The people in this village are those who have managed to escape Roman. We ourselves were put into danger when we went back to our father. Wellington wanted our heads. She knows she cannot harm us, but we decided to leave and come here to the valley. Roman has been here, but because he fears you, he has left us alone. He will return, and when he sees that we have left, he will know, if he does not know already, that the two of you have returned. So, in answer to your query no, we will not be staying behind."

"To be truthful, Joseph, I am glad that you will be joining us. I do not think I can do this without you. I feel a sort of comfort in knowing you will be beside me."

Charles spoke next, "Sabine, you are going to meet my oldest son. He will be my second in command. His name is Richard, and he will be me when I am not there with you. One of us will be with you at all times when we leave this valley. Try to go easy on him, for he has a tender heart, unlike me, who can handle your....um...let us say moods."

I could not hold my laugh in. "Oh, Charles, you make me smile."

"I am glad to accommodate you," he said with a smile. I could see his age lines around his eyes.

"Charles, if your son is tender hearted, is he the best man for the job. We are going to embark on far worse than when we went in search of Juliana. I cannot be held back by a man who thinks I might be harmed. I can fully take care of myself."

"He is well aware of the abilities you and Rebecca have."

"That may be so, Charles," Rebecca spoke up. "But Sabine has grown a great deal since we saw you last. You will be surprised."

"My love, everything the two of you can do apart and together surprises me. I would never have believed that the sword she wields could even be lifted by her small frame, but yet she raises it without any effort at all. The fact that she can put me on the ground and not even blink amazes me. So, my darling Rebecca, I say bring it on."

We all laughed. A young man appeared in the doorway. "Father, there are horses coming from the West."

"Roman, no doubt. Thank you, Richard. Please have the men stand ready, and we will ride out to the plain to greet him." Richard nodded and left. "Ladies, shall we go and meet this man we shall battle the land for. I am sure he is ready to meet you. He has been waiting a long time for this."

I looked a Rebecca. Her face was solid, but I saw that glimmer in her eyes. She was ready for the fight. As I stood, I heard Raiden in my head.

'Outside now.'

I turned and ran to the door. Standing outside was Raiden.

'Get on, NOW.'

I did not hesitate, nor did Rebecca. I was on Raiden, and he was flying through the village in the opposite direction. It was not even a breath that we were on the opposite side of the valley climbing the hills. When we hit the ground on the other side, we were gone. I did not understand why, not until we hit the river. We were going to the hidden valley. Once across the river, we hit his fastest stride. The mountains came fast. As we started our ascent, I could see the smoke. The valley was on fire.

"Hurry, Raiden! Are they all right?"

'Lean into me.'

I did as he asked. It took a flash of time before we were out of the passageway and heading down the mountain. I could see the valley floor, and it was engulfed in flames. I could not see Westin or the children, only the flames.

'Calm them.'

I climbed off of him and said the calming spell three times out loud and three times in my head. The flames calmed and then went out. Standing on the other side was Westin. I could not stop my feet from moving, and before I knew it I hit him in the chest with my body. He was crying, and I was crying. He had changed so much; he was older, wiser.

"Is it really you, Sabine?" I heard him say between sobs.

"Yes, my love, it is me."

"Where have you been? So many years have gone by."

"I know, and I am sorry. I had no idea so much time had passed."
We separated.

"You look the same, Sabine, and Rebecca looks like she did all those years ago. How is this truth?"

I giggled. "Oh, Westin, there is much to tell you, but first, what happened here?"

"I do not know. Juliana and Stephan were fighting, and all of a sudden the valley started on fire. Camille took the children to the tree, and I came to try and put it out. I remembered what you said about not starting any fires, but Sabine, if I had known it would bring you here, I would have done it a long time ago." He smiled at me.

"I am glad that you did not do that. I had some things I needed to do, and now they are done. Now we have to take care of one more thing, and then we can all go home."

"Good. I miss our home, Sabine. Hi, Rebecca," he said as she walked up and grabbed him and hugged him tight.

"Hello, Westin. Where is my little Stephan? I want to give him a squeeze."

Westin bellowed laughter. "Stephan is not so little. He is a man now, but we do have another little one you can squeeze."

He turned, and we followed his gaze. Walking, almost running, up was Camille, along with eight others.

Juliana was the one I was focused on. She looked just like Jenna, with her long dark hair and those beautiful amber blue eyes. She saw me, and it was just as the day when we saw one another when I found her as a child. She stopped and tilted her head.

"It is me," was all I said.

She was moving fast toward me. It was hard to scoop her up in my arms and spin her around, but I did. We ended up falling to the ground, giggling like little girls. The rest of the children just stood there looking confused, which caused us to laugh even more.

"I have missed you greatly," she whispered in my ear.

"As I have you, my love," I whispered back.

We gathered ourselves and got up. Camille was crying when I hugged her.

"We thought you would never return."

"I know, and I am sorry for the delay. Your brothers will be excited to see you and to know that you are well."

"How are they? My parents, are they still living?"

"Your brothers are all fine. Each one has married, and each one has seven sons and one daughter."

Camille started laughing. "As do I," she said as she waved her arm around.

I followed her arm to see seven sons and a daughter. We all started laughing.

"I know nothing of your parents, I am afraid to say. We had just found Charles a day ago. There was no time to chat when Raiden brought us here. What happened here?"

A young man walked up and said, "I am Stephan, first born."

"I know who you are. I am your aunt Sabine."

"How can this be? I am sure that I am older than you, and I know that my father's parents have been gone for a very long time."

"It is a very long story. You will learn it all when the time is right, so what happened here?"

Stephan turned to look at his father, who in turn nodded toward me and said, "She is the Queen of Whispering Wind, my sister."

Stephan turned back to me and bowed. "My lady, please excuse me for my ignorance. Juliana and I were down by the river, and I took a liberty with her and kissed her. She in turn slapped my face and screamed at me, 'Not without my permission,' and before I could respond, the flames were everywhere."

I turned to look at Juliana. She had a smile on her face and said, "He is my cousin. If he ever does that again, I will do more than just slap him."

"Yes, I do not doubt that you will. I think you and I have a lot to talk about."

"Come, you must be hungry," Camille said.

I took Juliana by the hand, and we walked to the camp. It was so good to be with them all. Westin introduced me to his children; Stephan, Julia, David, Edmund, Arthur, Henry, George, and Louis, more than enough to fill the halls of Whispering Wind. We ate the fine meal that Camille made for us, and I noticed that the dark of night was upon us.

"Will you excuse us? Juliana and I have much to talk about. Rebecca, will you join us?"

We walked to the base of the tree and sat down. Looking at Juliana, I said, "My love, did you start that fire?" I could see the fear in her eyes. "There is no need to be fearful."

"I am not sure, but I think I did."

"Will you tell me what happened to you right before it happened?"

"Well, Stephan kissed me, and it made me very angry. I do not want him to touch me. My body just grew hotter and hotter, like I was going to burst. Then something just beyond Stephan caught my eye, and when I looked at it, the plain just started on fire. It scared me. What if I had not looked away? Would Stephan have burned instead?"

"But you did look away from him, and he is fine. Do you under-stand what it is that you have done?"

"No."

"Do you think you can do it again?"

"I do not want to do it again. Westin told us that we must never start a fire, that bad people will come and take us all away, and that they would use us to make you do what they want."

"Yes, that was and is truth, but I am here now, and soon this will all be over. We will go back to our home then, back to the place of your birth. I need to know if you can do it again."

"I can try, but I still do not know what it is I did, or how I did it, or even why I did it. But if you want me to, I can try again."

"Yes, I want you to try again, but not here. We should go to the lake and try it there, that way nothing else will burn." I smiled at her as we stood. We gathered at the lake, and I told her, "Now I want you to think about what Stephan did, and I want you to look at the lake, only the lake, and when you feel like you are going to burst, thrust your energy at the water. Can you do that?"

She did not answer me; she just stood there staring at the water. I watched her carefully, looking into her eyes as she made herself angry.

Her eyes went from the beautiful amber color to deep, dark amber, almost reddish in tint, just before the lake burst into flames. When she jumped back, the flames ended.

Rebecca howled with laughter. "Now, that was something," she said.

"How do you feel?" I said as I put my hand on her arm. She was very warm.

"I feel like I am burning from the inside, and I have a funny taste in my mouth."

"Listen to me." I turned her toward me. "We have to leave, and you must stay here until I send Raiden for you."

"But..."

"No, you must learn to control this. You cannot let this gift get away from you. Come, I need to tell you what has happened and what is going to happen."

I took her hand, and we walked back to the camp. Westin and Camille had put the children to sleep, so we walked a bit away so I would not disturb them.

"Westin, Camille, what I am going to say to you is so far from real that I would not believe it, but seeing that we have lived through it and are it, I believe."

"Sabine, if you say it is truth, then I will believe you."

"Thank you, my love. Now let us sit." We all sat in a circle. "Our kingdom, Whispering Wind, is a very magical place. It is where time began. It is where life began. For all of time, evil has tried to take it from our family. We have been chosen to protect the magic. Raiden's father was the very first king to have that honor, only Raiden's sister was born first, and she wanted to rule. She knew her father's secret, and she wanted the knowledge, and you know that only the first-born son can become king. Well, his sister Diana made a deal with a very nasty witch to take the knowledge from Raiden's father when he died, instead of it going to Raiden. To stop Raiden from getting it, his sister Diana turned him into a horse and then murdered her father. Well, Merlin himself gave Raiden the ability to live forever until the chosen one came along to calm the land. Diana turned out to be Devious the witch, the one who took Juliana as a child. Father knew the legend of the Bringer of Peace, and he knew that I was that person the day I was born. Ardes and Simon knew as well. Without my knowledge, Father, Simon, Ardes, and even you, Westin, trained me. When I started to figure it all out, all of my memories came back. Each and every thing you all taught me made sense. There is a man who is the vilest form of evil named Roman. He is a very bad man, and that is why you need to stay here. If he gets his hands on you, on any of you, he will force me to give him my sword. He can only take control of the land if he has my sword and he finds the place that has stopped Rebecca and me from growing old. I need a jewel on his sword to stop the evil from taking control, so I have to kill him to get it."

"Sabine, does that mean he will have to kill you to get your sword?"

"Yes, Westin, he would have to kill me or find you. That is why I have you hidden here. When I get the jewel from him, and I will get it, we will need the four elements of magic to complete the ritual that will settle the land, and the evil will be no more. Then and only then will we be able to live in peace at Whispering Wind."

"Sabine, what are the four elements of magic?"

"Well, Westin, they are not what but who; earth, air, water, and fire."

"Who could be those things Sabine? That is funny. Who can be the air? Who could be earth and water, and then who could be fi..." His eyes got huge as he turned to look at Juliana then back to me. In a whisper he said, "Sabine?"

"I know, my love. That is why Samuel took her and gave her to the witch. They all knew what she could do, but they did not know about me or Rebecca or Raiden."

"I do not understand."

"I am Earth, Rebecca is Water, Raiden is Air, and Juliana is Fire. Only we can stop this, together. Do you understand, Westin? That day on the hill that you saved me, you saved all of us. It was supposed to be like this. Father and Mother knew, as did Ardes, Jenna, and Simon. Everyone knew except for us. I had to take this journey to figure it all out. It is so big that Father could not tell it all too any one person, only me, and he did it in a way that no one else would ever figure it out."

"Father was a very smart man, Sabine."

"Yes, he was, Westin, but do you understand what I am saying to you?"

"That you are magic," he said and smiled.

"Well, sort of, but Rebecca and I have to go. I will send Raiden to get Juliana when I have the jewel from Lord Roman's sword. You must stay here. Only she can leave. When it is finished, I will send Raiden and Spirit to get you. While I am gone, can you do something for me?"

"Of course, Sabine. I will do anything you ask of me."

"I need you to help Juliana control her gift."

"I will do my best. When are you leaving?"

"I am afraid it will have to be now, while the dark of night is here. Lord Roman knows that we are back, and he will be looking for me."

"In the dark it will be hard for him to find you."

"He does not need the light of day to find me, Westin, but this valley is magic, and he cannot see here, and Raiden moves too quickly through time to be seen. I just think it would be best to leave in the dark of night. Raiden will know if anyone finds you. He knew about the fire and brought me here, so have no fear, my love. This will be over soon."

Juliana reached for me. We embraced, and she whispered in my ear, "I love you. Please come back for me."

"I will, my love. I promise. Try not to start anything on fire, just the water, okay?"

She giggled and squeezed me tight.

I hugged Westin and Camille. "Stephan, I know we do not know one another, but please take care of your father for me," I said as I hugged him goodbye.

"I will do as you ask of me."

I smiled, and Rebecca and I left the valley.

CHAPTER EIGHTEEN

When we arrived in the village, Charles was waiting for us.

"What happened? Why did you run?"

"Hello, Charles. There was a problem that I needed to take care of," I said in a tone that was saying not here, not now.

"I see... Well, Roman came to visit. He knows you were here, and he left one of his men here. I believe you know him."

He nodded his head, and I turned in my saddle to see Toddzwga standing on the path leading from the stables.

"Well, hello again," I said and smiled. He looked like an old man. He did not move, he just stood there staring at us. Raiden turned to face him. "Should you not go back and report to Lord Roman that we are indeed back?"

"How can this be?"

Rebecca laughed. "It would seem that Lord Roman has led you to believe something other than what you see. Yes, you have grown old in years, and we have not changed. Your Lord Roman is said to be a great sorcerer, but he cannot change what time changes, can he? You may live long, but you still grow old."

"I told Roman that he was no match for these two. Perhaps you should go and share the truth with him. You are going to lose your life, Toddzwga, along with the rest of your men. All the killing you have done will be paid for with your life." Charles said.

"Do not think you can throw threats at me, Charles. You live only because Roman allows it."

Charles laughed. "I live because Roman cannot kill me. He must not have shared that knowledge with you.

"And you, Princess, you are untouchable as long as you sit upon that horse. I will find you without him, and then we shall see how powerful you are."

I looked at Rebecca, and I knew the look in her eyes; she was ready for the fight. I giggled and threw my leg over Raiden's back, jumping off him.

"Well, it would seem, Toddzwga, that I am no longer on my horse. Care to come and get me now?"

He drew his sword and smiled at me. His teeth were dirty and rotting in his mouth. He charged me. My sword hit his with a flash of light, and he was on the ground on one knee. I pushed my sword against his and got as close to his face as I could stand.

"See, I do not need my horse to take you down. Now before you force me to end your life, I would suggest that you return to Roman and tell him that I will meet him at Whispering Wind in five days' time. Tell him not to return to this valley, or his little army shall meet the same fate as your little band of misfits did."

He pushed me back a bit and gathered himself, but he did not leave. He swung again and again, each blow weakening him. I swung back three times, and he was down again.

"If you continue to attack me, I will be forced to end your life. You decide," I told him and then backed off.

Looking up at me from his knees, he said, "I will meet you in battle, and you will be the one who is kneeling before me. I promise you that, Princess."

"Lord Toddzwga, might I suggest that you do not make promises you cannot keep. You will not defeat me. Now go before you make Rebecca angry. She has a habit of cutting people's heads off."

He looked up at her, and of course she was smiling at him. "I will deliver your message. Five days' time..." He got to his feet and backed away. Looking past me to Charles, he said, "Do not think this is over, Charles. You will answer to Lord Roman."

Charles chuckled and responded, "I would die before I would answer to him."

"So be it," Toddzwga said as he turned to go to the stables. Moments later, we heard his horse as he left the valley.

Rebecca was giggling. "Did you see his face? He is scared, really scared."

"They all are, my love. They know now after seeing you that they do not stand a chance."

"I do not suppose that if I ask Lord Roman for the jewel on his sword that he would just give it to me?"

He chuckled. "No more than you would give him your sword."

"Good, because I do not want to miss out on a good fight, as unfair as it will be. Nonetheless, it will be great fun," Rebecca said as she slid off of Spirit into Charles' waiting arms. "You know we have got to stop meeting like this."

Charles laughed as he drew her close to him. "I have missed you all these years."

"So I have heard. Charles, we really need to talk."

"Yes, I suppose we do. Come, we can eat and then talk."

We all went inside to the kitchen. "Oh, Your Highness," the cook said as she bowed.

"Please, I am just Sabine. There is no need to bow to me. Would it be possible for us to get something hot to eat?"

"Please, go sit out at the table. I will serve you."

"No need to serve us," I said as I walked to the cupboard to retrieve some plates. "We are fine just sitting in here. Do you mind?"

"No, my lady. Please let me do that."

"It is not necessary for you to wait on us. So, what do you have on the fire it smells wonderful?" She just stood there looking at me. I smiled and walked up to the fire. "Looks like stew of some kind."

"Here, bring me your plates. I will fill them."

We each grabbed a plate. As we were finishing up, there was a knock on the door. We heard voices, and then Margret appeared in the doorway.

"Margret," Charles said.

"Come in and have a seat. We were just finishing our meal," Rebecca said, smiling at her.

"Thank you, Your Highness, but I am not here to stay. Charles, will you be coming home for our evening meal?" She looked at the table. "I suppose not," she answered for him, and then turned to walk away, but Rebecca stopped her.

"Margret, please do not go. As I told you before, we have nothing to hide."

"No, you do not have anything to hide, but my husband does."

"Please, you must understand. I know he is your husband, and I assured you that there cannot be anything between us. I am not here to come between you. You must know that."

There was a long pause before Margret spoke again. "With all due respect, Your Highness, you have been between us from the beginning. I am not a fool. Anyone who looks at the two of you can see it. Charles has loved you always, and he will love you beyond this life, but I love him as well. I will fight for my marriage, and I will fight for him."

Charles stood up. "Margret, you are my wife, the mother of my children. I love you."

"Yes, Charles, I know this, but I also know that you love Rebecca, and that you have always loved her."

"That maybe so, but you are the one I chose."

"You chose me because she was not here for you to choose."

"It should not matter how I feel about Rebecca. We will never have what you and I have," he pleaded with her.

"Charles, with all due respect, you and I share nothing like what you share with her. I have lived with this knowledge for twenty years, and I have never said how I feel about the fact that my husband will never love me the way that I love him. I have lost you, but I never really had you, did I? When they returned, I knew that I was never going to see you again after you leave here. I am trying my best to hold my head high while those in the village talk about me being poor Margret."

"Would you like it if I did not go?"

"Yes, I would, but I know that you cannot stay. Your father explained to me the night before we wed that when they returned it was your duty to protect Sabine, that you are her Guardian. Charles, I grew up hearing the same stories you heard. I grew up wishing and hoping, just as you did, that this legend was truth. However, I was unaware that the man I was to fall in love with and marry would be in love with one of the Bringers of Peace."

"Margret, I wish I could explain this to you, but I am not sure that I understand it myself. What I felt for Rebecca was so new and wonderful. I had never felt the way I did when I was with her. When she left, I knew that the years would pass with her never changing, but when I met you, it gave me hope that perhaps I could love again. You gave me that. You gave me the love I did not believe that I deserved. Yes, I love Rebecca, but I also know that our time was twenty years ago. It is not now, and it will never be. You are my wife. I chose you. If I wanted Rebecca, I would not have married. I would have waited. I will return to you, but you know that I must leave, for you know what will come if we do not."

The silence was more than I could bear, sitting there unable to move while I watched an innocent woman be reduced to tears. Charles moved toward her, and I was certain she would run, but she did not. He embraced her and said softly to her.

"I love you, wife, and I will return to you."

I could hear her sobs. I felt horrible, so I got up and went to hug them both, and Rebecca joined us. The four of us stood there in a most peculiar embrace, Charles holding his wife and the love of his life together. After a few moments, we separated. Margret apologized and excused herself, leaving the three of us standing uncomfortably in the kitchen of a cottage we once shared.

"Charles, I think you should go after her," Rebecca said softly.

"We need to discuss our departure."

"It can wait until the light of day. You need to see your wife and say goodbye to her."

He looked at Rebecca and reached up to touch her cheek. "How is it that I can love two women at the same time?"

"Sabine, what am I doing to that poor woman?" Rebecca asked after he had left.

"Oh, Rebecca." I hugged her. "You cannot help how you feel, nor can Charles. You both know that it will never be what it should have been. We need to leave here and end this, so we can both find our happiness. Yours, however, is not with Charles."

"It hurts so bad knowing he will never be mine."

"You should take with you the knowledge that he will always be yours, just not in the manner in which you both hoped. You will love him for all of your days, just as I will love Jared. It just is not your time. It is better to have loved once than to have never loved at all."

"I love you, Sabine. You are my sister in this life."

"I love you too, Rebecca. We should really get some rest. We have a huge day ahead of us, and I am not sure when we are going to have the chance to bathe properly or sleep in such wonderful beds."

She giggled. "You are right. I shall see you at the light of day. We are going on yet another adventure, Sabine. When I met you on that plain all those years ago, I never imagined that we would be here holding magical powers, preparing to fight the great sorcerer Lord Roman and save the land."

"Nor I, my friend." We smiled at one another and made our way upstairs.

The light of day was barely in the sky when Rebecca jumped on my bed. "Wake up, Sabine. Today is the day we fight our final battle and become the legends everyone thinks we are."

She was giggling, and I could see the excitement in her eyes. She really was made for this.

"Can we wait for another day to murder thousands, please? I just want to sleep in this very comfortable bed," I said as I pulled the blankets over my head.

She grabbed them and was right in my face. "No, now get up and let us finish this."

I complied and rose to dress in my boy clothes. We went downstairs together to the room where we ate our meals to find Charles and his brothers sitting at the table.

"Well, I must say that this is a pleasant surprise, Sabine, to see you on time for once in your life," Charles said smiling.

I stuck my tongue out at him, and we all laughed. "So what is on the agenda for today?"

"First, I would like to apologize for what took place last night in the kitchen. Margret should not have done what she did."

Rebecca interrupted him. "Charles, there is no need to apologize. Margret had every right. I will have to say that if I was in her place, I would not be so graceful. I am, after all, stealing her husband." She smiled her wicked smile.

"Thank you, Rebecca." He smiled back. "Now, back to the matter at hand. We are ready to go whenever you are. The men are preparing the horses. Our oldest sons will be coming as well. You will meet them all soon, and then we shall go back to Whispering Wind. I suggest that the two of you stay close, for we do not want you arriving before us."

"Blake, we are aware of the fact that your wife is no longer with us. Should you be leaving your sons to come along?" I asked.

"Thank you, Sabine, but Margret has gracefully offered to care for them until we return."

I looked at Charles; he married a good woman. This must be so hard for her.

"Charles, after we eat I would like to go see your wife, if you do not mind. I will need to know where it is that you live."

Blake laughed. "He lives next door."

"Fine then, I will meet you at the stables when I am finished."

"May I inquire as to what it is you need to speak to my wife about?"

"Yes, you may inquire all you like, however, I do not have to tell you," I replied with a smile.

We ate in silence, and when I finished, I excused myself and made my way to the cottage next door. I knocked on the door, and a little girl answered.

"Can I help you?" she said.

"Hi, sweetheart, is your mommy here?"

"Mommy, a very pretty lady is at the door for you."

Margret walked up, looking a bit startled to see me. "Can we talk?" I asked her.

"Of course, Your Highness. Please come in."

"Margret, my name is Sabine," I reminded her. She guided me into a small sitting area and motioned for me to sit. "I just wanted to say to you that I admire you. I hope that when I grow up, I am half the woman you are. I know that it is taking a great deal of pride for you to watch your husband ride off with a woman he once loved. I just want to tell you that there is no need for you to worry about Rebecca. She would never do anything to harm your relationship with Charles. She wanted him to stay here with you and his children, and she feels terrible about what you are going through."

"Sabine, as much as I appreciate you coming here, I have to say that you cannot possibly know how I feel."

"You are wrong. Are you aware that I had to cut the head off the man I love? His body was taken over by a witch. I do know what it is like to feel the loss of someone you love so dear, but you are not losing Charles. He will be back. He will not die. As long as I am alive, he lives. It is what being my Guardian means. Once this is done, he will return to you, and your life will go back to the way it was, only the threat of evil will be gone."

"But what if you lose?"

I could not stop the giggle. "There is no chance of that. Why do you think Roman has not harmed any of you? He knows what is coming, but he is just too arrogant to let it be. He thinks he can win, but he cannot. He will not. I know you have heard stories about us and what we can do, but I am sure that they do not do us justice."

"Well, the stories of your beauty have not done you justice."

"There are stories of my beauty?" I whispered to her.

She chuckled. "Oh yes, and let me say this, they do not even come close to your real beauty."

"Well, I think, as with most stories that they are a bit built up. I am just a girl who was thrust into an intrigue beyond any stories that could be told."

"You are anything but a girl. You are a strong young woman, as is Rebecca, who holds such beauty and grace that any woman would be worried."

"You are too kind. I just need for you to believe that Charles loves you and that he will return to you."

"I will take your words to my heart, Sabine. Thank you for coming here, but you should go. Charles is waiting for you."

"Will you walk with me to see us off?"

"I would like that."

We left the cottage and made our way to the stables. There were so many men waiting. Charles came up to us and asked, "Is everything all right?"

I looked at Margret, and she hugged me. "As right as it will ever be," she said. She let go and turned to Charles. "I will love you until I take my last breath. Please come back to me, husband."

He grabbed her and pulled her into his arms, telling her, "I love you wife, always."

They kissed, and I looked at Rebecca to see she had tears streaming down her cheeks. I climbed on Raiden and leaned over to wipe one of her tears away, whispering, "You ready?" She nodded and wiped the rest away.

Charles got on his horse. Looking at his wife, he mouthed, 'I love you always.'

Margret smiled and said to us, "Ladies, I give you my husband, and I send with you all the well wishes I have to your success."

"Thank you, Margret. We shall take care of these men and take your well wishes with us."

With that, we rode out of the village and to the plain, where there were thousands of men waiting for us. I turned to Charles and said, "My, you have been busy."

His bellowing laughter caused us all to laugh as we rode out of the valley, heading to Whispering Wind.

CHAPTER NINETEEN

We cleared the hills and hit the plains below, we rode hard. It was a five days' ride from there to Whispering Wind, and Roman knew we were coming. The fastest we could make it was in two and a half days, and that was riding hard without stopping. Rebecca and I could make it in no time at all, but Charles made me promise that we would stay with them. We stopped only to eat and rest the horses. We rode for two days and one night, and then stopped on the second night. As we set up camp, Charles introduced us to the first-born sons; his son Richard, Blake's son Gerald, Joseph's son Alexander, Steven's son Arthur, Aidan's son Brian, Edward's son David, and James' son Henry.

"I think you and Rebecca should get some rest."

"I will not give argument to that," I said as I rose from the circle, we were in.

I looked around for Raiden. I think he sensed my apprehension in being so exposed. He walked up to me and nudged me in the shoulder.

"Will you stand guard over me this night?"

"I would be honored," replied Richard.

Charles laughed again. "She was not talking to you, son. She was talking to her horse."

The look on his face said it all, so we had a good laugh.

"He has been with me from the beginning of this, and he has a sense of danger that no man can match. I trust him like I trust your father but thank you for the offer."

I walked toward our tent, and Raiden followed, along with Rebecca and Spirit.

I could hear Charles laughing at us. I was sure that Richard was shaking his head. Rebecca and I fell fast asleep, and thankfully, we had an uneventful night. When the light of day broke the sky, Charles was at our tent.

"Ladies, it is time to rise. We have a long ride ahead of us."

Rebecca yelled out, "Go away, Charles. We are sleeping."

He laughed, saying, "I have a pail of water here with your name on it, Rebecca, and it is not beneath me to use it."

She giggled. "We are coming."

We ate a quick meal while the men took our tent down, and then we rode. By dusk on the second day, we had come to the forest just outside of Whispering Wind. Blake and a few men went ahead of us to see if it was safe, but I already knew it was. Raiden would not have led me into a trap. When they returned, we rode into the village and then to the castle. It felt good to be home again.

"Charles, where are all these men going to sleep, and where did they all come from?"

"They will bunk in the barracks, and we will bunk in the castle with you." He looked up as the men rode in. "They came from everywhere really. Roman has destroyed many kingdoms, and these men survived. Many of them are the sons of those who did not. I told you that I would raise an army for your return, and I like to think I am a man of my word."

"You are a man of your word, that is truth, but why would they be willing to die for me?"

"Sabine, have you not figured it out yet? This is not only about you any longer. Since Roman came here to take this sacred ground, he has let everyone know how life will be once he has finished this. These men will fight to the death, not only for you, but to save themselves as well."

"Do you think Roman will come here?"

Raiden answered that with the stomping of his hoof and the bobbing of his head. I could not help but smile at him.

"I think you got your answer."

"Yes, I suppose I did." I patted Raiden's neck. "You will protect me always," I said into his neck.

He placed his giant head on my shoulder and pulled me close to him. When I pulled away, I noticed Richard watching me.

"He thinks he is human sometimes," I said to Richard.

'I was once.'

"I know you were, and that is what makes you so special," I said out loud.

"I am sorry, Sabine. Did you say something?"

"Not to you Richard. Perhaps your father should explain my horse to you. He is not an ordinary horse, and neither is Spirit, but I am sure you already guessed that by our departure from the valley the night Roman came. Charles, I am going to sleep. If you do not need to wake me when the light of the day comes, would you not?"

"I will do my best, Sabine, but you know me. There is always something I need to say." He smiled.

"Well then, I shall bid you goodnight." I started walking into the castle, and Raiden followed me.

"Is that horse going with you?"

I just smiled at him. "Richard, talk to your father."

As we were ascending the grand staircase, Rebecca, who had been silent most of the way here, asked me, "Have you noticed how very charming Richard is?"

I stopped. "No, I have not. Why would I?"

"No reason... I was just wondering."

"Rebecca, this is not the time. Let us sleep, and then we can kill Roman, take the jewel, and end this. I want my family home. I want to sleep my days away."

"You are right. Can I bunk with you?"

"Actually, I was hoping you would consider bunking with me," we heard someone say.

We both turned to see Charles standing at the bottom of the stairs. I looked from Charles to Rebecca, whose eyes were huge.

"I am not so sure that would be the most ideal situation to put yourself in, Charles."

"Let me be the judge of what is ideal for me and what is not. I have waited a very long time to see you again, and there is much we need to say to one another, things that should have been said before you left me. I am afraid that I will not take no for an answer. We may not have another opportunity, and besides all of this, I have missed you. Our time together back then has played over and over in my mind all these years."

I felt the tear fall from my eye. I looked at my friend standing next to me, my sister in this life, and she was crying. Before I knew what was happening, Charles was pulling her into his arms, muttering, "Oh, my love, do not cry." He lifted her into his arms, looked at me and smiled, and continued up the stairs to Simon's room. Charles was taking a huge chance on sleeping with Rebecca while his son was around, but they needed to be together. They needed to talk.

I went to my room, and as always, Raiden stayed at my door. I do not remember much after I crawled into my bed; clothes, boots, and all.

The light of the day was high in the sky when I woke. Rebecca was sitting on the edge of my bed, her eyes red.

"What is it? Are you all right?"

"I am fine, Sabine, better than fine."

"Do you want to tell me what happened last night?"

"In time I will, but right now I just needed to be close to you, so I came here to wait for you to wake."

I stretched out. "How long have you been sitting here?"

"A while now. Come, get dressed and let us go find some food."

I pulled back the covers and said, "I am already dressed." We laughed.

Again, sitting around the table in the dining hall were Charles, his brothers, and their sons. I glanced at Charles, who shyly smiled at me.

"Good morning, Guardians. What is the plan for today?"

The words no sooner came out of my mouth than Raiden was in my head.

'*Outside now.*'

I jumped out of my chair along with Rebecca, and we ran full force out the door, finding Raiden and Spirit waiting for us. We climbed up, waiting for them to take off, but they did not move. Then we heard the horn. They were coming, and from the feel of the ground, there were a lot of them.

Charles came busting out the door, shouting orders.

"Roman," was all I said.

"Sabine, you need to stay behind me no matter what."

"Charles, he cannot touch me. You will see."

"He is a great sorcerer. He does not need to touch you," he said as he climbed on his horse.

We rode out to the village to meet them. The guards made their way around them, surrounding Roman and his men. As they rode up, I could not help but notice that this Lord Roman was quite striking in looks; very well dressed and very good looking. I smiled as I thought to myself, '*Too bad I am going to have to kill him*'.

"Charles, old friend, we meet again."

"Roman, I am not your friend."

"That is a pity. If you were my friend, it would make it much more difficult to kill you."

Charles laughed. "Roman, you and I both know you cannot kill me."

We stayed out of his line of sight like Charles had asked, but he knew we were there.

"I have waited a long time to meet Princess Sabine. Are you going to make me wait even longer? I hear from Toddzwga that she is something to behold, a waif of a child with beauty that could blind a man. Are you going to keep her for yourself, Charles? What would Margret have to say about that?"

I could not stop myself; the words just flew out of my mouth. "You know nothing of who I am."

"What is this? The child hides from me? This great warrior who slaughtered my men and bested Toddzwga hides behind others."

Raiden moved forward at that statement.

"I hide from no one."

I heard the murmur from his men, and then I heard him gasp as I came into full view. I looked him in the eyes, and I could see the evil in him. I could feel it to my core.

"You are but a waif of a child," he said in a low voice as he tilted his head to look at me.

Rebecca and Spirit walked up next to me. "You are but a man," she said.

His eyes did not move from mine.

I smiled at him and said, "Your trickery will not work on me, Roman."

"No, I did not believe that it would." He looked at Charles, who was smiling as well. "So, this is the girl my men fear. This is the girl you think can save you."

"Roman, you know as well as I do that you cannot kill me, so your trickery with words does not affect me. This is Sabine of Whispering Wind and Rebecca of Blackmore. Ladies, this is Lord Roman."

"You are always the gentleman, Charles," Roman said in a mocking tone.

"I have a query for you, Roman," I said.

"Why of course, Sabine, but first, I must say that the stories of your beauty do not do you justice. You are quite breathtaking. Your father did right by keeping you hidden. I bet there would have been many a suitor fighting for your hand."

"Your flattery means nothing to me, Roman. Now to my query. What do you think you are doing on my land?"

I felt Raiden twitch under me; something was not right. Rebecca saw my hand reach for my sword, and she did the same.

"Well, you see, young Sabine, I have every intention of taking this land from you, and soon."

I sat there looking into his eyes, not saying a word. I had learned Raiden's body language.

He looked at Rebecca now, saying, "Yes, your mother told me that you were a feisty one. She had said that your sister was just like you. It saddened me when she threw herself off the tower. I really wanted to taste her, but now, here you sit right in front of me." He licked his lips. "I would imagine that you are a fine taste, and it will be glorious to feel your flesh between my lips."

Her reaction was not what I expected, for she laughed right in his face.

"Roman, if my flesh comes anywhere close to your lips, it will be when I kiss you as you die in my arms."

He did not like that response. "Do not think you can throw out threats such as those. You will learn to obey me, and it will bring me great pleasure to bring you to your knees in submission. You will beg for my mercy, and I will not give it."

Charles spoke, "Roman, I would not provoke these women if I were you."

"Oh, Charles, I know of their magic, and you must know that they cannot harm me, just as I cannot harm you. As long as she lives, you live."

I do not know why it happened, but I felt Raiden rear up. It was instinct to raise my sword, and the light was far brighter than I had ever seen. When he landed, the only thing left standing was Roman, and if I was not mistaken, it was fear I saw in his eyes.

"Very good trick, Princess. Is that all you have?"

"You may think you know me, and you may think you are a great sorcerer, but you are nothing compared to me. I was born this way while you were taught. My power is truth, not trickery. Yes, Roman, I see you are wondering if I know the truth, and let me tell you, the knowledge you seek is within me. You will never have it. It was instilled in me from Merlin himself. You cannot kill me, and you will not win. There is but one thing I need from you, and I will get it, then you will be nothing. The death you have cheated for all these years will come on its own. There will be no need for me to kill you. I can see it in your eyes, Roman, you know what I speak is the truth. You know that this will not end with you the victor, and I also know you will try anyway. So just let us know when you are going to return with the rest of your army because as you can see…" I paused, waving my arm. "Mine just might be a bit bigger than yours. I will be right here, so you come back when you are ready."

He was furious. I turned Raiden and started back to the castle. I felt him throw something at me, but I did not look at him.

I said, "Is that the best you can do? It did not even touch me. You cannot touch me, Roman."

He turned and rode off.

Charles rode up next to me. "It would not be wise to provoke Roman."

"I know that your intention is to keep me safe, Charles, and I appreciate that, but Roman cannot touch me."

"You have it then?"

I smiled at him. "Yes, Charles, I have it."

He chuckled. "Well then, this is going to get interesting."

"So, I was right all along. You do know everything that we were supposed to figure out?" I asked him.

"Yes, Sabine, though I am the only one who does. Before my father left this world, he instilled in me the rest of the knowledge. Roman was right. He cannot kill me as long as you are alive."

"Well then, it shall be interesting." We both chuckled. "I do not know about you, but I am famished."

"Well, it is my job to keep you safe, and that includes keeping you fed. To the dining hall it is."

We were all sitting around the table when Richard came into the room. He did not wait for the conversation to end before saying. "Would someone please explain to me what happened out there? Who are you people?"

"Richard, you would do well to mind your manners."

"Excuse me, Father, but what I saw out there was nothing short of trickery. I do not understand how you have managed to entwine our lives with these witches, or how you could betray my mother by spending the night alone with this one." He pointed to Rebecca.

I saw Charles' reaction on his face, but it was Rebecca who jumped out of her chair and answered him.

"I know you are Charles' first born son, and I may be out of line, but let me tell you a thing or two, you little fool. You know nothing of who I am or who we are. You should be on your knees in front of me. I am Princess Rebecca of Blackmore, and you have shown me a great dishonor by even being in my presence without showing respect. I could cut your head off for that alone.

"Apparently your father has chosen not to fill you in on all the details of what is happening here, and if he did, then you are not intelligent enough or mature enough to understand it. Either that or you are a typical man who thinks that women are beneath him. Well, I feel it my duty to inform you that you would be wrong on all accounts. I can, and I will if you would like, best you. I have been wielding a sword long before you were ever thought of and trust me when I tell you that it was your father who taught me.

"If you want to believe that we are witches, you should be very worried right about now. The fact that you are your father's son means nothing to me. If I were a witch, you would not be standing here accusing me and your father of betraying your mother. My virtue is still intact, as is your father's honor. If you knew anything about life and love, or even trust, then you would know that even though I love your father and your father loves me, he is bound by marriage to your mother. He is an honorable man, and he would never dishonor your mother as you have just dishonored him. I do not care what you think of me, but you will show him the respect he deserves, or I will show you just how good I am. I do not have a problem with putting you on the ground."

She did not wait for him to respond. I do not think he could have responded, but Rebecca walked out of the room, leaving him standing there with a very red face. I could not stop the giggle as it escaped.

"Charles, perhaps you should explain to Richard."

"I believe that Rebecca has already done that. Richard, you are out of line, and this manner of behavior is unacceptable."

I did not want to watch him be reprimanded by his father, so I left as well to find Rebecca. She was in my room walking back and forth and talking to herself.

"Can you believe that little fool?"

"Well, he did make a good argument. You did spend the night with his father."

She stopped walking and looked at me, and I could see in her eyes that her mood was softening.

"Oh, Sabine, it was wonderful. We talked most of night, and it felt so good to wake in his arms."

"I am sure that it did."

"His kisses are the same as they were when we left him."

"Rebecca, he is someone else's husband. You should not be kissing him."

"It was not like that. We were just talking and laughing, and he told how he met Margret and how he felt when Richard was born. I started to cry because I realized that it should have been me that he shared those feelings with, and I think he kissed me to make me feel better. I cannot stop how I feel about him, Sabine. I still love him, and he loves me."

"Oh, I know the feelings you share. I have them still for Jared. Rebecca, this is not a good idea. You do know that, do you not? I mean, when this is over, he will go back to Margret while we remain here."

"I know this in my mind, but my heart keeps telling my mind it does not matter. Sabine, what if we do not win? What then?"

"What if we do win? What then?"

"I know we are going to win, so I decided when I woke this morning in his arms that I am going to enjoy this time. Either way, I will have to say goodbye to him."

"I suppose that is a good way to look at it."

She hugged me. "I knew you would understand."

I laughed. "I do not understand either of you, but I do understand how you feel. Now I am going to find Blake as we have a few things to discuss."

"Discuss? Are you rethinking your feelings for him?"

"No, but while we were at the cottage, he was in my room when I woke."

"I know. I had him lift you from the tub and put you in bed. I covered you with a blanket before I let him in the room."

"Yes, I know, and thank you for that, but when I woke, I sat up in bed. The blanket fell away, and Blake saw me again. He made a comment before I asked him to leave."

"What did he say?"

"He said, 'You are still as beautiful as were all those years ago,' and I need to address this."

"He still has feelings for you after all these years."

"I think you may be right, but his wife has been gone for ten years now, so perhaps he is just lonely."

"Or perhaps he is like Charles and me."

"I do not know, but either way, I have to stop this. I do not feel the same toward him."

"Well, good luck. I think I am going to take a rest. Come find me when you get done. Better yet, do you mind if I sleep here?"

I smiled at her. "No, I do not mind. I will be back soon." I hugged her and left to find Blake.

As I wondered through the courtyard, I could hear the murmurs of the men. When I reached the barracks, the two men standing by the door bowed to me.

"Princess, how can we help you?"

"You can start by not bowing to me, and my name is Sabine, not Princess."

"Yes, my lady."

"I would like to speak to Blake. Would you be so kind as to see if he is available?"

One of the men entered the barracks, and it took a few minutes before Blake came out.

"Sabine, is everything all right?"

"Everything is fine. Would you walk with me? I think we have a few things to talk about."

"Of course." He turned to one of the men and said, "If anyone needs me, tell them they will have to wait for my return."

"Yes, sir."

"Come," he said as he put his arm out for me to take, but I did not take it.

I just proceeded to walk toward the courtyard. We were at the main gates to the castle before I started talking again.

"Blake, while we were at the village, you were waiting in my room when I woke. Again, you saw me with nothing on, which I do not like, but it was the comment that you made and the fact that you still seem to watch over me as you do. I am not comfortable with this obsession you seem to have to be so protective of me."

It took him a few moments to answer me. "Sabine, I know that you must have an inkling of my feelings for you. I am in love with you. I have been for a very long time. I know you do not feel the same for me, but as with Charles and Rebecca, I cannot stop how I feel."

"No, I suppose you cannot. You must understand, however, that I do not return those feelings."

"That is what I wished to discuss with you that day. Sabine, after all the time we spent with one another, there has to be at least something you feel for me."

"I do have feelings for you, Blake, feelings of respect, gratitude, and friendship, but that is all. I do not love you in the manner in which you love me, or at least think you love me. I do not want you to believe that there is something more from me. I value your friendship. I love that I can depend on you, and I trust you to always be there for me. If that is love, then yes, I do love you, but I am not in love with you. I just feel for you as I do my brother."

He stayed quiet for a bit while we walked, looking at me from time to time, though I could not read his eyes. After a while, he stopped and turned to me.

"Sabine, I understand what you are saying to me, and perhaps it is the reality that you have depended on me to protect you that I have been misled by my own emotions, but I give you my word that I shall not cross that line again. I will believe that your need for me and your vulnerability in all of this, and especially your trust that I will always be there for you, is not you returning my love for you. Keep in mind, however, that I cannot change how I feel, but I will not expect you to feel anything more than what you do. I will not fail you."

"Thank you, Blake. I am forever in your debt for all that you have given up for me. You shall always be in my heart and in my life, and I do need you more now than I did before."

He smiled. "As I need you. I want to say this to you, and when I am done, I will not say it again. Your beauty takes my breath away. The fact that you do not know just how beautiful you are makes you that much more. You are so innocent, and I am honored that I am a part of your life. I will do everything in my power to see you to the end of this, and when it is over, I will look forward to sharing life with you as your humble servant and friend."

I could not stop myself; I threw my arms around his neck and hugged him, and the tears just fell out of my eyes. "Thank you so much, Blake. I needed to hear that. I needed to know that I will have you forever, however long that may be."

He held me while I cried standing there in the road. All the emotions that ran through me ranged from fear to gratitude, and to be honest, it felt good to be held. It felt good to feel his breath on my neck, and it felt good to feel the warmth of another. We stood there in our embrace for a very long time. I was sure that those passing by wondered what was going on.

I kept my face buried in his neck so no one could see me crying. His arms did not fail me when I lost control. My sobs finally came under my control, and his arms loosened a bit, but he did not let me go, not until he felt me pull away. He put his hand on my chin and tilted my face up to his. With his thumb, he wiped the tears from my cheek, and without any warning, his lips were on mine.

I was so taken by surprise that I did nothing. I just let him kiss me. I let him lead my mouth with his. When he slipped the tip of his tongue in to gently mix with mine, my mind went blank, and my knees went weak. His arm tightened around my waist. I felt myself kissing him back. My hand reached up to touch his face, and the kiss deepened. Jared had never kissed me like this. My breathing started to come in short spurts, as did Blake's. The feelings that worked through my body were feelings I had never known. I felt like I was numb and at the same time felt tiny prickles all over. If he had let me go, I would literally have fallen to the ground. My legs were wobbly, my chest racing and pounding. I felt alive like I had never felt before. *What was happening to me? Why was I enjoying his kiss so much?* I did not want to stop, so I pulled him as close to me as possible.

He stood straight and lifted me off the ground, and my instinct was to wrap my legs around him. I had no control over my body. No matter what my mind tried to tell me, my body stopped it from working, from thinking. Our mouths did not part for a very long time. I found myself not wanting the kiss to ever stop; it was magnificent to feel that way. His hand holding my head, his fingers in my hair, his body pressed against mine, I wanted to crawl inside of him. I think he sensed my hunger to do just that, and our kiss felt as if it was coming to an end. I put my feet back on the ground just as our lips parted. He put his forehead on mine, and in a whispered husky voice, he said, "I love you, Sabine."

We stood there head to head with our eyes closed. I did not know what to say. I did not know if I could even move. It was Blake's son Gerald who caused us to lose contact, when he said.

"Excuse me, Father, but Uncle wishes to speak to you in the dining hall."

"Thank you, Gerald. Tell your uncle I will be with him shortly."

"Yes, sir," he responded and walked away.

"Are you going to be all right if I let you go?"

I could not speak so I just nodded. His embrace slowly loosened around me. As his hands slid off my waist, his thumbs gently brushed against my chest, sending a blaze of feelings throughout my body. I could not take my eyes off his. Somehow, they had changed; I did not see in them the man I saw before, but rather a tenderness that I had not known from Blake.

"I must go and see what Charles wants, although I can guess." He smiled at me. "Are you sure you will be all right?"

Not being able to find my voice, I just smiled at him and nodded.

He smiled back and walked away, my eyes following him. When he reached the gate, he stopped and turned to face me. There were no words from him, but I knew what he wanted to say. He paused for a minute and then continued on. I could not move, nor did I want to move. I closed my eyes, searching for that feeling, for I did not want it to end. I stood in the road for quite some time, feeling eyes upon me. I opened my eyes, but there was no one in sight. *'I should not be here alone.'* Somehow, I made my feet move, and by the time I reached the gate, I could hear them shouting at one another. I jerked my head toward the front of the castle, noticing the voices were coming from just inside the door. There were a few men standing there; I recognized Gerald and Richard among them.

As I walked up, I ask Gerald, "What is going on in there?"

He looked at me as if I was a ghost. "My father and uncle are fighting about you," he said matter of fact, as if I should know.

I pushed through them and opened the door to hear Charles say, "You will not go near her again. Is that understood?"

I do not know where the anger came from, but my mouth opened as I made my way between them.

"I am not sure what this is about, but I can guess. Charles, as I have reminded you on many occasions, you are not my father, nor are you my husband. You have no say over what I do."

"It is forbidden!" He shouted.

I must really have lost my mind because I burst into giggles. "Forbidden? Who are you to say what is forbidden? Have you gained some kind of control over my life that I was not aware of?"

"Sabine, you are but a child," was all that I allowed out of his mouth before my anger took control. Before I knew what was happening, he was lying flat on his back.

"For the final time in this life," I said and then shouted, "I am not a child! You do not control me!" I walked away.

Halfway up the grand staircase, I heard him say, "Well, you sure are acting like one."

I spun around and ran down the stairs to face him.

"You want to see me act like a child, Charles? Then you continue to treat me as one. You have no right to speak to your brother in this manner, and you sure do not have the right to pose your judgments on me or anyone else. How many lines have you crossed here? How many times is it acceptable for you to do one thing then FORBID others to do them? Do you not believe that you are holding double standards, Charles, or is Rebecca less valuable than I am?"

He stood there glaring at me. I knew he was angry, but I also knew I was right, as did he. There was nothing more said. He spun on his heels and walked out, slamming the giant door against the wall.

I turned to face Blake then. "I do not even know what to say to you."

I ran up the stairs and went to my parents' room, slamming the door and bolting it behind me. I did not want to talk. I was so confused about what had taken place on that road that I threw myself on the bed. To escape my mind, I went to sleep.

I had no knowledge of how long I was there, but Raiden speaking in my mind woke me.

'Where are you?'

'I am here. I am safe.'

I opened my eyes to realize that the dark of night had come. There was no light coming from the windows. I got up and felt my way across the room, and when I opened the door, it was darker still in the halls. I kept my hand to the wall and followed it to the main hall. At least I could focus now that I could hear voices. As I turned the corner at the top of the stairs, I heard my name. They were looking for me. I was sure that Charles was in an uproar. I started down the stairs, not looking where I was going, and my foot caught on the rug. The next thing I heard was Rebecca scream as I tumbled head over foot down the grand staircase, landing face down on the floor below. Darkness engulfed me.

Days had passed while I lay asleep. So many things were shown to me in visions in my mind, and everything I wondered about was made clear. Everything I was unsure of was shown to me. I could feel my body coming back to me. My eyes fluttered, and I heard myself say his name. I do not know why I was asking for Charles, but I heard him. He was with me.

I heard myself say, "I need you."

My body shifted as if someone next to me had moved away. My eyes opened, but I saw no light, so I closed them again. Was my mind playing tricks on me? I opened them again, but nothing, though I could sense people in the room, I could hear them breathing. I could taste the blood. *'Blood? Why is there blood?'* Then I heard Raiden.

'Do not be frightened. Trust that this is what needs to be.'

'I cannot see.'

'You will again. There is more you need to learn now. Trust.'

Then he was gone. I reached out to feel what was around me, and a hand grasped mine, soft and delicate.

"Rebecca, I cannot see. My vision is gone."

"I am right here. I will not leave you."

"I need to be alone with Charles. Do not go far."

I could feel her tension as she let go of my hand. I felt her weight lift off the bed, as well as the weight of another.

"Blake," I whispered as my other hand reached for him.

The minute we made contact; my skin felt like it was on fire. I pulled him close to me with no trouble. I could feel his face next to mine, and I whispered in his ear, "Do not leave me. When I am done with Charles, I need you."

He whispered back, "I will never leave you."

I felt him pull away. I sensed them all leave, and then Charles sat next to me, holding my hand.

"I am so sorry for reacting the way I did. I think I was in shock at seeing you and Blake on the road."

"No, Charles, it is I who is sorry. I know now why. I must stay pure in order to complete this. Rebecca and I must both stay pure. It is why my father died before I came of age, to keep me pure. I understand now. Jared needed to be removed from my life. We would have crossed the line, and it would not have been of my own free will. The witch knew that I could not achieve my task if I was not pure. I know everything now." I felt his body relax. "I do not know what happened in the road. I broke down and he held me while I cried. I told him that I do not love him, and he understood, but when he kissed me, it was like nothing I have ever felt before, Charles. When I touch him, it is like I am on fire."

He chuckled a little. "Yes, unfortunately I know exactly how you feel. That is what I feel when I am with Rebecca."

"Charles, I am fearful that it is not real. If we are to be pure, could this be trickery of some sort to make sure we are not?"

"I feel the same, Sabine, and that is why I was so angry with Blake."

"Charles, please put your trust in me. My sight is gone because there is something left for me to learn. Raiden told me to trust, so I must trust."

"I will not fail you again. I am here, and I will not leave you."

"Thank you, but I am going to have to ask you to leave me now and send Blake to me. Trust in me that I will remain pure."

"Sabine, I am a man with honor, as is my brother. It is not you I do not trust. If there is trickery about, then it is me and my brother who should not be trusted."

I could not help but laugh. "Charles, I can best you even without my sight. Do you believe I could not best your brother?"

He chuckled. "I would hope so."

He let go of my hand, and I felt him rise from the bed, but what I noticed was his presence leave and be replaced with Blake's; two significant differences.

"Will you come and sit with me," I said to him while I sat up and crossed my legs in front of me.

I felt him come closer, and then I felt his weight as he climbed on my bed and sat in front of me, his knees touching mine. I felt his hands move to mine, but I moved them out of the way and up to his face. I felt the tension pulsing through his body.

"Shhh, it is all right. I am fine," I told him.

When he went to speak, I placed my thumb gently on his lips to silence him. I felt every part of his face; his eyes, the length of his nose, his cheeks, his jaw, and his lips. He sat there motionless while I memorized him with my hands. When I finished, I pulled his face to mine and kissed him. I needed to know if the feeling blazing through my body was real. I did as he had in the road and gently moved my tongue to feel his lips, sliding it across first the top and then the bottom. I felt the murmur coming from his chest before I heard it. He let me explore his lips until I was ready to part them. I did what he did and separated them just a little to make sure it was acceptable to do so. As I did for him, he opened them and gently touched my tongue with his. Just as when in the road, my body reacted to this. I wanted to crawl inside of him; I could not get close enough. I felt my body move instinctively toward his, and my legs went around him as I slid myself on top of him. I was sitting on his lap with my legs wrapped around his waist, my chest pressed against his, and with our mouths in a luscious dance. Our kiss slowly ended, and we pulled apart breathless.

"I now know why Charles was so angry with you. It was not just you he was angry with, but also himself."

"Why did you kiss me again?"

"Because I needed to know if it was just in that moment that I felt the way I did. I was emotional and thought I might have needed the closeness."

"And now?"

"Now I am more confused than I was before. I have lost my sight, Blake. I cannot see you." I felt him tense. "Do not be fearful. It is the way it must be. While I was sleeping, I had visions if you will. I know why Charles reacted the way he did. I know why Jared had to be removed from my life. I need to remain pure, and Charles is fearful that we may cross a line. Jared would have compromised my virtue. He would not have stopped until he achieved his goal. That is what the witch did to him. She knows as well as Roman does that we need to stay pure. Charles believes that there is some sort of trickery being had on us by Roman, perhaps even by the witch, to enhance our emotions. I do not know if he is correct, but we must be careful. He believes that this is what has him tied in knots about Rebecca."

"Sabine, you must trust in me to never put you in that position. I am a man of honor, and to take from you your virtue without making you my wife first would not even be a choice for me. I have not been with a woman in that manner since my wife died, and I had not been before her either. If this is a manner of trickery, then these feelings we are having will be gone when this ends."

"I need to apologize to you for my behavior. I am sorry for discarding your feelings for me, and I am sorry for leading you into believing that I have feelings for you. I do not know what is happening to me. When Jared and I shared our kisses like this, I never felt the way I do when you touch me. My skin feels like it is on fire, yet I cannot get close enough to you. An overwhelming feeling of loss fills me when you walk away from me. I have never felt feelings like this, and right now, I cannot trust that they are real. I do however trust in you to keep my virtue intact. We cannot fail. If we do, we will never know if this is real or if this is trickery." I leaned forward and whispered in his ear, "And I want to kiss you again and again. I want to feel your body next to mine, and I want to smell you and taste you. I am fearful that I cannot get enough of you." I leaned back away from him. "I cannot trust those feelings."

He leaned into my neck and whispered, "I know you do not have knowledge of the union between a man and a woman, but I do. Sabine, what I feel for you is already beyond the feeling of that very union. I promise you, no matter what the outcome, I will not cross that line, just please do not stop kissing me."

As he pulled away, his lips brushed my cheek and set it ablaze. His lips found mine, and it was like never before. I do not know how long we shared our mouths with one another, but for me, it was not long enough. I could however sense Rebecca outside, and she was getting tense. I pulled away from him and rested my forehead on his.

Breathlessly he said, "Is it wrong to want more of you?"

"Yes, Blake, it is. We need to stay focused. We cannot do this again. We cannot take this temptation any further. If these feelings are real, if this is what is supposed to be, then it will still be when we have finished this."

"Well, if this is the last time that I can kiss you..."

He pulled me to his chest and covered my mouth with his, the soft and gentle thrusts of his tongue in my mouth. Feeling the heat of his breath caused me to press harder against him. We were losing control of ourselves. His hands came to my sides, and he gently moved me from his lap, pulling away from me.

"We cannot cross this line, Sabine. This is not you. This is not who you are, nor is it who I am. This is trickery all right. I would never take such liberties with you. We must wait. No matter what this turns out to be, I will be respectful of your decision when this is finished."

My head was spinning. I could not speak. I felt him shift on the bed and stand. I reached up to touch him, and he responded.

"You will always be here?"

"I will never leave you."

I nodded. He let go of my hand, and I could feel him moving away from me. I heard the door open, and a different energy came into the room; Rebecca. She was moving quickly, and I felt her slam against me before she ever touched me.

"I thought you were dead, lying there on the floor. Do you have any idea how long I have sat here, holding your hand and willing you to wake up? I could feel everything you felt. I could not let go of you." She leaned in. "I saw everything you saw."

"Rebecca, I have lost my sight."

"You cannot see me?"

"Not with my eyes, but I can with my mind. We have much to talk about, but I need you to do something for me."

"Anything you need I shall do."

"Gather up Charles and his brothers, as well as you, Raiden, and Spirit. Have everyone stand next to one another in the great hall. Tell them not to speak to me, then come and get me and help me to the stairs. I need to see something. Can you do that for me?"

"Will you tell me why you were kissing Blake in the road?"

I laughed. "I will even tell you why I was just kissing him in this bed."

I could see the smile on her face well, I could feel her energy change.

"You have a deal. I will be back shortly."

I felt her move across the room and out the door, and then I heard her talking to Charles. I felt them move anyway from me. A few moments later, I felt Rebecca coming down the hall long before I heard her.

"Are you ready?"

I reached out for her hand, and she helped me out into the hall.

"I want to see if I can walk on my own, but stay close to me."

I let go of her hand. Navigating down the hallway was easy. Everything seemed to have an energy to it; either that or I was just remembering where everything was placed. When I reached the stairs, I stopped reached out for Rebecca's hand, and she told me when to step.

"Take me halfway down and then you go join everyone on the floor."

I sat down and felt her as she moved away. I could feel the energy coming at me in waves.

"I asked you all to stand here for a reason. Something is happening to me, and I need to see if I am correct. I think I can tell who each of you are, so please do not say a word. If I am right, would you please bend to your knees? All right, from right to left Aidan. I felt him move. James." I giggled. "Raiden, and you do not need to bend to your knees." I felt him raise his hoof before I heard it hit the floor. "Next would be Charles, then Steven, Rebecca, Joseph, Spirit, and Edward? Where is Blake?"

"Sabine, how did you do that? How did you know Blake was not here?"

"I am not sure how. It is like each of you has a different energy. Everything has a different energy. Rebecca, would you get my sword for me? I want to try something."

I felt her rushing toward me and then past me.

"Charles, will you please help me down the stairs? I am unsure of their energy, perhaps because there are so many of them."

I felt Rebecca return.

"Good, you brought yours as well."

She stopped. "How did you know that?"

I reached out for my sword, noting that its energy was the most powerful.

"I am not sure, but if I hit someone with my sword, I might hurt them. Only you can test this with me." She handed me my sword. "I want you to fight with me, like we used to on the plain."

"Sabine, I am not so sure this is a good idea." I heard Charles say as I felt his energy change, becoming even more tense than usual.

"Relax, Charles, for she will not hurt me. You ready, Rebecca?"

I already knew the answer as she was bouncing all over the place. I felt her sword rise and strike down, and I met it with mine. Time and time again she swung, and each time I matched her.

"Now it is my turn. You ready?"

"More than ready. Let us see if you can find me."

"Oh, I will find you," I said as I swung and hit her sword.

We continued for some time. It felt good to fight with her; we had not done it for so long. I felt the energy of others coming into the grand hall. Soon the place was full of men, and I heard Richard say to his father.

"What is this quarrel about? Did Sabine make a move on you?" He then laughed.

I dropped my sword and turned to his energy. "Would you care to go a round, Richard, or are you afraid of hurting a girl?"

"I am not afraid of a girl, especially one as tiny as you," he said as he removed his jacket.

"Sabine, he is my son."

"Do not be fearful, Charles. I will only give him what he is due."

Richard laughed. "We shall see about that."

"Richard, I would not be so quick to judge her."

"Father, she is but a waif of a girl. Without her horse, she is nothing. We have all seen what that horse can do."

"His name is Raiden. Charles, do I have your permission to show him what I am made of?"

He laughed. "Indeed, you do, Sabine. Feel free to put my arrogant son in his place."

Richard put his hand on his chest and said, "Father, it pains me to think you believe I cannot best a girl at swords."

I felt him draw his sword. "Richard," I said.

"Going to beg for mercy already, Sabine?"

"No, I was actually going to put forth a little wager."

"Whatever you choose, but choose wisely, for you are going to lose."

It was then that I felt Blake rushing toward me. "Blake, how nice of you to join us," I said, stopping him dead in his tracks.

"What do you think you are doing, Richard? Did your father not tell you?"

I felt Charles reach over and touch Blake's arm and then shake his head no. Blake stood still.

"Your wager, Princess?"

"If I best you at swords, how about you and me have a go at some hand to hand combat?"

I felt him look away toward Charles, and Charles nodded.

"My father seems to think that would be a good wager, though I do not know why. If I win, then you have to refer to me as the almighty Richard for seven days' time."

"And if I win both, then you will stop your arrogant behavior and treat me with respect."

"Considering that will never happen, if my father taught me right. You gain respect, not demand it, and so far, you have done nothing to gain it, so you are on. Oh, this is going to be too easy," he said as he raised his sword and charged me.

He was such a young and arrogant man. I found great pleasure in countering him and dropping him to his knees on my first blow, my sword never flickering. I felt his energy change, telling me he was not so sure of himself now. I swung again and again, each blow weakening him. One last blow and down he went.

"So what were you saying?"

I heard Blake whisper to Charles through the laughter of Richard's friends, "How is she doing this?" I could feel Charles shaking his head.

"So it would seem, sweet Richard, that I have won that round. Would you agree to yield?"

I felt the rage in his energy pulse out. "I will yield swords, but you will not win in hand to hand. I am the best of these men."

"Yes, I would imagine with your size and quickness that you are, but the query here would be, are you better than your father?"

"No man is better than my father, or quicker."

"Well then, with that said, are you ready?"

"Father, do I have your permission to handle Sabine?"

Charles chuckled, saying, "If you can, then yes you do."

It was quite comical to watch Richard's energy dance around me; I did not turn and follow as it was pointless. I could not see him anyway. I just stood there and felt him. When he reached my back in his ritual dance, as Jared use to dance around the stables, I felt his energy grow. His confidence had risen back up. He thought he had the perfect position, and he lunged. I simply stepped aside and let him fly by me. Spinning around, he lunged again, though this time the energy came shooting from his hands. I felt it going for my neck, so I bent over, catching him at the stomach. I stood up and flipped him onto the floor, turned and jammed my foot to his throat, and then knelt on his chest.

"It would seem, young Richard that you have ended up on your back, making me the winner of this round as well. Is there yet another wager you would care to make with me, a mere girl?"

I stood and began to walk away. I did not expect him to jump up. His energy hit me in the back, but before he did, I turned and grabbed him by the throat and slammed him to the floor.

"The next time you want to cheat and attack me from behind, my suggestion to you, young Richard, is that you think twice about it, because next time I will not be so kind."

I picked up my sword and walked toward Blake's energy. I felt Richard coming long before I heard Charles yell, "RICHARD NO!"

With his sword raised and his heart black with anger, he swung at me. I spun around and slammed my sword into his. Though I could not see it, I could feel that the light was so brilliant that I think everyone in the room stopped breathing. I pushed him with my sword all the way to the wall. My knee came up and caught him in his lower parts. He dropped his sword to the floor, and I pushed mine against his throat.

"Your first mistake was believing that you could best me. Your second was attacking me with anger and fury. I trust you will not make those mistakes again and believe me when I tell you this Richard attack me again out of rage and anger, and it will not matter to me that you are Charles' son or his first born. A little education is in order for you, I believe. It was your father who taught me in hand to hand, and if you were not so arrogant, you might have gotten your facts correct. No man can best your father, but I am not a man, now am I?"

I pushed my sword against his throat one last time and then pulled away.

When I turned, the energy coming from those in the hall was ice cold. They were all frightened, Blake and Charles included. Rebecca was alive and vibrant, however, and I knew she was loving this. I could not help but smile.

Charles was walking toward me. "Thank you for not killing him."

I smiled at him. "I could not do that to you. He needs to be told the truth though, Charles. He holds much anger and contempt toward me. I feel his energy, and it is not good. Edward of Collingwood had the same energy. He will try again, Charles."

"I will see to it that he does not." He continued past me to Richard, telling him, "I would like for you to join me in my quarters. It is time you were informed. You are very lucky to be alive, and I am thankful Sabine is generous."

"She was lucky, is more like it," Richard said.

I turned toward his dark energy. He was still filled with rage and anger.

"Charles, if you do not mind, may I say something?"

"By all means, Sabine."

"Richard, you are filled with anger and rage toward me. May I inquire as to why this is?"

"My whole life I have heard nothing but praise about this Bringer of Peace. My father and uncles have put you on this pedestal, and we grew up hearing the stories of how this person is going to come and bring the land out of dismay and upheaval. My whole life I had to listen to this garbage. They made you some kind of mythical goddess, but you are nothing but a waif of a girl. Look at you. You have the body of a child, yet I am supposed to be grateful that you are going to save us all from Lord Roman? Please, to infer that I am less intelligent than you is an insult to me and to my father, but somewhere, somehow, you have twisted his mind into believing that you are someone we should all fear as well as praise glory for. You want to know what I think. I think my father has secretly been exchanging body fluids with that one, and my mother caught him, so he put you up to this just so he could leave her."

"Rebecca be careful. You have been named a harlot and a home wrecker. Richard, how do you think I just bested you?"

"Luck and magic. Otherwise, you would not have been able to, for I am two times your size."

"And yet your father is three times my size. Well, I cannot change your opinion of me, nor do I care what you think of me. Just let me leave you with this one thing to think about, when I fell down the stairs the other day..."

"A ploy I am sure to gain control of Blake," he interrupted.

"When I fell down the stairs the other day, and when I woke up today, I woke with no sight."

I felt his energy change, and I was done. "Rebecca, will you take me back to my room. I suddenly feel tired."

I could not see Richard's face, but I knew his eyes were on me. I knew he was watching me, and I knew that Charles was furious with his son. I was glad not to be the object of his anger.

CHAPTER TWENTY

Rebecca guided me to my room, and I felt Blake coming up as I climbed into bed.

"Rebecca, would you give me a minute with Blake?"

"Sabine, now I know you have lost your mind. Blake is not here."

"He will be shortly. I can feel his energy coming."

Just as I finished, he knocked on the door. Rebecca got up to open it and said, "I will be right out here." She smiled at Blake as she left the room.

"That was quite the show downstairs. May I inquire as to what you were doing?"

"The boy needed to be taught a lesson."

"A lesson? Sabine, you could have hurt him."

"He attacks me again with such rage, I will not hesitate. He holds contempt for me. He is a very angry young man."

"How did you do that? Did you get your sight back?"

"No, I have not, but where were you?"

"After I left you, I needed to clear my head. It got pretty intense in here. I needed to put myself in place. Sabine, I could have, and probably would have, taken some liberties with you that no man who is not your husband should take. I know how I felt, and I know how you felt to me, and you would not have said no to me. We cannot do that again."

"I know. That is what I wanted to talk to you about. I am sorry for doing what I did to you. I just do not know what has come over me."

"Nor do I. It has got to be Roman."

"Agreed, but even now I feel drawn to you. I feel the need to touch you."

"I feel it as well, but we must do our best to fight against it, however difficult."

I smiled at him. "You find it difficult not to touch me?"

"You have no idea." I felt him smile.

"Blake, I want to tell you something. I can feel your energy. It has a very powerful pull for me. I can see Rebecca's as well, and hers is very much alive. We did a test down stairs. I recognized everyone. Each of you has a certain energy, and I think this is what I am supposed to learn. Rebecca and I drew swords and fought one another. I matched her every swing, and when I swung at her, I did not miss. I could feel her sword coming at me, just as I did with Richard. I could feel his energy pulsing out from within him. That is how I knew he was coming after me that last time."

"When I saw you react, I had hoped you had gained your sight back, but now I see that you have not. This has got to be yet another gift you have."

"I think it is a test."

"A test? How could losing your sight be a test?"

"I am not sure, but how is it that I know who everyone is? I can see your energy. Each of you has a different feel, and my sword is the strangest of them all. It vibrates. Blake, even the furniture and the stone have an energy, as if everything that is not alive is. What else could this be? How else would I be able to fight Roman? I would wager that his energy is far worse than Richard's."

He chuckled as he raised his hand to touch my face. I felt him getting closer and leaned into his hand.

"You are so beautiful. Even without your sight, your eyes are something to behold."

"We cannot do this, Blake. We cannot take this any further."

"It does not mean I do not want you or want to do this."

I felt his lips on mine before he ever touched me. The fire deep inside of me ignited when he touched me. I could not contain myself and pulled him closer to deepen our kiss. His tongue gently trailed along my top lip, then my bottom, and in turn I did the same to him. His tongue gently entered my mouth, sending pulsing emotions through my entire body. His energy changed, becoming much more intense, and it drew me in. My mind wanted nothing more than to be one with him, with his energy; it was soothing, inviting, and most of all it was calming. In his energy I felt at peace. It was Charles clearing his throat that slowed us. I felt Blake change, though he did not pull away as I thought he would. Our kiss slowed and we parted. With his forehead on mine and his eyes closed, he sighed.

"Yes Charles."

"I am not so sure this is the best of ideas."

"It may not be, Charles, but for some strange reason I am finding your brother irresistible. You need not worry, however, for we are well aware of the cost if we move forward with this. We are not even sure what this is, but I just cannot stop myself," I said smiling.

Blake pulled away, and I felt a sort of loss when his contact with me ended.

"I suppose the two of you have a great deal to discuss, and I have some work to do." He reached up to run his finger down my cheek. "I will return."

I grabbed his hand and kissed his fingers, and then he was gone. I got up and walked to the chair by the fire and sat down, and I could feel Charles' eyes on me.

"Come, let us have our talk. I have much to tell you."

"As I do you," he said, sitting down across from me. "First, I want to apologize for Richard and to thank you for not killing him."

I giggled. "Charles, I would not end your son's life."

"You put him in his place that is for sure. He has a whole new respect for you."

"You sure his pride did not get the best of him? I did, after all, best him in front of his friends."

"Yes you did, but you also showed them you are not to be underestimated. He did not know that I trained you or that you had no sight. Would you care to explain how you did what you did?"

"Charles, I am not sure I can explain it. I discovered when I woke that there was some sort of energy in this room. As it turns out it was Blake. Rebecca was here as well, although her energy is much different from everyone else's. That is why I had her line everyone up. Even the furniture has an odd energy, and the stone. It is like everything is alive around me. Raiden told me to trust, so I did, and he was not wrong. I may not have my sight, but I can see you. I can see your energy, and right now you are very tense. Do not worry, Charles. Raiden told me that I needed to learn something, and I think Roman has a plan. While I was sleeping, I had some visions. I know why you were so angry when you saw us on the road. We must remain pure, and you knew this before we went into the cave. That is why you let go of Rebecca and married Margret. Why did you not tell me?"

"Sabine, it is not the easiest thing to speak to a woman about keeping her virtue intact."

"No, I suppose it is not, but Blake and I believe that what is happening between us must be Roman. When he is near, his energy draws me in. I cannot seem to get enough of him. It feels almost like I want to crawl inside of him to feel safe. But when he is not near me, I am fine. I do not think about him like I should if I was in love with him, nor does he, not anymore, not like he used to. So we have figured out that we can stop ourselves, or well, he can. In this instance, I would have to say that Blake is stronger than I am."

"I would think that in this instance, he is more experienced than you are. He would no way cross that line with you unless you were his wife. It would not be proper, and our father raised us well."

"I know that, so we decided that because we know what is going on, or think we know, that we are going to enjoy these feelings while they are here."

"Well, when you decide that you want to be alone, I think someone else should be close by to interrupt you before it goes too far."

"I cannot believe that we are having this conversation, but I could not agree with you more. It was in fact Blake who stopped me, but I cannot trust him to do that again. So what happened with Richard? The energy that was coming from him was dark, Charles, very dark. It would be just like Roman to use your son against you."

"Yes, Joseph and I thought the same thing, so we sent our sons back to the valley. They left right before I came up here."

"Is it safe for them? What if Roman's men are waiting for them?"

"I sent men with them, and Roman will not hurt my son. He fears me, you know."

I felt him smile. "He fears you?"

"Oh yes. To know that no matter what he does, we cannot die. As long as you live, we live."

"That is very interesting news. I forgot he did say that out on the road. Charles, did you send Richard away because you were afraid that I would kill him?"

"Yes and no. I remember what happened when you uncovered the jewels, how we were acting, and I realized when I saw Richard come at you with the intent on killing you how easily he could be influenced. Roman cannot harm us, but he can cause us to harm one another. Like you and Blake all of a sudden finding yourselves with this uncontrollable desire to be with one another, Roman is influencing us to do things we would not ordinarily do. I know you would not harm my son, but I am not naïve enough to think that you would not defend yourself against anyone who poses you a threat."

"This Roman is a pretty powerful sorcerer, huh?"

"More so than Devious, and we all know she was pretty bad."

"I need the jewel on his sword to complete the ritual to end him. I also believe that I am without sight because Roman has something planned. He cannot touch me to cast a spell on me, but he can use the elements to create dust that would blind us all. Perhaps he is planning something like this to try and kill me."

"That would make sense, Sabine, but he cannot kill you."

"If he gains ownership of my sword, I will be helpless, and he can kill me then. I know Raiden would never let that happen, but what concerns me is that it can happen, and if I were Roman, I would do the same thing. So, my test is to be able to see without my sight."

Just as I finished, we heard Steven shouting in the courtyard.

Charles jumped up to look out the window. "Roman is on his way here. I guess now would be a good time to keep you here."

"No, Charles, I need to go. I need to see his energy, so that when I face him I will know where he is."

"All right, but you stay behind me."

I giggled. "Charles, I am not afraid of him, and besides, Raiden would not allow him to hurt me."

We made our way to the courtyard, and it was interesting to see all the energy moving about. Raiden and Rebecca were the most energized. I started toward them both when I felt Blake walking up behind me. I turned to face him.

"Please do not tell me I need to be in my room." I could see the shock on his face in my mind, and I giggled.

"Now why would I say a thing like that? I just wanted to do this."

He wrapped his arms around me, picked me up, and gave me a hug. As his lips brushed against my neck, he whispered in my ear, "Be careful," and then he was gone.

I turned to see Rebecca's energy bouncing all over the place. I shook my head and made my way to Raiden. We made our way to the end of the village and waited for Roman to come. It was so strange to sit with Rebecca behind the seven brothers. Their energies were similar, but each one had a distinctive feel. I felt the ground vibrate as Roman rode up. Looking at Rebecca, I put my hand on my sword, and she did the same. I felt Raiden twitch under me, so I leaned down to his neck.

"I will be fine. I am all right." I felt him nod his head and calm.

"Well, Charles, it would seem you have a bit of prophecy in you to know I was coming and to greet me like this."

"Roman, what do you want? Have you come to give us what we need, or are you here to visit?"

His laughter was genuine and deep. "Visit? Charles, I do not visit. I came here to see the beautiful and lovely Sabine and to check on my future wife, Rebecca of Blackmore. I cannot seem to get that spunky thing out of my mind. Yes, I bet she tastes just as sweet as she looks. You would know, Charles. Tell me what I am missing."

"Roman, you will not get a rise out of me. You are not worth the energy."

Charles' energy was generating at a speedy pace. I knew he was getting angry.

"Lord Roman," Rebecca said as she moved Spirit into his line of sight.

"Ahh, there you are. Have you come to terms with things yet, my sweet Rebecca?"

"I will not engage you in such matters, for I am a Lady. It is beneath me to even think those thoughts."

"But you do, Princess, do you not, of Charles no less." He looked at Charles. "Pity he is married to another."

I could not stand the sound of that man's voice any longer. I moved Raiden up next to Rebecca.

"Roman, what is it that you want?"

"Why, Sabine, how nice to see you," he said with a chuckle.

His energy was black and cold. He knew I was without sight; he knew all along. This would be my test. He moved on his horse, and my eyes followed him.

"As I said before, what is it that you want?"

He was pacing back and forth on his horse, and my eyes did not leave him.

"I was just being a good neighbor. I thought I should come and bring you a welcoming gift."

He did something I was not expecting. He got off his horse. I felt Raiden twitch and knew he was walking right toward me.

"You should stop there, Roman," I said.

He did and tilted his head, looking at me. He raised his hand, as did I with my sword in it. He put his other hand in the air, and that is when I felt the energy from the jewel in his sword. My eyes left his and moved to his sword. It was brilliant, calling me to it.

"I mean you no harm, my sweet Sabine."

I could not stop what happened next. Raiden and Spirit both jumped. When they landed, all was gone except for Roman. His army, his horse, all had been reduced to nothing but ash. My mind could not stop my body as I slid off of Raiden and walked up to face him. Standing in front of him, I came to his chest he was a huge man.

"You have something I need, and I wish for you to give it to me now."

"I seem to be at a disadvantage here. The laws of nature will not allow me to touch you, yet you can do this," he waved his arm, "to me and my army. I was sure by now that your purity would be gone, but I can see that I was mistaken."

I felt him look at Blake. "Guardian, you are less of a man than most. With a woman of such beauty right there in front of you, yet you cannot follow through. Such a shame. It is no wonder your wife left you."

Roman's energy changed; he was getting nervous.

"I have been preparing myself for a great battle with you, a war of sorts, with all these men standing behind me ready to give their lives to protect me. You bring your men here, knowing what I will do to them, but yet you bring them anyway. I know there are more, Roman, and if you think that because I am off my horse that you are safe, you are wrong. My magic has been instilled in me from my birth. I did not learn this, as you have with your spells. Raiden is not where my magic comes from, and you know this, so why are you here facing me, knowing I am going to take what I want from you?"

"The battle, my dear child, is not a battle of war, but a battle of good and evil. It is a battle for this very land you stand on. It is a battle of wits and challenges, of courage and of strength. This battle, my child, is between you and I. I bring my men here so you can turn them to ash to keep them from interfering. I must be the one to end your life, and they want it so badly. Your men, the seven brothers will stand down. The rest I might have to deal with."

"Well, if this battle is between you and me, then perhaps we should get on with it."

"What? Here? Now? What kind of gentleman would I be if I took advantage of a sightless child?"

Charles' laughter startled even me. "Roman, you should be very careful what you wish for."

I felt Blake move. "Stay where you are, Blake. This is not your fight," I said softly, never moving my eyes from Roman's. "He does not intimidate me."

With no warning, his energy blew out from him. I felt it go around me and figured he must be casting a spell. He was fast, but not as fast as me. His sword was in his hand and cutting through the air. When it connected with mine, I felt it hard through my arms; it nearly knocked me back.

"So it will be like this. You are frightened, Roman. You know your life will end soon. I can feel your fear," I said as I raised my sword.

Swing after swing, he came at me, but not once did he find fault in my defense. His energy was weakening, his body tiring. It was my opportunity to take him down. I spun around with my sword coming down hard on his, and the light was blinding. I felt Rebecca coming up behind me.

"No, you must not interfere. "

I screamed at her as I swung again and again. Roman was moving backwards. He was going to run. I just kept hitting him down, and though he stumbled, I did not lunge at him. I knew he was waiting for me to think I had the upper hand. He may not have been able to touch me, but his sword could. He scrambled to his feet and swung again. I caught his sword and slammed it to the ground, breaking it in half. His energy froze. He dropped the hilt and turned to run. I dropped to my knees and slammed the hilt of my sword into the ground. What happened after that was spectacular. The ground shook, and wind started to blow, moving very quickly. I could feel things swirling around me, flying past me, and then the wind engulfed Roman. I heard his screams as he was tossed around in the circular funnel of air and wind. Then just as it began, it stopped. Roman was bound by the elements, unable to move. His energy had been captured by the elements of magic, the very magic that lived in this land. I reached for the hilt of his sword, for the glowing energy that called to me. The jewel fell into my hand, and just as my sight was lost, it was regained. I could see him. I could see the fear. Rebecca was behind me, and together we went to face him.

"You see, Roman, you were never going to win. Do you not understand truth? I am truth. I am this land. I was born here. I was made here. I am truth."

"You think that you can hold me here?"

"I am not doing anything to you. The land has a hold of you. This place, Whispering Wind, is done with you and you will stay here for the rest of your days. You will never leave this spot. You are bound now with this land. You were the final piece to all of this. You are the balance of evil and good. In order for the land to settle, it must own you and consume you."

"They will find her, your fourth element. She will not survive."

"You will remain here for all time. When I finish this, you will become one with this land."

I turned and walked away. I climbed on Raiden, leaned into him, and said, "Take me home."

In a blink, I was in front of the castle. Climbing down, I told him, "Wait here. I will be right back."

I ran into the castle to my father's study. I found a quill and some paper and wrote a note to Juliana.

My Love,

The time is now. Leave the valley with Raiden. He will bring you to me. Tell Westin I will see him soon. Do not look back, just lean into him and ride.

Love

Sabine

I folded the note and ran back to Raiden, tucking it into his bridal. "I need for you to go and get Juliana. It is time to end this."

'No, the time is not now.'

"I have what I need."

The time is not now.'

I stood there looking into his eye. What was he saying? "What did I miss?"

My mind searched for all the pieces, but it was done. I had the last jewel.

'Read your father's journal. The time is not now.'

I took the note and slipped it into my bodice. Rebecca, Charles, and Blake came riding up. I could feel his energy still. I could not help but wonder why that was; if Roman had cast some spell over the kingdom, then would it not be broken when he was captured? It did not matter right then. I needed to get to my father's journal. It was the only thing I took with us from the cave.

"Charles, I need to take Rebecca and go someplace. Can I trust you not to search for us? There are still things we need to do. I will not leave the castle."

I felt Blake's energy shift, so I turned to look at him.

"I have gained my sight back. When I am finished, I would like to find you. I think we need to talk."

"I will be in the barracks."

"Charles?"

"You have my word, just please do not leave the castle."

"I give you my word."

I reached out for Rebecca's hand and pulled her through the castle behind me. I went from this room to that room to at least three different rooms, just in case someone was watching us, before going into my father's study. I shut the door and bolted it, then unbolted it. If someone tried it, they would know we were in here. Rebecca stood there looking at me with a smile on her face.

"What?"

"You still feel him, do you not?"

"Rebecca, this is not the time, but yes, I do. Could you get the door?"

She rushed over and clicked the drawer, and in we went.

"Why are we back in here? Should we not be sending Raiden to get Juliana?"

"He will not go. He said it was not time yet, that we needed to read the journal."

We sat on the floor with our backs to the table, flipping through page after page, through all the pages we had already read. When I turned the last page, I looked at Rebecca.

"There is nothing more here. What are we missing?"

"I am not sure. Here, let me look, "she said, taking the journal from me.

I leaned my head against the desk. "I thought for sure that I would not feel Blake when we put an end to Roman."

"Well, Roman is not ended, so to speak. He is more captured, like Devious was, so it would be safe to assume his trickery or whatever would still be present. Sabine, have you not given thought to the idea that you really are attracted to him?"

"No, I have not. He is not my match, Rebecca. He is not my happiness. I do not feel it like I think I should. I only feel it when I am near him. When he is away, I feel nothing."

"Hey, look at this." She was looking at the back of the journal.

I looked over, reaching out to touch the leather. "It feels like something is written on it."

"Maybe you can use your new magic powers to read what it says," she said and giggled.

"It does not work that way, but I wonder if we do this…"

I reached over and took the candle and held it up to the leather. The closer the flame got, the darker the words turned.

"Can you read it?"

'When the light of the day turns to the dark of the night'

"What does that mean?"

"I have no idea. I wish we could ride. I really need to just be free for a while."

"Well, Roman, is trapped. He cannot harm us without his magic sword, and you fixed that."

I could not help but smile as I reached into my bodice and took out the jewel.

"You should hide that somewhere."

"I need to talk to Raiden. I need to know what this means," I said, tapping the journal.

We made our way out of the secret room and back into the courtyard. I found Raiden standing by the fountain.

"We need to talk," I told him. I looked around to see if anyone was watching. "I found the writing, but I have no idea what it means, and seeing as how you are who you are, and you sent me to find it, you probably know what it means. Care to explain it to me?"

His ears started to twitch. I knew this feeling all too well, so I climbed up and yelled for Rebecca. She was already on her way with Spirit. I leaned in to his ear, whispering, "Do not think this is over." Then I turned and yelled, "Charles, Blake, we have company."

They came riding up with the brothers and about a hundred men or so.

"Did our little army get smaller?" I asked.

Charles laughed. "No, they are all here. You just cannot see them."

"Oh, I see... sneaky."

We smiled and rode to the end of the village, where we found about a hundred men or so riding up and demanding that we release Roman.

"Considering we did not put him in there, we cannot release him."

The man in the lead position looked me up and down.

"The infamous Princess Sabine of Whispering Wind," he said and then laughed. "Roman and Toddzwga are afraid of this child." he said as he turned his head to talk to his men. "So, tell me child if you did not put our master in this contraption, then who did?"

Charles spoke, "You should take care in the words you use when you are talking to her."

"You do not frighten me, Charles. I am well aware of this child's magic. Toddzwga refuses to return here." He then noticed Roman's sword on the ground. "Was this your doing, Charles?" He pointed his head toward the sword.

Charles chuckled. "I could only wish that I had the pleasure of taking Roman's sword from him, but I am afraid that honor goes to Sabine."

The man just sat there staring at me and not saying a word. His energy was dark like Roman's. My hand moved to my sword.

"Are you going to draw on me, child?"

I did not answer him; I just stared back at him. He shifted on his horse, and I drew my sword.

"You can try and free your master, but you will not succeed, and when you are finished, you will leave my kingdom and not return again. If you do, you will suffer the fate of those who have come before you."

I lifted my sword and pointed the end to the piles of ash beneath them.

"Do you think your little army can stop us?"

"It is you who believes my army is little, but to be truthful, I do not need them."

I felt Raiden twitch beneath me. I saw in this man's eyes the anger that Roman had. He drew his sword and moved forward. Raiden and Spirit rose, and he was gone instantly. The other men moved back.

"Leave my kingdom or suffer the same fate."

I heard Blake chuckle as they turned on their horses and rode off. Roman was yelling at them to stop and to free him. I smiled at him, and Rebecca blew him a kiss, saying, "Remember what I said, Roman. You will taste my flesh as you take your last breath."

On our way back to the castle, I heard him in my head.

There is more.'

I knew he must be talking about the journal.

"Rebecca, there is more to this. Would you accompany me once again?"

She looked at me and tilted her head. "So formal, Sabine? You know I would follow you to the ends of the earth." She laughed. "Oh yeah, I already did that. Whatever you need."

We went back to the secret room. "Raiden said there was more."

She opened the book, and I got the candle. I held it up to the leather while Rebecca read it out loud.

When the ground is ripe
At midday you will find

The time will be right'

"So what does that mean?"

"I am not sure, but I believe that whatever we are supposed to do happens on the day that the fields would be harvested and at midday."

"So when do the fields get harvested?"

"I am not sure. Perhaps Charles knows."

"Sabine, can I tell you something?"

"Rebecca, you can tell me anything. You are my sister."

"Well, Charles and I nearly crossed that line everyone keeps talking about. I think what is happening to you and Blake is happening to me and Charles as well."

I was shocked. "Charles is married, Rebecca."

"I know, but neither one of us could stop it. It was in fact Spirit who entered my mind and told me to stop." She put her head down. "I had most of my clothes off, as did he."

"Are you all right? What was it like?"

"Yes, I am fine." She giggled. "It was like nothing I have ever felt before. His hands touched me in places they should not have, and his mouth was all over me."

"All over you?"

"Yes, Sabine all over me." She moved her hands to her chest and down her body. "I wanted him to touch me. I wanted him to do those things to me. I feel so ashamed, for I promised Margret that I did not want her husband. Sabine, I want her husband in the worst kind of way."

"When did this happen?"

"The night we returned to Whispering Wind."

"I do not think what happened between you had anything to do with Roman. Blake and I did not start until after Roman came the first time. I think what you did was about love. He still loves you Rebecca. This would explain why he was so angry with Blake."

"Yes, Blake," she said smiling at me.

"What?"

"Do not what me... give it up! Why were you kissing him in the road? Better yet, why were you kissing him in your room?"

"I am not sure. That day in the road we were talking, and for some reason I got very emotional. I started to cry, and he held me, and then it just happened. It was very intense. He is a very good kisser."

"Better than Jared?"

"Oh yes, way better. Jared would not have taken it to the level that Blake did. When he touches me, it is like fire burning my skin. When he leaves me, I feel empty. I am confused by this, and I am sure that it has something to do with Roman. We talked about it, and we decided that as long as it feels so good to kiss one another, we were not going to stop. Also, when we are alone, we thought it best to have someone stand guard, so to speak, and interrupt us from time to time so we do not cross that line. Perhaps you and Charles should do the same."

"After that night, Charles refuses to be alone with me."

"I know why. We must remain pure. I am sure that his anger is directed toward himself, for he knows that if our virtue is tarnished in any way that we will lose. Roman would win. If you were nearly without all your clothing, then Charles could have taken you and made you impure. Not to mention he would have been completely unfaithful to his wife. Rebecca, you must be careful here. I know how hard it is to resist these feelings, but he is another woman's husband. He is not yours any longer."

She stuck her lip out as only she could. "I know all of this, Sabine, but the way I see it, he was mine long before Margret had him."

"Yes, and they all married for a reason. He had no choice but to bond himself to another, just so we could remain pure and finish all of this."

"So what I am hearing you say is that he is still in love with me as I am with him, and because of that love, he married another."

"Exactly, as with Blake. You know, he told me that he was never with a woman in that way that men and women are together before he met his wife, and he has not been with a woman since his wife."

"I will be your look out, Sabine, if you will be ours. I cannot get enough of him. I will never get the chance to be with him until this is over. Even when it is over. I may not get that chance. I say let us live in this moment and enjoy this. It is quite enjoyable, is it not?"

"Oh yes, it is, Rebecca, and very dangerous. I would take my chances with the likes of Roman any day than take the chance we are taking with Charles and Blake."

"Yes, I do know what you mean, so I am going to find Charles and let him know what our plans are for keeping a look out for one another."

"I am going to find Blake and kiss him again. When you are done, bring Charles and come find me. I will probably be in the stables. Blake said he would be in the barracks, so that is where I am going."

CHAPTER TWENTY-ONE

We made our way out of the secret room and into the study.

"Rebecca, would you take your time finding me?" I asked her.

She giggled. "Only if you will give me the same courtesy when it is my time to be alone with Charles."

"It would be my pleasure."

She hugged me, and we made our way out into the courtyard. I went in the direction of the barracks while she went out into the village.

I felt excited to see him. As I approached the barracks, I could still feel his energy, and it made me feel alive. There was a man sitting on the stairs leading into the building that Blake's energy was coming from.

"Excuse me," I said.

The man jumped up and bowed.

"Yes, Your Highness."

I smiled and said, "Please, my name is Sabine. I was wondering if you would be so kind as to get Blake for me."

He smiled at me. "Of course, my lady."

"Would you tell him that I am in the stables? I am going to see my horse."

He smiled again and went inside, and I walked over to the stables. Raiden was in his stall with the door open.

"Hey, boy, I found what you said was there. I do not know what it means yet, but I found it. Rebecca went to find Charles, and I am going to discuss it with him." Raiden nodded his head. "I wish we could end this now. I am so confused by all that is happening."

I felt him before I heard him walk up behind me.

He put one arm around my waist and the other around me and up between my chest, so that his hand rested on my shoulder. He pulled me close to him, and when my body touched his, fire shot through me from the top of my head to the bottom of my feet. He breathed in my scent through his nose, and when he exhaled, I could smell the hunger on his breath. His hunger for me was the most intoxicating scent I had ever encountered. I wanted nothing but to turn in his arms and find his mouth with mine, but he held me tight.

"Gerard said that you were looking for me. Is everything all right?"

My mind was blank; the only thing I could think of was him and the way he felt against me. Then he whispered, "Sabine, are you all right."

"I have nothing in my head but the feel of your body and the way it sets mine on fire. I want to feel your lips on mine."

"As I do yours, but we cannot. This will have to do for us. I told you in your room that I will not, that we cannot put ourselves in that position again. I am a gentleman, and I cannot allow your virtue to be compromised."

"I know, and thank you for being so honorable, but Rebecca and I have come up with a plan. In fact, I must talk to you about some things, and this is not the place. Rebecca and Charles will be here shortly. I can feel her coming, and then we can go someplace a bit more private and talk."

I leaned my head against his chest, wanting his lips anywhere on me.

He complied and brushed them along my neck, whispering, "You are incorrigible, my lady."

With my eyes closed and my breath caught in my chest, I said,

"Me? Who is the one holding me in place and teasing me to the point of madness?"

He chuckled, and on cue Rebecca and Charles entered the stables.

"I found him."

Blake did not let me go; he simply lifted me off the ground and turned us both to face them. I felt like I was in a trance, a beautiful floating trance.

"Blake, I cannot think while you are touching me. My mind wants nothing more than to be submerged in the scent of you."

His hold on me loosened, and then he was gone from me.

"Charles, when are the crops harvested?"

"Just as the seasons change, when the hot months turn into the cool months. Why?"

"Well, something is supposed to happen in the sky on that day at midday. That is when we must complete the ritual, when the light of day turns to the dark of night. When will the seasons change?"

"I am not sure. I will ask the men if they know. Some of them are farmers and should know how much time is left."

"All right, but first I need to talk to you alone. Will you walk with me?"

He looked at Rebecca, and she smiled at him.

"Lead the way," he said as he bowed and put his hand forth for me to follow.

I reached behind me to find Blake's hand. My fingers brushed his, and I walked out into the sunshine. We walked a bit.

"Charles, I have something uncomfortable I need to talk about and to ask you about, so please do not get upset."

"I give you my word."

"Well, Rebecca has told me of your experience together the night we arrived here. She told me that the two of you did some things that made you angry for doing them. I am not going to judge you simply because I cannot stop myself from touching your brother, but what I want to know is, does this have anything to do with Roman?"

"No, Sabine, I do not think so."

"Would you please tell me why it happened?"

"I have loved her my whole life. When we were talking that night, I just could not stop myself. My heart was bursting, and I had to kiss her again. For me, she is like the piece of me that has laid vacant for all these years, and to be here with her again I felt whole. What we did was beyond careless. I nearly took her pureness from her."

"See, that is the part that confuses me. What does that mean?"

"Oh, Sabine, you are going to make this very difficult for me."

"No, Charles that is not my intention. I need to know so I do not make the same mistake. We are so close to finishing this, and I do not want to do something that will stop us, but I cannot stop these feelings I am experiencing toward Blake. Do you understand what I am saying?"

"Yes, I do. When a man and a woman become husband and wife, a union of two becomes one, one heart, one mind, and one body."

"Yes, Blake spoke of this union, but I do not know what it is. Is this something only men know of?"

"As innocent as you are, the answer would be yes. It is that innocence that must stay intact. Let me see if I can explain this a little better. When you are with Blake, how does it make you feel?"

"On fire, like I want to climb inside him and never come out."

"That is how he feels as well, only he can achieve that goal."

He stopped talking and was watching me. I did not understand how Blake would be able to climb inside of me and how I could not do the same to him.

"I am fearful that I have no clue what you are saying to me, Charles."

"Blake told me that you stirred something in him. Do you remember that?"

I thought about the encounters we had on my bed, the one with me on his lap.

"Would that be what I felt when I was on his lap, the reason he removed me and stopped kissing me?"

"That would be why."

"Charles, I am more confused now than I was before."

"I think that you should be having this conversation with Blake. I think he would do a better job of explaining it to you."

"Speaking of Blake, Rebecca and I have devised a plan so I can be with Blake and you two can be together. Because we are losing our control to stop ourselves, me and Blake because of Roman, and you and Rebecca because you are true loves, we have decided to stand guard over one another. When you are alone with Rebecca, I will interrupt periodically, so you do not take it too far, like when you were nearly totally unclothed, and then Rebecca will do the same for me. I know that you are married, and you should not be with Rebecca to begin with, but we all know that when this ends, it all ends. I will not judge you if you do not pass judgment on me."

"Well, Sabine, I like your idea. It would make being together a great deal easier, and it would allow me to be alone with her and to deal with these feelings I have for her. I think you have a deal."

I threw my arms around his neck and kissed his cheek.

"You are the best. Now I am going to find Blake and have this talk. I want to know what this all means. Maybe if I have a better understanding, I might be able to stop myself."

He chuckled. "Sabine, I do not think that will be possible. I will give you some time alone before I bring you that information you need. I will send Blake to your room. I think that would be the most private place for this conversation, perhaps even this interlude you will undoubtedly have."

"Thank you."

I watched as he walked back to Rebecca and Blake. He said some words to Blake and then looked up at me. I smiled and walked to the castle. I was halfway up the grand staircase when Blake walked in the door.

"Charles said you needed to discuss something with me, that you have a few questions for me that he could not answer."

I smiled at him and took off running; it felt exciting to have him chase me around the corner and down the hall to my room. I stopped at the door, knowing he was close. He slid to a stop just inches from me.

"You are so beautiful."

His lips were on mine then. His arms around my waist, he lifted me and walked into my room, kicking the door shut with his foot. He walked me over to my bed, his mouth never leaving mine, and gently laid me down, coming down on top of me. He was a big man in comparison to me, and the full weight of his body should have crushed me, but I hardly felt him. It was only when he pressed into me that my body lost control. My hands started on their own to explore his body; his arms, his back, his sides, and his waist. He was solid with muscles, many more than Jared ever had, and Blake was twenty years older than him. He slowed our kiss and pulled back.

"What is it you wished to discuss, my lady?" he asked as his fingers trailed down my jaw to my mouth.

I opened it and drew his finger in, gently suckling it like Juliana did to Jenna's breast when she was a baby. The rumble that came from Blake sent shivers through me. He pulled his finger out and pulled up off of me, bringing me with him so we were in a sitting position on my bed. I smiled and pouted at the same time.

"Well, some things have happened, and I am a bit confused about them. I discussed them with Charles as you know, and he said that it would probably be best to ask you, seeing as how you are the reason I am confused."

"All right, let us start with what are you confused about."

"Well, Rebecca told me about her encounter with Charles, the one that provoked his anger toward you when you kissed me on the road."

"Yes, and what did she say?"

"Well, the same thing Charles did, that they were talking and he could not stop himself, that he kissed her, and Rebecca had told me that they had taken the majority of their clothes off, and that Charles kissed her in a great many places that were not her mouth. She showed me where he kissed her."

"I do not wish to make you feel uncomfortable, Sabine, but would you show me where."

I nodded and got off the bed. He looked at me strangely. I turned my back to him and proceeded to undo the boy shirt I was wearing. As I slipped it off my shoulders, I felt his hands on me.

"What are you doing, Sabine?"

"I am going to show you where he kissed her."

He pulled my shirt back up on my shoulders. His mouth was near my neck.

"I did not intend for you to disrobe yourself in order to do that. You could have just pointed."

I could not stand it anymore. I turned and tilted my head up to kiss him. He complied deeply. My shirt was open with just my under garment between us, and when our chests touched, I felt that grumble come from deep within him before he pulled away.

"Sabine, I can feel the warmth of your skin through the sheer material that separates us." His eyes shifted down to my heaving chest. "I can see you through the material, and I need to stop before I lose myself in you." His hand came to my cheek. "Your beauty and inno-cence are like nothing I have ever known. I want nothing more than to climb inside of you and make you my own."

"That is what I am confused by. What does that mean? When I told Charles that is how I felt about you, he said it was impossible for me to do that, and then he said that you had said the same thing about me, and that is what this union between a man and a woman is about. What does that mean?"

His smile was gentle as his hands fastened my shirt, careful so as not to touch me. When he finished, he said, "Come and sit with me. I will do my best to explain it to you."

We sat on the bed. "Remember when you were on my lap and we were kissing?" I nodded my head. "Remember how you pushed against me here," he said, pointing to just below his midsection. I nodded. "Do you remember what you felt?" I remembered all right. I slowly nodded my head. "Do you remember when you kneed Richard here? I like that you referred to it as his lower parts." I nodded again.

He was looking at me, waiting for me to put whatever it was he was saying to me together. I guess the confused look on my face made him continue talking.

"For a man and a woman to become one, a union must take place, a union of bodies."

"Blake, I do not understand."

"Nor should you, Sabine. This is what I am talking about when I say your innocence is what draws me to you. What did you feel that day you were on my lap?"

"I do not know, but I felt like you belonged to me."

"I have always belonged to you, but that is not what I mean. Close your eyes." I did. "Now think back to that moment. Tell me what you were feeling."

"I remember pulling myself closer to you, and I felt something hard right here." I slid my hand down between my legs. "It was circular and very big." I opened my eyes. "Am I right?" His cheeks were flush. "Blake, are you all right? You look like you are not feeling well."

"Oh, my beautiful Sabine, do you trust me?"

I laughed. "About as much as I trust myself right now, which is not much, so no."

He smiled. "May I have your hand?" I put my hand out. "Now I am going to do something, and I do not want you to scream out. I want you to feel something." I nodded as he slowly moved my hand to his chest. "Do you feel that?" I could feel the hard thumping in his chest. I nodded; mine felt the same way. He slid my hand slowly down his chest to his stomach. "Do you feel that?" His stomach was as hard as his chest. Again I nodded. He continued to move my hand down further, and my mouth opened. It was as hard as his chest and stomach. I looked into his eyes, feeling fearful. I pulled my hand away.

"Blake, is something wrong with you? I do not understand. Why is that like that?"

"Sabine, when a man and a woman have this union we keep speaking of, this part of the man..." He pointed to the space between his legs. "...enters this part of the woman." He put his own hand close to the space between mine, though he did not touch me. "And they become one."

My hand fell from him, and I got up off the bed.

"So, what you are saying is that this is what you did to your wife? That is what Charles almost did to Rebecca? It is so big, and I am so small. Would it not hurt me?"

He was off the bed; he felt my distress.

"Yes, Sabine, it hurts, but only for a little while, then your body conforms to mine, and the feeling is undeniable."

I did not even look at him. I turned and ran from the room. I wanted to be as far away from him as I could...On my way down the hallway I ran past Charles and then Rebecca. I kept going past the grand staircase to the secret back stairway, down into the kitchen, and straight to my father's study. I popped the door to the secret room and entered, shutting it behind me and locking the world out.

Blake followed me out of my room, but Charles and Rebecca stopped him.

"What happened?" Charles was not happy.

"You happened, brother. Now move out of my way."

"Blake, what did you do to her?"

"I did nothing. You were the one who sent her to query me. You should have explained things to her. She was so frightened. She is so innocent that she does not have a notion as to what I was trying to say to her. This is entirely your fault. If anything happens to her, I will blame you."

He pushed past Charles, but by that time I was already in the secret staircase. He did not find me.

I sat in the dark for a long time, remembering everything that he had said and done in my room. None of it made sense. I did not want him to hurt me like that. *Why would Rebecca want that from Charles? I* was so lost in understanding, and it frightened me to think that Blake would want to hurt me. He told me that he loved me. *Why now, after all we had shared, did he want to hurt me?* Perhaps it was Roman again, like with the jewels, making them crazy. I sat in the dark on the floor for quite some time, with my knees drawn up to my chest while I shook. My mind began to wander again; he had put my hand on his lower body, and he said he wanted to put that huge thing inside of me. I shook my head. There was no way that was going to happen.

I put my head back against the desk and closed my eyes. I must have fallen asleep, for I was having visions again. There was nothing but vibration. I was in complete blackness, but I could hear giant booms so loud that the walls and ground vibrated. I could feel things on me, crawling on my arms; boom, vibrate, crawl. There were sounds that I did not know. What did it all mean? Then I heard him, or thought I heard him. It was muffled, as if someone was silencing him.

'Sabine, help me!'

Who was that? My eyes shot open.

"RAIDEN," I screamed.

The booms and vibrations were not in my visions. It was real. I felt my way to the latch, popped it open, and when I did, I could hear the fighting. My sword. I made my way to my room without being seen, grabbed my sword, and then made my way to the grand staircase. Everything was happening outside. I ran down the stairs, taking two of them at a time, and then ran out the door. I could hear Rebecca screaming my name, but I could not see her.

I turned to follow the voice and saw a man dragging her by the hair toward the barracks, striking down every man in his path. I do not know where the voice came from, but I screamed so loud the windows in the great hall shattered.

"NOOOOOO!"

I slammed my sword into the ground. The ground shook and rippled in the direction of the man. He lost his footing just as Aidan came flying through the air and cut his head off. Rebecca was on her feet and running toward me. She grabbed her sword that was lying on the ground just ahead of me in front of the fountain.

"Where is Raiden," I screamed to her.

"They took him and Spirit," she screamed back.

She slid as she came to a halt, and our backs were together. "Do what I tell you to do."

"Ready," she said.

"Put your sword in the air and spin with me in a circle. Close your eyes and do not lose contact with me."

With our swords in the air we turned, and turned, and on the fifth turn I said, "Air that I breathe, wind that moves me, bring your sons to me."

I could feel the wind getting stronger and stronger. We were in the middle of it, and it was projecting out, drawing everything in. Around we went five more times.

"Touch your sword to mine."

The tips of our swords touched, and a brilliant light came from the end, swirling around us and entwining with the wind. I could hear the yells, and then I heard him.

Do not stop.

"I have them, Rebecca. Do not stop."

We turned again and again. The wind lessened more and more, and the light started to fade. I opened my eyes and he was there; they both were. I dropped my hand and ran to him, throwing my leg over the saddle, and we were gone like the wind. Rebecca and Spirit followed right behind us. We stopped at the end of the village. I felt him twitch. My arm was immediately in the air, and then he was up. When it was over, there was only one left standing, the same one that was there before. I got off Raiden and walked up to him. He was covered in blood. I swung my sword at him. He raised his to stop me, and when they connected, he went down with his sword split in two. I pushed him backwards, angling the tip of my sword to his throat.

"No one touches my horse! I warned you not to return, and now you have sent these men to their deaths. You think you can stop me, but you cannot. You think you can release him, but you cannot. My magic is not taught. I was born like this. You cannot beat me. Now go and tell the rest of your scum that this is what will happen if you return to my kingdom."

I turned and walked away. The man got up and started to run in the other direction. I heard Roman screaming at him to return and free him.

I looked up at Rebecca and told her, "I am so sorry I was not here. Are you all right?"

"I am fine now. That barbarian got the better of me… well, him and three of his friends."

I smiled at her. "You are slipping, my friend. Perhaps you and I need to practice."

"Are you all right? Where have you been?"

Just as I started to answer her, I felt him, and he was riding up fast. I did not want to see him, so I climbed on Raiden, looked at Rebecca, and said, "Ride with me." She nodded, and we were gone.

I leaned into Raiden and whispered, "Take us someplace safe."

I could see in his eye that he knew just the place. We ended up on the plain where Rebecca and I first met. They rode to the middle where we got off.

"What happened back there?"

"Well, first you must tell me what happened between you and Blake. He was so angry at Charles that I thought they were going to end up in blows. It was bad, Sabine."

"I feel so foolish, Rebecca. I had a talk with Charles about what happened between the two of you, and then I told him what Blake had told me about this union between a man and a woman. He told me I should talk to Blake about it, that he would explain it to me."

She smiled. "And did he?"

"I am hoping he did a terrible job of it because the things he told me were horrible. He tried to explain it all to me, but I did not understand, so he took my hand and put it on his…on here," I put my hand on my body to show her, "and he explained that he would put that thing in me, and then we would become one." Rebecca giggled. "What?" I asked her. "His man parts are huge. I figure because he was so big and I am so small that it would most definitely hurt me. He confirmed that it would hurt, but then I would conform to him and like it. What does that mean? How would I conform to him? I do not want to conform to anything that big that it would hurt me. And where does he think he is going to put something that big anyway? He actually said that it would go in my woman parts. He is crazy if he thinks I want anything to do with that."

Rebecca started laughing. "You should hear yourself, Sabine. You are ranting. Breathe already." She continued to laugh. I did not find any of this funny, so I sat there looking at her. She subsided her giggles and said, "Oh, you poor girl." She then hugged me. "You really do not understand any of this, do you?"

"And you do? Why in the world would you want to do anything like that with Charles?"

"Because I love him," she said matter-of-factly.

I crinkled my face up. "To me, Rebecca, that is not love. That is torture and pain. Why would you want Charles to hurt you like that?"

"Calm down. Let me see if I can explain this better than Blake, who incidentally is really scared. He has been beside himself with worry."

"I do not care what he is. How dare he think I would want him to do that to me?" Then I whispered, "He did that to his wife, and he said she liked it. I am glad I do not know her."

"Listen to me. When you and Jared would kiss, what was that like?"

"It was very pleasant."

"Was it anything like what you feel when you kiss Blake?"

"Not at all. When I kiss Blake I am on fire."

"All right, so when you kissed Jared for long periods of time, did you notice anything that changed in him?"

"I do not understand."

"His body, did his body change?"

I thought about it. "Well, sometimes he would get very tense, and we would have to stop."

"Did you ever notice anything else about him?"

"No, Rebecca, I do not understand what you mean."

"Here is one for you, do you know how to become with child?"

I sat there staring at her. *Did I know this?* "I do not think so. Do you?"

"I do. When my father announced my marriage to Jared, my mother and I had a talk. Remember, when my mother said that Gerald did vile and disgusting things to her?"

"Yes, and that is what I think Blake wants to do to me. What does that mean anyway?"

"Well, my mother explained it this way; when you are given in marriage, you are given in body as well. I asked her what that meant, and she told me that when you get married, you sleep in the same bed as your husband, and he will do things to you that only your husband should do. For her, she did not like him, and she said that he was brutal to her, that he did not care to be gentle, that he took her by force."

"See, what does that mean, took her by force? Took her where?"

"You said you felt Blake's parts, right here?" I nodded. "Well, my mother told me that the man gets bigger here and harder when the man wants to fulfill himself, and he sticks that part inside of you here." She touched herself there.

"That is what Blake said. Would that not hurt?"

"According to my mother, it is horrific pain, but after the first couple of times, it does not hurt so much. She said there were times she found it quite pleasurable. But she was a liar because she was with my father before she was with Gerald. She also told me that after a few times with Gerald, he said she was worn out down there, and he moved to her backside."

I sat there horrified at what she was saying to me.

"Rebecca."

I turned my head, and what was in my stomach came out onto the grass. I kept heaving and heaving until there was nothing left to heave up.

"I understand now why you were so scared, sweetie. It will be all right. If you love Blake, he will not hurt you. He loves you so much, as Charles loves me, and as I love him. Yes, I want him to do those things to me, and I want to do those things to him. If what is between the two of you is real, when this is over, you will want him to do those things to you. It will be a natural progression in your relationship."

"Rebecca, I am scared, I mean really scared of what I felt when he put my hand there. You did not feel what I felt."

She giggled. "You are right, but I have felt Charles there, and let me tell you my hand," she paused as she held it up, "does not fit around it."

My eyes were huge as she spoke. "And you still want him to put it in there?" I pointed to her."

She smiled at me. "Someday I hope he will, but I do not think it will ever happen. He is married to someone else."

"I know, and I am sorry for that. I wish we were not who we are. Then you two could have been together."

"That is not truth. If we were not who we are, then I would not know him. You know how the cave makes time stand still for us?" I nodded. "I wish it could turn time back, so he was not married and twenty years have not passed."

"I wish the same." We laid back in the grass and looked at the sky. "So what happened today?"

"Well, after you ran off and disappeared... hey, where did you go anyway?"

"To the secret room."

"I should have known that. Anyway, Blake was going crazy, screaming at Charles, and Charles was screaming at him. Blake went out and got a bunch of men to go looking for you. It was kind of funny, but no one had bothered to look in the stables to see if Raiden was gone. I went to get Spirit to join in, and I found Raiden. I asked him if he knew where you were, but he did not answer me, so I figured you were still somewhere close. I waited for the men to leave and then made my way to the cave, but you were not there, so I tried to figure out how to get to the hidden staircase. I spent a great deal of time doing that, but then I heard horses. I knew it was not the men because they had just left, so I ran to my room and got my sword. By the time I got to the grand staircase, something hit the wall outside. I nearly fell down the stairs from the vibration. I ran out the door, and there were Roman's men all over the place. Four of them jumped on me, and I got two of them. I laughed when their heads flew off their bodies, and I heard Spirit scream my name. I turned as some men were roping them. They had so many ropes around them, Sabine. They did not stand a chance. I started to run after them when that man grabbed me by the hair as I moved past him. I slammed on the ground, and my sword fell out of my hand. I fought him, and he just kept saying that Roman was going to love this."

"I am so sorry," I whispered, reaching for her hand.

"I managed to get away from him when this other guy stepped right in front of me and I slammed into him. It felt like I hit a wall because he was huge. He smiled down at me with black teeth, and he was nearly drooling. It was disgusting. Then the other guy grabbed me by the hair again and started dragging me to his horse, and that is when you came out."

"They know that Raiden and Spirit are deadly with us on them. They probably thought that if they separated us they could overpower us."

"Hey, where did you learn how to do what you did to get them back?"

I laughed. "I have no idea. It was just there in my head."

"We have been gone for a while now. Do you think we should go back?"

"Well, after all that happened, I would imagine that they will be frantic, especially Blake. He was riding up when we took off."

"I did not see him."

"I felt him coming, but I could not face him, not after the way I acted. Rebecca, I am not sure I can be near him."

"Well, after the way you just tossed the contents of your body all over the grass, I would not blame you."

"Would you please intervene and tell him that I do not want to see him?"

"You know Blake. I will try to keep him away, but I do not think I will succeed."

"Can I ask you something before we go back?"

"You can ask me anything," she assured me.

"When that guy was dragging you away, were you scared?"

"I was a little, but I knew you would come and save me."

We laughed. We were back at Whispering Wind in the blink of an eye. As I was getting off Raiden, I could feel Charles coming up, and he was angry.

"You will not walk away, and you will tell me where it is you have been, Sabine, and where the two of you have been."

I spun around to face him. "Again, Charles, I am finding myself reminding you that you are not my father. I do not answer to you."

"You may not answer to him, but you will answer to me."

Blake had come out the door and picked me up, and then he literally threw me over his shoulder.

"I have this, brother. You can have your say when I am finished."

"Put me down, Blake."

"All in good time, Sabine. I have something to say to you, and you will hear it."

I did not fight. I let him carry me into the dining hall, kicking the door shut behind him. He sat me down on the table, placing his legs on either side of mine and his hands firmly on the table.

"Where did you go today? I was looking for you. I sent many men to their deaths because of you."

I just sat there staring at him. I could not help but feel guilty. My horse was nearly taken, our men died because of me. I fought back the tears and just stared at him.

"You will answer me."

I did the only thing I could do, and that was to fight this incredible urge to kiss him.

He opened his mouth to speak, and I covered it with mine. He responded for a moment, but then he grabbed my arms and pulled me away.

"You will not sidetrack me. Where did you go?" he yelled at me.

Now he had made me angry, and he was hurting my arms.

I pulled my leg up, planted it square in his stomach, and pushed with all that I had. He moved back, and I started in.

"First of all, I do not answer to you. Second, you man-handle me like that again, and you will be the one in pain. And third, where I go and what I do is really none of your business. You are forgetting your place, Blake."

"Do not think you can attempt to speak to me as if I were a child. First, you will answer me. Second, I will handle you any way I see fit. And third, it is my business where you go and what you do, especially when a hundred of my men die trying to keep you safe."

I slid off the table and went to walk away, but his arm came around my waist and slammed me on the table.

"I told you, you are going to answer my query. Where were you?"

This time I did not hold back. I laid back on the table, brought up both of my feet, and slammed them into his chest. It was so fast that he had no time to defend himself. He went flying against the sideboard, knocking everything to the floor with a crash. As I got up from the table, he was right there with his arm around my waist again. My reaction was to throw myself forward, causing him to bend with me. When he did, I flipped him over and onto his back. I put my foot on his throat and said, "Stay down."

I then went for the door. He grabbed my foot and then my leg and pulled me back on top of him. Before I could react, he had me pinned under him. He was up on his knees so not to put all his weight on me. I managed to get my leg between us and slammed him in his boy-man part. He rolled over in pain and landed on the floor next to me. I opened the door and slammed it shut behind me. Standing in the grand hall were Rebecca, Charles, and the rest of his brothers.

I nodded to Charles, who smiled and said, "Is he still standing?"

"See for yourself," I answered headed to the stairs.

The door flew open, and Blake was behind me before I hit the first step. He picked me up high so my feet were very far off the floor, making our heads level. I just threw my head backwards as hard as I could and caught him across the nose. He let me go and fell to the floor, screaming that I had broken his nose. I made it halfway up the stairs when he caught me again. He did not make the mistake of lifting me high up this time, but he flung me over his shoulder and continued walking up the stairs, down the hall, and into my room. He slammed the door shut and dropped me on the bed. I was up and moving toward the door when he caught me yet again. This time he pushed me back and sat on the floor in front of the door.

"You will answer me, Sabine. I can do this all day."

I stood there deciding whether or not I was going to fight him some more. He looked so beaten down and bloody and just done, so instead I went and took off my clothes and climbed into bed. He could sit there all night for all I cared. I was doing what I wanted to do all along, and that was to sleep.

The visions came again. I felt the fear that Raiden felt when they caught him with all those ropes. The men were mean to him. He felt trapped and could not escape. I felt the fear Charles and Blake felt when they could not find me, and then I felt the fear Rebecca said she did not have. What woke me was the screaming. I sat up in bed, listening to the screams, and Blake nearly fell over trying to get to me.

"Sabine, it is all right. I am still here," he said.

Though I did not understand what he was saying to me. *Who was screaming?* I jumped off the bed and fell against the wall, my hands flat on the wall, and he was right behind me. Then the door flew open, and Charles came running in with Rebecca behind him. The screaming stopped when I saw her. I ran to her and let her hold me.

I heard her say, "What did you do to her?" She was angry.

"I did not do a thing. I was sleeping in the chair, and she woke up screaming."

I was screaming? No, Rebecca was screaming. I looked at her; she looked so scared. Charles came over to us.

"Sabine, are you all right?"

I heard him, but I did not know what he was asking me. I just looked at him. *What did he do to her?* I looked back at Rebecca, and she had tears streaming down her cheeks.

I hugged her and whispered in her ear, "What did he do to you? Did he try to make a union with you? Is that why you were screaming?"

She looked at Charles with panic on her face then waved them out of the room.

"Come on, sweetie. I think we should have a little talk."

She walked me to the chairs by the fireplace. I sat across from her, and she asked.

"Sabine, what happened?"

"I heard Raiden screaming. I could feel his fear. Then I heard Charles screaming, and I felt his fear, and then...Oh, Rebecca, I am so sorry that I was not there. I felt your fear. You were so scared, yet you did not tell me. You told me you were a little scared. You were not just a little scared you were so scared, and you were screaming. I could not get you to stop."

"Sabine, I was not screaming. You were. What woke you were your own screams. You were having those visions again. I am fine." She leaned into me. "And no, I did not let Charles do those things to me. I was sleeping alone. I thought for sure Blake tried to talk to you again."

"Blake? Oh yeah. I hurt him, huh?"

"Yes, you did. I think you broke his nose." She giggled.

"Rebecca, I do not think we should be here. I think that witch has some kind of hold on this place. I think she is in my head again. The last time I had visions, Blake was here. I do not think it is Roman. We need to get her body out of here. Rebecca, I keep having visions of you dead. I watch you time and time again dying."

"Sabine, if I am to die then I am to die, but I will do my best not to, and when we finish this, that witch will die along with Roman. She will not be able to give you visions any longer. I spoke with Charles. He said the harvest is twelve days from today. So we know when, we know where, and we know how. We just have to survive the rest of the time."

"I am not sure I can take much more of this. As long as Blake is near me while I sleep, I believe this will keep happening."

"Well, he is here because he does not want you to be alone. How about I stay here with you? She cannot get into my head, so you should be safe."

"I think I would like that very much. Are you sure you would not mind?"

"I am sure. I will go and gather my things. Will you be all right while I am gone?"

I nodded. She left, and I saw Blake standing at the door.

"Are you all right?" he asked.

"I do not know what is happening to me."

"May I come in?"

I nodded, and he was at my side in an instant.

"I am sorry that I was rough with you. I was just so angry and worried."

I reached up and touched his face. "I know, and I am sorry that I broke your nose. Rebecca is going to stay with me until this is over. I think the witch is using you to get to me. I think she is trying to confuse me. I do not believe it is Roman who has cast this spell on us. I believe it is her. She is still alive in this land, and she wants us to know it."

"Would it be all right if I stayed in the room next to yours?"

"That would be nice to know you were close, yes."

"Then I shall bid you goodnight. Will you talk to me in the light of the day?"

"Yes, and again, I am sorry for my behavior."

"As I am for mine." He stood and left my room.

CHAPTER TWENTY-TWO

When the light of the day arrived, I woke with a sense of happiness. I opened my eyes to find Rebecca gone. I smiled and stretched my limbs. I could feel him close to me. "Are you here?" I said without opening my eyes again.

"How do you know when I am close?"

I giggled. "I can feel your energy, Blake. Can you forgive me for what took place yesterday?"

I felt him move toward me, and I made no effort to cover myself. I lay there with my arms stretched above my head with just my thin undergarments on and the blanket to my waist. I heard his breathing change when he got close, and although he did not want me to hear his breath, he inhaled deeply.

"You truly do not know the beauty you possess," he said, and then his mouth covered mine.

I did not fight him. I wanted to feel his kiss, to feel his tongue gently trail across my lips. When he sought permission with his tongue to enter my mouth, I greeted him with passion. I felt his grumble as he entered, and our tongues touched. At first it was gentle and sweet, with him kneeling next to me. I put my arms around his neck and pulled him down next to me, needing the feel of his body next to mine. It was not fair to my mouth to feel all this fire; my body deserved it as well. He rested his arm between my breasts, so his hand could hold my face. I am not sure what made me put my hand on his, but I did, entwining our fingers. I felt my back arch as our kiss deepened, pressing myself against his massive frame. I felt safe here with him. His leg moved between mine, completely covering it. As I brought my free leg over his, my knee and lower leg was the only part that made it around his waist. We stayed like this kissing one another, our bodies locked together, our hands entwined and our mouths never separating. He slowed his kiss and pulled back, breathing heavily.

"Sabine," he whispered putting his forehead on mine. "I know I scared you, and I am so sorry for doing that."

"Blake, when Rebecca and I left, I had a long talk with her about what you tried to explain to me. I understand now. I am the one who is sorry."

His mouth covered mine again, and it felt so wonderful with half his body lying on me and his warm mouth kissing me. I moved our hands to my neck then laid his hand flat on my bare skin just below my neck. He groaned from deep within him and pulled away from me. His eyes were wild with passion, and his energy became very calm, his expression serious but inviting.

"Touching you like this causes me to think those thoughts. Hell, kissing you brings those thoughts to my mind, but touching you is something I never thought I would or could do."

"Then touch me, Blake. Touch me like you would have touched your wife."

He closed his eyes and whispered, "I cannot,"

I felt dread seep into my body; he felt it too.

"If I start this, I will not be able to stop it. Do you not see? I have loved you for a long time, a very long time. We both know this is some kind of trickery, and we are foolish to allow it to enhance our emotions. I cannot allow this to hinder what you need to do to end this."

He put his head on top of his hand. I could feel his heartbeat racing.

"I think I might be afraid that when we do end this, that this, what we are sharing, will be no more. I was scared at first because I could not even imagine the things you told me that happen to a man and a woman. Do you not see, Blake? I do not want this to end."

He picked his head up, and I saw one tear fall onto his cheek.

"I waited a lifetime to hear you say that to me. If I had known you would ever feel like this, I would have not married. I would have waited."

I reached up and wiped his tear away. "Will you touch me just once?"

He held his breath. "With all that I am I want to touch you, but it would be crossing that line we cannot cross."

"Then may I ask you a question?"

"Anything you want."

"When this is done, when it is over, will you touch me then?"

His mouth covered mine, and his hand did not move from the place just below my neck. We parted, and he said, "Every day and night for the rest of your life. I want nothing more."

On cue, Rebecca knocked on the door. We did not move when she came in. Blake had rested his chin on his hand.

"Good..." she started. "Should I not be here?"

"No, come in. I am glad you are here," Blake said. "Your timing could not have been more perfect.

"That is what I am here for. I came in earlier, but you were busy, so I thought about how long it took Charles and I to get to... well, you know, and then I came back."

We both smiled. Blake got up, and I sat up. My chest was burning from where he touched me. My hand reached up to feel the warmth.

"I need to get some things done. You two have fun,"

Blake said as he gathered his things and left us.

Rebecca waited until Blake was down the hall before she spun around and said, "Well, that looked pretty intense."

I smiled. "It was."

"So all is forgiven with the two of you?"

"For now, yes. I wanted to know if you would go someplace with me. You up for some screaming men?"

"Oh, you know it."

I got dressed in some clean boy clothes, and we ate and then headed toward the barracks. The men stood as we passed. Joseph was watching us with a quick eye. We passed the barracks to the entrance to the dungeons, where accordingly, were two guards posted at the entrance.

"Do you two ever get to do anything other than stand here all day?" Rebecca asked as we started to enter.

"We have orders not to let you go in."

Just as he said that, Raiden came running up behind us.

"You tell him that," Rebecca said, pointing over her shoulder as she pushed past them.

"Princess Rebecca, we have strict orders."

"Tell Charles I threw you to the ground and passed that way."

I chuckled as we started our descent into the labyrinth of tunnels and stairways with Raiden and Spirit. "Do you find it odd that all the torches are lit?"

"Yes, I was just thinking that."

We made our way to the witch's cell. Looking in we could see that her body and her head were still here.

"It has been twenty years, Rebecca, and she is still intact. I would have to believe that it is her who has cast this spell over us. Roman cannot touch us. I felt him throw something at me that day we first met him on the road. It did not touch me."

"Yes, I felt the same thing. I wonder if it is just Whispering Wind that is enchanted." She turned to look at me. "Do you think we should leave the kingdom and see what will happen to us? I could pay my mother a visit. It would probably kill her to see that I have not aged."

"It would be interesting to find out. I think we should ask Charles what he thinks. Perhaps we should all go. I would not want to leave these men here unprotected. Roman's men will be back."

"Yes, let us go find Charles and see what he has to say," she said then turned and started to walk away. I turned in the opposite direction, toward where Jared's body was. "Sabine, what are you doing?"

"I have to see. I need to see if he is still there."

"I do not think that is wise."

I turned and looked at her. "Is anything we have done since we have been here been wise? Is lying down with men we are not married to wise?"

"I suppose you are right. I will go with you."

We walked slowly to the door. "You look. I cannot," I said to Rebecca.

She peered in and gasped. "He is still there, just like the witch."

I closed my eyes and swallowed. I made myself look, and there he was, his body still sitting in the same position it was when I cut his head off.

"How can this be? We really need to talk to Charles."

We turned and ran up and out of the labyrinth of halls and stairs. When we reached the top, Charles was reprimanding the men who let us pass. He stopped mid-sentence and turned to us.

"Rebecca, Sabine, are you all right?"

Breathless, we both shook our heads no. We bolted past the men and kept right on going. Charles called after us, but neither of us looked back. I could feel Blake's energy, and I ran toward it. He was coming out of the stables when I slammed into his chest, and his arms instinctively wrapped around me. Rebecca ran behind him and leaned into his large frame.

"What is going on here? Are you all right?"

I just shook my head no while it was buried in his chest. He removed one arm and grabbed Rebecca from behind him and pulled her into our hug.

"I got you both. It will be all right."

I could only imagine what he was thinking. Charles came running up, and I felt Blake's shoulders go up and then down again.

"What happened down there?"

I did not want to say. Rebecca pulled away from Blake and jumped into Charles' arms. They walked us to the barracks, to Charles quarters.

"You are safe. Please tell me what happened," Blake said in a very comforting voice.

I pulled away from him. "We went to the dungeons to see if the witch was still there, which she is. Then I wanted to... no, I needed to see if Jared was still there, and he is. How could it be? Their bodies have not changed in all these years. How can that be?"

"I know. Charles and I checked it out when all these strange happenings started."

I turned to Charles. "We must leave this place for now. If she still has power here, there is no telling what she can do."

"We can go and see my mother," Rebecca said. "That should give her a few more years to see me looking as I did the last time she saw me."

"I do not think it is wise for us to leave here," Charles said, still comforting Rebecca. "There is much to do in the days to come. We need to prepare for the coming."

I did not understand what Charles was talking about but decided I would ask him later.

"I need to ride with Raiden. I will return."

I pulled away from Blake and went to the stables. I heard Charles tell him to let me go.

He took me to the top of the hill. When I dismounted, he was in my head.

You cannot leave here. She will win then. You must stay.'

'How is it possible that they are still the same?'

'She was given powerful magic by her teacher. She turned me into a horse. She cannot defeat you. You are strong, and you will endure. To leave would only give her victory.'

'I am feeling fear and lust, things I have never felt. I want to cry, and when I am not crying, I want nothing more than to be with Blake. Is this her magic?'

'Yes, if you do not stay pure, then she will rise.'

'When will you go and get Juliana?'

'I do not want to leave you.'

'I know how to do what needs to be done. For you it will be an instant, but I have never been without you. How long will it be for me?'

'The light of day will come and go four times for you.'

'Should you go soon then?'

'Yes, I will leave when the light of day returns.'

We did not speak again. I just sat on the hill and looked at what was my home but was now tainted with trickery and witchcraft. There was much to be done. We needed to prepare, and I needed to be strong. I could see Blake riding through the village. I could only assume he was coming to look for me, but when he went in the opposite direction, toward Wellington, it made me wonder. I got up and climbed on Raiden.

"Take me to Blake." He did not move. "Raiden, take me to Blake."

'No, there is danger coming.'

"Then you must stop him. Go now. You are faster than any horse. Go. We must stop him." Without notice, he was moving down the hill and out into the plain. It was only a moment and I was side by side with Blake.

"You must return. There is danger on the rise."

He turned his horse, and we raced back to the castle. As we rode into the courtyard, Charles came running up, saying, "Our scouts just returned. Roman's men are coming. There are thousands of them, and they have strange contraptions with them. I have prepared the men, and they are getting into position. You and Rebecca must stay close to us."

I nodded as I climbed off of Raiden. I reached for Blake's hand. I found it, and before I knew what was happening, he was pulling me into the castle. Just inside the door, he pressed me against the wall and covered my mouth. His kiss was fierce and hurtful. He was full of this lust that Rebecca spoke of. His body pressed against mine. His energy was not like any other time we had been together. I put my hands on his chest and pushed. He pulled away and rested his head on mine.

"What is it, Blake?"

"Charles is keeping things from you. We know that they are

bringing huge contraptions that fling fire balls. Sabine, we may not survive this attack."

"How many days out are they?"

"As far as we can tell, four."

I pushed him back and took off out the door, running to Raiden.

"You must go now. You will get back in time but go now."

His ears twitched and then he was gone. I could only hope he would return in time. I spun around to see Charles standing there looking at me with shock on his face.

"What have you done, Sabine? Why would you send him away?"

"He went to get Juliana. We may not be able to stop them, Charles, but she can. Why would you not tell me the truth? Why would you keep this from me?"

"Because I cannot tell you what is coming."

"You are not being truthful, Charles. You could get us all killed."

I walked away and back into the castle. I went straight to the kitchen to see if there was anything to eat. Charles had sent for some of the women who were at the cottage to cook for us after the mist had lifted.

"Your Highness, would you like me to bring you something to eat in the dining hall?"

"No, I will eat in here, and please call me Sabine."

"Very well, my lady. Is there anything you would like?"

"Whatever you are making is fine. What is your name?"

"My name is Charlotte," she said and smiled.

"Charlotte, do you know anything about why men are so difficult?"

Her laughter bellowed through the kitchen. "My lady, I could tell you a few things about men."

"Would you please? Why do they think that they always have to be the protector?"

"Oh dear, you are the princess of this manor. You should not be carrying around a sword and wearing man clothes. Young women, well, women in general should not be doing these things. Men feel threatened I suppose, when a woman can best him. It is all in the upbringing. If a man's father is brutal, then it is to be expected that he be brutal. If a man's father is weak, then the son grows up weak. Your Guardians were raised to protect you and that is what they are doing. By not giving you information, they feel they are protecting you. I am sorry, my lady, but I have heard some of the arguments you have had with them. If I might say, it was nice to see you put that young Richard in his place. If you had not, I would have gotten him with a switch."

I giggled with her. "Thank you, Charlotte."

"There is no need to thank me, child, whatever you need."

"What I need is to understand men. Do you have a husband, Charlotte?"

"I did at one time, yes, but Roman's men took care of that, so I have a vested interest in seeing that you succeed. That is what brought me to the valley."

"I am so sorry that we were away for so long. And here you are, right here in the middle of a battle no one should experience."

"There is no need to apologize for leaving. We know that the time was not right, and I volunteered to come here to serve you. I was just a helper when you first came to the cottage in the valley. My mother was your cook, and my father was a guard, so it is a great honor for me to serve you now."

I sat there looking at this slightly heavy woman cooking food for me with great admiration.

"There are thousands of men coming. Apparently, they have contraptions that fling giant balls of fire. It may not be safe here."

"I am well aware of what is coming, my lady. I hear all sorts of things."

I felt my cheeks redden. "Then I would assume you know of this thing happening between Blake and myself, and with Rebecca and Charles. Please do not feel ill will toward him."

"I have known of the love Charles has for Rebecca my whole life. Margret and I are friends. She knew he loved her when they agreed to marry, and she knows that she stands to lose him to her. You just cannot erase a love like that. What bothers Margret is that she is so kind to her, and that makes it hard for her to dislike her. As for Blake, I knew his wife, and he never told her he loved her. She knew you would return, and she knew he loved you. He is an honorable man, Sabine. He would make a good husband for you."

"Thank you. I do know he is honorable, but I just do not know if what I am feeling is real. We seem to be under some kind of magic here. The witch would have my honor defiled if she could, but Blake would not do that to me."

"No, he would not. It took him years to bed his wife. He waited for you, and when you did not return, he knew he had to have sons. She told me once that it was just that and nothing more for him."

"That is so sad. I wish I would have known her. I am fearful, however, that when this is over I will not feel the same for him as he feels for me."

She chuckled. "You do not see your eyes when he walks into a room. No matter what you think, magic cannot cause that effect. When he kissed you in the road that was real."

"You know about that?"

"It was hard to miss, and then the fight after between Blake and Charles... yes, I know all about it. You will see it all in the end. Things will work out. Now here, I will let you eat in peace."

"Thank you." She set a plate of food in front of me and left the kitchen.

I sat there thinking about Blake and how he kissed me. I reached up to touch my lips, noting they felt swollen. He was so forceful. I think he might have been scared. *'Do I love this man?'* I did not want to hurt him. I finished my food and went looking for Charles, eventually finding him outside the barracks, barking orders at some men who could not be older than I was. He stopped yelling when he saw me.

"Can we go inside and talk please?"

He turned and waved his arm for me to pass. Once inside, he took the lead and led me to his quarters. There was a chair in the corner, and that is where I sat.

"I am sorry I yelled at you. I do understand that you cannot tell me what is to come, but you cannot leave out information that could end my life either."

"Sabine, you must understand the role I play in all of this. You already know that as long as you are alive, I cannot be killed, but what you do not realize is that Rebecca can be. I am not bound to her, only you. She is your compliment, not your counterpart. To end this, you do not need her. My fear in all of this is that she will not survive."

"What do you mean, I do not need her? She is water. I cannot complete the ritual without her."

"Yes, you can."

"So, if you had this knowledge, then that should have caused you to speak out and tell me so I would have had a chance to save her."

"I am bound by my oath as your Guardian to not interfere. It is too late. Blake already told you. He has already changed the outcome. By you sending for Juliana before it was time, I have already changed the outcome."

"Charles, that cannot be right, to stand by knowing that Rebecca was not supposed to survive this attack." My anger was building, but I needed to stay calm.

"Do you think I want to lose her after all these years of loving her? I cannot bear knowing that I may never see her again. I will give up all that I have to spend the rest of my days by her side. We may never marry, but I will never leave her again."

"What are you saying, Charles? That no matter what we do to prevent it she will die?"

"I do not know now. This morning I knew she would die, but now that Blake has told you and you sent for Juliana, I changed the outcome. I do not know."

His eyes were full of dread and fear. The great love of his life had been marked for death, and he had known it all along. I did the only thing I could do; I got up and held this man who would give his life for me. I held him tight.

"Charles, I cannot lose her."

I felt him sigh as if he was crying. "I cannot lose her either, not now, Sabine, not after all these years of waiting for her. Maybe I told

Blake so he would tell you. Maybe I put us all in the line of fire. You are now without your horse. We cannot stop them."

I pulled away from him. "Charles, perhaps this is the way it was supposed to be. I do not need Raiden to fight. I need Raiden to fry everyone, but not to fight. Maybe this final battle is what makes us stronger. We can and we will do this. Listen, you stay with Rebecca when it happens. As long as I live, you live, so you protect her, and Blake will make sure I am protected. Charles do not cross that line with Rebecca. She needs to remain pure." He nodded. "Give me your word, Charles."

"I give you my word, Sabine, but I cannot leave you."

"Then we will keep Rebecca with us. The four of us will stand and fight together."

He wiped his eyes and nodded at me. "Can I say something to you?"

"Yes, of course."

"Do not take this the wrong way, but I love you. I admire you. I am in awe of you. When we met, you were a scared little girl, and look at you now a warrior."

"Thanks to you." I smiled and hugged him again.

CHAPTER TWENTY-THREE

The dark of night came fast, and with all the emotion I had felt, I went to bed early and quickly drifted off to sleep. Rebecca did not turn in with me. She chose to spend time with Charles, little did she know that these next few days could be her life. I wanted to tell my friend, but I could not risk changing the outcome of this battle. I could not bear losing her.

It was in the middle of the dark of night when the screams came; visions of fire and Rebecca in the middle of it all. When I felt his arms around me, then and only then did the screams stop. I do not know how long he held me, whispering to me that everything would be all right. I needed him, and he was there for me, the warmth of his body next to mine, the safety I felt in his embrace.

"I cannot bear this," I whispered to him.

"I am right here for you always."

"Will you kiss me?"

He scooted down the bed so that our faces were equal.

"I would like nothing more."

He was gentle this time. His lips brushed over mine with just his tongue, teasing first my upper lip then my lower. My body filled with the heat that came from his presence. My mouth just slightly open, I darted my tongue to the edge of my lips so he could feel it as he passed across them with his. He opened his eyes and looked at me.

"I love you, Sabine. I have always loved you," he said, and then he covered my mouth with his.

I moved my hands off of his shoulders to realize his arms were bare. When I touched his skin, I felt him inhale deeply. He was wearing nearly nothing, as was I, just a thin covering of cloth between our bodies. I pulled him close to me, he slipped his leg between mine, and I lifted mine over his waist. That is when I felt him press into me. There was no mistaking what I felt, but this time I was not afraid. It felt hard against my hip. I lifted my body slightly to meet his, and the guttural moan that escaped him did not frighten me this time. It excited me and made me hungry for him. I moved my hand to find his. It greeted me with tenderness. As we entwined our fingers, gently touching each other, I brought our hands to lay on that spot just below my neck. He pulled back and looked at me.

"What are you doing?" he whispered breathlessly.

"I am giving you permission to touch me. I need to feel you touch me."

"I cannot. I am fearful I will not stop."

"I am not. You will stop. I know you will. You love me, and you will not dishonor me," I said and then kissed him.

He gently pulled away, and his hand lifted slightly from my chest so his fingers were the only thing touching me. He moved them down between my breasts, moving the material away. I could see the mounds that were slightly hidden beneath the cloth as he picked up the material and moved it off my left breast. I watched his eyes as they filled with so much love that it brought tears to my eyes. I had never known this feeling. Jared never reacted this way to me. He just looked at my breast, his finger just barely brushing across it, sending waves of fire through me all the way to the core of my being that I shook. His huge hand cupped my breast; it barely fit in his hand, and then he began to gently squeeze it. I closed my eyes and felt his head move, and then I felt the warmth of his mouth engulfing me. The pleasure was excruciating, causing me to yell out. He stopped.

"Did I hurt you," he whispered.

I shook my head, and he noticed the tears on my cheeks.

"Sabine, are you all right?" He kissed them away.

"I have never known such pleasure. My tears are from the feelings I have from your touches. Blake, I think I am in love with you."

I no sooner got the last word out and his mouth was on mine. The kiss was intense and deep, and it lasted a long time. He finally pulled away and looked down at me.

"I must end this now. I cannot stay here with you, Sabine. I want this union with you. I know this is the way it was meant to be for me, but I cannot cross this line."

"I understand, but..." I closed my eyes.

"Yes, I heard you, and they are words I have wanted to hear for a very long time, but I am not sure if you mean them or if it is this damn trickery that brings them to the surface. I will take them with me and leave you with this. I love you."

He gave me one final kiss then left my bed and my room. I laid there with my breast hanging out of my underclothes, my body on fire, and my mind whirling. I just told Blake that I loved him. I closed my eyes with a smile on my face.

The warmth from the light of the day woke me. Rebecca was fast asleep next to me, and I wondered when she got here.

"Hey, are you awake?"

She moaned, "No."

"I had a vision about you last night. When I woke, you were not here."

"I know. Blake was."

"Where were you?"

"I was with Charles." She sat up. "When I got here and came in, you and Blake were in bed together, so I waited with Charles in the hall.

"He was in bed with me because of my vision. I was so scared for you."

"You did not look so scared when we walked in," she said as she rolled over and smiled at me.

"I told Blake that I think I am falling in love with him."

She sat upright in the bed and turned to face me. "You did what?"

"Yes, I did that."

"This is wonderful." She hugged me.

"We have a great deal to do in the next few days. Raiden should be to Juliana by the dark of the night. I hope he makes it back in time."

"I still cannot believe you sent him away with all those men coming here."

"We will be fine. Our days are going quickly, and we have to be ready to return to the cave and perform the ritual. If we cannot stop these men from coming, then we are going to have to find our way there in the middle of a battle. Please, Rebecca, help me not to forget the days. For me they are becoming a blur. All of this emotion is making it very hard to focus. I am sure that is what that witch wants."

There was a knock on the door. "Come in," we both said together and then giggled.

Charles came in. "Oh, excuse me," he said as he turned his back to us. We rolled on the bed giggling.

"What can I do for you?"

"Um, Rebecca, when you are decent, could you meet me in the dining hall?"

Laughing, she said, "Of course, Charles. We will be down in a bit."

He left, closing the door behind him.

"What was that about?" she asked me. I shrugged my shoulders. "He has seen me with less on than this, and he is being so chivalrous now."

"Rebecca," I shouted and then smacked her on the arm. "Do you not have any pride?"

"When it comes to Charles, no, I do not, and you should be the one who is talking here. I saw Blake touching you last night."

"I know," I said shyly.

"So tell me what was it like?"

"Like nothing I have ever felt. It was beautiful. It set my body on fire."

"I know. I heard you yell out. I almost came in, but I know how I felt the first time Charles touched me like that, so I waited."

"The first time? There has been more than once?"

"Yes, and I am not ashamed to admit it. Trust me, Sabine, it gets better every time."

"Rebecca, you are scaring me. You have not crossed that line, have you?"

"No, he is someone else's husband, Sabine. I could not do that. We are just doing what this stupid spell is making us do, but we are both strong enough to stop. However, when it is over, and if we survive, I am going to cross that line, Sabine. At least one time I am. I have to be with him like that. I have to, at least one time."

I could do nothing but hug my friend. I knew just how she felt. Her feelings were real before this all started, so for her, it would happen. For me and Blake, I could not be so sure.

"What is the matter? You look so sad."

"I was just thinking about how your love for Charles is real, but mine for Blake might not be. It just makes me a bit sad, I suppose, to think that I may not feel this way in eleven days' time."

"Oh, Sabine." She hugged me again. "If you love him now, you will love him then. Come on. I am hungry."

"You go. I am going to have a bath. I will be down later."

"All right, I will send up Charlotte. See you later," she said and was out the door. A few minutes later, Charlotte knocked on the door.

"It will take me a few minutes to warm the water, my lady."

"That is fine. I will just wait here." I lay down in the bed and closed my eyes, letting my mind go back to the night before and the visions I had. *Was Rebecca going to die?* I could not handle knowing this truth. Charles told me, and that changed things. Perhaps we could still save her.

"My lady, your bath is ready."

"Thank you. I will be awhile."

She bowed and made her way out of the room. I dropped my underclothes on the floor and stepped into the very warm water. It felt good to soak in it. My mind went back to the night before, this time to Blake. His body was so big and so hard, his hands rough but tender. My back arched as I felt him pressing against me, heaving my chest out of the water. The moan that escaped my mouth was covered with his. I had not heard him come in. I was naked, and he could see me. He saw me heave myself out of the water. His kiss was tender but urgent, his tongue gentle but fierce at the same time. The position my head was in, tipped over the edge of the tub, had kept my breasts out of the water.

"Oh, Blake," I said rather loudly, and then just as quickly as he started he stopped. He dropped to the floor next to the tub and sat with his back to me.

"Oh my God, Sabine, I am so sorry. I do not know what came over me. Please forgive me. It will never happen again."

I could not talk; my body was sending shock wave after shock wave through itself. *Why would he say he was sorry?*

"I took a liberty with you I should not have taken. I am sorry that I violated your trust."

My body calmed down enough for me to lower myself into the water.

"Please say something."

In a whispered voice, I said, "I cannot seem to find my voice."

His head was in his hands. "I should be sent to the gallows for that. I am not an honorable man."

I did not understand why he was saying those things. I reached up with what felt like the last of my energy and put my hand on his head, running my fingers through his hair.

"I have never felt anything so wonderful in my whole life."

It was the best I could do. I could feel him shaking his head back and forth.

"That was so out of line, Sabine. I had no right."

"You have every right, Blake. I love you. I know now after that, that it could be the only reason you set me on fire. Rebecca said that is how Charles makes her feel, and she loved him long before we came back here. I love you. It has to be the reason."

"I can never do that again," he said and then got up and left my room.

I just smiled and laid my head back against the tub. *"Yep, I am in love."*

I washed my hair and dried myself off. I thought I would go for a walk. Yes, I felt like a walk. Perhaps I could persuade Rebecca to join me. Between me and Charles, we should be able to keep her with one of us at all times. I dressed, grabbed my sword, and went to the dining hall. As usual, everyone was sitting around the table.

"Well now, you look particularly cheerful today, Sabine," Joseph said with a smirk on his face.

"I am cheerful. Today is a good day indeed. Rebecca, would you care to go for a walk with me later?"

"I would love nothing more."

We sat and ate and chatted, just like it was any other day. No one mentioned the fact that in three days' time we could all be dead. I could feel Blake's eyes on me, but every time I looked up, he would turn his head away. I was finished sitting around. It was a beautiful day, and if I was going to die in three days, I was not going to sit around. I felt alive and free, and I wanted to be just that.

"Excuse me, gentlemen, but I think I am going for a walk. Charles, I am going to head to the hill and just relax. If you need me that is where I will be."

Rebecca seemed to be too into Charles to notice I was leaving. It did not matter, as long as she was with him, and I wanted some time to myself. It was nice walking through the village. The last time I had done so was when Jared and I burned all the bodies from Devious' attack on my family. Those who came after had done a nice job of fixing up the buildings, but now they just sit there empty. I was sure in the days to come that they would be burned to the ground.

I made it out of the village in record time, through the orchards and fields, and then up the hill. It was nice to smell the fruit on the trees. I stopped by an apple tree and picked two to have as a snack. Simpler times for me, it was only a few years ago, but for everyone else it was a lifetime. I made it to the top of the hill and then turned in a circle, looking out over my father's kingdom and remembering when I was a child.

"I miss you, Father," I said out loud. I sat down and looked at the sky.

For me it had been just over three years that I sat on this very hill, daydreaming about my life. I smiled; I could remember preparing myself to fight with Father about the man he would have chosen for me to marry. I wondered who it would have been. Perhaps he knew he would never have to choose. I knew too that he would never have chosen, for my mother told him that I was a free spirit. They knew that I would never marry, not in their lifetime. I could not help but wonder how they lived while knowing that they would die and never see me grow up completely.

I looked around the horizon, just like I had that day the barbarians came. I chuckled at the thought of their faces that day at the water's edge, the day I got Juliana back, the day Jared died. *Was he my true love, or was Blake?* Now I could not get Blake out of my mind. His mouth felt like nothing I had ever felt before. He saw me naked again; that made the third or fourth time. I guessed it did not matter, for in three days' time we were going to be in the middle of a full-blown battle with contraptions that threw giant balls of fire. I hoped Raiden got here in time with Juliana, not that I knew what Juliana was going to do to stop it all. I just knew that if this lasted longer than the eleven days left until the harvest, then there would be no way that Raiden would leave to go get her. He should be there as the dark of night arrived, and then they would be on their way back to me. This was the first time since he became mine that we had been apart, aside from the time we were in the cave. If he could not enter the cave, I wondered then how were we supposed to finish this? Charles said that I did not need Rebecca to finish this, so would that mean I did not need Raiden or Juliana either? What was I to do? Had I just sent Juliana to her death as well? I could feel the panic set in; I could feel the fear. No, this was the witch. I did not really feel this way. I outsmarted Samuel, and I would outsmart the witch and Roman. I looked down at the tree that had become Roman. He must have known what was coming. He must have known he was going to perish.

I stood up and started down the hill, through the fields and orchards, to the road into the village. I stood there looking at Roman.

"You will not win."

He smiled and said, "You keep going the way you are, Princess, and you will not be pure. We shall see who will win. Your one night of lust and passion will seal your fate. You cannot stop what is coming."

I laughed. "Roman, you do not know everything, and you certainly do not know me. I am good while you are evil. I am pure while you are not. I will win. My father has seen to it."

"Your father was an imposter. He took what did not belong to him and made you into some kind of goddess. You are just a mere child, Sabine."

"The jewels are what you are talking about? Well, Roman, I have seen them, touched them, and I know that they did belong to him. To possess them when one is not pure brings madness. Do I look mad to you? Samuel knew that the jewels I gave him were not the ones he sought after. He knew because he could not feel them."

His eyes grew large, and I knew he knew then that I had them.

"You cannot hide them. You have awakened them, and I will find them. They are alive with power, and it shall be mine."

Smiling, I said, "Yes, they were awakened, but now they sleep, waiting for me to finish this. You seem to forget your place in all this, Roman. You believe you were drawn here to claim the power, but really you were brought here to die. Evil such as you will perish in this land, and you are afraid because you know I speak the truth. You know I am the truth."

"We shall see, child. We shall see."

"No, Roman you will see." I walked away from him.

I made my way through the village and into the courtyard. Men were moving about, going here or going there. I could hear Rebecca laughing, but I did not see her, so I made my way to the kitchen. Charlotte was preparing food for the men.

"My lady, is there something you need?"

"I was wondering if we could talk."

"Of course," she said, then she flew her hands about, shooing everyone out the door. "Is everything all right?"

"I am not sure really. I know you are aware of what is happening between me and Blake."

"Yes, everyone is, and I am sorry that they are all talking about it. I do my best to not allow it in my kitchen, but he is a very handsome man. There are also a few of the girls here who do not understand why you would give him the time of day. He simply is not your equal."

"I am aware of all that, but I do not see myself above your station, or anyone's for that matter. I am just a girl with no kingdom and no father to give me away in marriage. He is just a man, and he has been my friend for a very long time. We have been through many a battle together."

"Yes, I am aware of that, but you are not just a girl. You are the chosen one, the Bringer of Peace, and most of all, you are a princess."

I sighed. "I know all of this, but what I do not know is men. Will you help me?"

She sat down next to me and took my hand in hers, saying, "Of course, dear."

"I do not understand why men think that because we are women that they have to protect us all the time and why they believe we cannot handle things."

She chuckled. "Men like to think that we need to be protected by them. It would make them seem less of a man if they allowed a woman to speak out of turn, have more knowledge then them, or heaven forbid, take control in the bedroom. It is bred into them to be the stronger, wiser, and certainly the more aggressive. It is just going against the laws of nature for a woman to be anything but a woman."

Just then, two guards came running into the kitchen.

"Princess, we were sent to retrieve you. Charles needs you in the barracks right away."

"Thank you, Charlotte. I will return if that is all right."

"It is fine, child. Now go."

We ran to the barracks. As I entered the gathering room, it was full, so I made my way to the front to hear what was being said. Charles was speaking.

"Our scouts just returned, and those troops heading this way are closer than we anticipated. They should be arriving sometime tomorrow. We need to stay calm and prepare for battle. I just want to take this moment and thank you all for standing with us and for fighting this battle."

Then the strangest thing happened all at one time, they yelled, "LONG LIVE SABINE!" I was shocked. I cleared my throat, and Charles beckoned me to the front.

"I just wanted to thank you all for being here, and I want to apologize in advance to you. Some of us will not survive this, and I will spend the rest of my days being sorry for that. There is still time for you to go back to your families. This fight is about me and Rebecca and this land. You need not die and suffer for us."

The emotion was too much. I was unprepared for what came over me. I ran out of there, wishing Raiden was there for me to ride. I ran into the stables and saw Spirit. I jumped on his back and leaned into him, asking.

"Will you take me for a ride?"

He nodded, and out the door we went. I saw Blake and Rebecca running out the door after me as we sped away.

He rode to the plain where Rebecca and I met. I stopped him in the middle and climbed off, collapsing in the grass crying. The dread washed over me, my confidence shaken and my will to survive gone. All of those men were going to die horrible deaths, and for what? There was nothing I could do to stop it. Raiden would not make it back in time. I had been a fool to send him away. I cried and cried. I was sobbing so much that I did not realize that Spirit had left. The dread filled me so, that I did not hear him ride up. I did not feel Blake, I just felt his arms around me. I felt him lift me onto his lap and wrap his arms around me. He held me for quite some time while I sat there sobbing into his chest.

"They are all going to die, and it is all my fault," I sobbed.

"Shhhh."

"You and your brothers are old, and it is all my fault. Rebecca is going to die, and I cannot do anything to stop it, and it is all my fault. I sent my magic horse away, and I cannot stop what is coming, and everyone is going to die, and again it is all my fault." I could not control the sobs. He just held me and rocked back and forth. Eventually my sobbing stopped, and I got control of my emotions. "I do not know what is wrong with me. Why am I so emotional?"

"Oh, I think I like this tender side of you," he said with a chuckle.

"Yeah, a slobbering crying mess, that is attractive."

He lifted my chin. "I have never seen you look more beautiful."

I smiled and laid my head on his chest. "Blake, how are we going to do this? Those men are all going to die. They have to leave here. They have to go back to the valley."

"Sabine, they are here because they believe in you. They believe in the legend that is you. To ask them to leave would only insult them. Do you not understand that they have nothing to go back to? That is why we sent our sons home. They will have to take care of the families if we do not succeed. These men have no families. Roman killed them all."

"But if they stay, they will have no chance of gaining new families."

"And if we do not succeed, they will have no families either."

"I was thinking about my family today. My father knew he would never give me away in marriage. He knew he would die before I reached the right age. My mother knew she would never have the opportunity to share intimate things with me. I cannot imagine knowing when you are going to die and continuing to live with no fear. Blake, these men know they are going to die, yet they go on living like they do not know. I cannot bear that I know they are going to die."

"You gave them a choice, Sabine. Some took the choice and are leaving. Others refuse to leave you, and well, we are kind of in this till the end, so we cannot leave you." He smiled.

"Gee, that makes me feel better. I could be sending all of you to your death as well."

"No, my beautiful girl you live, we live. Just do not go getting yourself killed. I have plans for the rest of your life."

"You do?"

"Oh yes, I do. I plan on doing this all day every day," he said, and then he kissed me, though it was not a long lingering kiss. In a husky, deep voice, he said, "And there is so much more than what happened in that tub that I plan to do with you every day." My body felt him all the way through.

"How did you find me?"

"Rebecca asked Spirit to come and get me. We should get back soon though, for I am sure Charles is beside himself." Blake laughed.

We got up and climbed on Spirit. We did not ride hard, just walked with me in his arms looking at one another.

"Will you stay with me tonight?" I asked him.

"Would that be wise, Sabine?"

"Probably not, but I do not want to spend our last night apart. Even if a wall separates us, it is still too far away."

"I agree, but I do not think we should be alone. Do you understand how I feel about you?"

"You are in love with me."

"Yes, Sabine, I am, and with that love is a desire to have you in a manner in which a married man and woman lay down together. These feelings grow very strong when I am with you alone, and if we spend an entire night together, I am afraid that I will not be able to stop, that we will not be able to stop. If that happens, then all of this will be for nothing."

"Do you remember before, when Jared was alive, and Rebecca and Charles slept with us in the same room? Perhaps we could do that. None of us will be able to cross that line then. Blake, I need to have you with me tonight. I do not know what tomorrow will bring."

"I cannot seem to tell you no. I will discuss it with Charles."

We rode in silence for a while, but when we reached the fields we started to run. Rebecca and Charles were walking through the court-yard when we rode up.

"Rebecca, I am sorry that I took Spirit."

"It is fine. Are you all right?"

"Yes and no," I said. Blake helped me down. "It would all depend on Charles."

"Me? What is it I can do for you, Sabine?"

"You can move a bed into my room, and you and Rebecca can sleep with us tonight. I want to spend the night in Blake's arms, but we are afraid we will cross a line, and well, if you and Rebecca are there, we are sure to not."

"Consider it done. I would like nothing more than to spend our last safe night with Rebecca."

There was shouting coming from behind us; men were running and screaming. Charles and Blake took off toward the men. Horses with men on them were running about. Men were dropping on the ground. Horses were dropping on the ground. It was panic, and then I saw it swirling around Blake's feet. The Mist.

Rebecca and I just stood there frozen, like that kitty in the water all those years ago. I watched in horror as innocent men dropped to their deaths. Birds fell from the sky; horses, cows, chickens all dropping. There was nothing I could do, nothing Charles could do. The men could not get away fast enough. I heard a horn blowing and then slowly stop. Those men that were at the outposts might have been able to get away. It took only minutes to happen, and then there was nothing but the nine of us standing like statues, with the green mist swirling around our feet. The bodies were everywhere, and the silence was the worst of it all.

CHAPTER TWENTY-FOUR

I finally broke the silence, saying, "How is this possible?" My voice echoed through the courtyard. "I thought it was gone for good. They all died anyway. All this was for nothing?"

Charles stood looking at me, and I knew he knew more than he was saying to me.

"You knew this would happen. You knew these men would die like this," I said as calmly as I could. "Why, Charles? Why would you not let them go home? Why would you not make them go home?" My voice was getting louder. "You keep things to yourself, things you say you cannot change. Are you saying, Charles, that you could not do a thing to save these men?" I was yelling now. "All those women in the house, are they dead as well?" I yelled at him. "Why, Charles? Why would you do this to them?" Blake started walking toward me. "NO! Do not think you can fix this!" I screamed at him, and he stopped halfway to me.

Charles said as calmly as he could, "I cannot..."

"Oh, that is right. You cannot interfere with the order of things," I interrupted him.

He took a few steps toward me. "Do you think I do not want to tell you? Do you think I wanted to watch these men die, Sabine? I know their families. I grew up with them. This was not easy for me. This is not easy for me, knowing what is to come. I am like you, Sabine. I was born with this knowledge. I knew it from the time I was old enough to think. Do you believe I want this for my life? It is what it is, and none of us are safe until this ends. You know that. WE have been your Guardians from birth, just like you are the Bringer of Peace. You were born into this, as were we."

"You stand here with all of these men lying dead around you, and you can hold your head high because you were chosen to survive this. How arrogant of you, Charles. You are not untouchable in all of this."

"I know my weaknesses, trust me, and I know that I am not as honorable a man as I claim to be, but there is an order to things. It must be the way it must be. I cannot change it. I have already done enough damage to the outcome of all of this. Perhaps this..." He paused and waved his hand across the courtyard, now filled with dead bodies. "Perhaps this is the payment for doing what I did."

"Charles, what have you done?" Joseph touched him on the shoulder.

"I have changed the outcome of this by giving Sabine information she was not supposed to have."

"Charles do not do this," I said.

"What information is that, brother?"

His eyes shifted from me to Rebecca. "Charles?" she whispered.

"I allowed Sabine to have the knowledge that Rebecca will not survive this battle."

I turned to look at Rebecca, standing there with tears forming in her eyes.

"No, I will not let you die. You are my sister in this," I said to her. I grabbed her in my arms. "I will not let you die," I said as I hugged her.

"You knew? You knew I was marked for death, and you said nothing to me?" she said to Charles over my shoulder.

"Rebecca."

"No, you do not get to say my name. You do not get to look at me. How dare you keep this from me?"

"Rebecca, please."

"How long, Charles? How long have you known this?"

I let her go and turned to face him. His head dropped.

"Always… I have always known you would not survive."

She turned and ran into the castle. I knew where she was going, and I let her go. Charles would not find her.

"Why would you tell her? Why on our last night together would you tell her she was going to die?"

"Because I cannot lie to her. She is everything to me. Do you not see that this is why I have done all that I have done? This is why I have dishonored my wife and sent my son away, because I love her. I cannot stop loving her, and believe me, Sabine, I have tried."

"You stand here and speak to me of love, but you know only of one kind of love. You know nothing of the love I have for her. You men and your arrogance toward women, thinking you are superior to us, you know of desire and passion that goes no further than your own satisfaction. You know nothing of love of the soul, the love of a bond one person shares with another. To you, it is just about how you feel. You think you know us, yet you know nothing."

"You stand before me, Sabine, and judge me. You knew and did not tell her."

"That is where you are wrong, Charles. She knew already. I told her of my vision that day we went to see the witch. I told her that I knew she would die."

I turned and walked away. I did not know where I was going, but I could not stand there and look at him any longer. I went to the kitchen, but Charlotte was dead; they were all dead. I went to the secret staircase and closed the door behind me, and then I sat down and cried. There was nothing more I could do.

I heard someone calling my name, and my eyes fluttered open. Gathering myself, I realized that I must have fallen asleep. I was still in the secret staircase. I listened again and heard nothing. *Was I having another vision?* Everything that happened came back to me. Everyone was dead. There were just the nine of us left, and Roman's men would be here by the time the light of the day left the sky the following day. *How were we ever going to do this?* Raiden would not be back in time. I concentrated on him, not knowing if I could reach him.

'The mist has returned.'

I sat with my eyes closed, listening for him, but I heard nothing.

I knew I should go find Rebecca. I got up and listened at the door, but I heard nothing, so I pushed the door open. There was no one in the kitchen. *'They must have removed the bodies.'* Then I smelt it, that smell from all those years ago when Jared and I burned the bodies of the villagers. I walked out the back door to find Aidan, Joseph, and James hauling bodies to the fire.

"Sabine, where have you been? Charles is looking for you. Have you been with Rebecca?"

Joseph looked relieved to see me. "Rebecca has gone missing. Charles and Blake are out looking for you."

I smiled at him and went back into the kitchen. Rebecca was still gone. I headed to my father's study, popped the latch for the door to the secret room, and made my way behind the tapestry and into the room. There she sat on the floor with her back to the desk. I sat next to her and held her.

"I am so sorry."

"It is not your doing. You told me that you knew I was going to die, yet he did not."

"Not that I want to defend him, but he could not tell you."

"Did he tell you?"

"No, Blake told me what was coming, and I put it together with my visions. I confronted Charles, and then he confessed. I will not let you die."

"Sabine, you and I both know you cannot stop this. It will be what it will be. I am all right with that. What our life is now is not what it should be. You and I should have lots of children and be married to men we fought our parents over not to marry. We should not have been stuck in time and then emerged into a world where everything that we knew was either old or dead."

I could not speak, so I just held my friend. We sat like that for a long time.

"It is our last night together. Roman's men will be here tomorrow as the light of the day leaves and the dark of the night comes. We will survive this, Rebecca. We have to. I cannot lose you."

"No matter what happens to me, just know that I love you. You must stay alive to finish this," she said.

"I love you as well. You are my greatest friend and my only sister."

We must have fallen asleep. I was awaked by Raiden's voice in my head.

'We are nearly there.'

I sat straighter, and Rebecca shifted.

'The mist has returned.'

'She will be safe.'

'They will be here soon.'

'I will make it through to you.'

"Rebecca, we must get up. I believe we slept through the dark of night. We need to eat and prepare, not to mention face the wrath of Charles and Blake."

She rubbed her eyes and stretched. "Is Raiden coming?"

"Yes, but he will not make it in time."

"What about the mist and Juliana?"

"He said she would be fine. Come, we must go and make our plan." We made our way out of the room and into the great hall before anyone had seen us.

James was walking out of the dining hall.

"Where have the two of you been? The dark of night has come and gone and is nearly here again. We have been searching everywhere for you."

Then I heard a chair slam to the ground. Charles came bolting out of the room, pausing only a second before he grabbed Rebecca up in his arms.

"Where have you been? I have been frantic with worry. We do not have much time before they arrive."

She pushed him away. "Do not touch me."

Charles let her go and just stood there looking at her.

"Sabine, we have much to do and little time to do it."

"Well, they cannot enter the village or the castle grounds with the mist here."

"The mist is gone."

"What? How?"

"As quickly as it came it has gone. They have already entered the kingdom and are less than a half a day's ride away from the castle. We need to prepare."

I could not stop the giggle. "Prepare for what, Charles? We are but nine people. We have no power to stop this assault. They are not coming for us. They are coming for the jewels. I have but seven days left. We need to survive this for seven days. How is that going to be possible?"

The nine of us just stood there in the doorway of the dining hall looking at one another.

"We should ride to the edge of the village and wait for them. If they destroy the castle and the grounds, they will destroy the jewels. Without them, Roman cannot take control," I stated.

"Nor will you be able to finish this."

"Perhaps that is so, but I have this."

I reached in my bodice and pulled out the jewel from Roman's sword.

"Roman cannot kill me. The witch cannot kill me. In order for Roman to complete the ritual, he needs this. Well, he needs this and to free himself from the ground that holds him because I cannot be killed by them, we are at an impasse."

"Roman and the witch both know you sent Raiden away. The power you and Rebecca have is unattainable without him."

"Oh, ye of little faith Charles, have you not heard I am magic? Come on, Rebecca," I said as I grabbed her hand, and we went out into the courtyard.

"Remember when they took Raiden and Spirit?"

"Yes."

"Stand with your back to me. You need to clear your mind and concentrate on the air and the wind." Charles, James, Blake, Aidan,

Steven, Edward, and Joseph stood at the doorway of the castle and watched.

I closed my eyes and leaned my head against Rebecca's. "We must not lose contact."

Blake ran up. "Here, tie this around your waists," he said, holding a rope.

He put it around us and tied it tight then went back to the doorway.

"Turn to the left. Do not stop turning, and you must concentrate. You ready?"

I felt her nod her head. We began to turn, and I started the chant.

"Winds arise and flow from the east."

I could feel the breeze pick up around us. We turned three times, and each time the wind blew stronger.

"Scream through the trees like a roaring beast."

The wind picked up more still. I could hear it roaring as it blew harder, and we started to turn faster.

"Take these souls to be leaves. Blow them clear and never cease."

I raised my sword into the air above my head, and I felt Rebecca do the same. We were turning at a very fast rate, not of our doing. The wind roared like thunder.

"Touch our swords," I screamed.

The tips of our swords touched, and lighting shot out of them, and just as we started we stopped spinning. I was so dizzy that I fell to the ground, as did Rebecca. The wind roared around us, the dust from the ground blowing in my face. I felt hands on me, lifting me, but I could not open my eyes. We made it through the doors of the castle, Blake leading me and Charles leading Rebecca. James and Steven pushed the great doors shut.

Rebecca was yelling, "Let me go! I told you not to touch me."

Charles let her go, as did Blake with me.

"Well, that should hold them for a bit," I said and smiled.

"So it would appear we have a powerful sorceress on our side," James said.

I went to Rebecca. "See, I am not without the ability to save you. I will do my best to make sure you survive this."

"If you cannot, I am prepared for whatever will happen to me. Do not be sad if you cannot save me. You must finish this. I know now that you do not need me to do it. Just do not let my death be for nothing. You must stay focused."

I hugged her. "Your death will not occur if I have anything to do with it."

"Should we be doing something?" James said looking around.

"What should we do? They cannot reach the castle, and even if they do, the wind will not allow them to use their contraptions. It will be a hand to hand encounter, and I think we could beat them."

"The nine of us against thousands?"

"When the wind is finished, there will not be thousands."

"Sabine, can we talk?" Blake said as he walked up to me.

I smiled at him. "Yes, of course," I said.

I led him into the sitting room where Simon was killed. I had not been in here since that day. As I walked by the spot where his blood marked the floor, I stopped.

"This is where Simon died."

Blake put his arm around me and pulled me close. I walked away to sit on the chair by the window. He knelt in front of me.

"I am sorry for what took place last night. I was worried about you when I could not find you, but I understand how you must feel. I knew those men very well. I also wanted to tell you that I will regret for the rest of my days not being with you last night."

He picked up my hand and kissed the back of it.

"It was for the best that we did not, for my feelings for you are so intense right now that it would have taken a great deal of effort for me to stop you. Blake, this is all going to end soon. We may not get another chance to speak to one another like this, and I just want you to know that no matter what happens when this ends, that today, this day, I love you. I want to spend every night with you and every day with you, but I do not know if I will feel this way about you when it is over. I just wanted you to know that I do love you."

"Those words are words I have waited my entire life to hear from you. I have loved you always, Sabine, from that first day when we rode into Whispering Wind with Wellington and I saw you in the window. I knew that you might not ever return my feelings, but it did not matter to me. I knew I would never feel the same about another woman my whole life."

I placed my hand on his face. "I am fearful that we are not going to have our happily ever after."

"As I am, Princess. After all, you will be ruler of a kingdom, and I will be just a mere servant. You will not be able to humble yourself to look in my direction."

I giggled like a young girl and slipped off the chair and into his lap, into his arms. It felt good to feel his love, to feel the warmth of his body. I looked into his eyes and whispered, "I love you."

He smiled and covered my mouth with his. My legs made their way around his waist, and we sat there kissing and breathing hard. If I could have crawled inside this man, I would have. Out of nowhere, Raiden was in my head.

'Open the doors!'

I pushed off Blake without any warning and ran to the doors. He was right behind me.

"Help me," I yelled.

I pulled one while he pulled the other. The wind was whipping around, blowing everything inside the great hall. The others ran out with Charles yelling.

"WHAT ARE YOU DOING?"

I could just hear him above the voice of the wind. I turned just as Raiden blew in the open doors and skidded to a halt just at the base of the stairs. I looked past Charles to see Juliana sitting on top of Raiden with a huge smile on her face.

She jumped off Raiden and was in my arms. "My love," I said in her ear.

"I have missed you so much," she whispered.

Blake and Charles finally got the doors closed again.

"Is this little Juliana?" Charles asked as he walked up to her.

"Do you remember us?" asked Blake.

She looked them both over and shook her head very slowly.

"Should I?"

They both laughed. "No, I suppose you should not. I am Charles, and these are my brothers Blake, Joseph, Aidan, Steven, James, and Edward."

"Hello. I am Juliana of Whispering Wind. Where is Rebecca?"

"Right here!" she screamed. Juliana turned and ran into her arms.

It was so good to see her smiling.

"How are Westin and Camille, and the children?" I asked her.

"Westin is beside himself. He was more excited to see Raiden than all of us combined. He knows he will be coming home soon. He told me to tell you to stay safe."

"So now there are ten of us."

"That is it, just ten of us?" I heard the fear in her voice as she turned to look at me.

"Come for a walk with me. We need to talk." I held out my hand. We walked into the sitting room and sat down. "So how have you been?"

"Good, besting Stephan at everything. It is fun to see him get so angry," she said and smiled. "I have been practicing like you told me to, and I am quite good at controlling it now. I do not need to be angry, but it is much more intense and hotter when I am angry."

"What exactly can you do?"

"I can send it out like a finger, I can make it into a ball and throw it with my mind, and I can make it explode anywhere I want it to. When we rode in, the wind was so strong. We have nothing but blue skies in the valley. I have never seen the wind like this."

I smiled at her. "Rebecca and I made this wind to slow down the men that are coming here. I do not know how long it will stay."

"You made it?"

"Yes, are you hungry?"

"I am a little, and I am tired."

"Come, you can eat and then have a sleep in my old room."

"Sabine, will you show me where my parents died?"

"Are you sure you want to see it? I have not changed anything."

"Yes, I am sure."

We went to the dining hall where she had some bread, and then we went upstairs. I took her down the hall that led to Ardes and Jenna's room. I stopped just before the door.

"This is where your father died while he was trying to protect you and your mother."

She knelt down and felt the floor. The stain of blood marked the stone. I watched her run her hand on the floor. I wished that I could hear what was running through her mind. We entered the bedroom; the blood-stained blankets were still on the bed, the blood stained cot still in its place. I sat in the chair and let her have her emotions.

"Where was my mother?"

I pointed to the cot. "She was there."

"She was protecting me?"

"I believe she was. She gave her life to save you. Your mother and father knew who you were, just as mine knew who I was. They knew what was coming, and they knew that they could not stop it."

"Why were we marked for this?"

"It is a very long story, and someday I hope to figure it all out. I only have pieces of it, but perhaps together we can find the truth to it all."

She nodded. "I think I have seen enough. I am tired, Sabine, and I wish to sleep."

"Come, my love."

I took her in my arms, and we made our way to my room. She took the blanket off the bed and was making a place on the floor.

"What are you doing?"

"I am going to sleep. Why?"

"You can sleep in the bed."

"I do not know what a bed is."

"This is a bed," I said, patting the blankets. "Climb up here and lie down, get under the covers, and rest your head on this."

She did, and her face was that of a child, a small smile forming on her lips.

"I have never slept in one of these before," she said as she snuggled in. "It is very soft." She laid her head back. "What do you call this thing?"

I smiled at her. "That is a pillow for your head."

It only took a few minutes before she was sleeping. I sat in the chair and watched her. She was so beautiful, part Jenna and part Ardes. I missed them so much. I must have fallen asleep because I woke by arms surrounding me and carrying me to the bed. I opened my eyes to find Blake's arms around me. He laid me down, kissed my forehead, and whispered.

"You sleep, beautiful, and I will watch over you."

I smiled at him. "I love you," was all I said as I fell back to sleep.

The roaring of the wind woke me. I looked over and saw that Juliana was still asleep; she had a smile on her flawless face. Beauty such as hers I had never seen before. She was so innocent. I looked over to the fireplace, and Blake was asleep in the chair. I carefully got out of bed and went to him. Kneeling down in front of him, I gently pressed my lips to his. I could feel the smile form on his lips as his hands came around me to pull me closer.

"Good morning," I mouthed against his lips.

"Good morning," he mouthed back, and we kissed again.

When we separated, I took his hand and led him from the room. We made our way down to the dining hall, and for the first time ever, we were the first to arrive.

"We have four days until the harvest, and I have no idea how we are going to pull this off."

"You will succeed, Sabine. I have known you a long time, and you do not fail."

"Thank you, but you do not understand. When we enter the cave, time will stand still for us. A day is a year. How will I know when it is midday?"

"How did you know how to cause this wind to do what you wanted? How did you know how to get Raiden and Spirit back when those men took them? How do you do the things you do?"

"I do not know, it just happens."

"Well, I think you have your answer. It will just happen. You will know what to do, and you will know when it is time to do it."

It was enough for me to know that he had so much confidence in me. I kissed him, and it was Charles clearing his throat that separated us.

"Good morning, you two, although with this wind, I am not so sure I know if it is morning. How long will this go on, Sabine?"

"I do not know. I thought it was just a temporary thing, like when I got Raiden and Spirit back. I thought it would end when our swords were no longer in contact. Should I try and stop it?"

"Eventually, but I think we should first discuss what we should do. We have enough food in storage to last another month, but after that we will be in trouble. We cannot get to the fields, and the animals are all dead."

"We have four days until the harvest. We should be all right."

"When everyone gets down here, we will need to discuss what to do. I think it would be best if Rebecca stayed with me."

I laughed. "She will not be harnessed, Charles, and you know it. You will not convince her to stay out of this fight."

"Yes, I know, but I will at least try."

"Someone talking about me?" Rebecca said as she wandered in the room.

"We were discussing where Charles thinks you should be when I stop the wind. He thinks you should be with him, and I said that there would be no way to stop you from being a part of this fight."

"You would be correct, Sabine, and Charles would be wrong." She turned to look at him. "As far as I am concerned, I would like to be on the other side of the battlefield."

"Rebecca do not be a child about this. Someone has to protect you."

She laughed at him. "Trust me when I say this to you, Charles you destroyed any chance you had of protecting me when you failed to tell me all those years ago that the reason we could not marry was because I was marked for death."

"We could not marry because you needed to stay pure."

"Are you kidding me? If you knew I was going to die before we accomplished this task, then what difference did it make? You really should get your story straight. Either you love me and you want to be with me, or you felt sorry for me because I was going to die."

He slammed his fist on the table. "I love you! I have always loved you, but you forget, Rebecca, that I knew you would disappear for all those years. Was I supposed to marry you and then spend twenty years of life alone, waiting for you to return, when I was doubting it myself? I am but a man."

No one said a word. The silence was evident, even with the howling wind swirling around the castle. They stood there staring at one another until Rebecca broke the silence.

"You are one of the most egotistical men I have ever met. I would have waited for you!"

Then she turned and left the room. I looked at Charles, and I could see the pain in his eyes as I watched a tear fall.

He hung his head and said, "I am not worthy of her."

"Not to add salt to your wound, brother, but she does have a point."

"I know she does, and that is the most painful. I should have waited, and she was right. I knew she would die, and I was selfish."

I did not want to make light of the situation, but we still had much to discuss.

"We cannot waste time dwelling on these things and what will be. We have so much to do. Charles, please gather yourself so we can figure things out. Rebecca will need to stay with me. I cannot strike the lightning without her. There are things I can do on my own, but we need to be together for everything else. If you feel the need to be close to us then that is what you will do."

"I am your Guardian. My place is by your side."

Blake interrupted, "I will keep an eye on Rebecca."

"Blake, we are going to have more to do, and keeping an eye on either of them is going to be difficult at best. It will be what it will be. I have already come to terms with the fact that there is a great possibility that she will not survive this. All I can do is hope that we can do this with no loss of life."

"Charles, what scares me is that the only life that is in danger here is Rebecca's. They cannot kill me, and as long as I live, you will live. Is there anything in your knowledge that says the same for Rebecca?"

"No, and there is nothing about Juliana either. I do not know if she can or will perish as well."

I giggled. "They could not get close enough to her. You will be surprised when you see what she can do."

"Oh, you will indeed," I heard from the doorway.

We turned to see Juliana was standing there. "Good morning, my love," I said as I got up to hug her. Behind her came the rest of my Guardians and then Rebecca.

"I must apologize for my behavior earlier. This is not about me and Charles. We have a battle to fight, ten of us against all of them, so let us plan."

"It seems a bit unfair, do you not agree," Juliana said. The laughter that filled the room was strange. Here we sat, ten of us, laughing about the possibility that we could possibly win a battle with ten thousand or more men; men who would do anything to eat us, with their leader wrapped in the roots of the earth just outside the village.

"They should be close, the ones that have survived the wind." I turned to the window. "I think we should have a look to see just how many have arrived."

"I would agree, Sabine, but how are we supposed to get through this wind?" James asked.

"Well, I can calm it so we can go out." Raiden stomped his hoof and neighed. Then I heard him in my head.

'I will go. Do not stop the wind.'

'Be careful.'

"Raiden will go."

"You and that horse have your own language," James said with a smile on his face.

Blake and Charles went to open the huge doors in the grand hall. The wind was fierce, but Raiden went out.

"Leave them open for him. You know how fast he is."

We all stood in the hall, waiting and trying to see the grounds before us. There was nothing but dirt circling around and around. I had never seen the wind do such things. In what seemed an instant, he was back and they were forcing the doors closed.

'What did you see?'

'More than I wanted to see. Sabine, many men have come. They are camped just outside the village. They have surrounded Roman to protect him. I think they are trying to free him.'

'How many men are there, Raiden?'

'Ten times more than the barbarians, and there are more coming.'

I spun around to look at everyone. "We are in trouble. There are ten times more men than the barbarians, and there are more on the way. How are we going to do this?"

"We have our horses, Sabine, and we have Juliana."

"I do not think our horses are going to save us, Rebecca, and I am fearful that we may not make it through this."

'You will survive this, Sabine.'

I turned to look at Raiden. "Perhaps I will, but what of everyone else?"

"As long as you live, we live," Charles said.

"Yes, but what about Rebecca and Juliana? Will they live?"

Juliana came up to me and said, "Sabine, you do not know what I can do, and I am not afraid."

"I know, my love, but you do not know what Rebecca can do either, and yet she is not safe."

"Charles, would you open the door please?" she asked walking to the doors.

"Juliana, you cannot do this with the wind," I tried to plead with her.

Charles opened the doors. Juliana stood there not moving, just concentrating on something. I watched her eyes as they grew a dark amber red color, and then out of nowhere a huge fire ball blew from within her out into the wind. I could not see where it had gone, but I heard it and with it I heard men screaming. I watched her as she calmed down, and when I touched her hand, she was very warm to the touch.

James spoke, "Now there is something you do not see every day," He chuckled.

Juliana came out of her trance. "Do you see? Nothing can stop this, not even your wind, Sabine."

I chuckled also. "No, I suppose it cannot."

Charles and James closed the doors. "This might work to our advantage, Sabine," he said. "If her fire can work its way through the wind, then perhaps we stand a chance of not losing…" He looked at Rebecca. "…of not losing anyone in this fight."

I turned to see Rebecca flinch. I knew she was scared. I went to my sister, my friend, and hugged her.

"I will do everything I can to not let you perish."

"I am not afraid, Sabine. We need to stop this, and if me dying is the only way to do it, then so be it."

"You may be ready to die, Rebecca, but I am not ready to lose you."

"Oh, you have that all wrong. I have no intention on dying. My plan is to live and torture Charles because he will never have me, and living will do just that. See, as long as you live, he lives, and he will have to live with being selfish and never knowing what could have been."

I saw the sparkle in her eyes, and I knew she was ready for a fight.

"Well then, if that is the case, then perhaps I should calm the winds and let us go have some fun with these men. Besides, we should probably take care of them before the rest of them get here."

Charles spoke, looking right at Rebecca, "Whether you live or die, the regret will never leave me. Sabine, I think we should wait before we go out there. We still have four days left until the harvest."

"Yes, I know, but I can also bring the wind back again."

"And I can make a wall of fire," Juliana interrupted with a huge smile on her face.

"Really?" said James, completely amazed.

Juliana nodded her head like a small child would if they were asked if they wanted some sweets.

"Well then, I suppose, Sabine, we should get on with this." Blake smiled at me.

"As you wish, sire," I said as I bowed to him. We all laughed. "It is time for us to see just how good we are." My hand raised, and I closed my eyes as I chanted,

'I call upon the element of air,
'It is your time to be fair,
'Bring yourself to peace and cease'

I opened my eyes, and we all stood still, listening to the wind roaring in anger as it slowed and calmed itself. "You know, Sabine," Joseph said. "I am truly glad that I am on your side."

I turned to face him. "I am too. Shall we go out and welcome our guests?"

Blake laid his hand out in front of him. "After you, my lady." I kissed him on the cheek, and with our swords drawn, we made our way out into the courtyard. James and Steven ran to the stables to get the horses, while Rebecca and I climbed on ours. With the wind still roaring, we made our way to the middle of the village. As the wind started to ease up, I could make out the camp they had made.

"How did they do that with all the wind?" Juliana asked.

"I am not sure. Perhaps next time I should make it a bit stronger."

That will not be necessary.'

'Do you know something I do not?'

Just as I said that I felt him twitch under me, and I looked at Rebecca to see she was smiling. I put my hand on my sword, and Raiden moved forward. Toddzwga rode out of the camp on his horse, followed by about a hundred men.

"I believe I told you to leave my land and not return."

He laughed and said, "Yes, Princess, you did, but I brought a few of my friends to meet you. I see you have added a sweet little thing to your party."

He looked past me to Juliana, who was riding with James.

"If I were you, I would not be looking like that at her, Toddzwga. You might not like how you feel when she gets done with you."

"Why, Charles, you always seem to make things sound so eerie. She is but a child and a very beautiful one at that." Then he looked at me. "Sabine, I think this child might have your beauty beaten."

"I will not ask you again why are you here?"

"Oh now, come on. Can we not be friends and have a nice chat? I suppose not. I am here to free my master, of course, and to annihilate you in the process. There now, see how rough you make me sound."

"I do not hold Roman. The ground holds him, and you will not free him. You seem to have forgotten where you are. Oh wait. Roman did not tell you why you are here. Let me guess he promised you treasures beyond your comprehension."

"It is none of your concern what he promised me."

"Well then, it would not matter to you to know that I gave the jewels to Wellington."

His face changed just enough to notice. "You lie," he said.

"No, Toddzwga, I do not lie. Go ahead and ask Roman yourself. When Devious and Wellington murdered my family, I found the jewels and gave them to Wellington. He in turn gave some to the barbarians to kill me, and as far as I know, they are still in Wellington. Perhaps you should go visit there and see if you can find them."

He turned to face Roman. "Is what this child says truth?"

"Why would you listen to her and not me?"

"She has no reason to be untruthful to me. You on the other hand promised me wealth beyond anything I could imagine. All I had to do was follow you and take care of a few men and two small children."

"The jewels are here."

Toddzwga turned to face me. "I will pass, and I will take that castle down stone by stone, and I will find them."

I parted with Rebecca to leave an opening for him to pass.

"You have my word that I will not stop you, but it will be the task for the rest of your days." I leaned in and said, "The castle is rather large, and you will be the only one passing through."

"You will not thwart me, child."

I have no idea where it came from, but a giggle escaped me. "You can try and sound all tough and bad, but you know as well as I do that you cannot harm me. I gave you my word, but no one else shall pass. You know what I can and will do to you and all these innocent men you have brought along with you to die."

I looked past him at the men, but they were not afraid. In fact, they seemed eager to fight. I drew my sword and pointed it at one of his men.

"Shall I show you what I can do with this sword?"

He smiled, showing his rotten teeth. "Oh, Princess, I have been waiting for this day for a very long time. Even your wind could not stop us, and I would wager my life that you will not succeed."

I felt him move, and I saw Rebecca out of the corner of my eye draw her sword. Before I knew what was happening, Raiden was in the air. The light was tremendous, and the screams of the men left standing was loud. When Raiden landed, the only men left on their horses were Toddzwga and the man who spoke to me. I looked him straight in the eyes.

"I can do this all day. Now leave my land or suffer the fate of your men."

"You will not tell me what I shall and shall not do," the man screamed.

I felt Raiden twitch again, and up he went. The brilliant light that flowed from our swords felt different from the last time. It was more calming. When Raiden's feet touched the ground, I looked out past the men. He had caused a fire to glow, surrounding the men in their camp. No one could leave.

"I am tiring of the two of you. You have until the light of the day to leave Whispering Wind, or we will seal your fate accordingly."

I turned Raiden to head back to the castle. I felt something come at me before Juliana screamed my name. I jumped off Raiden, and when my feet hit the ground, I turned, swinging my sword and connecting with the neck of his horse. The horse fell to the ground, and then the man jumped up and swung at me. My sword connected with his, the flash of light slamming him to his knees. I pushed my sword against his to the hilt, making an X with his head in the middle.

"This would be goodbye," I said.

I pushed harder, his throat touching the blade. I watched the fear grow in his eyes as he realized that his life was going to end, but I did not turn away. I leaned into my sword, and his head fell to the ground. I turned to look at Toddzwga.

"You will leave by the light of the day. I will not ask this of you again."

I got on Raiden and headed back through the village.

I heard Charles as I rode away. "Roman, you cannot win this. If you chose to keep these men here, they will all die."

Roman laughed at him. "We shall see about that, Charles."

Then I heard a strange swishing sound. As I turned in my saddle, I saw a fireball flying through the air toward the castle. I looked at Juliana, who had her eyes closed sitting behind James, and then I saw James' face. I could not stop the giggle, for he looked terrified. Juliana held up her hand, and a fireball flew from within her at the fireball flying through the air. Connecting with it caused a shower of fire to reign down to the ground. I spun Raiden around and kicked him in the sides. I pulled on his reigns just short of Roman. I jumped down and drew my sword, putting the tip on Roman's throat.

"You will not destroy my family home."

He smiled. "You cannot kill me, Princess, and I will do as I please."

I do not know what came over me, but I shoved the blade through his throat. The look on his face made me giggle. I was pretty sure he did not believe I would do it. I pushed it to the hilt.

"I may not be able to kill you, Roman, but you will not be freed from this place. The ground will take you when I am done, and then I will not have to look at you again."

He tried to speak, but he could not. I tilted my head and looked at him.

"Well now, this is new. Would someone be so kind as to give me a sword?"

Blake walked up, picked one off the ground, and then handed it to me. I pulled mine out of Roman's throat and inserted the new one. I closed my eyes and said.

With this sword I bind you'
Now and until the end of your days'
Let no man have the power to remove'

'Silence'

Then I leaned into Roman and kissed him.

"You shall die here silent. That was my kiss of death. Be very afraid of me, Roman. I am going to destroy all of them, and then I am coming for you."

His eyes gave him away. I knew fear, and that is what I saw. I turned to find eleven pairs of eyes on me, yet no one said a word.

"What?" I said.

Charles chuckled and said to Roman, "You would not listen to me. I told you she would destroy you."

Roman struggled against the blade but could not move nor could he speak.

"I am hungry. Shall we eat?" I said as I climbed up on Raiden.

Blake rode up next to me. "I wish to see you in the stables," he said, and he rode off.

We took our time going back to the castle. I made my way to the stables, where Blake was pacing back and forth. I climbed off of Raiden and he grabbed me by my arms and pushed me against the wall, covering my mouth with his. I stood there, pinned and unable to move, matching his tense passion. He pulled away breathing heavily and said.

"You scared me to death out there. Do not ever do that again."

I tilted my head and smiled at him. "What are you talking about?"

He let go of me and started pacing back and forth again.

"Where do I start, Sabine? First, you provoked that man. Then, you dismounted Raiden to fight with him, and I thought I was going to die watching you. You cast some sort of trickery on Roman. Where did you learn to do that, Sabine? That is magic of the darkest kind. I am sure that my brothers are all talking about what you did out there."

"Are you saying to me, Blake, that it is acceptable for me to cast a spell, as you would call it, to bring the wind forth to save us or gain us more time, but it is not acceptable to silence a man who most assuredly wants me dead?" I was confused at his implications.

"I saw you bring the wind, and it was nothing like what I witnessed with you and Roman. And why did you kiss him? I wanted to grab you and scream at you not to touch him. He is evil at its worst. I pulled on that sword, Sabine, and I could not remove it. That is magic at its darkest."

"You keep saying that but saying it over and over is not going to make it go away. Blake, I do not know how I can do these things, nor do I know where these incantations come from. When we entered the cave, I was given this, or it was enhanced. I cannot explain it though. It just happens. Are you afraid of me now that you know I can do these things? Is that what this is about?"

He stopped moving and turned to face me. He was fast but not forceful as he approached me. His hands went to my waist as his mouth covered mine. He lifted me up, and I wrapped my legs around him. His hands rested just below my bottom on my thighs as he pressed me against the wall of the stables. I put my hands on his face so I could push my tongue deeper into his mouth. I felt myself sliding down the wall, and soon Blake was on his knees, and I was sitting on him. He slowly tipped me onto my back and positioned himself over me. I was ready for the weight of his body, but it did not come like I thought it would. He was very gentle as he pressed his chest against mine. Our lips did not part, not even when James came in and interrupted us.

"Excuse me, but Charles sent me to find you," James said.

We parted our lips but not our eyes, and I could see the change in his; they were a deeper color of green, the blacks of them huge. Breathlessly he said, "Tell Charles we will be in shortly."

I heard James leave, and then Blake said to me, "Does that tell you if I am afraid of you?"

I shook my head no and smiled at him. I pulled myself up to his mouth with my arms around his neck, and I kissed him again. He pulled away.

"I cannot continue, or your virtue will be no more," he whispered as he sat up with me on his lap. "You will be the death of me yet, woman."

"Apparently I am the death of many," I said giggling, then kissed him and got up. "Come on. Charles has beckoned us."

I held out my hand, and he took it. We walked back to the castle hand in hand. I noticed the campfires at the edge of the village, and as we passed the gates, I saw Rebecca sitting by the fountain in the middle of the courtyard. I stopped, letting go of Blake's hand.

"Will you help me? They will not be warm tonight. Blake, do you have that rope we used before?" I said.

He undid his wrap around his waist and handed it to me. I in turn tied it around me and Rebecca.

"Just like before," I said to her, and she nodded.

I closed my eyes, and we began to turn.

"Winds arise and flow from the east."

I could feel the breeze pick up. Around we turned three times, each time with the wind getting stronger.

"Scream through the trees like a roaring beast."

The wind picked up again. I could hear it roaring as it blew harder, and we started to turn faster still.

"Take these souls to be leaves. Blow them clear and never cease."

When we were done, Blake untied us and helped us inside. As we closed the doors, Charles came out of the dining hall and asked, "What is going on?"

"I started the wind blowing. I am going to bed. Juliana, do you want to sleep with me tonight?"

"If you would not mind, I think I will bunk with Rebecca."

I looked at Rebecca, and she mouthed 'please' to me, so I smiled at her.

"That is fine. I will see you all in the light of the day. If anything happens, please wake me."

I started up the grand staircase, and of course Raiden followed. I could not help but giggle.

CHAPTER TWENTY-FIVE

Once in my room, I peeled off my clothes and slipped on my sleeping gown, crawled into my bed, and closed my eyes. Sleep came fast and easy for me. I felt the bed sink down, and I naturally rolled over into the dip. I felt his arms around me as he drew me closer to him, and the darkness took over once again. It was the warmth that woke me, his warmth. I opened my eyes to see a rare glimpse of his face completely relaxed. He really was quite beautiful for an older man. I tried to remember why I did not find him attractive when he was younger. Perhaps it was his arrogance and the manner in which he declared his love for me. I think I was more of a princess back then, while now I am just a girl who has a huge task set before her. I sighed at what I needed to achieve. He felt me stir and pulled me close to him.

"Good morning," he whispered.

"Yes, it is a lovely day, if you do not mind the howling wind." I giggled.

"Is it all right that I am here with you in this bed? I slept in the chair for a bit, but it was not very comfortable. Well, nothing is more comfortable than lying here next to you."

"It is fine that you are here. I think I slept better in your arms than I did alone."

I felt his lips on my forehead. "I could get use to this, you know?"

"Yes, I could as well, but we have much to do today. I have some more men to torture." I giggled again.

"You seem to be in a good mood, knowing you are going to end the lives of many men this day."

"My mood, sire, is of your making, nothing more." There was a knock on the door. "Come in."

Charles came in. "Oh, excuse me. I did not know you had company."

I laughed. "It is fine, Charles. We were just talking. Come in."

I sat up on the bed, but Blake put his hands behind his head and stayed lying down. I looked him over; he had no shirt on, and the muscles in his stomach and arms were quite impressive.

"What can I do for you," I said as I winked at Blake.

"Steven went out in the wind. Roman's men have moved into the village during the night."

"That can be a problem."

"The real problem, Sabine, is the cave. When you and Rebecca went into the cave before, you said it was like a day was a year, correct?"

"Yes, why?"

"Well, I was thinking last night, that if a day is a year, then it would seem that a minute would be like a day, right?"

"That would make sense. What exactly are you saying?"

"Do you know how long it will take you to do whatever it is that you need to do in that cave?"

"I never really thought about it."

"I think you should. I will meet you in the dining hall," he said then turned to go out the door.

"Charles, will you find Rebecca and ask her to meet me in my father's study? I will be down in a few minutes."

"Of course." He walked out and shut the door behind him.

I felt Blake's hand before it touched me, his spread open hand covering most of my back.

"What are you thinking?"

I shook my head. "What I am going to say to you now, I need for you to keep close to your heart. I may not get the chance to say this to you again." I turned to face him, and he sat up. "Blake, in this moment, the feelings I have for you are like none I have ever felt in my life. I believe that I am in love with you, and I want nothing more than to spend my days waking up in your arms. When this is finished, I may not feel this way, and you will. All we have is right now. What is going to happen next will be a blur in our life. Please, no matter what happens, do not worry about me. They cannot kill me, and Roman knows this. He also knows that if he can get the jewels he will win, and I will spend the rest of my days fighting a no-win battle. I cannot let that happen. Right now, you are everything to me, but in three days' time, you may just be Blake again. Do you understand?"

He smiled. "I have known this all along, Sabine. It will hurt me, perhaps crush me, but I will never stop fighting for your love, for this love you have shown me."

I smiled at him. "I love you today. I need to find Rebecca. If we have just three days, then I have just three minutes to complete the ritual."

I got out of bed and put my boy clothes on. I did not care that Blake saw my back as I pulled my gown over my head. I turned when I was covered and kissed him.

"I will see you on the other side. For now, this is goodbye, and remember do not worry."

I grabbed my sword and was out the door.

I took the stairs two at a time and flew into the dining hall.

"Did you find her?" I asked Charles, and he nodded.

I took off running to my father's study, where Rebecca was waiting in one of the chairs. I slammed the door shut.

"Get the latch," I said to her.

She jumped up and sprung the secret door, and we made our way into the secret room behind the giant tapestry.

"What is going on, Sabine?"

"Charles came to see me this morning, and he made a valid point about time in the cave. If a day is a year, then a minute would be a day.

We have but three days until the harvest, which means we will have only three minutes to complete the ritual. That means I can save you. We can go now. Well, we have to go now."

"Sabine, I am not supposed to go with you."

"Yes, you are. If not you, then who is water?"

She looked at me and said. "Well, if Raiden is air, then it would make sense that Spirit is water, not me."

I did not know what to say to her. "No,"

"Yes, it is truth. I figured that out while we were in the cave. Spirit is my father's horse, and if Raiden was your father's horse, then it makes sense that Spirit is Raiden's younger brother, the one who got the knowledge but somehow, he was changed into Spirit. I do not know the details, but I am sure that Raiden does."

"How could that be? Tristan grew to a man and had children, my father's bloodline."

"As is my father's bloodline. Devious must have cast a spell on him as well, or someone did."

I looked at her. I was in shock, but she kept going, saying. "This is you, Juliana, Raiden, and Spirit." I felt the tear fall onto my cheek. "Oh no, sweetie. It is all right. You need to do this. I have been your companion and your compliment, not your other half. You are the chosen one, Sabine, not me." She hugged me tight. "I love you as my sister. You must not fail. My death must not be for nothing."

"I love you so much."

"You must go. It is time. Do not look back, Sabine. You take the horses and Juliana, and you go to the cave, and you finish this."

We hugged for a few more moments. I did not want to let her go. She pulled away from me and said, "Get the jewels, and I will get Juliana ready. We will meet you in the grand hall."

I nodded at her as she led me out of the secret room.

"Go get the jewels,'" she whispered. "Hurry."

I took off running. I was halfway to my room when I heard Raiden in my head.

'It is time.'

'I know. I am coming. Meet me in the great hall.'

I reached my room and searched it for the leather satchel that I had taken from Westin's room, finding it under the bed. I then whipped open the trunk, tripped the latch, and gathered up all the jewels. I went to the fireplace, reached up and took Roman's jewel from its hiding place, and slipped it into my bodice before running out the door. I could see everyone gathering at the doors.

"What is going on?"

Charles yelled to me. "They are moving on the castle. You must go."

I searched around for Juliana, finding that she was already on Spirit, then I looked for Blake, but he was nowhere to be seen. I ran down the stairs and jumped on Raiden.

"You ready for this?" I said to him. "Juliana, you stay close to me. Spirit will not fail you."

I looked at Rebecca and said, "I will do everything I can to stop this. No matter what happens, you are my sister. I love you."

I could see the sparkle in her eyes and knew she was ready for a fight.

"I love you too. Now go and finish this."

Charles was looking at her. In his eyes I saw passion and fear. He knew she would not survive this.

"You must go now," he said. "And do not look back, Sabine."

"Thank you, Charles. I love you."

"As do I, Sabine."

He turned and flung the giant doors open, and Raiden and Spirit took off. Just a few feet out the door, we were met with hundreds of men. Blake, James, Steven, Aidan, Joseph, and Edward were already fighting. We were blocked in, and Rebecca was not on her horse. I could not stop them. Raiden stopped and waited for a path to be cleared, but it seemed that every time one was made, it was filled with more men. I looked over at Juliana sitting on Spirit, her hands in front of her; she was in her trance. I did the only thing I could do. I climbed off Raiden and began to fight alongside my Guardians. I turned at one point to see Juliana send fireball after fireball at men, setting them ablaze. The smell of burning flesh reminded me of Jared and those days we spent burning the bodies of the villages. My sword struck time and time again, taking the lives of every man I fought with one blow. Blood and burning flesh; it seemed to go on and on. I needed Rebecca and Spirit to end this, but she was behind me somewhere. I screamed her name but heard nothing. Juliana held her own, and even Raiden did some stomping. We fought for what seemed a lifetime with these men, and they continued to come. The wind whipping around us did not seem to stop them.

They were pushing us backwards to the castle. They were coming, hundreds of them, pushing and pushing.

'Can we get out?'

'No.'

'What do we do?'

'Juliana is our only hope.'

I looked at her sitting on Spirit. "Juliana," I screamed her name. "Create a wall of fire between us."

"I am trying, Sabine, but the flow is not coming."

I look at Raiden. As I did, I felt a pierce go through me right to my heart. I stopped moving. Everything stopped moving. I was frozen. I could not breathe. I felt like everything that was, was no more. The light faded from within me, and I felt nothing. I closed my eyes and then opened them again, but no breath came. The world turned dark, and dread filled my body. *What was happening to me?* My knees gave way, and I found myself on the ground. I looked around to find Blake standing just a small distance away, looking at me. There was nothing left in me. It was as if time froze, and then I heard him scream. My eyes never left Blake's, but it was not him who was screaming. I spun my head around to follow the voice, and it stopped when I made contact with Charles. A sword was being pulled from his chest in slow motion, covered in blood, but the blood did not come from him. I looked behind him to see Rebecca looking at me. She looked down, and I followed her eyes. The blood was hers. It was pumping from her chest.

"No," I whispered. "No, no, no!"

I made my legs stand, my eyes never leaving hers.

"NOOOOOO!" I screamed.

It all happened too fast. I was running, slicing through men to get to her, cutting their heads off as I moved so slowly through them. I heard Juliana behind me screaming, and then I felt the heat on my back and the smell of burning flesh in my nose. I made it to Rebecca as her knees gave out, and she started to fall. I caught her in my arms.

"No, no, no, no, you cannot leave me," I said through tears.

"I love you," was all she said before she closed her eyes and was gone. I sat there holding her to my chest, crying and rocking her. Juliana was next to me before anyone else, and then she was holding me. Charles just stood there, not moving. I looked past him to see a wall of fire surrounding us then back to Juliana.

"You did it."

She did not answer me; she just sat there brushing Rebecca's hair and crying. I could not let her go. I did not want her to be dead. I looked up at Charles and asked, "What happened? You were supposed to protect her."

He just shook his head.

"Sabine," Blake said from next to me. "I am so sorry."

"Sorry for what, Blake? This was not your doing. Charles said he would protect her, that he would not let any harm come to her."

"We all knew this was going to happen, my love. We just did not know when or how. Come." He put his arms around me to lift me, but I pushed his hands away.

"No, I cannot leave her."

"Sabine, you need to get to the cave. I will tend to Rebecca."

"Do not bury her. Do not put her in the ground. I will be back." I stood and faced Charles.

"For the first time you have let me down, and now my sister in this life is dead."

"I do not know what happened. I thought because I could not die that I could protect her with my body. Sabine, I am sorry. No one feels the loss of her more than I."

"There is no time for this. Sabine, you must go," Joseph said,

321

picking up Rebecca's sword and moving me from in front of Charles. I let him guide me to Raiden.

"Joseph, do not put her in the ground."

"I will not."

"Give me your word that you will wait for me."

"You have my word. Now go."

I climbed up on Raiden. Joseph handed me her sword, and I looked back at my friend, my sister, lying on the ground in Blake's arms. Juliana touched my arm.

"Sabine, we must go while we have the chance."

I could not make myself turn away. This could not be the last time I would see her. But Raiden walked away, toward the stables and then to the back entrance to the courtyard.

Juliana moved the wall of fire so we could leave, and before I knew what was happening, we were in the forest by the river. This time, Raiden did not stay behind. Both he and Spirit followed the path to the steppingstones.

Once across, we moved to the entrance to the cave and stopped. I think I was in shock because Juliana had to help me down. I just stood there, looking at her beautiful face and her glowing almost red eyes. I sank to my knees on the soft grass.

"My friend, my sister is dead. I have nothing left inside. I cannot do this without her." The grief was too much, and I let the darkness take over. I felt her hand on my head. She laid it on the soft grass gently as the darkness engulfed me.

CHAPTER TWENTY-SIX

'No.'

Was that Juliana? Someone was in the darkness with me. Rebecca? How could that be? My heart wanted nothing more than to be with Rebecca.

'Sabine, open your eyes, darling.'

Mother? Was it my mother I heard? It could not be. My eyes fluttered. I could see the light of the day, so I knew I could not be dead. Juliana was there with me.

'Sabine, open your eyes. I am here.'

I had to fight it. I was having a vision or something. This could not be. My eyes struggled to open. I needed to get out of this. "Mother," I whispered.

"Sabine, it is me Juliana. Please wake up. I am so frightened. I am hearing voices, and yet there is no one here. Please, Sabine, wake up."

She was crying. Why could I not wake?

'Darling, please open your eyes.'

'No, I do not want to go on,' I said in my head.

I could not force myself to wake. Rebecca was gone. Jared was gone. My heart was empty and cold. There was nothing left for me. I did not want to live in a place where they were not.

'You must enter and finish this, my love. The time is now. All will reveal itself. All is not lost, my beautiful daughter. Your happiness will come when it is done.'

'There is no happiness in this world. Let the darkness take me.'

My mind went deeper into the darkness, into the place where I was happy, back to the time before the thunder came. I could see my mother. I could smell her beautiful scent as I entered the dining hall. Her presence filled the halls of Whispering Wind. I heard my father's bellowing laughter, and my brothers yelling at one another over who had bested who at swords. The house was full of activity. The smells from the kitchen were everywhere. The memories kept me safe in the darkness. The memories were what held me here. I did not wish to wake and face the reality that all was lost. All that was my life was gone. Westin was an older man with a family of his own, and he would survive in the valley until his time. If I stayed here, then they all would live in my mind. I did not know if Jared was here, but the hope that I would know him one day because of Jenna stayed alive in my otherwise dead and cold heart. Outside of the darkness was nothing but pain.

'Sabine.'

The voice in my head had changed. It was Father's voice I heard now.

'Sabine, you must wake and continue on this path you have been set upon.'

"No, I cannot," I mumbled.

"Sabine, do you hear that? What is it? Please wake up. I need you," Juliana was crying, shaking me as I lay on the soft green grass.

I could not pull myself away from the beauty and the love I felt in the darkness. I could not bear the emptiness I felt within me, without her, without them. How was anything in the world right, now that she is gone?

'Open your eyes, Sabine.'

"No," I whispered.

"Oh, Sabine, please wake up," Juliana cried.

Then Raiden was in my head.

'You must wake up NOW!'

My eyes fluttered open, but I tried to fight it. I wanted nothing more than to give in, but I could not. I was lying on my back, looking into the sky. I heard Juliana gasp. Turning my head to look at her, I expected she would be smiling down at me, only her head was turned away, looking at something else. I struggled to sit. Juliana was helping me, but she was not turning her head to look at me. I sat up and looked in the direction she was. There was a golden light growing from the rock face, as if the rocks had turned gold.

"I know this light. It is the same light from the tree in the valley, but how could this be?"

'Sabine, the time is now. You must finish this.'

"Mother?"

"Do you hear that," Juliana said as she gripped my arm.

"Yes, my love, I hear it." I tried to stand, but my legs were shaky.

"Look, the rocks are glowing." She pointed to the opening of the cave.

"I see that. Help me stand." Juliana helped me get up. I could feel the warmth, just as I had when I saw them at the tree in the valley. I searched for him in my mind.

'How is this possible? Is this you, or is this Roman?'

'It is neither. It is them.'

"Sabine, I am scared." Juliana grabbed my arm and moved herself behind me.

"I cannot explain this. It makes no sense to me."

The golden hue grew brighter, and I heard the voice again.

'My darling daughter, come.'

"Sabine, who is that?"

"It is your grandmother, my mother."

"How is that possible? She is gone and has been for a very long time."

I turned to look at her. "I have seen things that I should not have. I have done things I cannot explain, and where we are going, Juliana, is a place that time does not know," I said as I took her hand and moved toward the glowing rocks.

'Come inside. Time is moving fast.'

"Where are we going?"

"To finish this," I said to her. I looked back at Raiden. He nodded his head, and the four of us walked through the wall.

CHAPTER TWENTY-SEVEN

The inside of the cave was glowing in a golden hue. We did not need to light the candles. As we made our way into the center of the cave, they were there; Father, Mother, Ardes, Simon, and Jenna. Juliana stopped.

"What is this place? What is happening?"

"This is where Rebecca and I came for all those years we were gone."

I heard Jenna's voice saying, 'My daughter, she is so beautiful.'

"Did you hear that? Sabine, there are voices here, and I am not sure we should be here."

"It is fine, but right now we need to finish this."

I took Simon's satchel from my shoulder and laid it on the floor, and then opened it and dumped the jewels out. I heard Juliana gasp. I looked up and smiled at her. Reaching into the jewels, I felt them. Each of them had energy. Then I heard Raiden in my mind again.

'Close your eyes and you will see.'

I did as he said, and I could see that some of them had more energy than others. I selected the seven that were the most powerful, setting them aside. I then reached in my bodice and took out Roman's. This made eight, one for each of the holes.

"We need to place these eight jewels in the right slots in those holes."

Juliana turned to look at the holes in the back wall of the cave.

"Then we need to burn the rest of them in a certain order. You are going to need to use your gift to ignite them." I looked at Raiden and Spirit and asked, "Are you ready for this?"

They both nodded their heads. I laid all the stones out in the order in which we needed to burn them. Blue, White, Green, Violet, Red, Pink, Black, and Amber.

"Juliana, I need you to concentrate."

She nodded, so I picked up the eight jewels. Their energy was very strong, and for some reason, they seemed to have gotten heavier. I went to the back wall of the cave and looked into the first hole. I found the jewel that went in; a blue one, so I figured they must go in the same order. The next one was white, then violet, red, pink, black, and then the one from Roman's sword. When I placed the Amber jewel in its spot, the ground started to shake. I made my way back to the center of the cave.

"Now, when I tell you, I need for you to burn these."

I held up the blue jewels. She nodded. I laid the blue jewels in the center of the ground and said, "You ready?"

She nodded and concentrated on the stones. I looked at Raiden; both of the horses were staring at the jewels. I could hear them pop, and when I looked down, they were glowing. Juliana's eyes were turning that beautiful deep amber color, almost red. Then out of nowhere, I saw and felt the heat come from within her, and the stones burst into flames. I gently placed the white ones on top of the blue.

"Now these," I said.

She did not move, and soon those jewels were in flames. Next were the green ones. These seemed to take longer to ignite, but when I placed the violet jewels on top of the green ones, their energy seemed to make the flames larger. Juliana became hotter and hotter as each jewel was placed on top of the next. When it was time for the amber jewels, I noticed she was shaking.

"We are almost done, my love."

Raiden and Spirit had become restless and were moving in a circle around us.

When the amber stones ignited, there was a loud boom, and Juliana fell to the ground. I wanted to go to her, but I needed to finish this. I waited for the colors of the flames to change. The first colors were beautiful, and when they turned amber, I slammed my sword and Rebecca's on the ground. After the first strike, a howling started. The second strike caused the ground to shake more violently. At the third strike, I could hear screaming. The fourth strike made the wind start to blow, and the fifth strike caused the flames to grow bigger and bigger. They were so big they touched the ceiling on the cave. I said the words once.

'In this time, in this place, seek the refuge that brings you peace'
The wind slowed. I said them a second time.

'In this time, in this place, seek the refuge that brings you peace'
The screaming stopped. The third time I said them.

'In this time, in this place, seek the refuge that brings you peace'
The flames exploded, and I went flying through the air and slammed against the wall. Before the darkness came, I saw Spirit and Raiden change from horses to the men they use to be, and then there was nothing.

In the darkness, there was nothing; no visions, no sound, nothing but empty blackness. I could not tell how long I was in the darkness, for time had no meaning there. I felt at peace. There was no pain, no sorrow, nothing. It was as if I was floating through time, and there was nothing. It was the soft gentle voice that aroused me.

'Sabine, come back to us.'
I did not know this voice. I started to move through the emptiness. I had no idea where I was going, but I just kept moving, letting the sound of the voice guide me.

'That is it. Follow me. Follow me out.'
It became less and less, the empty darkness. The light came to a faded black, and then was the color of the sky just before the rains came.

'I am here with you,' the voice said.

I continued to follow it, and soon the color changed to a very light, almost white color. Soon the light turned to golden, like the golden hue in the cave. My eyes fluttered open. Yes, the golden hue was very prominent. I opened them wider, and that was all I could see at first. My eyes adjusted, and I could see people, lots of people. My eyes focused, and Jared came into view.

"My love," I whispered.

He smiled at me. "Yes, my love, it is me."

"But how? How are you here with me?"

"We are all here, Sabine." My eyes moved beyond him to see my mother, my father, Ardes, Simon, and Jenna.

"How is this possible?"

My father spoke, "You have accomplished the task that was set before you. You have achieved the impossible."

I looked at the fire, and just on the other side was Juliana lying on the ground. I crawled to her and held her in my arms.

"Beautiful girl, wake up," I said as I stroked her face.

I watched her eyes flutter as she tried to come out of the darkness.

"Come, my love, there are some people here who want to see you."

She opened her eyes and smiled at me. "Did it work?"

"Yes, my love, it worked," I said as she sat up.

"Juliana, my beautiful child," Jenna said.

Her head turned to the voice, and she whispered, "Sabine, I am scared. Who are these people?"

I helped her up and watched her face transform as she pulled from her memory the voice that was speaking to her. "Mother?"

"Yes, my love, I am your mother."

Before I could stop her, she was running toward them. Jenna opened her arms, and to my shock and surprise, they wrapped around her.

"How is this possible?"

I looked at Jared, and he was smiling. I walked slowly toward him, but he did not move. I reached him, and his hand came up and touched my face. The tears came freely, with him wiping each one away.

"My love, how I have missed you," he said as he drew me into his arms.

It was wonderful to feel him against me. I did not know, nor did I care, how any of this was possible. As I stood there in his arms, I felt my mother and then my father embraced me. I turned into their arms.

"How is this possible?"

They pulled away, and Simon then Ardes came, and then Jenna.

My father spoke, "This is possible because of what you have done. You have healed this land, and as your reward, we are allowed to say goodbye to you."

"Goodbye? You cannot stay with me?"

"No, my darling, we cannot. The powers that be have allowed this," my mother said.

Jenna and Ardes held their daughter, and I went back to Jared.

"I want you to know, Sabine, that I am whole because of you, but it was never meant to be for us. There is another who loves you as much, if not more, than I, and I think if you search deep within yourself, you will find that you love him as well. He will make a good husband for you."

"I love only you," I said through tears.

"As I love only you. You freed me, Sabine. You gave me life, but I am gone now. Your happiness awaits you in Whispering Wind."

I looked at my parents, at my brothers. "How long?"

"Only a few more moments, my darling daughter," my mother said as she took my hand.

Father took the other, and we stood looking at one another.

"Sabine, you have made me the proudest father to have ever lived. The world outside is new again, never to be tainted in your lifetime. I knew you had it in you to accomplish this monumental task."

"I am after all your daughter."

His laughter filled the cave. Oh, how I missed that sound.

"You are indeed," he said as he pulled me into a huge hug.

I felt Jenna's hand on me, and father turned me to face her.

"I cannot thank you enough for finding her and protecting her. I was so frightened when they took her. Even as I died, I tried to get her back. She has grown up to be a remarkable young woman, and I have you and Westin to thank for that, and Camille."

"Westin," I said as I turned to my father.

"Yes, we will see him before we leave. I have much to say to him. I am so proud of him and the man he has become. I cannot thank him enough for saving you. I tried so hard to get to the hilltop to hide you, but I guess I did not have to, and now you will have Raiden to look after you, just as he looked after me."

I turned to look at Raiden. "He is a remarkable force in my life. I do not know where I would be without him."

'Nor I you.'

My father laughed. "Still scaring people with that ability you have, huh, old friend?"

Raiden nodded and stomped his hoof, and we all laughed.

Father looked past him to Spirit. "Brother," he said as Spirit walked up. Father hugged him.

"Thank you for watching out for them. I have missed you all these years."

I saw what I thought was a tear fall from Spirit's eye.

"I am sorry, Sabine, but it is time for us to go."

"No, please, can you stay longer?"

"You have already been in this cave far too long. You must go and see all that you have accomplished. It is time to bring Westin and his children home. You are now the first Queen of Whispering Wind. Your kingdom will prosper, and you will be kind and endearing to those who wish to live in your midst. We will always be with you, my beautiful daughter. To me, there will be nothing you cannot accomplish. Just remember there will be those who will still try, but the real evil is gone. It has been absorbed back into this ground where it escaped."

I turned to face Jared. "I do not want you to go."

"I do not want to go, but it would seem that fate has different plans for me. Thank you, Sabine, for loving me, and for showing me love."

"I love only you."

We all stood together, holding one another. I could feel them fading away, and soon it was just the golden hue, me, Juliana, Raiden, and Spirit.

Juliana was crying. "Where did they go, Sabine?"

"Wherever it is you go when you leave this world."

I held her while she cried it out. "They love you always, my love."

"It is so unfair. I never knew them, and I will never know them."

"I know, my love, and I did not get the chance to thank you for being you. I love you so much, and I promised them a long time ago that I would keep you safe. I have fulfilled my promise to them. We have fulfilled our destiny, even at the cost of Rebecca's life. We need to go back to Whispering Wind and send the horses for Westin and Camille. It is time to go back home."

"I have no home. My home was the valley. Is that where we shall live?"

"No, my love, your home is at Whispering Wind with me, and this time, I do not have to leave you."

She smiled and hugged me tighter. "I love you."

"I love you too."

I took her hand, picked up mine and Rebecca's swords, and together as we entered the cave we left. As we passed through the rock, the light of day was high in the sky. Raiden and Spirit followed us. We made our way across the river to the other side and climbed up on the horses. I leaned in to Raiden and said, "Take me home." He nodded his head, and I could have sworn he had a smile on his face.

Looking at Juliana, I smiled and asked her, "Are you ready?"

She was looking at the cave. "Will we ever see them again?"

"I do not know. I wish they could have stayed with us, but they are with us always, as long as we keep them here."

I put my hand on my chest. I felt the locket that Jared had given me. I took it out, and for the first time since he gave it to me, I took it off. "I love only you," I said as I tucked it into the folds of my boy pants.

"I will say this, I am looking forward to wearing my gowns again." We giggled.

Raiden turned, and we made our way back to the castle. As we rode through the fields, I could see the spot where Roman was captured by the ground. It had turned to stone. I could not help but smile.

"I told you that you would not win."

I said as we walked past him and into the village. I could see the gates ahead of me, and there was no movement in the courtyard. I could feel the fear welling up within me. Where were they? Were they all dead? As we made our way through the gates, I looked to the spot where Rebecca had died, but it was vacant. Raiden walked up to the doors, and we got off. I turned to him.

"Take Spirit and go to the valley to get Westin, and then bring him home."

He nodded, and in an instant, they were gone. Not even dust was left in his path. I reached out for Juliana's hand, and together we walked through the doors into the grand hall.

There was no movement, and the silence was great. I heard footsteps echoing through the rooms, so I drew my sword. Had the bloodgutters survived? Raiden would not have left me here if they had. I tried to figure out where the sound was coming from, but the echo was too great. Closer and closer the footsteps got. I looked toward the kitchen when I saw a shadow move across the wall. When I heard Juliana gasp, my eyes tried to focus on what I was seeing. I must have been having some kind of vision; there was no way I was seeing what I was seeing. I closed my eyes, trying to stop my mind from playing this trick on me. I heard Juliana whisper.

"This cannot be," and I opened my eyes.

Standing in the doorway that led to the kitchen was a sight I could have only dreamed of seeing.

"Well, it took you long enough."

The darkness came, and it came hard and fast. I felt my body slam onto the stone floor. My head hit the stone, but there was no pain. There was nothing.

Thank you everyone who has fallen in love with Sabine and Rebecca. Writing their story has been one of the greatest times of my life.

Whispering Wind The Awakening is the third book in this series. Here are a few lines to make you wonder what is in store for Sabine and her Guardians.

I lay in the darkness filled with dread and sorrow, I cannot recover. I cannot let the light in. I want to be dead just as my sister, my friend Rebecca was, my family is gone, my Jared is gone, everything and everyone I have ever loved is gone and I want to be with them. I can feel Juliana shake me I can hear her cry but my eyes will not open.

I feel nothing, I am nothing without her. I felt that sword pierce her heart, and I felt her fear as she realized that she would not survive. I felt her love for Charles, I felt her strength drain from her, I felt her sadness, I felt her regrets and I felt the life leave her. How can I do any of this without her?

As I lay in the darkness our lives played out in my mind, our first meeting on the plain which was the work of Charles and his brothers. I think of that time seeing her hair the color of the golden sun flying through the air as she flew out of the forest and onto the plain. The friendship we built unknowing who either of us were. Finding out she was to marry Jared, our scheme to outwit Samuel and her father, who really was not her father.

Learning to fight together, all those talks we had, how she helped me realize what love was, discovering that our horses were magic and that they did not start out as horses but men, men who were to be our saviors many times but not this last time, Spirit could not save her, finding out she was my cousin all along, saving one another from ourselves time and time again, watching her fall in love and then holding her in my arms as she took her last breath. I wished I had died along side of her. How would I be able to live in this world without her? The way she would bounce into my room to wake me. Her energy was so alive and different from everyone else's. To hold her in my arms as that energy ceased to exist was more than I could handle. I had watched as the thunder came across the plains and seen the aftermath of my life when they were done. I had lost my parents, my brothers, my life.

Being turned into a killing machine, a warrior to avenge my family's death's, finding Juliana and then starting all over again. Standing still in time, Jared dying at my hand. I do not want to wake. I want nothing more than to stay in the darkness. I want to be with my family.